VELLUM

HAL DUNCAN was born in 1971, grew up in small-town Ayrshire during the Eighties, and now lives in the West End of Glasgow. He is a member of the Glasgow SF Writer's Circle, and works part-time as a computer programmer, while completing his follow-up novel, *Ink*.

HAL DUNCAN

VELLUM

The Book of All Hours: 1

PAN BOOKS

First published 2005 by Macmillan

First published in paperback 2006 by Pan Books
an imprint of Pan Macmillan Ltd
Pan Macmillan, 20 New Wharf Road, London N1 9RR
Basingstoke and Oxford
Associated companies throughout the world
www.panmacmillan.com

ISBN-13: 978-0-330-43836-0
ISBN-10: 0-330-43836-0

1 3 5 7 9 8 6 4 2

A CIP catalogue record for this book is available from
the British Library.

Typeset by SetSystems Ltd, Saffron Walden, Essex
Printed and bound in Great Britain by
Mackays of Chatham plc, Chatham, Kent

All Pan Macmillan titles are available from
www.panmacmillan.com
or from Bookpost by telephoning +44 (0)1624 677237

To my Dad, for the quirks and convictions

To my Mum, for the food parcels and forbearance

And above all else, to Ewan

Forever

VOLUME ONE

The Lost Deus of Sumer

The Road of All Dust

The Journals of Reynard Carter – Day Zero

– A burning map. Every epic, my friend Jack used to say, should start with a burning map. Like in the movies. Fucking flames burning the world away; that's the best thing about all those old films, he said – when you see this old parchment map just ... getting darker and darker in the centre, crisping, crinkling until suddenly it just ... *fwoom.*

That was Jack for you; if you asked him what he wanted for his birthday, he'd tell you he wanted an explosion. Jack was crazy, but as I flicked forward through the Book, faster and faster as each page fed in me a growing sense of horror and awe, I thought of what he'd said. I thought of gods and tragedies, legends and histories, and movies that opened with scrolling tales of ancient times. The vellum pages beneath my hand flickered under a light that wasn't fire, however, but rather the pale blue of the underground vault's fluorescent lights; and if there was a burning it was in my head, a fire of realisation, of revelation. Still, I couldn't shake the feeling that at any second the world around me would be torn away in flames and ashes, stripped back to reveal a scene of carnage choreographed as in some lurid Hollywood flick, and soundtracked with a crashing, clashing music over screams and sounds of war.

The Book. I slammed the thing closed, checking a suspicion. Its outward, leather, cracked and weathered carapace was thick and dark, embossed with strange sigils – an eye-like design, a circle within an ellipse, but with four smaller semicircles on its outer edge at three o'clock and nine o'clock, and at five and eleven; overlapping this but offset was a rectangle. The framework of embossing around it looked, for all the world, like the stolen architectural plans that lay abandoned on the floor, and with a glance around the vault my suspicion was confirmed – it matched. The long, rectangular room with the doorway in the bottom right-hand corner; the left-hand wall thicker, as it should be, a supporting wall for the building above; the two blocks of wall on either side jutting out a foot or so into the room two-thirds of the way up, as if the original end wall had been knocked through at some point, extended into a forgotten recess; the tiny alcove at the far end which I'd found hidden behind a tall glass-panelled bookcase and which was barely legible on the stolen plans, drawn in pencil where the rest was marked in ink.

I felt a bit guilty, looking at the piles of Aristotle and Nostradamus and Molière and who knows what else, lying on the floor where I'd put them so I could heave the solid bookcase out from its place. Fragile, priceless artefacts of the university's Special Collection, books a student would sign for, with his tutor's name and research subject, and have brought to him by the curator, in the Reading Room upstairs, lain gently on the desk before him on foam supports, their brittle pages to be turned so delicately, so tentatively in case they crumbled to dust between unthinking fingers. And I'd treated them like paperbacks dumped on the floor by someone rearranging furniture. But they were worthless in comparison to the Book; they were already dust.

I wiped away some of the blood that ran down from my forehead and opened the book again, to its first page.

The Book of All Hours

The Book of All Hours, the Benedictines called it, in the Middle Ages, believing it to be the Deus's own version of some grand duke's book of hours – those hour-by-hour and day-by-day, week-by-week and month-by-month tomes of ceremony and meditation inked by monks in lamplight, drawn in brilliant colours on vellum, pale but rich in tone, not bleached pure white but yellowed, brown, the colour of skin, of earth, of wood, old bone, of things that were all once alive. Princes and kings would commission these books and they'd take years of hunched backs and cramped hands and fading eyesight to produce by hand. It was said by the Benedictines that God himself commissioned such a tome from the one angel allowed to step beyond the veil and see his face and listen to his words, and write them down. The patriarch Enoch, who walked with God and rose to Heaven to become the angel Metatron, had made this book at his master's command, they said, and it held God's own word on every instant of eternity, the ultimate instruction manual for he who dared to live what He commanded, fully, absolutely. But no man was perfect enough to live in such devotion; so they denied the Book existed in this world at all; said it could be found only in Eternity, where the spirit was freed of the weakness of the flesh.

– The Book of All Hours, my father had said. Your grandfather went looking for it, but he never found it. He couldn't find it; it's a myth, a pipe-dream. It doesn't exist.

I remember the quiet smile on his face, the look all parents have at some time, I suspect, when they see their children repeating their own folly, a look that says, yes, we all think like that when we're your age, but when you're older, believe me, you'll understand, the world doesn't work that way. I'd come to ask him about these fanciful stories I'd been told, about the Carter family having ancient secrets, not just skeletons in the closet, but skeletons with bones engraved with mystic runes, in closets with false walls that hid dark tunnels leading deep, deep underground.

– But Uncle Reynard said that when grandfather was in the Middle East—

– Uncle Reynard is an incorrigible old fox, said my father. He tells a good tale, but you really have to ... take what he says with a pinch of salt.

I remember being shocked, confused; I was young, still young enough that it had never occurred to me that two adults whom I trusted absolutely might believe entirely different things. My father and his brother, Reynard – my namesake uncle – they knew everything after all, didn't they? They were grown-ups. It had never occurred to me that the answers they gave to my questions might be entirely incompatible.

– Of course, you should listen to your father, Uncle Reynard had said. Honestly, you shouldn't believe a word I say. I am *utterly* untrustworthy when it comes to the Book.

And he held my gaze with complete sincerity . . . and winked.

– Almost as bad as the Cistercians, he said.

The Cistercians called the Benedictines fools. They were quite convinced that the Book existed in this world, but they feared it as they feared the Devil himself. They damned the manuscript as the most diabolical of grimoires, a Book of the Names of the Dead, of every being that had ever lived or ever would live – human, angel, devil. They made reference to the Bible, to the Torah and the Koran, to Christian apocrypha and Jewish and Islamic legend . . . Didn't the Revelations of St John talk of a book made by God's scribe, a Book of Life containing names that were no mere christenings but the true and secret names, names which the owners could not refuse to answer when called before the Throne of God? But if this was to be carried out into the world only in the End Days, where then did Solomon learn the names of all the djinn? They were burning old maids at the stake in those days, herbalists and midwives; they believed the world was riven with darkness; they feared the evils of knowledge. So they said there had to be a *copy* of the Book of Life, a dark counterpart made by Lucifer himself before he fell, when *he* was God's right hand. And they said that perhaps he'd written into it the very name of God. Perhaps this was why he fell. If so, they whispered, it was a book that might be used to summon and bind even the Almighty to an audacious mortal's will.

The only binding that concerned me right now, though, was the makeshift bandage of torn sleeve stemming the bloodflow from my wounded hand. If I'd been thoughtless with the other books of the Special Collection, if I'd been rough-handed as I heaved the bookcase out to reveal the dust-smeared glass that fronted the alcove – like a painted-over window, or an inset museum display of a priest's hole, or a smuggler's secret cellar – I had been careful with the suction grip and diamond-tipped cutter as I carved the circle in the glass panel that fronted the alcove. The last thing I'd expected, though, was for it to shatter with a blast that threw me back across the room. I had been lucky. Only one of the shards had been large enough to do more than surface damage, embedding itself deep in the palm of my right hand when I'd thrown it up to cover my face. The rest of the shards had left me with only minor cuts, plenty of them, but most no more than skin deep. It was a mystery to me, why the case had been so pressurised as to shatter the very moment the seal was broken; it was a trivial mystery, though, in comparison with the book itself, sitting there inside its circle of salt.

The Legends of a Lifetime

– A book of hours, I said. Or a book of names. Nobody knows.
    – Bullshit, said Joey. You're making it up.
    – Shut up, said Jack. I'm listening to this.
    He slid the G'n'T across the table to me, handed Joey his Guinness and sat down in his own seat with his ouzo, sniffed it with a wrinkle-nosed grin.
    – Go on, he said.
    – Right, I said, voice hoarse from trying to talk over the thumping bass of the juke-box in the Student Union. So there's a Jesuit scholar in the seventeenth century, and he says that *both* these ideas are heresy. According to him this is the book from which everyone's sins will be read out before the Throne of God. The Judgement of All Accounts, or the Account of All Judgements, he calls it. Not so much a book of the names of the dead, but of everything that anyone's ever done, or ever will do, every deed, past, present and future.
    – It'd have to be one fucking huge book, said Joey.
    I shrugged, smiled, took a sip of my drink.
    – Maybe the language it's written in is more ... concise. I don't know. That's what I'm saying. Nobody knows exactly what it is. But *where* it is ... that's another matter.
    – You read too much, said Joey. Man, I bet if you look on their library database every university has a copy of—

*

7

– *The Macromimicon*, said Uncle Reynard. You know, you do have to wonder where Liebkraft got his ideas from. Elder gods; a book written by a mad Arab; a translation of an even older text. Where did you get this?

He turned the battered paperback over in his hands. Yellowed pages, broken spines, bent corners, lurid cover – this wasn't ancient mystery, just modern pulp, not truth, but trash. And it was everything my uncle had been telling me since I was a child.

– Second-hand bookshop, I said. Fifty pence. You ... you ... I don't believe you strung me along for ...

I was lost for words. The legends of a lifetime, told over glasses of milk or – these days – beer, and all of it just an elaborate fiction. And a stolen one at that. He just sat there in his armchair, smoking his cigarette.

– You know, this has been out of print for decades, he said, handing it back to me. You should read it. Honestly. I'm sure you'll enjoy it.

He had that old smile of mischief on his face.

– Sure, I've read Liebkraft, I said to Joey. Everyone in the Carter family has to read Liebkraft at some point or another. You especially, Jack.

I lit a cigarette and took a long draw, milking their attention. I'd fallen in with Jack and Joey in our first year at the university – Jack, the flame-haired wild boy with a tendency to climb out onto window-ledges while drunk ... another Carter, strangely enough, but no relation to the best of my knowledge; Joey Pechorin, the dark-voiced nihilist who struck you at first as someone trying too hard to be cool until you got to know him and realised, no, he really was that sullen and dismissive. Fire and ice, they'd been friends since school, inseparable until Jack hooked up with flighty, flutter-eyed Thomas. Thomas Messenger, so full-on a fairy that we couldn't help but call him Puck. Puck, who was, as usual, late. I saw Jack check his watch, look towards the door.

– Why do you think he has his character called Carter? I said.
– *Bullshit*, Jack coughed into his hand.
But I could see how the idea intrigued him.
– God's honest truth, I said. He knew my grandfather when–

– Oh, fuck off, said Joey. Fuck right off.

I shook my head, gave him a sad, resigned look. *Your loss.*

– Don't believe me. Doesn't bother me. I know the Book exists. I know where it is.

The legends of a lifetime, a lifetime of legends, of interest piqued, of curiosity sharpened, honed into a tool – I hadn't come to study at this university because of its academic reputation. I didn't give a damn for the mock-gothic tower and the quadrangles, for the droning lectures about Shakespeare and Spenser and Milton, for the pomp and ceremony of this or that professor still stuck in a previous century with his black robe and solemn voice. My three years of study in the library here were three years of research into its corridors, not its books. I knew the building now, inside and out, like I'd lived there all my life, every floor, every corner, every doorway. I'd studied the architect's plans. I'd struck up friendships with security guards, librarians. I'd worked there part-time for the last year and a half. I knew where the cameras were, what times the guards did their rounds at night, who manufactured the security system, how it worked, how it could be disabled. And I was finally ready.

– I know where it is, I said.

– I'll believe it when I see it, said Joey.

So will I, I thought. *So will I.*

Between Kabala and Calculus

Three years for me, and as many generations for my family – maybe more if my uncle was right. In the Middle Ages, he'd told me, every guild, every craft or trade had their own mystery play based on a story from the Bible or from the apocrypha. The Masons would put on a play about the Tower of Babel. The Wine-merchants would put on a play about the drunkenness of Noah. And there was a play he'd heard of, he told me, about the angels who fought neither for God nor Lucifer, but instead fled from the War in Heaven, down to Earth, and carried with them the Book of Life, so that it should be safe from the destruction. They carried it across the earth, from one hiding place to another, always on the move. The play, of course, was performed by the Carters.

– Well, of course, my father said, that's where the whole story comes from. The Carters travelled all over the place. The mystery plays were performed all over Britain, and on the Continent. And everywhere they went, you get these stories appearing about this ancient book. Myths based on a play cobbled together from a legend written in the margins of scripture. Stories created from stories created from stories. None of it's true, but eventually people start to forget what's fiction and what's fact. The Masons don't have a monopoly on spurious mythology, you know. But it's ridiculous. The idea that the last of the earth-bound angels hired a young carter to take a secret book across Europe to . . .

He went suddenly quiet; he must have realised from the confused expression on my face that I'd never heard this part of the story before. He sighed.

– That's what your grandfather believed, he said. That the Carters had taken over from the angels as guardians of the Book. But they lost it. And they've been looking for it ever since.

– Your grandfather was a sick man, he said, quietly, sadly. He was in the Great War, you know. He wanted to believe in . . . something greater. War changes people. Death . . . changes people.

Death changes people.

I remembered Jack and Joey fighting; I remembered watching as Jack self-destructed; Joey pulling a bottle of ouzo out of his hand and shouting at him; Jack screaming at him over and over again – *fuck you, fuck you, fuck you.*

You describe people as crazy – you say, *that Jack, he's crazy* – and it doesn't mean anything until you see them really, truly, going crazy.

There was a Jewish scholar, Isaac ben Joshua, in Moorish Spain who said that the Book drove everyone who saw it crazy. He said that it held not deeds but laws, that it was, in fact, the original Book of the Law – not the Mosaic Torah but an even older covenant known only in the most marginal of apocrypha, dating from the antediluvian time of Enoch and the rebel angels, binding the physical world in principles somewhere between kabala and calculus. He referenced an Islamic source, a story saying that all but one solitary page were blank, and on that page there was only a single simple sentence, an equation which captured the very essence of existence. This, he said, was why all those who'd ever looked upon the Book had gone insane, unable to comprehend, unable to accept, the meaning of life laid out in a few words of mathematical purity.

After what happened to Thomas, I remember thinking that I knew what that sentence was. Two words.

People die.

The page I looked at now, though, the first page of the Book, had no words on it, only a blueprint of the maze of concrete tunnels and chambers that surrounded me, here in the bunkered depths of the old building. Gold illumination traced out conduits, ventilation and wiring, heating ducts, while the same eye-like logo on the cover of the book was inked in black here, smaller though, more cursive; I felt that burning feeling rising in my head again. There was something wrong about an artefact as ancient as this with content that was so ... modern. This wasn't some doggerel prophecy before me, not a vague prediction but a precise plan, a schema. And, flicking forward to the next page I recognised the library as I'd seen it on the architectural plans I'd been studying for so long. Again that symbol in the centre of it. Pages two and three together mapped out the building in its context, the network of roads and footpaths, the buildings and grassed areas of the campus around the library. I recognised it; I had recognised it instantly and it was that recognition that had made me close the Book and reopen it, as if the act might change it, as if looking at it again, I might this time see something more rational, more sensible.

Instead it seemed even less rational. Now that I studied it more closely, it worried me even more because, in the tiniest of places – only here and there, mind you – the location of this pathway, the outline of this building – it seemed just a little different from my memory.

– What time is it? asked Jack. I checked my watch, but Puck answered before me.

– Summer, he said. It was April, actually, but there was time and there was Puck Time, where hours and minutes were described as quarter past a freckle and any day sunny enough to lie out on the grass and smoke cigarettes was summer. It was glorious that day, sunlight pouring down on us where Puck and Jack lazed like dogs on the slope of walled-in grass between the library and the reading room, the squat block of the campus cafeteria lowering behind us where we couldn't see it and the tower of the university reaching up into the blue, too solid and archaic to be quite a dreaming spire but still, in the fluted intricacy of its anachronistic design, denying the reality of its Victorian construction for a fantasy of antiquity. It was glorious that day, so it was summer.

The sunlight slanted off the glass exterior of the library to my right, and painted the white pebble-dashed areas of the walls with Moorish or Mediterranean warmth, flashed on the glass doors into the Hunterian Museum as they revolved, students passing in and out. At the ground level the library and the museum fused into one building, blockish and modern, all cuboids and cylinders, an abstract iron sculpture nestling in curved simplicity on the flagstones outside the doors, before the low steps that led down onto cobbles running down towards University Avenue. Following them down you passed the Mackintosh House, a museum-piece replica of a tenement home filled with furniture and fittings designed by one of Glasgow's most famous sons; built onto the Hunterian and accessed from inside the museum, its false front-door perched absurdly in mid-air with no steps to reach it. To my left there was the reading room, built in the Twenties, low and circular with tall slender windows and a domed roof – Art Nouveau, I thought, though I was never sure of the distinction between Nouveau and Deco. And though the Sixties brown-brick, smoked-glass block monstrosity of the Hub at my back, with its cafeteria and student shops, deserved a bomb for its sheer ugliness, I never loved any little corner of the world so much as that slope of grass walled in with rough-hewn sandstone between the reading room and the library, never loved anywhere so much as there and then.

I sat on a wooden block that was a recent addition to the slope. The university had hired a modern artist to commemorate their 550th anniversary by turning that green slope into a sort of art installation and I'd watched with some trepidation as they'd fenced off the area and torn up the grass. But when it was finished, I had to admit, it made that little area even more serene. The artist had laid ten of these long wooden blocks in pairs, each pair of blocks offset as if to mark out diagonal corners of a long, thin rectangle, the other corners marked out by low shrubs, five of these thin rectangles dividing up the space of the slope. Each of the dark wooden blocks had a white porcelain pillow at one end of it, and thin panels of glass text, buried in the ground running along either side of the blocks – lit up at night – told the story of the piece in ten sections. The shrubs were all herbs with medicinal properties, a reference to the university's first physic garden, a record that had only recently been turned up by some academic burrowing through archives. The blocks were replicas of old-style anatomist's dissection slabs, in memory of the oldest faculty of the university.

I lay on one of them, that day, head resting on the cool white pillow, or swivelled round and sat upright on it to slug back beer out of the cans we'd brought with us because, of course, you couldn't study for exams on such a day without refreshments.

– It's half two, I said.
   – Fuck, said Jack. How long have we been here?
   – A couple of hours, I said. Not long.
   I picked up the *Norton's Anthology of Poetry* splayed face-down beside me on the block, glanced at it and closed it, lay it down beside Jack's biography of John Maclean.
   – John Maclean. What? As in *Die Hard*? Puck had said.
   – As in the founder of Scottish Socialism, scrag.
   Jack had shaken his head.
   Of all the students lounging and laughing on the slope, sat on the grass in circles, cross-legged on the blocks with sandwiches, cans, packets of cigarettes or tobacco scattered around them, nobody

was really doing any work. It was the Easter break; we had exams coming up soon, so soon, but it just felt like we had all the time in the world.

I looked down at Jack and Puck, Jack with his hands under his head, Puck at right angles, using Jack's stomach as a headrest, one arm flopped across his chest – a scritch of fingers at his ribs – and the other stretched out to the side with a cigarette between his fingers, smoke rising from its tower of ash like slow, solemn incense, rising up into the still cerulean air.

Angularities and Curves

I flicked forward to pages four and five. A map. Again the scale had changed, zoomed out by another magnitude. Now all the streets and roads of the whole bohemian district in and around the university were clear, with the river and the park marked off, the museum and art galleries, all drawn with the precision of a modern cartographer. But all altered alarmingly, if only subtly, from the bohemian district I knew so well. Christ, my Bank Street house should have been on the map at this scale – I lived less than five minutes walk from the old cloistered quadrangles at the very heart of the campus – but instead the street wasn't even marked. The river seemed to twist to flow over where it should have been, and the rough grid-work of streets and tenement buildings was shifted to accommodate it. Two main roads that should have crossed at right angles met and merged instead in a Y-shaped junction. It was as if the smallest changes at the lowest level cascaded upwards.

The map of the city on pages six and seven was completely unfamiliar.

I remember, as a child, looking at an architectural model of my school and its surroundings that stood on display in the main hallway of the school itself, where the principal, the deputy principal and suchlike had their offices. One tiny discrepancy – a set of stone steps leading down from the raised car park of a block of flats, steps that had never been built but were shown on the model – and, as a child, I could not grasp the idea that the model was wrong. It wasn't that I thought the steps should be there in reality if they were on the model, or vice versa – I was too young to understand exactly why it bothered me – but I remember the vague unease, the confusion at the inconsistency. I felt that same disquiet now, but more profound, so many years later.

I turned another page and there I saw the city in its environs, the coastline and the countryside around it. Now it was definitely not the city that I knew; the city that I knew sat on a river, but not at its mouth. The whole geography was wrong, but, at the same time, I did recognise it. I knew the shape of the coastline well enough, and I recognised the island sitting out a short ferry-ride from the city's docks; I even recognised those docks as being where, in reality, a small seaside town of ice cream parlours and amusement arcades sat, gathering retired old folks and families on Sunday outings. It was as if the city of my own experience had been picked up and dropped some thirty miles to the south-west of its natural location, and had to warp and weave itself into a slightly different shape as it settled, to accommodate its new surroundings. Where the city should have been, on the map, was only a small village in the midst of farmland.

The Macromimicon. Was it then a book of maps, not of what was, but of what might have been, of a world that had taken a different course, with this village growing into a town instead of that one, this town burgeoning into a city instead of another? I turned another page. Even the language that marked out the streets and roads, the cities, towns and villages, seemed the product of some parallel development, composed of angularities and curves, bearing a similarity to the Roman or Cyrillic alphabets, but again not quite the same. Strangely – in retrospect – it never occurred to me that this book might actually be nothing more than mere invention, a work of fancy: perhaps the accuracy of the blueprint of the library held that idea from my mind; perhaps it was the power of the old family legends engrained so deep within me. All I know is what I felt: a growing conviction that this book spoke somehow of a larger truth.

– Jack.

He didn't answer.

– Jack, I said again.

– For fuck's sake, Jack, called Joey. Let us in.

– Come on. Please, I said.

We'd been there for maybe half an hour and all we'd got from the other side of the door was silence. I was worried myself, but I could hear from the fury in Joey's voice, the way he swore at Jack, insulted him, told him again and again how stupid and pointless all this was, that he was really terrified. If you didn't know him you'd have thought that he was more concerned about this ... waste of time he had to suffer, more bothered about his own inconvenience than anything else. But I could hear the edges and points in his voice, the tightness in his throat. Joey was coming to hate Jack because he couldn't stand what he was doing to himself; it hurt too much.

– Open the fucking door, ya fucking bastard. Just fucking open the fucking door, fucking ... *fucker*!

And he exploded at the door, kicking, snarling, spitting.

After a while, after a long while, when Joey had fallen silent, there was a click, and the door opened.

Jack sat back down on the floor, a Gideon's Bible in front of him together with a print-out of – I looked closer – columns of numbers, letters, other characters – colons, semi-colons, question marks – each with a numeric value beside it. It was the ASCII values for the keys on a computer keyboard, I realised, the set of numbers between zero and 255, used, in a computer to represent text in the binary form that a computer could work with, language boiled down to zeros and ones, to a series of electronic on and off values. Text was stored as *bytes*, each byte made up of eight bits, eight binary places representing 1s, 2s, 4s, 8s and so on up to 128, the same way decimal places represent 1s, 10s, 100s and so on ... 00000000 to 11111111, zero to 255. Jack was using it as reference.

*

On one side of him, he had a stack of paper, reams still wrapped or torn open, sheets scattered, piled on top of each other. I watched as he took a fresh sheet, from the top of the pile, looked at the Gideon's, finding his place with the point of his pen, then found the character in the print-out of ASCII values and started working out, on the fresh sheet, what its binary representation was. There were sheets of these workings scattered behind him where he'd discarded them and I crouched down to pick one of them up. He'd scrawled out columns for the places, scribbled numbers – 45, 37, 56 – down the left-hand margin and then ticked off places in the columns. 37, that was 1 plus 4 plus 32 … 10100100 in binary. Looking at other sheets, I realised that he'd worked out some of these numbers over and over again. He could have just put together another reference sheet of all the binary values for the letters and numbers he needed, but instead he was working them out each time. Every letter, every colon, every full stop, he was looking up on the sheet of ASCII values and calculating the binary for it, even when he'd worked it out just moments before.

As I watched, he took another sheet, already almost full of ones and zeros, each byte of eight places separated by a dash, and transferred a number from his workings to this page. And then went back to the Bible, back to the sheet of ASCII, back to his scraps of workings, to find the next value. When the page was full, he stood up and walked over to the corner of the room. He was barefoot.

In the corner of the room, the tower of finished sheets, piled face-down one on top of another, was up to his chest.

– What the fuck is …

Joey was walking over to the corner. I just knew that he was going to pull the first sheet off the top of the pile, hold it up in Jack's face, demand to know what the fuck was going on. And I could hear the creak of the loose floorboards of Jack's cheap rented room as Joey stamped across them, catching one of the piles of reams as he stepped over it; and I could see the white of his knuckles, the set of his shoulders, and I knew the tower was unsteady. Christ, it was a pile of loose paper up to Jack's chest and it was in the corner but it wasn't even leaning on the walls for support. It was a wonder Jack had managed to get it this high without …

And I watched as the tower of translated Bible, quivered with the floorboards under it, and leaned, and fell, pages scattering out into the air and avalanching out and down, sheets sliding across sheets and catching air and flipping and crashing like paper aeroplanes coming down.

And Jack was lost to us that day; we were all lost to each other, because Thomas was dead, and Jack was mad, and Joey was closed, and I . . . all I could think of was the Book of All Hours.

The Big Picture

As I turned the pages, taking care not to drip blood from any of my numerous cuts onto its priceless pages, I barely even heard the alarm that had been ringing in my ears ever since the shattering of the glass. I was transfixed by this strange sense of certainty; I just wasn't sure what I was certain of. A page, another page, and yet another, and Britain lay before me – a Britain without a Glasgow or a London, or any of the major cities I should have been able to point to, or rather with these cities in the wrong places, in the wrong shapes. A map of the past, or of the future, or of an imagined now?

– The Macromimicon. The Big Picture, my uncle had said. Whatever form it takes – and there's some who say it takes a different form for everyone – I think somehow – I'm not sure how but I think it's some sort of mirror of the world, or of something greater that includes the world.

Another page – Europe – and then another, and the world lay before me, the globe projected and distorted as it had to be to fit the rectangle of the two pages. The cartographer had elected to sacrifice the inhospitable polar regions, showing the coastline of Antarctica split and splayed to run along the bottom of the page, the tops of the northern continents stretched out and skewed in the transformation from three dimensions to two, running along the top of the page so that the Arctic Ocean was reduced to a mere channel bordering Greenland on either side.

– It's a fucking good story, Jack had said, as we sat in the Union. I'll give you that, he said. Don't believe a word of it, though.

He checked his watch again, glanced at the door.

I felt feverish, and I knew that it was more than lack of blood. I should have been out of there by now. I should have been getting the hell out of there with the book, not browsing its pages as if I was just one more student in the university library – in the university library in the dead of night, tooled-up with glass-cutters and tooth-picks and all the other implements of burglary, waiting to be caught quite literally red-handed, with fingerprints in my own blood all over the broken case and the wooden desk where I now studied the Book. I couldn't leave.

– Who's coming for a drink, then? Joey had said, one foot up on the wooden bench beside me, leaning on his knee as he looked down at Jack and Puck on the grass.

– Fuck that shit, said Puck. I'm not moving.

The alarm rang on, and no one came, and I found myself reaching out with my bloodied left hand to turn the next page, knowing that I had to leave but stuck there as if caught in a moment of determinism. I knew that I was smearing blood over Siberia, and over an invaluable artefact. I knew that the security guards could be no more than seconds away. I knew I could end up in jail for this. Christ, the Book was real, I had it in my hands, here and now. And still, with blood pounding in my ears, and blood dripping in my eyes, running from my cut hand, blood smearing everything that hand touched, I still turned the page.

New Unfamiliar Terrain

The coastline of a greater world lay before my eyes. It was a world where Antarctica was only the tip of a much larger southern continent. It was a world where Greenland was an island in a river's mouth, where Baffin Bay on one side and the Greenland Sea on the other stretched north, fused as an enormous estuary. Asia and the

Americas were mere ... promontories, headlands on a Hyperborean expanse, and the Arctic 'River' that divided them had its source far north and off the edge of the map.

To east and west the story was the same, a whole new unfamiliar terrain; the western seaboard of America extended up well past Alaska, north and west, while Antarctica continued round and down; the eastern coast of China curved round to a gulf the size of the Baltic where the Bering Strait should be, another massive 'river' running north from here. An entirely different land-mass jutted in from the east, out at the far edge of – I wasn't even sure if I should call it the Pacific now – the Eastern Pacific, perhaps, the Western being, on this map, an entirely different body of water. I turned another page.

Again the scale moved out and, on this map, the world I knew could have taken up no more than a sixteenth of the area shown. The north-east coastline of that Greater Antarctica curved up to meet the strange land in the east, which itself carried on to meet the coast that curved around and down from China; pincered by its own Gibraltar Strait formed by the tip of South America, the bump of Antarctica, this *Eastern Pacific* was no more than a landlocked sea here, like a larger Mediterranean, dwarfed by the lands surrounding it on three sides. Hyperborea to the north, I thought, the Subantarctic to the south, and an Orient beyond the furthest Orient we've ever known.

Another page, and another, and the world I knew was only a minus-cule part of an impossibly vast landscape. I'm no physicist, but I know enough about matter and gravity to know when I'm looking at the surface of a world that couldn't possibly support human exist-ence. This was a world on the scale of Jupiter and Saturn. I turned more pages, two or three at a time, and still each map was at a larger magnitude than the one before, and still the world revealed was only a quarter of the world mapped out on the page to follow. Continents became islands off of coastlines that became continents. Ten pages, twenty. The world I knew wasn't even visible at this scale, but there was still a world to be marked out, a fractured collision of earth and water, in areas so vast that terms like 'continent' or 'ocean' now seemed meaningless.

I kept turning the pages.

The Silent World

And as my heart pounded in my chest and my head swam, I realized that the alarm bell I'd been hearing was only a vague and distant ringing in my ears now. No one was coming. No one would ever come. I knew it with the certainty of dream knowledge. I knew it with the same certainty that told me this archaic text before me was no piece of whimsy, that it was real, it was true, truer than reality.

I knew it even before turning to the very last page of the Book, to the very last map in which this ancient cartographer had laid out the edges of his known universe, a blank and featureless plain extending in all directions at the centre of which, tiny and intricate, the world of worlds was only an oasis, with a dotted track leading out of it to the north as if to mark some unimaginably long road to the inconceivably distant.

I knew it even before I staggered out through the deep corridors of the library and out into the silent world, as I wandered through a campus entirely empty of human life, and out into streets of sandstone tenements and tarmac roads, traffic lights that still cycled through their sequences of red, amber and green although the empty cars just sat there, oblivious to their commands. I knew it even if I couldn't find the words to shape my tongue around in order to express that vague, disturbing certainty.

I shouted, but there was no one to hear me.

I didn't know at what point I had crossed over into this, my new reality: whether it had been my blood upon the Book that had somehow, like some magical anointment, released its power; or whether it had been simply my opening of the tome that had opened a gateway around me; whether that blast of shattering glass from the

Book's cabinet had thrown me clear out of my own world and into the next; whether the case itself had held not air under pressure, but something even less substantial, some aetheric force unbound by my meddling which even now might be travelling in a shock wave outward from its focus, transforming everything it touched.

Transformations

We stood there at the back of the church, Jack and Joey and I. He had a lot of family, a lot of friends, Puck did, and the church was full. I've heard it's often like that when someone young dies. Young lives leave a lot of mourners. But we'd almost had to drag Jack there; he wouldn't come at first, said he wouldn't sit and listen to a minister reciting platitudes and singing fucking hymns, fucking praising fucking God in fucking Heaven. That's how he put it.

I glanced at the two of them, Jack and Joey standing by my side, silent in black – black suits, black mood. And I had this absurd thought, this stupid, crazy idea, that the two of them looked like some kind of clichéd bloody Hollywood vision of secret agents, or Rat Pack gangsters, assassins, men in black. Angels of death, waiting patiently to collect.

They turned to look at me together, precisely in synch, like two parts of the same machine, and their hollow gazes sent a shiver down my spine, because I felt exactly the same emptiness.

I actually wonder now if nothing in this world has changed but me. It occurred to me as I wandered the empty streets of the world, walking down the middle of roads known and unknown – maybe the world was as it had always been and it was me that had been transformed, seeing for the first time the whole scope of it and myself alone within. I knew, as I wandered those streets so subtly familiar, that the whole world around me was abandoned, desolate; it didn't make sense in any rational way but somehow I knew the world I'd walked into, whatever kind of hell it was, was mine and mine alone. It was like that moment in a dream when you realise you're dreaming and wake up into the real world . . . and then you realise you're still dreaming.

*

I don't know how long I walked aimlessly around my new environment, struck by the surrealism of these buildings in all stages of abandonment, some overgrown ruins, some pristine with lights on in their rooms, child's toys left sitting on carpets, radios hissing white noise. It was as if the city's inhabitants had all simply dropped whatever they were doing and left, but over a period of centuries with none of them noticing the others' departures, even until the very last, who, it seemed, had left mere seconds before my arrival.

– You really believe in this Book? Jack had asked me. You really think you can find it?

He finished off his glass of ouzo, loosened his black tie and poured himself another. We were in his room, after the funeral, and the place was scattered with empty beer cans, empty bottles, and plastic bags with more for us to drink. We were going to get wasted. We were all of us going to get completely wasted that night. Fucked out of our minds.

I shook my head, laughed sadly.

– Maybe it *is* just some fucking old, old hoax. But ... I just want to know. My whole life, I've wanted to know if ... it's real.

– Nothing's real, said Joey.

– Everything's real, said Jack. Everything is true; nothing is permitted.

I thought, *that's a quote*. I thought, *I recognise it*, but I couldn't place it and it didn't sound quite right.

I looked from one to the other, all of us sodden with drink and grief, and felt one of those moments of acid significance, where you're sure you've just realised something important and forgotten it instantly.

No Comfort, No Answers

So I sit in this pub now, writing, and there are pints poured sitting on the bar, packets of cigarettes left with lighters on tables – Christ, when I walked in there was one still burning in an ashtray – but no humanity. Only the remembrance of it. I've spent the last few hours turning everything over and over in my head and I'm no closer to making sense of any of this. I can find no comfort, no answers, only that same sense I feel each time I look upon the Book, a mingling of dread and wonder, horror and elation.

It sits before me on the table as a mystery.

I think maybe I'm dead, that this world exists for me alone because it is no more, no less, than my own personal gateway to ... whatever lies beyond. And the Book? Maybe it's my own invention, my own creation, placed here, waiting for the moment when I could finally face my own mortality and cross the boundary into the unknown. Was my life before now imagined ... or reimagined, recreated with a path to lead me to this book of maps, with a family history filled with myths and legends, a drive to know, to grasp some secret, sacred mystery? And friends found and lost. All leading me inexorably to the opening of the Book, to the discovery of my state.

I miss Jack and Joey and Thomas. Nobody ever wonders if the dead grieve for the ones they leave behind, it seems, but I miss them, even if I'm not sure that they ever existed. If my whole world up until I found the Book was just the fantasy of a dead man wishing he was still alive, maybe they were only ever little parts of me that I snipped off and carved into a human shape to keep me company in that dream of life. I think of Jack and Joey, fire and ice, light and dark. And I think of Thomas and I feel cheated, betrayed. I can't accept that Puck was just a lonely ghost's imagination. No. I think – I want to think – that they were all real, that I knew them, that that day on the grass outside the library was real, true, even if it happened differently. I think I had a life without the Book, without any of those stories, just a simple life, replayed in death with transformations as a quiet way of bringing me to this point. And when I picture Jack and Joey standing in that church, I picture Thomas standing beside them in my place. Maybe his death was just another signpost of my imagination, pointing the way. I hope that's the truth. I dearly hope so.

So where do I go from here? It's a lonely world, this limbo, and I only hope that it's a borderland. The Book itself is evidence of something out there, surely, something greater than the scope of one man's memory, of a world beyond the world beyond; and if its opening was my awakening then the content of its pages must be the story of my life – my death – from here on in. I've found myself alone within a world that's only a minute portion of a larger whole. Somewhere out there, surely, other corners of this vast realm hold their own souls, born in death into their own imaginings. And will they know that they are dead, or does it fall to me to wake them? Are there already roads between the worlds, travelled by others? How many will have left their empty worlds in search of company, and what cities have been built where souls met in the great landscape of the afterworld? My God, this book might hold the Maps of Hell, but maybe it also holds the Keys of Heaven in the sigils that inscribe it. I don't even know if every dead man has such a book to guide him through his death or if I have the only copy. I won't know until some way into my journey, I imagine. I imagine there are many things that I am yet to know.

The Road of All Dust

I plan to set out tomorrow. I have the Book after all, calling me to this great adventure, and guiding my every step. As it sits on the table of the pub in front of me, I can see now what I did not understand at first. The cover of the Book no longer shows the vault I found it in. I didn't notice it changing, but it happened; now the embossing of the leather cover maps out the tables and the chairs around me, and the first page shows the architecture of this abandoned pub. The Book changes as its reader moves. The map stays centred on its observer. And the glyph, the strange eye on its exterior that is repeated on the maps inside? A symbol of the reader – the keeper, the maker – himself, an oval of a body seen from above, a circle within it to mark out the head, and four semi-circles to symbolise the limbs. And the rectangle that intersects it is, of course, the Book, the Macromimicon, the Great Copy, which I carry, perhaps as a part of me. Wherever I go, those first few maps, I'm sure, will show the world around me in all the detail I will ever need, even as I venture into regions as yet shown only at the widest scale.

*

Tomorrow my journey really begins. I'll set out down this road I knew in my world as the Great Western Road, to where it joins another familiar but altered street. That it joins with Crow Road in an unfamiliar junction, fusing to become a new and unknown way seems sort of significant – the road of the carrion bird, the bird of death, and the road towards the land beyond the sunset, the Western Lands. Perhaps I'm reading all this wrong, but it seems to make a sort of sense, as much sense as anything does now. What I'll do when I get to the coast I really don't know, but I suspect whatever lies in the far West is still only the beginning of my journey. I remember stories of New Mexico, that dusty, desert Land of Dreams, and of a road known as the Jornada del Muerto, the Journey of the Dead Man, and I wonder ... but I can't even imagine the road I'm setting out to travel, how I can hope to cross those oceans and continents that are mere puddles and islands in the greater scheme of things. I must be a fool to face distances that dwarf everything I've ever known.

So I sit here in the empty pub, as a final act of hesitation, uncertainty.

I know my destination though. I think of that final page in the Book of All Hours and the road leading north out of the minuscule oasis in the centre of the map, out of this world the size of a universe, and out of the scope of even this Book. I wonder if it is a road we all must travel eventually, even if it takes us eternity to get to its beginnings, and an eternity of eternities to walk its way. It may be the road to Hell or out of it, to Heaven or to something more profound; after all, if this whole empty world is my Limbo, Heaven and Hell may be no more than rural backwaters in the metaphysics mapped out by the Book, and maybe I'll pass them on my way like some pilgrim passing a village, his heart set on his destination, his gaze set on a distance further even than the far horizon, the dust under his feet the dust we all become, the life we cast off in the skin we shed.

I finish off the beer that I've poured for myself from the taps in this deserted but plentifully stocked pub and, I think, it's time that I was looking for a place to sleep. I wish that my own home was still here in this remade world; I'd like to sleep one last night in my own bed. But perhaps there is a reason for that comfort being denied me.

Perhaps I'd wake tomorrow back in a world busy with people, in an illusion of reality reconstructed from my memories as a buffer against the cold truth. I know a part of me would like that. But I have the Book, and in the pages of the Book, I have the map and, on that map, I have the way that I must travel marked out. There is another part of me that wants to wake tomorrow with that truth.

But, yes, it's time for me to sleep – even if it is only an imagined sleep within the sleep of death – so I can wake to face tomorrow fresh. The irony of it all does strike me as I sit here, but it seems that even in eternal rest I need ... rest.

I have a long road ahead of me, a long and winding road of dust ... perhaps the road of all dust.

1

A Door Out of Reality

From the Great Beyond

From the Great Beyond she heard it, coming from the Deep Within. From the Great Beyond the goddess heard it, coming from the Deep Within. From the Great Beyond Inanna heard it, coming from the Deep Within.

She gave up heaven and earth, to journey down into the underworld, Inanna did, gave up her role as queen of heavens, holy priestess of the earth, to journey down into the underworld. In Uruk and in Badtibira, in Zabalam and Nippur, in Kish and in Akkad, she abandoned all her temples to descend into the Kur.

She gathered up the seven *me* into her hands, and with them in her hands, in her possession, she began her preparations.

Her lashes painted black with kohl, she laid the *sugurra*, crown of the steppe, upon her head, and fingered locks of fine, dark hair that fell across her forehead, touched them into place. She fastened tiny lapis beads around her neck and let a double strand of beads fall to her breast. Around her chest, she bound a golden breastplate that called quietly to men and youths, *come to me, come*, with warm, metallic grace. She slipped a golden bracelet over her soft hand, onto her slender wrist, and took a lapis rod and line in hand.

And finally, she furled her royal robe around her body.

Inanna set out for the Kur, her faithful servant, Lady Shubur, with her.

— Lady Shubur, said Inanna, my *sukkal* who gives wise consul, my steadfast support, the warrior who guards my flank, I am descending to the Kur, the underworld. If I do not return then sound a lamentation for me in the ruins. Pound the drum for me in the assemblies where the unkin gather and around the houses of the gods. Tear at your eyes, your mouth, your thighs. Wearing the beggar's single robe of soiled sackcloth, then, go to the temple of the Lord Ilil in Nippur. Enter his sacred shrine and cry to him. Say these words:

– O father Lord Ilil, do not leave your daughter to death and damnation. Will you let your shining silver lie buried forever in the dust? Will you see your precious lapis shattered into shards of stone for the stoneworker, your aromatic cedar cut up into wood for the woodworker? Do not let the queen of heaven, holy priestess of the earth, be slaughtered in the Kur.

– If Lord Ilil will not assist you, she said, go to Ur, to the temple of Sin, and weep before my father. If he will not assist you, go to Eridu, to Enki's temple, weep before the god of wisdom. Enki knows the food of life; he knows the water of life; he knows the secrets. I am sure he will not let me die.

Thick with Trees and Thunderstorms

North Carolina, where the old 70 that runs from Hickory to Asheville cuts across the 225 running up from the South, from Spartanburg and beyond, up through the Blue Ridge Mountains and a land that's thick with trees and thunderstorms. It's on the map, but it's a small town, or at least it looks it, hidden from the freeway, until you cut down past the sign that says *Welcome to Marion, a Progressive Town*, and gun your bike slow through the streets of the town centre with its thrift stores and pharmacy, fire department, town hall, the odd music store or specialist shop that's yet to lose its market to the Wal-Mart just a short drive down the road.

She rides past the calm, brick-fronted architecture that's still somewhere in the 1950s, sleeping, waiting for a future that's never going to happen, dreaming of a past that never really went away, out of the small town centre and on to a commercial strip of fast-food restaurants and diners, a steak house and a Japanese, a derelict cinema sitting lonely in the middle of its own car park – all of these buildings just strung along the road like cheap plastic beads on a ragged necklace. She pulls off the road into a Hardee's, switches off the engine and kicks down the bike-stand.

The burger tastes good – real meat in a thick, rough-shapen hunk, not some thin bland patty of processed gristle and fat – and she washes it down with deep sucking slurps of Mountain Dew, and twirls the straw in the cardboard bucket of a cup to rattle the ice as she looks out the window at the road, hot in the summer sun, humid and heavy. The sky is a brilliant blue, the blue of a Madonna's robes, stretching up into forever, stretching –
– and she stands in front of the mirror in the washroom, leaning on the sink a second, dizzy with a sudden buzz, a hum, a song that ripples through her body like the air over a hot road shimmers in the sun. The Cant. Shit, she thinks. She must be getting close. She looks at the watch sitting up on top of the hand-dryer. The second hand flicks back and forth, random, sporadic, like one of those aeroplane instruments in a movie where the plane is going down in an electrical storm.
It's August 4th, 2017. Sort of.

Steady again, she studies her eyes, black with mascara and with lack of sleep, and pushes her dark red hair back from her forehead. Even splashing more water on her face she still feels like a fucking zombie. *Fucking zombie retro biker chick*, she thinks. Beads in her hair, a beaded choker round her neck, a chicken-bone charm necklace over a gold circuit-patterned T-shirt. Shit, she looks like her fucking techno-hippy mother.
She picks up her watch and slips it over her wrist, reels out the earphones from the stick clipped to her belt and puts them in, clipping them into the booster sockets in her earrings so her lenses can pick up the video signals. The Sony VR5 logo flickers briefly across her vision as she shoulders her way out through the door, tapping at the datastick to switch it onto audio-only. She doesn't need a heads-up weather forecast with ghost images of clouds or

sunbursts, or a Routefinder sprite floating at every turn-off to point her this way or that. Not today.

She grabs her helmet from the handlebar of the bike and puts it on as she swings her leg up over the seat, flicks up the stand, zips up her leather biker jacket, kicks the engine into life.

The antique creature of steel and chrome growls between her legs, and another antique creature – one of leather and vinyl – screams in her ears.

– Loooooooooooooooord! howls Iggy Pop, and the murderous guitar of the Stooges' *TV Eye* kicks in, as Phreedom Messenger opens up the throttle on the bike and roars out of her pit-stop on the way to hell.

Whore of Babylon, Queen of Heaven

And Inanna continued on her way towards the underworld. She journeyed from ancient Sumer up the land between the rivers Tigris and Euphrates, through the whole of Babylon and into Hittite Haran. She travelled into Canaan with the Habiru who called her Ishtar. She went with them into Egypt and they called her Ashtaroth when she returned, leaving behind only a memory, the myth of Isis. She saw god⁄kings and city⁄states rise and fall, patriarchs murdered by sons who took their places and their names, armies and wars of territory and dominion. She travelled with the armies, with the whores and the musicians and the eunuch priests, offering solace in their tents, in tabernacles of sex and salvation. She had bastard sons by kings. She washed the feet of gods amongst men.

She saw villages burned and statues toppled. She saw kingdoms become federations, federations become empires. She saw whole dynasties of deities overthrown, their names and faces obliterated from the monuments they'd built so, unlike them, she took new names, new faces. Times changed and she changed with them. She never accepted the new order that was tearing down the old around her but she knew better than to fight it, watching the others stripped of honour, stripped of reverence, stripped of godhood, still calling themselves Sovereigns even as the Covenant shattered every idol in their temples. So she travelled as supplicant, as refugee, with mystery as her protector rather than force, cults rather than armies. She saw the seeds she dropped behind her take root in the earth and grow only to be crushed by military boots. She travelled with slaves and criminals.

She went from Israel, to Byzantium and Rome, this Queen of Heaven, Blessed Mother, full of grace, her new name and old titles echoing amongst the vaults of stone cathedrals, spaces as vast and hollow as the temples left long empty in Uruk and Badtibira, Zabalam and Nippur, Kish and Akkad.

She travelled in statues and pietàs, painted in indigo and gold in old Renaissance frescoes, Russian ikons; travelled to the New World with conquistadors and missionaries, to plantations where the slaves danced round the fires at night, possessed by gods, by saints, by loas and orishas; journeyed across time to a New Age of carnival mythologies and stars worshipped in glossy parchments sold at newsstands, of rosaries and Tarot cards and television earth mothers fussing over the broken hearts and wounded prides of soft, spoiled inner children.

She journeyed on the road of no return, to the dark mansion of the god of death, the house where those who enter never leave, where those who enter lose all light, and feed on dust, clay for their bread. They see no sun; they dwell in night, clothed in black feathers of the carrion crow. Over the door and the bolt of the dark house, dust settles, moss and mildew grow.

She stopped, this Whore of Babylon, this Queen of Heaven. Inanna stopped before the entrance to the underworld, and turned to look back at her servant who had followed her down through the centuries, the millennia.

– Go now, Lady Shubur, she said. Do not forget my words.

– My Queen, says Lady Shubur.

– Go.

She shifts the engine to a lower gear, a lower growl, swings low and wide around the corners, slower as the bike climbs the steep, winding road into the mountains. White wooden churches stand with bible quotes lettered on hoardings at the side of the road, and shabby prefab houses perch in their little plots with leaning porches and pots of dying flowers in hanging baskets. They nestle in amongst the deep trees of bear and deer; this is hunting territory, a place of pickup trucks and men in armoured vests with high-powered rifles and coolers filled with beer. Stars and Stripes on every house. On a dirt track coming off the road at her right-hand side a rustbucket of a car sits up on bricks, the legend *#1 Dawg* scrawled in paint across the battered panels of its side.

The bike swings left and right in wide curves round the tight corners and she leans down into them, following the flow, the rhythm of the constant turns and twists. The road snakes on right up into the hills and she snakes with it, like a cobra reared up ready to strike but swaying side to side, charmed by the music in its contours, switching gears, from growl to roar and back again. Slow and wide. Fast and tight. Left. Right. Left. Right. Sunlight flickers blinding white through the canopy of trees like the end of an old celluloid film rattling through a projector.

The road cuts deep into the sharp-carved shadows of tall trees for a second, slices between dark juts of moss-slicked rock and through a concrete underpass; and she takes the circling slip road off to the right and turns and turns, and then she's up and out and on the Blue Ridge Parkway, riding the wide road that runs from mountain spine to mountain spine along the length of the whole range. And the sun is hot but the air is clear and crisp as a cool spring and she can look out to her left and to her right and see the world on either side, the hills in the beyond, the valleys in between, the vast, green, rough, soft sculpture of time and space, of earth and sky.

*

It's places like this that you can't tell where the world ends and the Vellum begins, she thinks. For all its asphalt artifice, for all the wooden mileage signposts scattered along its way, for all that you can look down into the valleys and still see the houses and churches, schools and factories of small towns cradled in the folds, up here reality, like the air, is thinner. The road is just a scratch on the skin of a god; if you came off it, she thinks, if you smashed straight through one of the low wooden fences and shot out into the air, you might crash right out of this world and into another, into a world empty of human life or filled with animal ghosts.

But those aren't the kind of world she's looking for, not by a long shot.

Inanna at the Gates of Hell

— Gatekeeper, open up your gate for me, Inanna called. If you refuse, I'll smash this door, shatter the bolt, splinter the post. I'll tear these doors down and raise up the dead to feast upon the living, until there are more dead souls walking in the world than are alive.

Inanna stood before the outer gates of Kur, and she knocked loudly.

— Open the doors, you keeper of the gate, she cried, her voice fierce. Open up the doors, Neti! I come alone and ask for entry.

— And who are you? asked Neti, surly chief gatekeeper of the Kur.

— I am Inanna, queen of heavens, on my way into the West.

— If you are really queen of heavens, Neti said, and on your way into the West, Inanna, why, why has your heart made you a traveller on the road of no return?

— My sister, Eresh of the Greater Earth, Inanna answered, is the reason. I have come to see the funeral rites of Gugalanna, Bull of Heaven, her dead husband. I have come to see the rites, the funeral beer of his libations poured into the cup. Now open up.

— Wait here, Inanna, Neti said, and I will give your message to my queen.

And Neti, chief keeper of the gates of Kur, turned and entered the palace of Eresh, the queen of the underworld, of the Greater Earth.

Mary or Anna, Esther or Diana, Phreedom flicks through the many cards she carries in her wallet, all the identities she travels in. She picks one out almost at random – an Anna, this time – hands it to the clerk behind the counter. He smiles at her and she can't help herself from thinking of the cheap motels she's stayed in where the clerks are all sim sprites, electronic ghosts with just enough AI behind them to take care of check-ins and check-outs. Sim answerers are the cheaper option, now, than the old service sector wage slaves of the past; she's kind of surprised that this place has a flesh receptionist. But maybe they just haven't caught up with the times.

Another town, another Comfort Inn, she thinks. This time it's Marion, but it could be anywhere. She watches as the clerk slashes the card through the machine and turns to watch the screen, waiting for confirmation. And she pauses, pen poised in her hand over the book, flicks her eyes up to the clock on the back wall and sees the second hand tick round, once, twice, then stop. The clerk is still, stopped in his stoop, one hand laid on the monitor, his drumming fingers caught between the beats. She flicks backward through the pages of the book, scanning the names for one that has a different look. She's no idea what name he might have used here, but she knows she'll know it when she sees it, by the little signs, not in the handwriting, in the snake of an *s*, the round mounds of an *m*, but in the imprints that it makes, not in the paper but in reality itself. The unkin can wear whatever names they want, whatever guises, but they still wear their nature in their attitude, in their actions. They leave traces.

And as it turns out, he hasn't even bothered to use a false name. *Thomas Messenger.*

It's black ink on white paper but she sees it glowing white with a black aura, like its own afterimage. So her brother was here right enough.

She lets the second hand tick forward on the clock, and the clerk rises from his stoop, turns back to her.

*

– My queen, said Neti, a maid stands at the palace gates. She stands as firm as the foundations of a city wall, tall as the skies and wide as all the lands. She comes prepared, the seven *me* gathered into her hands. Her eyes are shadowed with dark kohl and in her hand she holds a lapis rod and line. Across her forehead fall her fine, dark locks of hair, arranged with care. She wears small lapis beads around her neck, a double strand of beads across her breast. Around her chest a breastplate calls, speaks to all men, says *come, come to me*. On her head she wears the *sugurra*, crown of the steppe, and there's a golden bracelet on her wrist. My queen, she wears the royal robes wrapped round her body.

And Phreedom swipes the keycard through the lock and opens the door into a room that's just like every other room in this Comfort Inn, in every Comfort Inn, in every cheap hotel in every nowhere town in every state she's been in. She dumps the helmet on the wooden dresser as the door clicks shut behind her, drapes the jacket on the back of a chair. She slips the chicken-bone necklace off over her head, unhooks the choker, slips the watch off of her wrist, and unclips the data stick at her hip, lays them all on the dark wood veneer. She peels the T-shirt off and lets it drop on top of the double bed's thin fitted quilt of green and garish flowers, heads for the bathroom where–

The water from the shower head rains over her hand, hot patterings and trickling trails between her fingers. Her blue jeans lie crumpled on the floor but Phreedom has no memory of taking them off. Fuck, she thinks. Another cut. Another fold in time, a little nick in the Vellum. She's on the threshold here.

She steps into the shower.

Broken Minutes and Bent Hours

– She is here, your sister Inanna, who carries the great whipping stick, the *keppu* toy, to stir the *abzu* up as Enki watches.

When Eresh of the Greater Earth heard this, she slapped her thigh, bit at her bottom lip. When Eresh of the Greater Earth heard this, she raged.

– What have I done to anger her? I eat and drink with the Anunnaki, clay for my bread and stagnant water for my beer. What brings her here? I weep for young men and the sweethearts they've abandoned without choice. I weep for girls torn from their lover's laps. I weep for children born before their time to die before they've lived.

Her face turned scarlet as cut tamarisk, her lips as purple as a *kuninu*-vessel's rim. She took the problem to her heart and brooded on it. After a while she spoke:

– Come Neti, my chief keeper of the gates of Kur, and listen carefully to what I say: Lock up and bolt the seven gates of Kur, then, one by one, open each gate and let Inanna enter through the crack. Bring her down. But as she enters, take her regal costume from her, take the crown, the necklace and the beads that fall across her breast, the golden breastplate on her chest, the bracelet and the rod and line. Strip her of everything, even the royal robe, and let the holy priestess of the earth, the queen of heaven, enter here bowed low.

Neti listened to his queen's words, locked and bolted all the seven gates of Kur, the city of the dead. Then he opened the outer gate.

– Come Inanna, enter, Neti said to her, and as Inanna entered the first gate, the *sugurra*, crown of the steppe, was taken from her head.

– What is this? asked Inanna.

– Quiet, Inanna, she was told, the customs of the city of the dead are perfect. They may not be questioned.

And: Click. The door of Phreedom's room swings slow upon its spring, snicks shut behind her as she steps out into the corridor, plastic magnetic keycard in her hand in her pocket.

Other unkin, she knows, have other methods for finding those who don't want to be found. Some use the old ways: scrying in mirrors for a vision of their quarry on a corner, standing under a street-sign; or sniffing out a psychic scent like bloodhounds, following it on foot across whole continents; or listening, head cocked, for the faintest echo of a unique sound, a voice-print rippling across the atmosphere, half a world away. The Cant travels far.

Then there's those who use absurd artefacts of their own invention, reinvention, mojo compasses and geiger counters with their guts rewired to chitter randomly, palmtops with programs compiled into trinary, designed to print onscreen displays of names and assignations written into history before history even existed, the ancient *me* written in modern media. Some just find someone they think might know and rip an address straight out of their head. Phreedom's no stranger to these methods.

– Where's your brother, little girl, he'd said.
– I don't know.
– We'll see about that, he'd said, his fingers curling round her throat.

No. Phreedom's no stranger to these methods, but she works by something more like instinct, intuition. The unkin leave their traces in the times they travel through as much as in the spaces and the things, and Phreedom's following a trail of broken minutes and bent hours that's as . . . legible to her as Tom's signature in the hotel guestbook, even if it is a little . . . confused. In terms of time, her brother's trail reads like some chain gang fugitive crashing through bushes, crossing rivers, doubling back to cross again, stealing a car, exchanging clothes with a hobo and riding the railroad in a whole different direction – trying everything, anything, to get the bloodhounds off his trail. Phreedom knows that there's some hounds you just can't shake. She knows she has to find her brother before they do. Scratch that. She knows she has to find her brother before they *did*.

A Speck of Dirt Under a Fingernail

As she stepped through the second gate, the small lapis beads were taken from around her neck. And once again Inanna asked, What is this?
– Quiet, Inanna, Neti told her. The customs of the city of the dead are perfect. They may not be questioned.

Click. The bar-handle of the door into the stairwell unlatches at the press of her hand, and she steps past the vending and ice machines on the landing, down the stairs towards the exit.

– I've found a way, he says. A sort of loophole, a door out of reality . . . In Ash–

She cuts him off, fingers across his lips, and shakes her head.

They sit in the roadhouse – it's about a year ago – sipping at their beers and looking across the booth at each other. Their bikes are parked outside and in a little while they'll both go out, they'll give each other one last hug before they kick the stands up, gun the engines and head off in different directions. She's spent the last two years looking for him, praying that he doesn't know what she does, that he isn't like her, like Finnan. But she can see it in his eyes, like fear or fury. And he shows her his mark, on his chest, under his shirt, over his heart. Most people would just see smooth flesh, the beads and the mojo bag, the silver cross and dog tags. She sees his graving, his secret name written in light in the unkin script, like a luminous tattoo. He might as well have a halo, or horns.

– Don't tell me, she says. It's too dangerous if I know.

And all she wants right now is for the world to be the way it was when they were kids, before the simple surface that they knew was stripped away and all the flesh and bones of its metaphysique shown underneath, the rippling sinews of paths twisted out of time and space, the tendons stretching between centuries, the white bone structures of an eternity jointed, articulated, rebuilt by creatures that had stepped out of the mundane world long before either of them were even born. Creatures like they'd become, not even knowing it, and, in doing so, damned themselves to this insane existence. What do you do if the end of the world is coming and you're an angel who doesn't want to fight? Where do you go?

– The Vellum, he says.

The Vellum. Like giving it a name makes it any more comprehensible, any more sane. A world under the world – or after it, or beyond it, inside, outside – those ideas don't even fucking apply. Where's the Vellum? Outside the mundane cosmos, as the ancients thought, further by far than they could possibly imagine in their measures of the heavens dwarfed by actualities of galaxies and clusters? Or buried in a speck of dirt under a fingernail? Where do the gods come from? Where do people go when they die? Where do angels travel in packs for fear of being slaughtered by their own shadows, huddle in fortress heavens against a void they need a fucking God of Gods to conquer? Phreedom's seen a glimpse of it, just once, a plain of bird skulls stretching for as far as she can see, a vision given to her as a threat the day that she herself became one of these inhuman things. It was a warning given to a little girl who knew too much already, a message: this is what you're getting yourself into. As desolate and vast as that vision might have been, she knows, it was only a tiny corner of the infinite Vellum.

She looks at him, her brother, Thomas. His eyes are brown flecked with green, as hers are green with flecks of brown; where his hair's brown pushing for auburn, hers is rust red, streaked with ginger. They're both autumn – if you listen to that kind of Eurotrash fashionazi shit on the webworlds – but where he's kicking through the first Fall leaves, she's dancing round a Halloween bonfire.

– I'll go into the Vellum, Thomas says. The Covenant won't find me. Finnan–

– Fuck Finnan, she snarls. If it wasn't for that fucker, we'd have never . . .

Never what? Never touched infinity? Never heard the Cant that resonates in every fibre of their fucking bodies? Never learned to hear that language, read the gravings of it in the world and in themselves, their own secret names? Never become unkin?

But she knows it isn't true, that there was something in her that couldn't help but be attracted to the crazy guy who lived in his castle of junk in the trailer-park out in the middle of the desert where they came every winter, year after year, with their Mom and Dad, a snowbird family of the semi-nomadic Winnebago tribe. He didn't hunt them out. He didn't come to them and offer them eternity in the sand under their feet. They'd gone to him, first her brother then herself, because they just knew – in the way he touched the dry wind like a blind man feeling someone's face, in the way he turned his head to watch vortices of cigarette smoke curl in the air – they knew he had some kind of way of reading the secrets hidden in the world around them. If it hadn't been him who showed her – showed them both – the world beneath the world, it would have been someone else, some other place, some other time.

But still, she can't help hating him a little for the hell that hunts them both now, both her brother and herself. Or the heaven, rather.

*From her breast the double strand of beads were taken at the third
gate.*
    *– What is this? Inanna asked, but, Quiet, Inanna, she was told again.
The ways of the underworld are perfect. They may not be questioned.*
    Creak.
    – Thanks. The old guy smiles as he steps past her through the
door she's holding open and she nods – You're welcome – and walks
out into the car park.
    – Angels on your body, he calls after her, some misplaced Califor-
nian craziness of a blessing.
    She swings her leg over the bike.

Most people have it wrong, she knows now. They think the unkin –
wandering through their myths and legends, calling themselves
gods here, angels there – they think these creatures rule eternity,
own it as their realm. But eternity, the Vellum, is like … the media
of reality itself, the blank page on which everything is written, on
which anything *could* be written. The Vellum isn't the absolute
certainty of some city-state of Heaven; no, it's the vast wilderness
of uncertainty, possibility, the fucking primal chaos itself, and this
angel empire of their dreams is just a colony of settlers trying to
tame it, make it fit with their mad puritan ideals, a town of walls
and fences, of warped zeal, of hatred and fear, holding out
against the storms and the strange natives, and riding out with their
cavalry and swords and guns to slaughter every painted savage and
naked squaw who won't accept their righteous laws of sin and
purity. Angels and demons. Or the Covenant and the Sovereign
Powers, as they like to call themselves. To the angels, even eternity
itself is just another hell of redskin enemies to be purged and
rebuilt, New Jerusalem … their New World. She wonders if they'll
have slave ships ferrying dead sinners to their Western Lands to toil
in plantation purgatories.
    For a second, looking across at her brother, in the roadhouse, she
has a sudden image of him in a Civil War uniform, all the braiding
torn from it and gray with dust so you can't tell what side he's on, or

was on before he started running. She blinks and he's normal again. That's the thing about eternity. It gets fucking everywhen.

– They won't find me, he says.

– You won't find him, she screams, and she twists, snarling and cursing, sobbing, spitting blood and tears as one of the bastard fucking unkin pins her arms, wrenching them back behind her, cracking electric pain through dislocated shoulders, while the other gathers a fistful of her hair to snap her head back with one hand and, with the other, pound his fist into her face, into her jaw, again and again and again, till all that she can do is moan. *I'll kill you. I'll fucking kill you,* she's thinking. *I'll fucking kill you all.*

She can feel his mind touching on hers, a whisper inside her head, *where is he*? The cigarette still burns in the ashtray on the Formica tabletop of Finnan's long-abandoned trailer. *She shouldn't have come back here.* The smoke curls upwards, languid; the cigarette itself is mostly ash now.

He turns to look at the table, then peers into her face.

– Ash? he says. What *are* you thinking, little girl?

She looks at the cigarette, stares at the cigarette, the ash, that ash, not any other, not the spoken syllable of an interrupted word. She's not giving these fuckers anything.

– Fuck you, she says, and he punches her again.

– We'll find him, the one holding her arms is saying in her ear. You can make it easy for us, easy for yourself, but either way we'll still find him. Please.

Good cop, bad cop. Carter and Pechorin, they introduced themselves as. Golden Boy and Count Dracula, she thought with a sneer, dismissing them until they took off their shades and she saw just how empty their eyes were.

Fuck you. Fuck you, she thinks. *I'll fucking kill you. And you won't find him.*

The punching stops. She can't see anything any more, for the blood and the blinding buzzsaw sparks of pain, but she can feel him pawing at her now, pulling at her jeans, ripping her T-shirt. It's six months since she last saw her brother, but the scent of memory is strong on her; it's what led them to her in their hunt for him. They're gearing up for the apocalypse. Most of the unkin are already signed to one side or the other, and it's only the odd new blood, born in a backwater, living on the move, who've managed to evade the gatherers. For all she knows its only her and Finnan and her brother that are still free. And she's not even sure about herself.

I'll fucking kill you all.

She can feel his hand pushing inside her jeans; she's falling into herself, the only escape from the brutality of angels. He starts to grunt, his fingers pushing, probing.

You won't find him.

But I will.

Hunter Seeker

When she entered the fourth gate, the breastplate was stripped from her chest.

– What is this? asked Inanna.

– Quiet, Inanna, she was told, the customs of the city of the dead are perfect. They may not be questioned.

Doom. She catches a glimpse of past or future, an echo across reality, across the present ... across the road: a car door thudding shut as two men in black suits stand, arms folded, bug-eyed in black shades, beckoning to the person standing where she is now, to her brother Thomas. It's superimposed over her view just like a sim world in her lenses would be, but she knows this is no electronic apparition. She knows those fuckers; her personal demons, they are, those angels of death, hired gods. Fucking unkin. She can spot them a mile off. She can spot them a month off.

The vision only lasts a second, but it's enough to follow.

Asheville, she thinks, as she rides past another old Volkswagen Beetle slapped with peacenik bumper stickers. Haight-Asheville, more like.

It's weird. It's not at all what she expected after days of small towns with flags flying and motels with We Support Our Troops on their roadside signs instead of Vacancies or No Vacancies, after twiddling the dial on the alarm clock-radio in her room and finding only Country and Western, evangelists and Classic Rock. Or maybe she should have expected it, realized from the Jim and the Janis and the Jimi that if the small towns were stuck in the 1950s, the big city here would be sitting stoned and tripping in a haze of 1969. So the war is in the Middle East this time, instead of South-East Asia, so the rednecks are talking about sand-niggers and towel-heads instead of gooks; still seems like nothing ever changes.

It's a college town, she supposes, and this four-block area at the centre of it is a little bohemian ghetto for the intellectuals, all music shops and cafes, bars and bistros. A British double-decker bus sits in a beer garden, windows and seats taken out, replaced with tables and chairs, all retro European quirkiness. She walks past what looks like an old garage, painted in sky-blue and multicoloured flowers and rainbows – a fucking commune or cooperative of some sort. There's a kid in a Che Guevara T-shirt, graffiti that says Fuck The Alamo, Remember Guantanamo. No fucking wonder that Tom ended up here, she thinks, the latter-day hippy that he is, or was.

She turns onto College Street, and parks the bike outside a bank, circles the area on foot, working by this sort of sixth sense, like she's playing a childhood game again, her brother's voice laughing at her. You're getting colder. Warmer now.

They used to play Hunter Seeker among the trailers of Slab City, one of them hiding in some burnt-out automobile or oilcan, patched into the view in the other's goggles – that was before the first lenses came out – and directing them with clues and taunts whispered across the airwaves into their earphones. Like they were heat-seeking guided missiles with cameras on the front, straight out of the CNN coverage of the war in Syria.

– Ah, now you're really getting warm, he'd say. Hotter. Now you're burning. Red hot. *White hot.*

The Resonance of Another Moment

Doom. This time the car is real, parked up on College Street, the owner – some guy in khaki shorts – slamming the door shut and pinging the central locking down with the little black electronic key he points at it. She feels dizzy as the world buzzes around her. You could call it deja vu, but it's not that she feels like she's been here before in this exact moment, more like she knows that someone else has, that her brother has. Just like before, she has this deep uneasy feeling that she's standing in the same spot that her brother stood in. And just like before, she has that same peripheral vision of two men in black suits and black shades, one of them beckoning to her brother with a slow hook of his finger. *Come here.*

She has to fight the urge to turn and run, even knowing that these hunter seeker unkin, with their cold and knowing clichéd mafioso poise, aren't here, right now, but in another time, that it's her brother that they're after, not her. She can feel Thomas's terror, burning in her chest, red hot . . . white hot.

The car is real, the moment has no meaning, but she feels the resonance of another moment in it, the moment her brother stepped out of a car, stood where she's standing now and turned just as she's turning—

When she entered the fifth gate, the gold bracelet was taken from her wrist.

– What is this? asked Inanna.

– Quiet, Inanna, she was told, the customs of the city of the dead are perfect. They may not be questioned.

And she's close. She can feel reality stretch thin around her, like the world itself is only a skin, translucent, tenuous, the Vellum rippling underneath what's real, underneath, beyond, behind. She's followed the path her brother's ripped through time, pitched back and forward in his wake, cresting the waves and working her way inward to the source, the impact zone, where he broke through, like a comet smashing into the ocean. And she's . . . here.

She turns to find it staring at her.

The tattoo parlour is adorned with psychedelic patterns everywhere, painted over the royal blue of the woodwork and on photos and display-boards in the window. The glass panel of the door has a logo of an eye painted in black, intricate and old-fashioned like an engraving. Iris Tattoos. This is the place she's been looking for. If she wants to find her brother, wherever or *whenever* the hell he is, this is . . . the door she has to go through.

She lays her hand on the brass handle, curls her fingers round it, tender, tense. She pauses.

Ting. The bell over the doorway of the shop rings, brass like the handle that she turns again to push the old glass-panelled door shut, juddering in its misfit with the too-tight frame.

When she entered the sixth gate, the lapis rod and line was taken from her hand.

– What is this? asked Inanna.

– Quiet, Inanna, she was told, the customs of the city of the dead are perfect. They may not be questioned.

And the beaded curtain rattles as she pushes through it into the dark room where the woman in the veil looks up and pauses in her work, a buzzing tattooist's needle in her hand. And there's another hand, grabbing at her arm, the assistant's.

And when she entered the seventh gate, from her body the royal robe was removed.

– What is this? Inanna asked.

– Quiet, Inanna, she was told, the customs of the city of the dead are perfect. They may not be questioned.

– What's that? asks Phreedom.

– I said, you can't go in. Madame Iris is with a customer.

– She'll see me, Phreedom says.

Naked and Bowed Low

Naked and bowed low, Inanna entered the throne room of Eresh of the Greater Earth who arose. She started from her throne. The Anunnaki, judges of the underworld, came from the darkness to surround Inanna, passing judgement on her. Eresh of the Greater Earth fastened the eye of death on her. She spoke the word of wrath against Inanna, uttered the cry of guilt against her, struck her down. And as the judgement and the gaze, the wrath, the guilt fell on her, as the darkness fell on her, Inanna fell, and when she rose again out of the darkness it was as a corpse, raised up in the hands of the

46

judges of the underworld, raised up to hang, a piece of rotting meat, a carcass hanging from a cold hook on the wall.

Phreedom looks at the woman in the veil with quiet, grim detachment, ignoring the assistant who still holds her arm. Madame Iris looks more like Gypsy Rose Lee as far as she's concerned, looks more like some two-bit fortune-teller than a guardian of the threshold. Some fucking Sovereign. Better to rule in a fucking tattoo parlour in the middle of nowhere than to serve in Heaven.

The woman in the veil waves the assistant away, sends her customer out through the beaded curtain with just a whisper in his ear, and:

– You've got your mark, little goddess, she says. I can see it on you ... in you. What do you need me for?

She has an accent – vaguely European, Phreedom thinks, but she can't quite place it. There's an inconsistent mix of guttural Germanic, lilting Latin in it and she wonders if it's actually just an affectation, like the veil, a mask designed to give an air of phoney mystery. Madame Iris. Yeah, right. She's unkin for sure – she's radiating power that Phreedom feels prickling her skin like something between heat and static electricity. But, really. *Ditch the hokum, sister*, Phreedom thinks.

– I'm looking for someone, she says.

She reaches into her jacket pocket to pull her wallet out, to fetch a photo from it, but her hand is barely halfway out before the woman nods.

– Thomas, she says. Your lover?

– Brother.

The woman gives a *hmmm*.

– You know he's gone. Gathered, gone into the ...

– Vellum, she says. I know.

He said they wouldn't find him, but they did. They found him and he escaped. Somehow he got away from them and, skipping this way and that, the bloodhounds snapping at his heels, he made it here, to Madame Iris's tattoo parlour in downtown Asheville where the boundary between reality and the Vellum is so thin that you could stick a fingernail into it and drag it down and scratch a doorway between this world and the one beneath.

– I know he's gone, she says, her voice ragged with memory. That doesn't mean I can't go after him.

– He's dead, says Madame Iris.

– That doesn't mean I can't go after him.

Madame Iris is silent for a second.

– Where angels fear to tread, eh? You know that path is one-way.

– I don't care.

And Phreedom knows it's true. Under the grief and the rage, under all the bitterness that drives her, is an emptiness. The real sorrow, the true anger, is at what's been cut out of her heart. The pain she nurses when she lies awake at night in some hotel room bed is only a ... stand-in for the pain she *should* feel but just isn't capable of, not any more. Like a dead hunk of meat hung up to drain its blood, stripped of her dignity, flayed and gutted, dead inside. She belongs in hell, a carcass hanging from a cold hook on the wall.

– I'm going over to the other side, says Phreedom.

– You're already here, says Madame Iris, dropping the accent, lifting her veil, showing the face that Phreedom looks at in the mirror.

Phreedom at the Gates of Hell

Phreedom steps into the shower, pulling the glass screen shut behind her, and shakes her hair loose under the water, feeling the grime of the road and the sweat of the heat sluice from her body, weariness wash from her bones. She closes her eyes, closes her mind and lets it all drain away in the water, all the shit of memory, all the dust of identity, letting her hands take care of all the lathering and rubbing, working their way over her body, with a soldier-like efficiency in cleaning every part of her. If she enjoys it, if she relaxes in the warm water and enjoys the feel of it, scalding and soothing on her flesh, it's in an abstract way, a distanced and mechanical awareness of some object labelled *pleasure* that barely registers as real awareness.

*

If she was aware, you see, she might remember another shower where she scrubbed herself and scrubbed herself till blood and tears ran with the water down the plughole but no matter how she scrubbed she couldn't get the filth out of her soul, she couldn't get the black filth of the fucking angel out of her head, out of her heart, out of her cunt and all the places inside where he'd probed her with his fingers and his words and his prick, and in the end she just sat there, in the corner of the shower, arms around herself and bleeding from the wounds made by the angel and the wounds made by herself. She might remember that, you see, if she was aware.

So Phreedom washes like a robot, with a military efficiency.

She gives herself the once-over in the mirror before leaving the hotel room, fixing her mascara and her hair – it's still a little wet – making sure the choker's tight around her neck and that the chickenbone charm is sitting right, the way it falls across her T-shirt. She zips the leather jacket up and checks her watch to see the hands all moving independently, the hour hand moving faster than the minute hand, and both of them spinning anti-clockwise even as the second hand ticks forward. She has the earphones in already but they're silent, waiting for her to decide what music is appropriate to her mood.

With a wry stab at humour, she thumbs the toggle on the datastick, tapping and flicking it this way and that until the heads-up display in her lenses scrolls what she's looking for across her vision.

Hotel California.

She was never a big fan of The Eagles but as she lays her hand on the door of her room in the Comfort Inn, and pushes it open, and looks out into the bland corridor, it seems somehow appropriate as a bitter joke. Thomas. Fucking hippy fucking Thomas; he always loved that song.

It would have been his birthday today.

The door swings shut behind her.

Click.

Errata

The Book of Life

– So tell us about this Book then, says Jack. The Book of All Hours.

Joey snorts derisively and heads off to the bar to get another round in; Puck, arms draped over Jack's shoulders, sticks a tongue out at his back. In his long, black coat and brooding silences, I can't help but think of Joey Pechorin sometimes as a sort of latter-day version of his forebears. His family come from Russia, originally; White Russians from Georgia, they came over after the revolution and he acts like he has cossack in his blood, maybe even a little of Ivan the Terrible's oprechnika – half orthodox monastic order, half secret police. I've seen him in a fight – defending Jack, of course, who'd managed to insult some yob – *clear latent case*, said Jack – by coming on to him while out of his face on ecstasy – and I've wondered what he would be capable of in other circumstances. Puck doesn't like him at all, but then Puck is only jealous because Jack and Joey go back such a long way. They've been through high school in a nowhere town housing scheme and they're like a double act that nothing can break up – Carter and Pechorin, Pechorin and Carter – except for maybe flighty fairy Thomas.

– OK, I say. So this Book was written by the angel Metatron before the world even existed and it's actually God's plans for, well, everything. Except that being God's Word, it's not just the plans. I mean, it doesn't just describe reality; it defines it. God says, Let there be light and, bingo, there's light, and it's good, of course. He says, Let there be this and let there be that and all of reality pops into existence, and it's all good. Smashing. But what happens when the sound of his words dies out? I mean, eventually the echoes fade away and you're left with silence again, the big black void. So, of course, God has his private secretary write it all down for him, make it all a little more permanent. Written in stone, signed and sealed, here we go, mate, sorted, this is reality the way it is, was and ever will be. Boxed up.

I sip my G'n'T.

– But then, of course, his right-hand-man decides to stab his boss in the back and take over the business for himself. Everything goes tits-up and war breaks out in Heaven. Most angels stay with the Big I Am, but there's enough of them on Lucifer's side that maybe the outcome isn't as certain as you might think, so some of them, some of them just panic and leg it for Earth. Either that or they're sent there, secret mission and all that, because anyway, they have the Book. Maybe God *is* going to fall. Maybe Lucifer's about to get his hands on the Book and rewrite reality the way he thinks it should be. Whatever the reason, the Book winds up on Earth, hidden or lost, for all of history, just waiting for the day that it's discovered. Gathering dust in some library somewhere.

– So if you change what's written in the Book, you change reality? says Puck.

– Exactly, I say. Write someone out of history or write them back in where they don't belong at all.

– So what happens? says Jack.

– I haven't decided yet, I say. I mean, I know I want to have the angels and demons both hunting for the Book. I could write it as a straightforward fantasy adventure, you know? Some normal human finds the Book and gets drawn into the whole big cosmic struggle thing. Blond-haired, blue-eyed heroes and black-hearted villains, and all that. But, it's just . . . that seems a little escapist.

– What's wrong with that? says Puck. Escapist sells. I'd buy it. The Book of All Hours, by Guy Reynard. Cool.

– War isn't an adventure, I say. There's no glory in war.

– Bollocks, says Jack.

He grins as he flicks the Zippo open, lights up another cigarette.

– You don't fucking get it, Guy. Of course war is bloody glorious. Flamethrowers and Agent Orange. Deforestation bombs. Fucking beautiful. That's the true horror of it, mate.

– Jack, I say, sometimes you worry me.

– Cheers, he says.

The Search Engine

I trace the course of the River of Crows and Kings with one fingernail, running it softly over the vellum of the Book and looking down to the real thing below, down through the glass desk on which the Book sits, down through the glass floor of the ship's bridge under my feet, down through the clouds towards the churning course of mud and filth; I am thankful that at this height I can no longer smell the rot. Reaching over with my free hand, I grasp the ivory handle of the lever and pull it back. The low hum of the *Search Engine* heightens slightly, becomes louder as its monstrous turbines rise out of sloth and into life. There is no lurch, no feeling of inertia broken, and at this height it's almost impossible to see any visible shifting of the world beneath me. Only the glittering light displays of dials and indicators, projected on the glass in front of me give any sign that we are moving forward. That this leviathan of the sky is rising from its indolence and moving slowly, saurian, across the oceanic clouds, following the path marked out for me in the Book of All Hours, north, ever north, towards the end of the world.

In scale and style somewhere between a steamship and a cathedral, the *Search Engine* is the product of some technology far surpassing the world of my origins. I found it in a city as pristine in its desolation as if it had never had inhabitants at all, berthed among a score or so designed on the same principles in a wide docklands of glistening grey warehouses full of steel cargo containers and wooden crates, plastic sheets covering bales of hay, huge reels of cotton or silk thread, canisters of sugar, tobacco. In a way, the whole scene was quite mundane – a dock or port like any other dock or port I've come across in my travels. It was only the black river of unspeakable mire and the great hulking sky-ships floating in the air above like zeppelins, grounded by spiralling threads of silver staircase, that made the vision quite different from anything else I've seen.

I have no idea how these contraptions fly; if I were to describe them as having wings it would be the type of wings that a mansion has rather than those upon an aeroplane. From the main hull of the ship, transepts project, three at each side as in the crosses to be found in a

Greek or Russian Orthodox church. From below, that hull appears as an inverted vault, like the ribcage or armour plating of some great beast, curving up and opening out to araeostyle intercolumniations, panes of stained glass and pillars between them. Parapeted towers rise above, with spires topped by vast thuribles spewing a blue-green steam, presumably some by-product of their power source, though I really have no idea. I have no idea how they float in the air impervious to the winds buffeting, no idea how they glide smoothly forward or back, up or down at the touch of this lever or that. But thankfully, the controls are rather less inscrutable than the principles underlying their construction. When I finally found my way to the glass bowl of the cockpit-bridge that hangs from the tip of the machine's prow like some World War Two gunnery emplacement on a bomber, I was relieved to see, at the bottom of the steps leading down into that segmented swimming pool, at the centre of this vertigo-inspiring glass bowl, only a deep green leather armchair with a crescent-shaped glass desk and console and a few bronze, ivory-tipped levers and wheels around it. It's taken me less than a week of experimentation to get the hang of it all; I'd have to say I'm really rather impressed by the elegant simplicity of the design.

And so now, I am off again, a thief at the helm of yet another stolen vehicle, leaving behind me yet another caravan of sundry acquisitions, souvenirs of my seemingly eternal travels. This time, I have to say, I have little regret.

I have been finding it increasingly difficult, these last few centuries, you see, to maintain my memories of the world I left so far behind, and I realise now that it was a mistake to start collecting these various scraps and parchments of the transfigured realities I travel through, the places I have come to call the Folds. I have collected so many birth and death certificates, journals and photographs, newspaper clippings and suchlike, in all relating to perhaps a thousand different variants of what appears to be myself – or Jack, or Joey, or Thomas – so many and so varied that I think my poring over them has begun to blur the boundaries of what I was – what I am – and what I might have been. Perhaps I thought that I might find some pattern among the congruencies and dissonances, as if this whole journey had been laid out for me as a lesson by some greater power. I did work, for a while, on the theory that all souls travel such a journey, drifting through the worlds of other choices, other chances, so that, when they finally reach their destination, they should understand exactly who they are, by understanding who they're not and why. Now, though . . . sometimes I get confused. I forget if this scrap of journal or that was written by myself or by some other Guy Reynard or Reynard Carter or whatever bloody name I was born with.

2

The War Against Romance

The Journey of the Dead Man

The angel walks into Slab City off the Jornada del Muerto, the journey of the dead man which runs north from Kern's Gate, El Paso, through a dry plain of natron and uranium, salt, sand and dust, and the moment she looks up and sees him she just knows that he's an angel, because, although she's only fifteen and has never seen one of *them* before, one of what Finnan calls the unkin, she recognizes right away what she's been taught to look out for, the particular kind of graving, the mark of their essence carved into them, into their words, their actions, their existence.

Nearly everybody has some kind of graving in them, Finnan's told her, because nearly every *thing* does. Every thing in the world has its true name, its name in the Cant, the unkin tongue, and humans are no different. It doesn't have to be physical, although sometimes people wear it in their eyes or on their skin for everyone to see, a thousand-yard stare or a knife-scar or tattoo. But what makes it a graving, a name that you can read and maybe even use, is that it's real close to the surface, some event has brought it out, a welt on the surface of reality. You get it for your own reason, if you ever get it at all; maybe you get it the first time you fuck, maybe the first time you kill, either way it's your own special graving, it's *you*, that secret name carved into your consciousness at that precise moment when you suddenly, instantly realize: I know what I am. Just a moment, just a day like any other, like today, April 12th, 2014. But what happens on

55

that day marks you for the rest of your life, says Finnan, and maybe even longer.

Of course she doesn't have her graving yet, so she can't really be sure he's not just shitting her about it; first time he told her, in fact, she said so in her foul-mouthed tomboy terminology. Except. Except since then Finnan has been teaching her to read those secret names, to read them in the squint of an eye, the set of a jaw, the hunch of a shoulder, a rap of a knuckle on a table. For most people it's like a gambler's tell, a little characteristic that gives away their whole hand, their whole game, but for some that mark is just a little bit more defining and a little bit more definite. They wear it like an aura and it flickers through the air around them, ahead of them even, turning heads when they walk into a room, hushing conversation. Nearly everybody has some kind of graving, all right. But not everyone has it graved so deep that it goes right down through them and under the skin of reality itself. Not everyone has the Cant.

So she knows he's an angel, all right. She knows he's unkin. She could damn near *smell* him on the dead, desert air, even before he came into sight over the low brow of the Jesus Hill.

He's black; at first she thinks it's just shadow, but, no, the sun is due east, still rising, and he's coming in from the south, so he isn't in silhouette. He stops at the top of the hill for a while and stands under one arm of the large, wooden cross like a man waiting to be hanged calmly scanning his audience, and though the air is shimmering around him she can suddenly see him in perfect focus, his black leather clothes, his black leather skin, his dreadlocks and goatee, his deep hooded eyes. He's carrying what looks like a small but thick leatherbound book in one hand. As dogs, chained to their owners' trailers here and there, bark at the dawn, and somebody, somewhere, plays 'Crawling King Snake' on a tinny radio, she hears him clearly as he whispers to the wind: Finnan.

– Never saw anyone *walk* into Slab City before, says a friendly voice behind her.

– Morning, Mac, she says. Maybe ... uh, maybe his car broke down ... or something.

She's pretty sure that that's not even near the truth, but she doesn't want to start on the subject of unkin with Mac. Mac, he's this weird fusion of old-style Christian evangelist and acid-crazed flower-child who never quite made it into the ministry, just a bit too eccentric for any orthodox faith to handle. Instead, he took to his vocation in his own, individual way. He took to painting a hill.

He started his mission before she was born, before her parents even started their semi-nomadic lifestyle. For as long as anyone can remember here, in fact, he's been painting one side of the low hill that marks the southern boundary of Slab City, decorating it inch by inch in whites and pinks and corn-yellows and sky-blues, with giant hearts and massive flowers. Originally he'd just freshened up the paintwork as often as he could afford it, but as time went on the thing took up more and more hillside and more and more paint, so that Mac found it hard to keep up with the wear and tear of New Mexico weather. Then someone suggested using clay as well and the Jesus Hill took on a whole new dimension. By the time her family arrived to spend their first winter in Slab City, it had become a permanent adobe sculpture, a landmark-sized masterpiece of Christian kitsch.

She remembers watching it growing larger still throughout the warm winters of her childhood, its bible slogans in six-foot letters proclaiming love to the world and salvation for all. Despite her neo-pagan upbringing she's always found it a welcome sight to return to this in the Fall, after a summer spent around the cool Great Lakes up in Canada, and she's always sort of sad to leave it in the spring as they follow the other mobile families, snowbirds escaping from the coming heat of the Mojave summer. Between May and September, Slab City belongs only to the real desert-rats, non-mobiles like Mac or Finnan who, it's generally accepted, have long since fried what's left of their brains.

– Hey, by the way, she says. Mom picked up some paint over in Santa Fe; some guy she was doing hackwork for had it lying around, she said to ask if you could use it.
    – Sure could, says Mac. What colour is it?
    – Eggshell . . . puke yellow, perfect for the hill.
    Mac laughs.
    – I'll bring it over before we head off. Maybe you can have a big 'Jesus Loves You' done for when we get back. Real tasteful, like.
    – So cynical, so young, says Mac. In trash lies truth, remember. The Good Lord loves a glow-in-the-dark Madonna much as he loves the biggest cathedral – hell, more so, if it means more to one of his lost sheep.
    – Baa, she says.

A Heart-Shaped Window

You don't argue theology with Mac, she reckons; he's too nice a guy to take away his sense of Grand Purpose in the Simple Act. Nuts, sure, but 50 percent of trailer-park society as a whole, and about 75 percent of Slab City in particular, is at very least eccentric if not outright certifiable. There's her own dad, trying to map Atlantis using regressive hypnosis to access the mental database of his prime incarnation's experience. Then there's their neighbour at the moment, Mr Willis, who thinks they should all be buying up NASA leftovers and trying to colonize Mars as autonomous collectives. He already has his own spacesuit. Up in the parks around Lake Superior you get a lot of people who're real 'tolerant' of this sort of weirdness, but she's always hated their patronizing attitudes. Sure, she thinks Mac and Mr Willis are bugfuck crazy lunatics but she respects them for that and, in the same way that she hates to be treated like a little girl, she hates the way some of the middle-class mobiles talk down to people she considers her friends.
    – Hey, says Mac. He's coming down.

*

The rasta angel starts slowly down Jesus Hill, climbing round 'LOVE' and over the Sacred Bleeding Heart, cracking 'CONSIDER THE LILIES' under his feet and scuffing dirt on 'THE LIGHT OF THE WORLD'. She waits with Mac at the foot of the hill for him to arrive, her standing in the open, trying to look bored by kicking at the dry grasses under her feet, Mac leaning out the heart-shaped window of his junk-augmented schoolbus-cum-shack, scratching at his grey stubble. The black guy jumps the last five feet or so down the hill and lands damn near in her face.

– Can I bother one of you for a little water? he asks, looking at Mac, then shifting his gaze to her.

The bastard is fucking tall.

– My . . . car broke down on the freeway other side of the hill there, he says. This desert air's given me one mother of a thirst.

– I'll get you a bottle, says Mac. Offer you a beer, if you want one.

– No . . . thanks, but water'll be just great.

The heart-shaped wooden shutter snaps closed as Mac disappears. The angel is still looking straight at her.

– What's your name, little one? he says and she hates him instantly.

– Phreedom, she says, but spelled PH instead of F.

She loves her techno-hippy parents – really she does – but she used to be a little jealous of her brother, Tom, with his normal name. Went through a phase, in fact, where she would only answer to 'Anna'. She's kind of grown to like it now, though. It's a good way of judging people, how they react to it if they ask, and you tell them, and you just stand there with that look on your face – *yeah, and your point is?*

– Is it? – he smiles – Tell me . . . Phreedom . . . do you know of anyone around here good at fixing things . . . cars, that is?

Finnan.

– You mean like a repairman? A mechanic or something? she says.

– Exactly.

Don't lie to an angel, she thinks.

– What kind of car is it?

– Here's your water, says Mac, stepping out of his open front door and handing a bottle of mineral water to the stranger. What's up?

– I was just asking young Phreedom here if she knew anyone who might be able to fix my car.

– You want Finnan, says Mac. The guy's some kind of a wizard. Electrical, mechanical, you name it – if it's broke he can fix it. Slab's over that way, all corrugated iron and old rubber tires, you can't miss it. Phree'll take you, won't you, Phree? Her and Finnan are great buddies. You're not doing anything just now, are you, Phree?

She looks from one to the other then down at her feet.

– Guess not, she says.

Staring Down an Angel

– So, how come you're up and about while everyone else is still in bed? asks the angel.

He's walking about two paces behind her as she leads him the short distance to Finnan's slab. She takes her time.

– Just heading out to gather some peyote buttons for Finnan, she says. You get better mojo if you collect them at dawn, he told me.

– I imagine he's told you a lot of things.

– I like your coat, she says.

It's long and black, with a high, turned-up collar, the leather scuffed and dusty like he's walked around the world in it.

– It looks good and warm for the cold, desert nights, she says.

– I wouldn't know, he says. I'm never usually this far from civilization . . . no offence.

– None taken.

Slab City *is* pretty primitive, she has to admit. When trailer-parks first took off in the Home-of-the-Future 1950s a lot of white-collar families wanted trailers and campers for second homes. By the last decades of the last century, these recreational vehicles were the only thing a lot of shit-poor people could afford as a *first* home. So you got some trailer-parks which were like holiday camps, with leisure-facilities and every amenity you could name – just drive up, rent your slab and plug into the water, electricity and disposal pipes, or, better still, get a valet to do it while you take the kids for their tennis lesson.

Other places were cheaper and nastier, with fewer and fewer amenities. Slab City's really just a flat piece of dirt where people started to park one day. With no charges and no power or water, its denizens are pretty much confined to the self-sufficient or the financially desperate.

– So what kind of car was it you said you had, again? she asks the angel.

    – A red one, he says. Tell me about this Finnan.

    – I don't know much about him.

    – Mac said you were his friend.

    – He doesn't talk a lot.

    – Perhaps he's got something to hide.

    – Finnan doesn't have anything to hide.

    – We *all* have something to hide.

    – So what are *you* hiding?

The guy stops and she turns, shoving her hands in the pockets of her oversize biker jacket – a hand-me-down from Tom before he lit off to find . . . she doesn't know what exactly . . . his fortune, she guesses. There's a part of her that's still pissed off at him for it, but . . . But he left her with his jacket and she wears it with his attitude.

So, she stands there, trying to stare down an angel.

– I imagine your friend Finnan would call it my . . . graving, he says.

It's like he's throwing out the word as a fishing line, seeing if she'll bite. She looks away, at the dog lying sprawled out on the makeshift porch of a nearby trailer-home. Gazing over at them, without lifting its head, it wags its tail, thumping it lazily on the wooden planking. She looks back at the angel.

– You're not doing a very good job of it, she says, and he laughs, the air wavering around him, dust swirling in barely perceptible vortices and currents. He raises a hand like he's playing with the breeze. And way off in the distance: a high hollow note like the coda of a song played on a flute carved out of bone.

    – Don't try to teach a birdman how to fly, hatchling.

    – *Birdman?*

    – What does Finnan call us? Angels . . . gods?

– Unkin, she says. And he looks at her like she's eaten his grandmother, pushes past and starts straight for Finnan's slab … as if he's known the way all along. She hurries after him.

A Plain of Bones

– I thought you said your friend didn't talk much.

His voice is clipped.

– He never told me what it means.

– Ignorance is bliss.

– Bullshit, she says.

The angel glances back at her and the dog they've just passed starts to howl.

– Did he think we wouldn't gather you as well? asks the angel.

– I don't know what you're talking about.

– Then your friend Finnan didn't tell you everything. Ask him sometime what it's like to walk the road of all dust. Ask him about the dry wind that blows across the fields of lost days. Ask him.

And he mutters something under his breath and suddenly she's dizzy, her mind filled with this image of a long, dry dusty road, and the angel walking down it, dust devils spiralling in the air around him, whipping up the sand and grit, the dusky-grey and ochre-red and bleached-white dirt of centuries, of millennia of … she sees his black leather boot coming down on a bird's skull, in her mind's eye, and she sees a whole plain of bones, a whole desert that isn't the Mojave at all but somewhere else, somewhere far, far away. And there's a word that's running through her head, something she can't quite make out … villain? volume? valium? … vellum?

She shakes her head to clear it, shake off the image and the ringing sound, but she still feels … sick.

– All I know, she says, is what he taught me about mojo, about voudon and santeria, which is nothing you can't learn in books. And all I know about you unkin is that some people let the mojo take them over, carve it into their own souls till they think they're some sort of fucking superior race, some kind of 'living manifestation of divinity', and sure, they've got power, but they're so fucking full of themselves, so fucking self-righteous, so fucking . . .

She loses the word she's looking for; all she can do is spit on the ground in disgust.

In some ways it's true. The little that Finnan's told her is really just kitchen magic, charms, little gravings on the world. Even the word *unkin* only slipped out when he was drunk that time and got all weird so that she couldn't tell if he was sad or angry, at her or someone else. But if this bastard's going to play fisherman with her then fuck him; two can play at that game.

– There are righteous unkin and there are fallen unkin, says the black man, and there are fools like Finnan who think they can stay neutral, who think they can hide from their duty in the middle of nowhere and pray it never finds them.

– And that's your job, right? she says. Finding them?

– It's time for your friend to decide where he stands. On the side of the angels or with those who would . . .

He tails off into a silent scrutiny of her.

– You have no idea, little one, just what our enemies are capable of. You have no idea what the demons of this world would do to you if we didn't . . . draw the line.

– So you're a recruitment officer for the War in Heaven? she laughs. Hunting down draft-dodgers and deserters? You going to press-gang him or shoot him at dawn?

– I've come to gather him, says the angel. I've come to gather your good friend Finnan.

And Finnan's slab comes into view ahead.

An Old Sepia Photograph

The place has the look of an old sepia photograph, with its sand-scoured chrome and rusted steel and everything all dusty faded brown. The old Airstream trailer stands high up on red brick piles and girder stilts, forming the centre of a large structure of retrofitted salvage. Canvas, corrugated iron and even old car hoods form the walls and roofs of annexes built around and under the main living area, accessed by an old rusting ladder.

Round the back of this industrial gothic folly, rubber tires are piled up to form three walls of an open garage-workshop area, roofed with obsolete twelve-foot solar panel and linked to the Airstream by wires and cables. In front of the main construction, the sandblasted shells of two dead automobiles stand like two stone lions at the steps of some grand City Hall. All around, the place is littered with electrical and mechanical equipment, old and new, broken and fixed, with computers, TVs and satellite dishes, with stripped-down washing machines and motorbikes built up from spare parts.

It was Finnan who'd built the bike her brother Thomas left on, just picked up and left one day, without a note or a word of goodbye. She knew the two of them well enough to know that if anybody had an answer for her it would be Finnan. Finnan had an answer for everything. So she had stormed up to Finnan's slab and started throwing stone after stone against the aluminum of his trailer, stood there, hands on hips, cursing him and shouting at him to come out, demanding to know where Tom had gone. That's two years past now and she still isn't convinced that Finnan doesn't know exactly where Tom is, but she's learned to trust him in so many other ways . . . she's learned to trust him that Tom had a reason for just disappearing.

Part of it is, she's seen what Finnan can do. His slab is a junkyard in its own right and Finnan . . . Finnan is the junkmaster, the man who can take a broken food-processor, a Frigidaire, an electric boiler and a bus-engine, and rebuild them into a single unit that turns raw sewage into fresh water, fertilizer and sterile non-toxic dust. But he can do other things as well. She still remembers when Mac had his 'episode' and they found him lying on the ground, and before she knows it Finnan is down beside him, one hand on his chest, and he gives just a little flick – it wasn't a laying on of hands or nothing, she wouldn't say that exactly, but no way was it a cardiac massage. She was trying to take Mac's pulse and it just wasn't there, she remembers, she couldn't find it there at all until Finnan gave that tiny flick of the wrist . . . and then it was.

And right now, Finnan is standing in his dead-car gateway, waiting for them patiently with his staff in his hand and a cigarette in his mouth.

Finnan

Finnan looks about twenty and has done for as long as she's known him. He claims to be in his late thirties, but there's nobody who knows for sure. The clothes he wears seem always the same, the same white button-neck T-shirts, the same sandstone-coloured chinos and the same scuffed desert hiking boots, everything always smudged with the same black engine oil and grease that slicks back his dirty blond hair. Short and skinny, but with muscles that look like they're made of steel cable, every fibre of them showing under the taut skin of his arms, shifting as he moves them as he works on whatever his latest project is.

– That's the demon inside me, he's joked with her a few times, but she's never been sure just how much of a joke it really is. Got a little bit of something in me, he says, seems to just eat up all my body fat.

She's sure there's something underneath the joke. Finnan has an air about him, a sense that he's constantly on edge, constantly restrained, like he's burning all his energy just holding back, holding himself back from doing God knows what. As she's come to know him, from the late nights when the three of them would get wasted, back when Tom was still around, or chasing him around in the months after her brother left, trying to get some answers out of him, she's come to realize that, in a way, it isn't a joke at all.

We've all got a little bit of demon in us, she thinks, and a little bit of angel. Finnan talks about it in terms of the graving, about the way everyone has an . . . ability to find the Cant inside themselves, to open up a locked door in their heads and let it loose. She thought he was talking in metaphors until the day he held his hand out in front of her, closed in a fist, then opened it up to show her the palm of his hand, closing it again quickly. It might have been some magic trick, but the scar looked real for that instant, the weird shape that looked like it'd been carved in with the point of a knife; she didn't get that good a look at it but she caught a glimpse of something that looked vaguely like an eye in outline – an ellipse with a circle inside – but with four little bumps coming off the outside of it.

Then he opened up his hand again and it was gone, just the rough skin of his working man's hand. He closed his hand into a fist again, flexed his bicep, looking at his arm like it didn't belong to him.

At the moment, she can see the tension in those arms of his, the knotted muscles and wire veins, as one takes the cigarette from his mouth and flicks it away, while the other grips the iron railing that functions as the shaft of his staff. A TV-aerial is fixed at the top of the railing, pointing downwards, its crossbars hung with chains and charms, wound round with barbed wire and crowned by a plastic doll's head. Finnan holds the thing with white knuckles like it's his only connection to sanity. He calls it his *disruptor*. Magic for the TV generation, he says, for an electronic world of nanotech and simware. There's mojo in skin and bone and graveyard dirt, of course, but you have to keep up with the times. The Cant is powerful enough just whispered in an ear; and in these days of *bitmites*, nanite surveillance systems blowing in the wind they breathe, riding on the dust they taste on it, well, the Cant is even stronger as a whisper in the head.

She doesn't know what powers it, but Finnan's disruptor gives a low buzz if you listen close to it, as he grips it in his hand. Like now.

– Well, he says. Good morning, reality. Let's go inside and talk.

The Book of Names

– There's nothing to talk about, says the angel.

He and Finnan are sitting at the Formica top of the little dinner table in Finnan's Airstream, one drinking bottled water, the other bottled beer. She noses round the fridge, looking for a Coke, but watching them all the time out of the corner of her eye, and listening intently to everything they say.

– Your name is in the book, says the angel.

The angel's leatherbound 'book' – actually a tenth generation palmtop with slick packaging – is sitting up on the table in front of him, open and switched on. Scrolling over the screen, row upon row, is a sequence composed of four different glyphs arranged in seemingly random order, and she can't help thinking of an image she saw on a documentary once, a computer-generated graphic of As and Ts and Gs and Cs, scrolling behind a slowly spinning model of a double-helix. The letters represented a gene sequence, she remembers, four basic building blocks that combine along the helix of a DNA molecule to write out the pattern of a living creature.

As she watches, the scrolling gradually accelerates until the screen becomes just a gray blur.

– The book is wrong, says Finnan. You've got the wrong man. Maybe you should check the original. Oh, that's right, I hear you lost it.

He smirks.

– Pity, he says. You really can't expect a cut-rate copy like that to be worth a damn. Those scribes in Aratta hacking the old Cant into gravings that–

– Seamus Finnan. Born in Ireland, in–

– That's not my name, he says. You don't even have my fucking name. Fucking angels. You want to get yer fookin facts straight before ye come barging into someone's fookin life.

It's not the first time she's noticed the hint of an Irish accent in Finnan's voice, but she's still surprised. It's as if the name has just this moment sparked something off inside him, and despite his denials she's suddenly sure that Seamus is the name he was born with. But she's also sure that isn't what Finnan means when he talks about his name. He's talking about something deeper.

The angel leans forward, peering at the book as if the blur actually means something to him.

– The book isn't wrong, says the angel. The record is complete.

– The little black book of your master's conquests, eh?

– A book of unkin, the angel says. Covenant and Sovereigns and those who're not yet signed. All of them. Times and places of callings and gatherings. Crossings of paths. Reckonings.

He moves a finger across the trackpad and the screen flicks sideways, up, down, scrolling, panning, faster than he can possibly see, surely. He taps it and it stops.

– Slab City, April 12th, 2014, says the angel. He turns it round to show Finnan, like the gibberish of sigils proves his point.

Finnan lights another cigarette and takes a draw. She wonders how long he's been here, that his accent's so ... sporadic.

– I don't see my name in there, he says.

– Slab City, April 12th, 2014, says the angel. And there's only you and me here.

– You can't take me without my true name. You've got no hold over me, and you sit here at my table by *my* invitation.

– You *will* be gathered, says the angel.

– Not by you.

– Then by the others, by the Sovereigns.

– You think a nut-job megalomaniac like Malik wants me for his private jihad? Not fucking likely.

She picks up Finnan's lighter from the table and starts playing with it.

– When *they* come for you they'll be less ... diplomatic than I am, says the angel.

– And I'll be less hospitable, says Finnan.

– They'll rape your little apprentice here, the angel says, and drag you down into hell by your greasy matted hair.

She blinks and flicks the lighter open, sparks it.

– Don't underestimate the girl, says Finnan. She can look after herself.

– A chicken-bone cross around her neck is going to save her from hellhounds?

She fingers the charm-necklace that Finnan made for her. Finnan blows smoke in the angel's face.

– You know ... birdman, he says, your organization will never beat the opposition, and they'll never beat you, because underneath the bullshit you're exactly the same thing. Oh, it may be *unkin* with a little 'u' and not a grand and self-important capital letter. But it's Covenant with a capital 'C' for cunt, isn't it? The Covenant and the Sovereigns. I bet they have a book just like that one. How's the score

68

looking, anyway? All even in the final minutes? Waiting for that golden goal.

– You never did understand us, Finnan. The point of the struggle is not to 'beat the opposition' as you put it, but to separate the ... chaff from the grain ... the good seed from the bad seed, and if it means burning the world to dust and fire, well, the most fertile fields have come from ashes.

– I always thought you fuckers were inhuman. You've forgotten where you came from.

– We're *more* than human, boy. We've seen what's out there, you and I. We know what we could build on the ashes of this world. We don't need this ... squalor. We can burn the filth away and build humanity a new world, one of order ... out there ... in the Vellum. You know this world is nothing. This whole universe is ... a mote of dust, a smear of ink, on the surface of the Vellum.

The Last Big Rumble in the Sky

He turns to smile at her, condescending.

– At most, little girl, your history, your reality is ... a groove, cutting its way through what might be, curving so slowly that you see it only as a straight line stretching ever-onward, just deep enough that someone like you can't even conceive of the worlds that run in parallel on the other side of your reality's walls. And it's still nothing more than one tiny whorling line of a fingerprint on the Vellum.

She looks at the angel with his coat covered in the desert's dust, and at Finnan, face smeared with engine oil. He's never mentioned any of this to her.

– I took the King's Shilling once, says Finnan. Once was enough. I was a fookin eedjit then and I won't do it again. Not again.

– You know, Finnan, says the angel, it doesn't really matter to us whether I leave with your heart or with your head; all that matters to us is that you make the choice.

– The Last Big Rumble in the Sky, says Finnan. Is that what you're fookin wanting? Wake up, birdman, the gangs are dead; the Anunnaki, the Athenatoi, the Aesir – they're all long gone–

*

– What do *you* know about that? the angel snarls. Were you there when those *gangs* were throwing children into furnaces in case – just *in case* – they might grow up to be rivals? Did you see Irra march across Akkad, laying waste to everything in his path? What have you seen, Seamus Finnan? What petty little human wars have you seen?

Finnan flicks ash on the linoleum floor. Phreedom fidgets with the alphabet magnets on the fridge door.

– You think I want the old days back? the angel carries on. You think this is nostalgia for *that*? This is an age of reason, and it's the Covenant that built it. This is a war against all that. Against the god-kings and emperors.

He turns to her.

– Against those great romantic lies you humans seem to hold so dear. I would have thought that you'd appreciate that, Seamus Finnan. But you weren't there, were you, when we signed the Covenant to bring an end to all the bloodshed?

Seamus Finnan. She's wondered about his past before, and now she wonders again. The King's Shilling. So he was in the army, in a war? Syria wasn't that long ago, but then again she's sure – the way Mac's talked about him – he was here before that. Iraq? Before that? She suddenly realizes that she doesn't know shit about history. And in all the times he's talked about the unkin, up to his arms in wires or engine-parts, she's never really imagined him anywhere but now.

– No, says Finnan, I wasn't there. But I knew a man who was. A long time ago – maybe not for the likes of you, mind, but for someone like me who still remembers his mother's face and the like – a long time ago for me. I knew someone who was there through it all, who was there when yer fookin Covenant was signed. And he told me it was a big pile of horseshit.

Finnan flashes a grin at him.

– And that he fucked yer mother.

She's waiting for the angel to come flying across the table at him, but he just sits there, staring at Finnan with absolute fury.

The angel sits silently for a moment, while Finnan takes another draw on his cigarette and a swig of his beer, then he punches a few buttons on his palmtop. It starts to scroll again. He looks across at Phreedom, then at Finnan, then out the window at his side.

– My name *is* in this book, you know, says the black man. You may not have decided where your graving goes – yet – but I'm in here.

The scrolling stops again and the screen starts flashing up matrix after matrix of those four glyphs repeated.

– Would you like to know my true name, Finnan, or should I tell the girl so she can call on me when the demons–

– Neither of us want to know your name, says Finnan, cutting him off. I'm not interested. She's not interested.

– What is it – Rumpelstiltskin? she says, and immediately feels stupid.

– It's–

– I won't join you and I won't fight you, snaps Finnan. I won't be named, numbered, called, gathered, saved or damned, and you can–

– Metatron, says the angel.

Metatron

– Metatron, says the angel, and it hurts. He says it real quiet, but she can feel the resonance deep in her skull and it's like a thousand dog-whistles have been blown in both of her ears and for a second – for less than that, for a fraction of a second – she feels like the sound is carrying a living information into everything in the trailer, herself included; that by speaking that single stupid-sounding word the angel has stamped his name into her and into everything around her. For that fraction of a second it seems totally natural, totally logical to think this way, and then the room is spinning but the world has stopped ringing and she leans back against the fridge, looking at Finnan to see if this new development is good or bad, even though she doesn't really need to, because she knows already. It's bad.

Finnan's anger flickers through his body, in the wire vein in his forehead, in the cables of his tensed neck muscles, in the twitching of his arms and clenched fists. His eyes, though, are as calm as ever, cool ice-blue and never blinking.

71

– Nice of you to introduce yourself, he says.

– You *invited* me in. It's only polite, says the angel.

– Polite, sure, but there's no need to be so . . . formal.

– I always think courtesy is the basis of any good working relationship.

– We have no working relationship. We never will.

– Then 'know thine enemy'.

– We're not enemies. I ask you into my home. I offer you hospitality–

– And in gratitude, the angel says, in return, I give you my name; I'm in your debt.

– You don't owe me a thing.

– But I *have* to repay your hospitality. If you refuse me that then you offend me, and if you offend me then you're my enemy. Which is it?

– I release you of your debt. I take back my hospitality. Get out of my home.

Phreedom notices that some of the magnetic letters on the fridge have arranged themselves to spell out a word – M E T A T R O N. It looks like some inane comic-book superhero's name, spelled out in all its pompousness. It looks harmless.

– You're expelling me? asks the angel.

– I'm requesting that you leave.

– Just say the word and I'm gone.

– Please, snarls Finnan.

– Not that word, boy. You know what I mean.

– *I* know what you mean, you arrogant fucker, she says.

Finnan shakes his head.

– Don't even think of it, Phree. I taught you how to read the marks, but the name would just be a word in your mouth . . . and it's a word they'd damn you with.

– Let the little girl try, birdman. Let the hatchling chirp her first angel-call.

– Don't patronize me, you bastard, she says.

– Leave her out of this, says Finnan, half-rising from his seat. Get the fuck out of my house, now.

He bows his head, as if in prayer or invocation.

– I command you in your own name, I command you twice, and I command you for the third time—

– Metatron, she says.

Golden, Burning Sound of Fire and Rust

The empty bottle in the angel's hand shatters, and the shards themselves shatter, and sand rains across the Formica table-top.

Metatron, she says, again for the first time, time echoing itself.

The world is screaming in her face, a golden, burning sound of fire and rust. The angel is white and Finnan is green and her own hand is crimson as she raises it to try and stop the Cant from shaking her whole existence apart.

Metatron.

And it feels like she's going to be saying that one word for the rest of her life, forever in that one moment, living, reliving the reverberations. The air is liquid in front of her, its intricate flow tracing sigils and symbols, all instantly understood, all woven into a single living word, that name. She reaches into the deepest part of the mark carved into the world inside Finnan's Airstream, and, with thumb and forefinger, she twists it at its heart. She makes her first graving.

The angel throws back his head and laughs, and weeps.

Finnan stubs out his cigarette on the table-top.

The world becomes normal . . . almost.

– I'll be leaving now, says the angel, picking up his palmtop, switching it off and closing it as he rises from his seat. His voice is tight and one small bead of sweat runs down his forehead, but he has the faintest hint of a smile around his mouth.

– It looks like I was wrong, he says. It seems I wasn't here to gather your soul after all. Young Phreedom's bought you a little more time.

– Maybe I'll do the same for her some day.

– I don't think you'll have to. She's a fighter, that one; she's made her choice already and she's not even named yet.

73

– My folks called me Phreedom, she says. That's all the name I need.

– My father named me Enoch, says the angel, but when you walk with God you soon find those human names too small a fit. Phreedom is what they call you, yes, but is it really who you are ... *what* you are?

– As long as I'm alive, says Finnan, it will be.

– You'll protect her, birdman? You damned her to hell the day you taught her that the gods were real. And when the desolate ones have gathered her into their arms – because that *is* the choice she's made – she'll probably thank you for it as she rips out your heart.

– Get out of here, she says. Get the fuck out of here.

He pushes past her to the door and opens it, but stops at the threshold as he turns to go down the ladder. Finnan walks over to the fridge to pull out a bottle of beer; he twists the top off, holds the bottle up ... *cheers*.

The angel flicks his hand in a sort of John Wayne salute.

– Be seeing you, he says.

The Fields of Lost Days

– How long has Finnan been here? she asks Mac as she puts the last tin of eggshell-yellow emulsion down on the ground at the foot of the Jesus Hill. Mac grins and shrugs.

– Longer than me, he says. And I been here near forty years.

– So how old is he?

Mac shrugs, and laughs this time. He pulls the baseball cap off his head and scratches at his scalp.

– Looks like he's about twenty. But I reckon he must be over a hundred.

As Mac replaces his cap, he grins at her with a carefully cultivated innocence.

– But, hell, my memory isn't what it used to be. Who knows, maybe Finnan only got here yesterday.

*

And she's thinking to herself about just who this Seamus Finnan is, the war he fought in and the war he's running from, the history he never talks about, the future he rejects, and she's wondering if, with that one word, she's stepped into a role that he won't play. The angel's name still echoes in her head and there's a part of her – something that's always been there, but she just never noticed it, she thinks – a part of her that wants to burn it out, to burn it all out.

– You know what Finnan is, don't you?

– No. No, I'm just another old drugfucked hippy hermit; I don't push my trip on Finnan, and he doesn't push his trip on me. If someday he comes up to me and tells me, hey, I know where the fountain of youth is, I can take you back to the garden, man, well, maybe I'll follow him and maybe I'll just stay here and paint my hill. I figure you got to make your own way through; you can't walk another person's journey.

– So you never asked him where he came from or anything?

The road of all dust, she thinks. *The fields of lost days.*

– I didn't ever think he *wanted* to be asked, says Mac.

Nearly everybody has some kind of graving, Finnan told her. With some folks it's cut so deep in them that they forget there's any *them* except that little mark. Cut so deep it's carved into reality itself and you can see it in the air around them, smell it on the wind. There's a hole inside their heart that goes right down to hell, right up to heaven, and what's on the other side's so bright, so dark, so fucking pure they let it take them over, walk the world in their bodies. Angels and demons.

And she knows he's right. She knows why he's walked away from all that shit. But she doesn't know if she can walk away from it herself.

The Song of Unknown Lands

– Are you sure about this? asks Finnan.

Evening is falling and she lies in his arms in his bed in his trailer in his world. The last echoes of the black angel's true name are fading now, but she can still feel the call, the Cant, the song of the land, in the rhythm of Finnan's breath, in the beat of his heart, and in her own breath and her own bloodstream. She touches his thigh and life quivers.

– Nothing I've ever done felt so right, she says. I want you to be the one who graves me, and I want this to be the ... the sacrament.

– It's not *me* graving *you*, he says, shaking his head. It's not like that it's – shit, you know I could go to jail for this, he says, a little slurred, smiling gently.

– We're unkin, she says, knowing it now, knowing that there's something between them, that there's always been something between them, that's more than friendship.

– We're different. Other people, they–

He puts a finger to her lips.

– No they, no us, just you and me, OK?

– OK.

They stay there for a while in silence, not doing anything. Then Finnan slides his hand down to her ass, almost absent-minded, like he's thinking of something else.

– What does it feel like to you, she says, the Cant, I mean?

– It's like a million tiny wires firing charges through my flesh, he says, down into my bones. Sometimes it's just a low buzz, other times feels like I'm burning in the fucking electric chair. It's like a fucking magnetic force and every cell in my body is just a little piece of iron being shaped by ... interfering fields.

– With me it's like a song, like something calling me ... from I don't know where. It's like everything is resonating around me, inside me.

– 'Everything is broken up, and dances', he says.

– That's it exactly.

– I envy you.

She turns over to lie on her back, looking out the west-facing window, where the red and golden sunset seems almost artificial in its numinous washes of light, like the painted backdrop of some 1950s Technicolor and Cinemascope movie – it all seems so staged.

– How long do you think I've got, she says, before they come for me?

– Not long, he says. Seems like they're gearing up for a final showdown. The gatherers will be scattering across the face of the earth right now, hunting down, one by one, every last rogue, every last free unkin. They want me, and, sooner or later, they'll want you. They're already looking for . . .

He stops, as if thinking better of something.

– Fucking angels, he says. Christ, save us from the fucking angels.

– Maybe . . .

She hesitates.

– Maybe it's a war we have to fight.

– A fucking glorious battle for the kingdom, Phreedom? You and me saving the world?

– Maybe.

He shakes his head.

– Promise me, when they come for you, you'll run, just fucking run. Don't be a hero, Phreedom. Don't play their game.

But she realizes she can't promise that.

– Why didn't you tell me about the Vellum? she asks.

– Cause it's a fucking pile of shite, he says. A fucking dream. This is reality, here, now, and anything else is just . . . smoke and mirrors. The Cant is real but the Vellum's just . . . myth.

She can hear the lie in his voice, though. Hell, she can feel that other reality pressing on her, trying to push through. Smoke and mirrors. There's no smoke without fire, and there's another world through the looking-glass.

– I'm ready, she says. I want to know my name.

He rolls over so he's on top of her, resting his head on her shoulder, kissing her neck as he fingers her clit. She can smell the beer, bitter on his breath. He started drinking as soon as the angel left and she could have stopped him. She could have stopped him, but she didn't. He might not have done this sober.

– Fuck, she says.

And his other hand presses down through her and curls electric fingers round her heart, reading her, writing her, fusing sacred and profane in grace and obscenity, and he leans close to her and he whispers it in her ear.

A Half-Empty Pack of Cigarettes

She wakes in his bed in his trailer in Slab City in a new world, her world, and he's gone. Outside, Mac is up early, working on his Jesus Hill, but she's alone in Finnan's castle of junk. Even the air is empty of his sepia lifelight and steely soulscent. She looks around inside the Airstream for any clues to why he's gone or where he went, a note, a goodbye message of some sort, but all there is is a half-empty pack of cigarettes, his Zippo lain on top of them. And a lot of empty beer-bottles.

Tomorrow she's supposed to leave with her family for the north, head out of here before the scorching sun becomes too fierce with the heat of summer, head for somewhere cooler, less harsh. She's not sure that she wants to go with them, but it's not that she wants to stick around in case Finnan comes back; she's guessing that he's never coming back.

No, it's more that she just knows she doesn't belong here any more. One strange thing about being a mobile is, she thinks, wherever she's been she's always felt like she was home. It seems strange, maybe, but that's the way it is. Slab City or way up north, travelling or camped, she's never felt that she was anywhere she wasn't meant to be. Now it's different.

She looks out over the junkyard where, she notices, one of the bikes is missing, but another of them has its heavy green tarpaulin thrown back off of it, its keys in the ignition – an invitation, an offering. Promise me you'll run, he said, but she can't do that. There's something out there, gathering in preparation for a war to burn this earth to dust and ashes, and she doesn't want to be a hero – really, she doesn't – but that doesn't mean she won't fight. Fuck it, she thinks. Fuck Finnan. He doesn't know everything. He's just fucking scared. He's just—

*

And she remembers that image of the plain of bones, of a boot crushing a bird skull underneath it and she knows that whatever this so-called Vellum is, whatever the black leather angel with his book was talking about, this road of all dust, these fields of lost days, she knows that Finnan had a right to fear it. But she won't live like that. If she takes the bike it won't be to run from the angels or demons but to find them. Maybe she'll go looking for Finnan, maybe she'll go looking for Tom – she doesn't know. All she knows is she's not going to wait for it to come to her.

Before she leaves she rearranges the alphabet letters on the fridge door so they spell out PHREEDOM, then she lifts her chicken-bone necklace, the santerian charm to ward off bad mojo, from the Formica tabletop where she laid it last night, last night when she was still a human being. She has the language of the angels in her head now – in her body, in her blood – so she doesn't really think she needs it any longer.

But then again. Maybe that means she needs it more than ever.

Errata

The Journals of Guy Reynard Carter – Day Infinity

The trailer-town they call Slab City, in the world where I belong, sits four miles or so out of Niland, off the 111, down there on the east coast of the Salton Sea in the south-eastern corner of California, with the Sonoran Desert all around, and the Mojave somewhere far up to the north. It gets its name from the foundations of the buildings of an old naval base abandoned after World War Two, slabs of concrete that now serve as parking spaces for the RVs and the trailers of those who travel with the seasons, to Canada in the summer, California in the winter. Snowbirds, they're called.

New Mexico, with its Jornada del Muerto, is a whole state of Arizona away.

The Jornada del Muerto, the Journey of the Dead Man, runs from Kern's Gate, El Paso, north through a dry plain of natron and uranium, salt, sand and dust, up to Santa Fe, up to Los Alamos and Trinity where they shattered atoms, those destroyers of worlds. It's a section of the old Camino Real by which the Mexicans came north, from Teotihuacan into the Land of Dreams, and Peter Kern must have known this when, on his return from the Alaskan Gold Rush, he built his suburban housing development and gave it a towering gate of wrought iron, two pillars branched and bedecked with silver globes, swastikas and other occult ornaments, joining across the road more like an entrance into Chinatown than into Suburbia. Or like an entrance into Hell, more accurately. This Gate of a Thousand Doors stands open, for anyone to drive through.

To get to Slab City from there, in my world, you'd have to walk ... how many thousand klicks?

I lay the maps I've gathered of this corner of this world on the Formica tabletop of the old Airstream trailer, spread out edge to edge

– New Mexico, Arizona, California. In this world, Slab City stretches across them all.

The handwritten pages of the girl's journal – if it is a journal – hang on the door of the fridge, pages of errata overlapping like scales on a fabulous beast, stuck there by magnets covered in the shapes of plastic letters just like the ones she mentions. I'm trying to understand what process must have gone on in her mind to shift and skew a world so certain, so solid, into the terrain of artifice where her strange tale of angels takes its place. Is it possible that she, like me is not from here, that this journal or fiction with its reinvented world is, like myself, a traveller on the long road.

The journey of this dead man, Guy Reynard Carter of Eternity as I wryly style myself these days, began 527 worlds south of here. I've been travelling north for how long now? I don't know. I stopped measuring it in days and weeks and months and years and centuries and millennia about two hundred worlds back. Even worlds is an inadequate measure of the distances; I'm not counting the wide plains of broken bones, or stretches of marble causeway across shallow tranquil oceans without tides, places where I've walked for decades in a straight line, waking every morning to a sight the same as yesterday. It's just that every now and again the area that I find myself in has been defined enough by those who were its denizens that you can walk into a library or bookshop and pull out all the atlases and encyclopaedias and know its boundaries the way they did. These are the places I count as worlds. I'm not counting the wide areas in between I've had to walk to get from this one to the next – the Jungle of Filigree, the Bay of Afternoon.

The Jornada del Muerto

This world is one of only a score or so I've been in that resembled my own place of origin so well that you could lay a tracing of the continents of one across a map of the other and see only the smallest differences – a missing Ireland, a Britain without a land-bridge to Europe, a California split right down the middle by catastrophe.

There are always more errata in the encyclopaedias or dictionaries, assuming those mundane texts are decipherable – Nazi victories in Europe, actors as presidents, British Empires on which the sun never set. It's the similarities that really interest me though. A world might have no Christianity at all and yet still have a Holy Roman Empire founded by a Constantine, even Crusades against the heathens in the Middle East who did not worship Dionysus on his cross. Mona Lisa with the eyes of a cat, but still that same so-famous smile.

I left my last truckload of mouldering journals in the truck outfitted as a library in its articulated trailer, left it two hundred worlds back there in a place where the crescent sun just couldn't power its solar engine any longer. I've done that only once or twice, abandoned my records of this endless pilgrimage into Eternity when, for whatever reason, I no longer had the means to carry them with me. But both times I managed to salvage maybe a backpack's worth of notes, maybe a summary of a century's experience in a page or two, maybe a sketch of a plaza in a Renaissance city that I settled in for a decade or so, before the emptiness became too much and, for all that I was loath to leave somewhere so beautiful, I knew that it was time for me to move on.

Sometimes I make small sacrifices – leaving an encyclopaedia that I picked up in one world on a shelf in a bookshop in another – or elaborate projects – filling a warehouse with silvery computer disks of scans – whatever I'm carrying in whatever fantastic vehicle I've managed to obtain in whatever world of awesome technological advancement. I always keep the Book, though, of course. As long as I have the Book, I know the road I'm on, even in a world where po-faced humans in the garb of burgermeisters, in the oil paintings in the galleries, have glittering fairy wings and horns.

Slab City, California. The trailer-town sits four miles or so out of Niland, on the east coast of what once was Salton Sea, where sundered California's new coastline cuts in a ragged rip from north to south, from one-time desert town to one-time desert town, all now ports, but ones with parking lots as wharfs, jetties of downtown commercial districts, crumbling into the Pacific. Sometimes, at night,

I stand where broken roads end at a clifftop with a road-sign marking out the distance to a city now sunken, cities of saints – Diego or Francisco – or the very City of Angels itself, now swallowed by the sea. I imagine Hollywood as a new Atlantis, glittering in the depths.

3

All Eternity or Nothing

A Vague But Passionate Way

Asheville, July 13th, 2017

Thomas watches the blond frat boy sit his glass down on the table so he can use his hand to argue with a crow-haired friend – who shakes his head, sneering. He watches the wild gestures of that cutest member of the frat pack; there's six or seven of them, all crew-cut and clean-shaven, mostly decked out in the red-white-and-blue of their trendy logoed togs so out of place in this college town bar with its foreign beers and alt-rock ambience. The only ones who look at all like they belong here, in their leather jackets and boot-cut jeans, are that lion of a golden boy and the one he's arguing with; the rest are square to the hair, the legal eagles and football bulls of the future. They're arguing about the war, it sounds like, the golden boy – the delicious closet case with the sideways glance – going on about freedom and democracy in a vague but passionate way that Thomas finds dumbly endearing. It's at least a little better than the ones who're using words like *sand-nigger*. Jack, his friends call him.

He darts another glance at Thomas again, losing his train of thought apparently and finishing his bluster with a wave of his hand. Thomas keeps his eyes on him as he looks away again just as quickly.

You know you fucking want it.

– You've got to be fucking crazy, says Finnan. This has the stink of demon all over it. Honest-to-God, bona-fide, 'kill your own soul rather than let the Covenant have it' demons. Sovereigns. Jesus, the fuckers who think of themselves as angels aren't bad enough for you?

– All I want is a way out, says Thomas.

He's still watching the frat boy.

– You think the Vellum is a way out? It's not an escape. It's fucking death.

Thomas turns back to his friend.

– No. Death is *this* world. Death is a suicide-bomber on a bus. It's a car on the road going too fast. It's that poor, gorgeous bastard over there getting old and fat and dropping dead from a heart attack in his fifties. Death is reality and if the Vellum is anything, it's what ... it's what starts where reality ends. You told me that yourself.

– Well, maybe I was talking shite.

Thomas notices that Finnan's accent kicks in when he's pissed – pissed-angry or pissed-drunk, it doesn't make much difference – and he wonders again just what the Irishman's story is. Seamus Finnan. Where do you really come from? *When* do you really come from?

He fidgets with a beermat.

– Come on. You're the fucking original drop-out, angel-eyes. Huckleberry Finnan. Man, I thought you'd be with me on this one. You and me, Butch and Sundance, we could–

– Shite. Will ye just fookin listen to me for fookin once, Tommy. Tom. Yer fookin twenty-odd years old and ye think ye know what death is. Yer barely graved and ye think ye know what the Vellum is. This isn't a fookin game. It's not some fookin doorway into Never-Neverland that we're talking about here.

Thomas runs a finger over a gouge that cuts across the grained surface of the table. He thinks of the tree it was made from, its trunk of capillaries drawing water and minerals up along them, streams of ... time all arranged as a thin skin round the inner rings of dead matter. Like the Vellum, their world just one stream. He's been cutting across from stream to stream these last few years, up and down, and side-to-side, looking for a way to get out of it entirely, to dig his way out onto the suface of it, or in, into the quiet, solid wood. Neverland? He smiles.

– Second star to the right and straight on till morning.

Finnan says nothing for a while.

– OK, says Thomas. OK, I'm sorry. I know this isn't a game. Fuck it, Finnan, I wouldn't be living out of motel rooms and hopping freight-trains between decades if I didn't know it was serious. I'm not dumb. The thing is . . . what other choice is there?

Thomas has been on the run now for nearly two years, hasn't seen his sister or the folks for that long. It's not so hard roughing it when you're what Finnan calls *unkin*, not as hard as it would be otherwise; there are plenty of . . . tricks you can use. He takes a sip of the beer he paid for with a smile and looks past Finnan at the blond frat boy. And there are plenty of tricks you can use.

But, still, he wouldn't be running at all if there wasn't good reason.

– Do we just keep running forever, Finnan? I mean, do we? You've heard about the weird shit going on in Jerusalem. And we've got a fucking fundamentalist in the White House who's obviously a Covenant man, whether he knows it or not. How long before the whole shithouse goes up in flames?

– I don't know, says Finnan.

– How long?

– I don't know.

Destination Apocalypse

Thomas picks up the business card lying on the table between them and starts turning it between his fingers like a magician playing with a coin. He turns it up and out to face Finnan, who slumps back into the red faux-leather of the booth, shaking his head. All it has are a name, a logo and an address – no phone, no email, no link. It's not even smart, just printed white card, like something from the last century. But then – Thomas looks around – the whole fucking city of Asheville is an anachronism. Not that that's a bad thing. It's in these kind of places that it's easiest to step across from one time to another, following the flow of similitudes, the folds of commonalities.

Like airports, he thinks. You go from one transfer lounge to another and you look around you and, if it wasn't for the plane-ride, you wouldn't know you'd gone anywhere. Thomas has walked into a john in George Bush International in Texas and come out of another in Mexico City. And out on the back-roads through these sticks of States, the desert roads, mountain roads, you can step across whole decades. He managed to spend last summer hiding out in 1970, moving from commune to commune, July through May; only reason he's back now is to see Finnan and his little sister Phree one last time before he takes that last big step ... sideways. You can skip up and down the railroad track as much as you want, back and forth, back and forth. Pick a year, any year. At the end of the day, there's still a freight train coming that'll either run right over them or pick them up and slam them all the way to the terminus. Destination Apocalypse. Better to get off the track entirely.

– Madame Iris Tattoos, says Finnan. You don't have a fucking clue what you're dealing with, Tom.

Thomas lays the card down on the table. The logo is a black, stylized eye, radiating lines and curves, like the eye in the pyramid on a dollar bill, like the Eye of Horus used on all the New Age head shops around here ... and quite different from either.

It fucking screams unkin. He can hear it in the bones of his fingers where he touches it, the way it resonates inside him, simpatico with his soul. Thomas is one of them, you see, unkin. One of what they call angels, or demons, or gods. The birdmen who sing the morning world into existence with their Cant. He found it out three years back and he's been running ever since.

– So are you born unkin or made unkin, he asked Finnan one night, before he was sure about himself, when he could just feel something tingling in his bones. A sense of something. They were on peyote, the two of them, out in the desert outside Slab City and the world seemed like a dream that he was suddenly lucid in.

– Fucked if I know, Tom, Finnan had said. I'm not sure it's either. Maybe it's a bit of both.

He wonders if it was chance, meeting this crazy hermit in his ramshackle cave of junk with his young face and old eyes, or if Finnan somehow found him, somehow knew before he knew himself and was just waiting for Thomas to realize what he was. Looking out for him in the meantime, while the Covenant angels and their enemies walked the earth, gathering their armies.

– This is our way out, he says. Away from the whole fucking bullshit war. Into the Vellum. It's all or nothing, he says. All eternity or nothing.

– *bullshit war?*

The frat boy's voice isn't loud enough for him to make out the whole sentence, but the tone of it and the stares in their direction carry more than enough information, more than enough threat. Thomas waits for the crow-haired hawk to calm his fuckwit fascist bull of a buddy – the queer lion just sits there of course, avoiding all the confrontations, external or internal, that might arise from any actual action. He wouldn't want people to think ... whatever. Thomas waits until the bull is soothed – *leave it, man, leave it* – and they've turned back to bludgeoning each other with their blunt opinions, then leans over to Finnan, speaking quieter now, serious.

– We don't belong here, Finnan. None of us do. And we all know it; we all feel it. We get that graving cut into us, burned into us, we get a little glimpse of what's out there and, you know, from then on, we can't get it out of our heads.

Thomas became unkin at the age of nineteen, wasted on peyote out in the Mojave desert, saw eternity in a grain of sand, and didn't like what he saw, a vast and ancient power moving under the world around them, like muscles under the smooth skin of some slouching panther. Not God but something older, something colder. A glimpse of scales and feathers.

Finnan finishes his beer and peels a twenty out of his pocket, drops it on the table to cover their tab, stands up.

– God help you, Tommy boy. You don't know what you're doing. God help you.

– Which one? says Thomas.

But as they say their goodbyes and Finnan walks away and pushes his way out through the door and into sunlight, as Thomas sits back down to finish off his beer and eye up the blond frat boy over at the other table, he thinks to himself that he knows – he *does* know – that he's playing with fire.

But there's a whole Vellum out there to hide in.

He checks the clock behind the bar – he doesn't wear a watch himself these days, not much point the way he lives. It's 5:45 or so. Where to, he thinks, where to?

Pick a year, any year.

The Voice of God

The Voice of God has a name – Metatron – but it's a made-up name, a chosen name; it's not the name he was born with and it's not even the first name that he's taken since abandoning the one his mother and father gave to him, back when he was still human. Needless to say, it's not the name on the passport that he hands over to the painted china doll of a woman at the check-in of the KLM flight from Schiphol Airport, Amsterdam, to Newark, or at customs and immigration, or the transfer desk in New York; on the passport, he's Enoch Hunter, a solid, straightforward name that's not going to raise any eyebrows. Traveling to the States as Enki Nudimmud, in this day and age, would be just plain foolish. Slipping through the cracks in reality requires subtlety; and given the . . . situation in the Middle East, the last thing he wants is to draw attention to his origins. It would be ironic if the very architect of the new crusade was detained under the Homeland Defence Act for 'motivational profiling' as they call it. He could beat the lie detectors and the truth drugs, but it would waste his time, and he would be tempted just to tell them everything.

– You want to know the truth? he might say. You *really* want to know the truth about your war on terror?

And then he'd whisper one word and they'd see it all, the Dead Soul Deeps and the demon Sovereigns walking in the shape of men, angels begging for their lives on Al Jazheera. And Malik in Damascus, at the heart of it all, graving Shariah law and hatred of the West into his followers. The real Cant under all the rhetoric.

Charlotte, July 13th, 2017, 11:45 a.m. Six hours before the Messenger boy and the Irishman will meet.

He takes the passport back from the guard, nods and smiles at him as he leans forward, putting his eye to the retina-scanner and his thumb to the sampler. The guard runs his gloved fingers over a non-existent keyboard, and stares through him for a second as data scrolls across his lenses; Metatron watches it like a reflection in the man's pupils, little arcane flickerings of light drawn out of a distant database – birth and citizenship certificates, criminal record query, tax records. It all pans out as tidy and safe, as it should. Enoch Hunter is an African-American, unmarried, a professor at the University of North Carolina, based at the Asheville campus, specializing in Anthropology and Archaeosociology, a taxpayer and an honest citizen. Metatron puts the passport in the inside pocket of his long black leather duster, flicks back his dreads and gives the man a *You too* in reply to his *Have a nice day.*

It's not that the passport is forged. It's not that Enoch Hunter doesn't actually exist. The identity is a construct but it's an airtight, solid-as-mahogany one. Here and now, at this exact point of time and space, in this little corner of the Vellum, Enoch Hunter is as real as the guard, with the same memories of childhood and adulthood, in his head or in other people's, the same tracks and traces left in the world around him, among his friends and family, as any human leaves in their path. Metatron remembers his lecture at the conference in Paris. He remembers laughing in the seafood restaurant as he dined with colleagues. It's just that all this is temporary. Even as he walks out through the silent slide of automatic doors that open out into the North Carolina sunshine, Enoch Hunter dissolves back into the field of possibility that he came from, forgotten as quickly as he was created. As Metatron takes the small black leatherbound palmtop out of his pocket and flips it open, Enoch Hunter ceases to have ever existed and reality slides back to where it was and should be. There was no conference in Paris now. The KLM flight from Schiphol to Newark, the Northwestern flight from Newark to Charlotte – neither have any record of an Enoch Hunter traveling in business class.

Carter and Pechorin are waiting in the airport car park, his spear-carriers. Carter looks like what you'd get if a farmboy of the Mid-West married an Elven princess – all corn-colored hair and jut of jaw but greyhound slim, more a gymnast than a quarterback. Pechorin has a Slavic face of angular curves, all cheekbones and quiet, catlike intensity. In their mafioso black suits, they're clean-cut all-American angels, the paragon of efficiency. They should be; Metatron graved them himself.

The other five sebitti will be following them in some unmarked van presumably, back-up in case any demons have picked up on his movement, caught sight of the wake, the ripples in the Vellum as he slides through it from one time and place to another. It's unlikely, but there's always the chance.

– Glad to finally meet you, sir, says Carter as he reaches out a hand to shake, sliding down off the car's hood where he's sat. Neither Carter or Pechorin have any memory of their graving, of course, or of much else at the moment. Sebitti don't function very well under those hindrances of humanity.

Metatron shakes his hand absently, busy studying the scrolling sigils on his palmtop. He lets Carter open the door for him and slides into the back seat, still looking at the screen.

– I understand you've had some problems tracking the boy, he says.

– Slippery little fucker, says Carter.

– He always was, says Metatron. Or could be.

Thomas Messenger, he thinks, looking at the sigils in his electronic book of life. Metatron wonders if the boy even really knows what he is, what they all are. Or could be.

– We'll get him though, sir, says Carter. We will get him.

– I know you will. He's history.

Golden Apples and Green Leaves

In Uruk, under a tree of golden apples and green leaves, Tammuz, the lover of Inanna, sat, sheened in his *me*-garments, lounging, still, upon his throne. Inanna fastened on Tammuz the gaze of death, spoke out against him words quiet in wrath, uttered against him cries of shame, of blame:

– Take him! Take Tammuz away!

The *ugallu* grabbed him by his thighs, spilled milk out of his seven churns, smashed the reed pipe the shepherd played. The *ugallu*, who know no food or drink, who eat no offerings and drink no libations, who accept no gifts or invitations, grabbed Tammuz. They dragged him to his feet; they threw him down. They punched the husband of Inanna, slashed him with their axes.

Tammuz wailed. He raised his hands to heaven, to the god of justice, Shamash, begging him: O Shamash, my brother-in-law, I am your sister's husband. I brought cream – I brought milk – to your mother's house, to Ningal's house. It was me who brought food to the sacred shrine, me who brought the wedding gifts to Uruk. It was me who danced upon the holy lap, Inanna's lap. Shamash, you are a god of justice and of mercy. Change my hands into a snake's hands. Change my feet into a snake's feet. Help me flee my demons; do not let them catch me.

Shamash in his mercy heard the tears of Tammuz, changed the hands of Tammuz into snake's hands, changed the feet of Tammuz into snake's feet. Tammuz fled his demons and they could not catch him. He slipped away, slid from their grasp and off and out and down, down into the eternal tales of transformation, metamorphic, mythic, Tammuz, Dumuzi, escaping out of Arcadia into the Fields of Elusion. Even now the shepherd boy, the king, Dumuzi, runs across cornfields in his mother's white dress, Tammuz, veiled like a bride, a priestess or a whore, his skin, beneath the silk, the smooth and golden gleam of a gazelle under the sun. He stops to drink from a stream, hunted, alive. Sees a reflection and looks up. A dark man, a shadow, some kind of friend or brother, perhaps – or something entirely other – stands on the opposite bank, across the water.

Who are you?

Carrion Comfort

Lightning. The rivers rise in rain, deep ochre down among the greenery and rising, brown bubbling up out of the drains, red ruin flowing over where the road should be. The day is dull with thick clouds of a summer storm but somehow still too bright, fierce with an unearthly light, blue-green, grey-blue, the tarmac mirroring the sky, sky mirroring the tarmac. Out on the road, out on the run, the boy flicks up the collar of his sodden afghan coat against the downpour, wondering if somewhere there's a new ark for this broken covenant. This hail of liquid light – *a flash of white* – electric flame over the earth's primordial blood, this second flood ... is this to kill more sons of angels? He draggles long hair from his face with fingers of one hand and, with the other, reaches out a thumb, hoping – in vain, it seems – to hitch a ride.

Poet, prodigal, pilgrim Thomas still wears a silver cross around his neck, a half-forgotten article of childhood faith buried among the beads of his new age, an age of adulthood, of newfound, foundering, floundering identity. He feels it in his fingers, behind a wooden amulet, the leather mojo bag that Finnan gave to him back in another time and place, a world away. It's North Carolina. It's not 2017 though. Screw that. Pick a year, any year. Let's make it 1971. New age. New gods ... or older ones. The cross is cool, crisp-edged, metallic amongst its rough, organic brethren. He shakes wild rain from his hair, snorting, a horse, and laughs up at the sky, opens his mouth to it. If he had any remnant of that superstition anyway, he shrugs, the situation calls more for Saint Christopher. And anyway, he has his own charms now.

Thunder. He writes in his journal. Sleep is a dark comfort from the dreams of day, sleep in the arms of a stranger. Sex is play. Picked up in a bar, fucking in a motel. Awake. Aware. Await. Away. It's always the same, he thinks, in roadhouse after roadhouse; there's the one that calls you beatnik, and the one that calls you faggot, and the one that doesn't call you anything, just watches, drinking his beer with dry lips, dry mouth, drinking you. Long hair – *hey girly-boy* – and hippy badges – *which way you heading, Canada or Mexico* – blue boot-cut hustler hipster jeans ripped at the ass – *you selling that, girly boy*.

And all you have to do is wait for him to leave with all his friends ... and wait for him to come back in alone.

– Get the fuck out of here. Just ... here, take this and go.

He shrugs. He wasn't going to ask for money, but if it's offered ... He slides his fingers through the scruff of rough hair running from his navel down – he shifts position, settling cock into the comfort of its natural canter, pulls on his jeans and buttons them, buckles his belt. It's getting light again outside. And inside the motel room, attraction sated, revulsion burns in the redneck's face now, redder still with shame. Thomas offers an indifferent shrug.

– Good Book says it's a sin to lay with a man as if he was a woman. Don't say nothing about laying with him as if *you* were.

Carrion comfort for this guy, he thinks.

– Fucking hippy draft-dodger, the man mutters, that's what makes me sick looking at you.

– Sure. Whatever.

And Thomas feels, under his shirt, against his chest and buried amongst all the beads, the dog-tags ... cool, crisp-edged, metallic. *You don't know shit.* This Thomas is a nineteen-year-old veteran. Nineteen years and as old as war itself.

He pulls his coat on and walks out the door into the river of rain that washes his tracks away behind him as he walks. If he walks far enough in the rain, he thinks, maybe it will wash away his scent.

But it would have to wash his scent off the skin of the Vellum itself and he's pretty deep engrained in that.

The Lioness and the Gazelle

His heart, the shepherd's heart, Tammuz's heart was full of tears. Tammuz staggered across the steppe, stumbled and fell, and sobbed:

– O steppe, sound a lament for me! O crabs in the river, mourn for me! O frogs in the river, cry for me! O Sirtur, mother, sob for me! And if she cannot find the five breads, if she cannot find the ten breads – if she does not know the day I'm dead – then you, tell her, O steppe, I beg you, tell my mother. On this steppe, my mother will weep for me. On this steppe, my sister will grieve for me.

And on that steppe, the shepherd boy lay down to sleep. Tammuz lay down to sleep and, as he lay among the buds and rushes, dreamed a dream.

Tassili-n-Ajer or Lascaux, 10,000 BCE or today.

It is a dry, hot and sun-bleached day in the savannah, and a lion slouches slowly through the tall grass. A slender buck twitches nostrils at the scent of

94

predator in the air, and looks at us, and blinks long lashes over deep dark eyes. Vultures wheel lazily overhead. Turning to look around us, we can see the herd of aurochs grazing on the open skies and, superimposed like ghost-forms over this vision of a veldt, lithe copper-skinned and dark-haired villagers dance, recline and hunt. A dog lies curled up beside (beyond? behind?) a strange figure wearing animal skins, a beaked mask and what might be perhaps a feathered cloak or wings. Everything is still, poised in the moment.

– These animals in the cave-paintings, he says, they've got no fences, no boundaries, no parameters, no perimeters, you see. It's . . . it's not *where* they run that matters, only *that* they run.

In ochre sketch, an antelope looks back over its shoulder, eyes wide, nostrils flared, seeing and scenting its own golden, pouncing death. The lioness's teeth touch to its neck, claws dig into its shoulderblades.

– There's no ground to them, you see, no frame, no mud under their feet . . . no wire caging them. Look, see where these two bison here just overlap . . .

– Sure and the artist probably just ran out of space there, Tommy boy.

– No. No, it's more than that. It's like there is no space.

It is a dry, hot and sun-bleached day in the savannah, and a lion slouches slowly through the tall grass. A slender buck twitches nostrils at the scent of predator in the air, and looks at you, and blinks long lashes over deep dark eyes. Vultures wheel lazily overhead. All are aware, awake, in an acute sentience of the tensions of the situation. Turning to look around you, you can see the herd of aurochs grazing on the open skies and, superimposed like ghost-forms over this vision of a veldt, lithe copper-skinned and dark-haired villagers dance, recline and hunt. For each group it is the sense of community that sustains them. A dog lies curled up beside (beyond? behind?) a strange figure wearing animal skins, a beaked mask and what might be perhaps a feathered cloak or wings. It is known as the Shaman of Lascaux.

Unbound by either frame or forum, the figure turns, and steps out of the moment.

Tassili-n-Ajer or Lascaux, 1916 or today.

– Tommy boy, sometimes ye talk as much rot as I've got between me toes here. Sure and I don't know what ye're on about half the time.

Seamus looks at the small sketchbook that the boy treasures more than anything, more than any of them treasure anything, he thinks sometimes, more even than all the tattered, battered photographs of sweethearts and mothers, and the lockets, and the father's watches, and all the decks of playing cards with the nudie women on them and all; and he thinks the boy's daft, so he does, but, in a way, he understands. Seamus looks at the drawings that the boy spent so much time on, so much care, last month on leave in Lascaux when he could have been whoring it with all the rest of them, whooping it up, sure, the way a boy his age stuck in this shite to fight for someone else's King and Country should be; and all that Seamus sees when he looks at the little sketchbook is yellow paper and brown pencil lines. But Tommy now . . .

Tommy reaches over and takes the book out of his hands, shaking his head.

– Ah, you've got no soul, Seamus, no soul.

But the boy is blushing shame even as he tries to play the old game of young lads, sure, they way they bandy abuse about but with a twinkle in the eye and a nudge of the elbow, because, *aye now, ye know I don't really mean it*. The boy can't really carry it off – too shy, he is, and too much of a young gent even if he wasn't quite born with a silver spoon in his gob, not that he comes on all Lord Muck-a-Muck, like. He's just . . . ach, he's just a good lad what misses his mother and his home like the rest of them, only he shows it more. O, but he gets a right roasting from the other lads of the pal's battalion sometimes, he does, just like he got back home, and where would he be without Seamus sticking up for him, as ever?

Seamus wanders over towards the door of the dug-out where, apart from the mud and the mud and the fookin more mud, ye can just see a wee blue hint of sky up there, if ye're hunkered down a bit so ye're looking up at the right angle, sure, which ye are anyways on account of the fookin low ceilings. He reaches into the inside pocket of his jacket to pull out a cigarette from the crumpled packet of Gauloises in there – fookin nasty shite that they are, but what's a man to do when he's smoked all of his and the quartermaster's as crooked as a British politician, sure, and he's just putting it to his mouth—

DOOM!

– Jesus Fookin Christ!

Tommy's howling like a fookin wean and it's fookin dark but Seamus can feel the fookin dirt raining down on him.

– Jesus Fookin Mary and Fookin Joseph! Fookin shite! Fookin Hun fookin bastards! Seamus is down on the ground, hands over his head – Christ, and he wasn't even wearing his helmet – and he doesn't even fookin remember diving down there, but he's sure as fook happy to be there and he'll just stay right where he is for the time be, thank you very much, ma'am, and . . .

– Jesus. Tommy are ye all right there? Ye're not hit or nothing, are ye?

The boy's panting like a dog, gasping for air like he's fookin drowning, sitting there, just right there at Seamus's elbow, with his arms wrapped round his knees and his teeth biting into his trousers, panting and kind of whining like a sick animal; and as Seamus touches his knee, he flinches.

He looks at Seamus like he's looking right through him, eyes wide, nostrils flared, seeing and scenting his own golden, pouncing death.

Dumuzi's Dream

He awoke from his dream, still trembling with the vision, rubbed his eyes, felt terrified. Dumuzi called out: Bring her . . . bring her . . . bring my sister, Geshtinanna. Bring my little sister, the wise singer with so many songs, the scribe of tablets who knows what words mean, my sister who can read my dreams. I have to speak to her, to tell her of my dream. So, he spoke of his dream to Geshtinanna, saying:

– Sister, listen to my vision.

*

– I see rushes rising all around me, rushes thick about me, sprouting up out of my dream. I see a reed with one stalk, trembling in the wind, a reed with two stalks, one of which – and then the other – is removed. Then I am in a forest grove and trees rise all around me even as the fear rises within, tall shadows swallowing me. I see water poured over my sacred hearth; the base of my churn, broken, drops away. I see my drinking cup fall from its peg.

I look everywhere and cannot find my shepherd's crook. I cannot find it anywhere, and I can only look on as an eagle swoops into the sheepfold, snatches a poor lamb. I watch a falcon catch a sparrow on the reed fence. Sister, I can see your goats, their lapis beards all dragging in the dust, your sheep scratching the soil with broken hooves.

– Sister, the churn lies quiet, and no milk is poured into a shattered cup. Dumuzi is no more; the shepherd's fold, like dust, is given to the winds.

The Great White Hunter

DOOM!
   Thomas trembles, flinches again as the tin mug falls from its hook – a rusting nail banged into the wood post of the bunk and bent up – as the tin mug falls to clatter rattling on his kit box, knocking a tin of boot-black off. He jerks away, pushes himself back to the wall of the dugout, back into the wall, into the rough wood shoring with the gaps where all the dirt comes trickling out each time a shell hits and—

DOOM!
   – It's all right, lad, come on now, calm down, hush now, sure and we're safe as houses here and Jerry can do all he wants and – Jesus Fookin Christ! – O Jesus, aye and I nearly shat myself there, sure, and did ye see the look on my face there, aye, but it's all right, see, we're all scared, see, and we all just want to get the fook out of here alive but – hush now, come on lad, look, here, see, ye've gone

and dropped yer drawings, here – aye, Tommy boy, I know, I know, come on, lad, don't be crying like a babby for its mammy, here now, hush now – *shhh* – that's right, that's right, it's all right – *shhhhhhh* – I know, Tommy, lad, I know it's fookin shite it is, it's all just fookin shite but – aye, that's it, that's it, lad, Tommy boy . . . come on now, sure and haven't I promised yer darling sister, Anna, I'd look after ye?

And Seamus cradles the poor lad in his arms and just keeps talking to him, talking to him and rocking him like a mother with her wean, and it's not fookin manly and it's not fookin brave and it's not fookin *our* fookin *boys* going out on fookin horseback, with their shiny fookin sabres flashing in the sun and cutting down the Huns all fookin noble-like, and fook that, fook that fookin shite and any shitebag who tries to tell you it's like that and, Jesus, how he wishes he could have a good greet himself and just curl up in a corner and wish it all the fook away, but he can't, he can't, he can't . . .

– O Jesus, Tommy, Jesus, it's all right. Don't you worry, lad. I'll see you safe home if it fookin kills me.

Tassili-n-Ajer or Lascaux, the Somme in 1916 or—

DOOM!

– Damn it, boi! Didn't I tell you, not a sound. Bloody kaffirs!

Kenya. Pick a year.

The hunter throws the rifle to the native boy – at the native boy? – sideways so that the boy can catch it, but with all the force of his frustration, making the boy flinch and fumble backwards before he gets a grip. He doesn't even look at the boi, but bites his bottom lip and glares out over the tall grass.

– Reload it.

His face red, the great white hunter rearranges the fawn-coloured hat he's wearing, holds his hand out past the brim of it, shading his eyes from the savannah sun. He's a good shot and he would have made it if it hadn't been for the bloody native boy. And the bloody sun. The bloody sun doesn't help one bit.

Out in the tall grass, the Thomson's gazelle – his bloody Tommy – bounds high and far, in leap after graceful leap, saved by the sun, away, away, away.

The Somme.

– That's good, boy. Bloody good.

Thomas jumps, startled, dropping his sketchbook and fumbling the pencil, goes to pick up the book and stops, puts the pencil into his pocket and stands to salute, trying to do so many things at once he doesn't do anything right.

– Sir, he says.

– At ease, Messenger, says Captain Carter.

He smiles at Thomas with a sort of amused superiority for a second but clears it from his face quickly, looks away and back, jaw set now, eyes so intense that Thomas drops his gaze.

Carter crouches down to pick up the sketchbook, flicks through it to the page of Thomas's drawing. He looks up at him from down there – blue eyes with a piercing fire in them. Thomas feels uncomfortable, exposed.

– Saint Sebastian, isn't it? Mantegna's? says Carter, standing up with the book in hand, studying the picture for a moment before handing it back. On the yellow page, grey lines mark out the martyr in a classic contrapposto pose, the sensual snaking of one shoulder lowered towards a raised hip, face turned to one side and up. Arms tied to the Corinthian column behind his back, his soft shaded skin is pierced with arrows. Thomas takes the offered edge of the book, nods silently. Carter lets go and Thomas closes the book.

– You recognized it?

As embarrassed as he is, Thomas is pleased at the compliment; working from his memory as he did, he's surprised the Captain was able to place it.

– I'm something of a classicist myself, says Carter. What is it Mantegna said? The works of the ancients were more perfect and beautiful than anything in Nature.

Of course. Mad Jack Carter is notorious for his obsession with the ancients.

– I'm not sure I'd agree with that, sir, says Thomas, relaxing a little. Not that he said that, I mean, sir, but the sentiment, I mean. I'm not sure I agree with that.

Carter nods. He looks around the room absently, walks over to a small shaving mirror on the wall to take his hat off, brush his blond hair back and place the hat back on his head. It would seem like vanity except that Thomas notices the eyes studying him in the mirror rather than the Captain's own reflection. He looks out the door of the dugout but you can't even see the sky from here, just the sandbags of the wall of the trench outside.

– Was . . . was there something you wanted, sir?

Carter turns back to him, those eyes scrutinizing like they're looking for a weakness, like a predator studying its prey.

– I just . . . heard you had a little . . . turn, says Carter.

Thomas bites his bottom lip.

– I'm OK now, sir.

– Good. Good. Just wanted to be sure.

They stand for a while in silence.

– You know, says Carter, you really do have quite a talent there.

He nods at the sketchbook Thomas still holds in his hand.

– Thank you, sir.

– Saint Sebastian, eh? Interesting choice.

Thomas says nothing. The story of the Christian legionnaire put to death by his commander for refusing his advances is one of chastity and virtue but it is one told down the centuries in sensual painted flesh of a body bound and twisted, sublime in surrender as the arrows penetrate the smooth and semi-naked youth. Of all those ecstatic deaths of saints, Mantegna's subject is either the most ambiguous or not ambiguous at all. So Thomas says nothing.

– Interesting choice, says Carter again as he leaves the dugout.

Objects Out of History

– My brother, Geshtinanna said, I beg you not to tell me of a dream like this. Tammuz, don't tell me of a dream like this. The rushes which rise up all round you, yes, the rushes sprouting thick about you are your demons, who will hunt you and assault you. The reed with one stalk which trembled is our mother, mourning for you. O my brother, and the reed with two stalks, one of which − and then the other − is removed ... Tammuz, those stalks are me and you. First one of us, and then the other, will be lost.

Oxford, 1936

Professor Samuel Hobbsbaum − Sam to his friends − stops at the Olivetti, finger poised just touching the smooth, curved shape of the carriage-return lever ... then quite suddenly slaps his hand down on the surface of his mahogany desk as a sharp breeze, drafting from some distant doorway, flicks at his notes, blowing one page into the air the merest fraction of a second before he would have caught it. Cursing, he gathers the cuneiform drawings and scribbled fragments of translation and places them under a paper-weight before bending down, still seated on his chair to claim the fugitive scrap. The gas light flickers on the wall, in the breeze.

− In the forest grove, the tall trees which rise all around you are the terrible ugallu who will fall upon you in the sheepfold. The fire doused in your sacred hearth means that the sheepfold will become a cold and empty house. If the base of your churn is broken, dropped away, it means the ugalla will capture you. Your drinking cup falls from its peg; this means that you will fall into the mud, into your mother's lap. And when your shepherd's crook is gone ... Tammuz, the world will wither under the ugallu then. The eagle snatching a lamb from the sheepfold is the ugallu who'll scratch your cheeks. The falcon catching a poor sparrow on the reed fence is the ugallu who'll leap that fence to snatch you.

Around the study of Professor Samuel Hobbsbaum, objects out of history − some real, some replica − litter the room with time and culture, as chaotic as the desk itself, on shelves and bookcases, filing cabinets and anywhere there is the smallest space: plaster repro-ductions of alabaster vases carved with ceremony in processional friezes; cylinder seals once rolled over soft tablets of damp clay, to leave behind an image in relief; a stele on which an *ensi* stands in victory over the bodies of his fallen enemies, twice their size; a scorpion king in victory on a palette; a black-and-white framed photo, detail of a statue of a youthful king whose soft round face and serene smile make him think of the kouroi and buddhas of much later sculpture, holding the architectural plans of a temple or palace. A calendar on the wall shows the month as July 1936, outdated because Sam has neglected to change it for the last few months. Ancient history holds as much meaning for him as current events, perhaps more.

Given to the Winds

A Phoenician carving in ivory coloured with gold, where a youth – Adonis perhaps or some half-conscious reference to the imagery of his myth – supine and naked from the waist up, propped up on his arms, head lolling back, is caught in the moment of his death, as a lioness's jaws clamp round his throat, the creature standing over him, embracing him, like a lover. This is his personal favourite, so ambiguous, so sensual, almost erotic in its portrayal of the intimacy of victim and killer, predator and prey.

The lioness is one animal aspect of the goddess Inanna, Dumuzi's wife who gives him to the demons that have followed her from the underworld, so that she herself can be free. And yet Inanna does love him. Even as she damns him she is recast in his story as his sister, Geshtinanna, so that she can try to save him. Dumuzi has his sister and his brother-in-law, Geshtinanna and the sun-god Shamash, both trying to save him. But in the maelstrom illogic of myth, Geshtinanna is also Inanna who damns him in the first place, and Shamash may well be the unnamed friend who tries to save him, and in the end betrays him.

– *Tammuz, you see my goats, their lapis beards all dragging in the dust. My head will swirl through the air, my hair will flail, as I wail. You see my sheep scratch at the soil with broken hooves. O Tammuz, tears will gouge my cheeks in misery for you.*

And she looks at him with eyes wide, blinking back the tears that fill her heart and Phreedom Messenger reaches across the wooden table of the roadhouse up in the mountains to take her brother's hand.

She doesn't understand. Like Finnan, she's still thinking linearly; she still thinks this is a simple tale of the three of them, all changed by the way they've touched eternity, touched the Vellum, all on the run from angels and demons, fleeing from State to State across America. She thinks maybe if they keep running long enough, the two warring factions of the unkin will just wipe each other out and, one day, they can raise their heads out of the ditches that they're hiding in and the world will be empty of Metatron and his Covenant of angels, and all those others in endless rebellion against it.

But Thomas has traveled so long, he's slipped through so many interstices in reality, in the Vellum, that he's beginning to realize just how deep the story runs. She thinks they're on the run from death, but he knows that in the malleable and multi-faceted reality of the Vellum it's not a little temporal thing like death they have to fear, but oblivion. The angels want a world that's stable, a history that's sure and certain. Rogue unkin have no place in the story Metatron is writing in his little book of life. This year or that year, sooner or later, later or sooner, their futures will catch up with them. They have to weave, side to side, in and out. It's all eternity or nothing.

Dumuzi in Sumer, Adonis to the Greeks and Adonai Tammuz in all the city-states of Phoenicia, all the sinful cities so reviled in the Bible for their decadence, for their luxuries and their softness, for their crimes of sensuality. Damu, *dumu-zi*, child, shining lovechild, Thomas, nipper of gnostic gospels, twin of the Christ, kid brother, kith and kin, kidskin to lambswool. O, how the women of Jerusalem wept for him. How many times and in how many places has he died and been reborn, under how many names? Like a kid, the Orphic initiates in white linen once intoned, I have fallen into milk.

Forgotten for millennia, Dumuzi's tale might have been lost forever. But instead, in the buried cuneiform, Dumuzi is not dead but merely hidden, and Sam retells his tale, transforming it from cuneiform to Roman alphabet, black ink impressed onto white paper by the clattering keys of his typewriter. His sister cannot save Dumuzi because she is also the wife who has already given him to hell, but maybe Sam can, bringing his excavated text back into the light of day, translated for this modern era of motor-cars and megalomaniacs.

– *The churn lies quiet, said Dumuzi's sister, and no milk is poured into a shattered cup. Dumuzi is no more.*
  – *The shepherd's fold, like dust, he said, is given to the winds.*

And the problem is, thinks Sam, that Dumuzi's tale itself is also shattered, given to the winds. His translation is, of necessity, a reconstruction, filling in the gaps where the clay is cracked, footnoting meanings for words with no true parallel in English. Are the *ugallu* 'demons' or 'soldiers'? In one version of the tale, Inanna gives her lover up to them, to take her place in the underworld; in another, Dumuzi is a military conscript on the run. Perhaps there are yet other versions, still buried, waiting to be unearthed. And perhaps the true Dumuzi is not to be found in any one version, but somewhere between them, in the transformations.

Errata

The Vellum

Talmud, Midrashim and Pseudapigraphia of Jewish myth – and later sources – all agree that there are seven heavens. Highest of all is Araboth, where the souls of the righteous sit before the Throne of God or walk amongst the ophanim and seraphim, feet treading through the morning dew by which the dead shall be restored to life some day. Beneath this is the heaven of Makhon with its carved ponds of water, caves of mist, chambers of wind and doors of fire. Closing those doors behind us, we would walk on down into the Maon where the ministering angels sing by night, silent by day. In Szebhul, we might walk the streets of the city of Salem, where the prince of angels, Michael, offers sacrifices in the temple, at the altar there. And down. In the Shekhakim, the millstones grind, manna is made for pious mouths. In the Rekhia, the moon, the planets and the stars are fixed, like motes of dust in the sun's rays. But the sun itself has its home in the Villon, in the Vellum.

I find it an interesting congruence that, in the cheap paperback of myths of Ancient Israel which sits beside me on my desk, folded face-down and open at the page, the writer, Angelo S. Rappaport, simply includes an alternative name – Vellum – in brackets after the more traditional and orthodox *Villon*. He makes no comment on it, no note that one word is translation of the other, simply offers it up as an abstract aside, even as he describes this first and closest heaven as a veil, drawn between our world and the other so that the watchmen angels, peeping through windows in it, can view humanity unseen. Down in the world, flocks follow their shepherds through the valleys, to their folds, while eyes of angels follow them from their own vales, veiled within the folds of the Villon, the Vellum. A thin skin between reality and eternity.

*

Outside, the sun is setting, off to the west, off to my left, its red light burning on the terracotta tiles of the rooftops of the terraces far below, and the chimneys and towers of the towns that string the hillside cast their shadows upwards, impossibly tall, stretching towards the sky like the cedars of some mountain coast. It might well be a coast, for all I know, down there beneath the clouds; on days like this the Rift can seem like the very edge of a continent, slipping down into an ocean of cumuli and tumuli. It's only on clear days you can see just how far down the terraced hillside goes with all its strips of farmland hugging to its side, its roads winding along the contours of its steep stepped edge, and strata of cities coating it here and there. It's only on clear days you can look out north across the great gulf, searching for the far side of this vast valley, for a sign of a mountain-top shrouded in mist in the far-distance, and letting your eyes drop gradually down and down and down and down, realise properly that you might never find it.

The maps in this fold of the Vellum are strange, showing the world not from above but from a forty-five-degree angle, looking south and down into it, the view of a midwinter midday sun. I suppose that does make sense, though, for a people living on the diagonal, living on the staircase of the gods. But it's also that when you look at the maps you realise just how defined their orientation is. Roads run across the way, from left to right, from right to left, like the plodding square-by-square path of a snakes-and-ladders game, only occasion-ally going up or down in serpentine zigzags, wide and shallow, where they seek to climb from one ridge to another. Here and there a more vertical path is marked in black where, as I have discovered, great funicular railway carriages haul themselves on grinding pulleys up or down the mountainside.

The Sheer, Skewed Slant of Their Perspective

It is a peasant culture, generally, an agricultural system of terraced farming, with only a little industry, quarrying or mining, some chem-ical works, and sundry other technologies. I would not underestimate their ingenuity, but it seems the sheer energy involved in travelling upwards must have inhibited the people who once lived here in many ways – conquest or trade, communication in all forms – forcing them into a stratified existence. In the rural areas, the villages are strung out like clothes on a washing line, like layers of sediment exposed in a landslide, long thin veins of lamplit civilisation marbling the green and grey of earth and rock. The tracks that run between them may be precarious ledges or wide shelves but they almost always link towns on the same level; red rooftops visible over the canopies of trees below or lights glimpsed between crevices in the rocks high overhead may be no more than half a mile away, but might as well be half a world away. So, where on a flat world, one small town might have a dozen villages scattered around it feeding its market with produce and desire, each town here really has only its most immediate neighbours on the same level to the east or west to deal with.

But, no, as I say, I would not underestimate their ingenuity. The cities that they have here – those that I've seen – are something spectacular, like sights from the imaginings of a Brueghel or a Grimmer, not in their medieval or renaissance architecture, not in their picturesque and painterly grandeur – though they have that, they have their castles and their steeples, archways and domes, bridges and buttresses – but in the sheer, skewed slant of their perspective. As in those tourist maps of old towns where important buildings are drawn side-on so that the wandering stranger recognises the famous towers or ancient palaces and can navigate to them, the cities of the Rift lay out their edifices for all to see, on shelf upon shelf upon shelf of street upon street upon street, rising up and tumbling down the slope. Andean mountain villages were never so perched as the cities of the Rift, pouring like waterfalls downwards, reaching like forest-fires to the sky. A man would be a fool to call these people backward.

And I have only seen one tiny fraction of this culture of the Rift; I do not imagine for a second that having seen their tilted Tuscany and their rising, falling Rome, that I have seen their world. The geography of the Rift may have limited these people's awareness of the full extent of their world, but I have the Book that brought me here in the first place, with its maps showing Rift cities quite unknown to the people of this region, far off to the west or the east, thousands of miles downhill or up. I can see that some of them dwarf the cities that I've been to so far; there are shelves further down, deeper into the Rift, that look, on the maps marked out in the Book at least, as if they must be miles in width.

The sun is nearly down now. At eight o'clock – the angle, not the time – it's almost sunken beneath the burning shrouds of clouds, among the apple trees of an orchard beside a red-brick building with a tower and a low white wooden fence around it marking the sheer, sudden drop beyond. And beyond? Beyond that ledge some miles away and down, the glare of the setting sun is just too strong to make out anything, and the even-more-distant lower terraces are just a melted impressionist blur. It's beautiful.

I consider staying up to watch the dawn – the nights are short, it won't be long – but I find myself yawning and decide it's time to rest. I plan to make my first test flight with the wings tomorrow, and I'm not as young as I used to be, to say the least; I should be ready for it.

4

Gravings of Destiny

A Sister of Sorts

Inanna, fierce goddess of war, whose dance was the moving of battle lines towards each other. Inanna, lion-headed thunderbird of the showers of spring, the rains needed for pasture by the shepherds. Inanna, Ninana, mistress of the date clusters, who received her lover Dumuzi Amaushumgalana at the gate of the storeroom, at the bringing in of harvest. Inanna, Ninnina, protector of harlots, *mistress owl*. As soon as Inanna went down into the Kur, it was said, no cow was fucked by bull, no mare was fucked by stallion, no girl was fucked by any young man in the street. The young man slept in his private room, the girl slept in the company of her friends, the ancient myths say. Inanna, goddess of the evening star, goddess of the morning star, queen of heaven, thief of the Tablets of Destiny. Determined, ambitious Inanna. The little girl who stole the world.

– I'm going over to the other side, says Phreedom.
– You're already here, says Madame Iris, dropping the accent, lifting her veil, showing the face that Phreedom looks at in the mirror. The woman doesn't look any older than her but she's not sure that matters; Phreedom still wonders if she's looking at her future, because she knows that she's not looking at her past. Maybe it's possible. The unkin aren't as stuck in time as everyone else. It takes real skill, or desperation, to really cut loose, the way her brother has, but maybe that's what's on the cards for Phreedom.
– You're ...
– No, says Iris. I know what you're thinking, but you're wrong.

I'm not your twenty-seconds-into-the-future other self; I'm not your one-step-to-the-side alternative self. Time isn't that simple. Time in the Vellum isn't that simple.

Forward and back. Side to side. There's an ... up and down as well, Phreedom knows, dead worlds under her feet, and emptiness above – or beyond and within, maybe – and all of it together making up the Vellum. So this woman isn't her future or a version from a parallel stream ...

– Who are you, then? asks Phreedom.

Eresh, Eris, Iris of the Greater Earth, queen of the underworld. Just as they placed their heavens far above the visible sky, the ancients had their hell beneath the known earth. There in the dust, those with no sons to make burnt offerings for their ancestors would live as beggars, but small children, lost and loved, would play with golden toys, gifts of their parents' grief. An Assyrian prince who visited in a vision once described the demons dwelling within the walls of the dark city of the dead, and Ereshkigal who reigned over it all, the woman in the mourning dress who raked her fingernails across her own flesh, pulled at her hair, and wept forever for all dead. She never played as other young girls did, for all her joyless life; marked for her role, her only childhood songs were elegies.

– Let's say that I'm your sister of sorts. Does it matter? Does it really matter if I'm your second self twice removed or ... whatever. You want to break on through to the other side? Think of me as your ... foot in the door. I'm a part of you, yes. But then I'm a part of a lot of people.

Madame Iris drops the veil back down over her face but by now her accent is abandoned and her words sound genuine.

– I am the part of you that feeds on dust and ashes in the darkness, that died, that *is* dead, and that will *always* be dead.

– Good, says Phreedom. Then you'll help me.

The needle buzzes, wails on her shoulder, low at this point or that, a sickening sound like it's grinding on the bone, and Phreedom feels a little queasy even though this isn't her first tattoo by any means. The pain – the physical pain – is distinct and strange, the needle moving at such speed she doesn't even feel the individual tiny pin-pricks, just the pressure and the nip of it, a sharp but dislocated mass of feeling moving across her shoulder, across her skin and under it, and the tickle of trickling, warm here, cool there. Iris pulls the needle away, dabs at the raw area with a pad of sterile, white cotton wool that turns the blackened red of blood mixed in with ink, deep spoiled soiled crimson, and drops it into a steel tray on the counter behind her. Vapours rise from it.

On the counter, the black ink swirls in the bottles. Glimmers and vortices of involution. It might be nanotech, she thinks. She hears the angels are using high tech shit for their gravings these days; no reason why the other side should be behind the times. Then again it might be plain old-fashioned magic.

The needle touches skin again. The pain – the physical pain – is nothing, just another threshold that she has to cross.

– You understand that this will not remove the graving that's already there, only obscure it? says Madame Iris. You'll still be, at heart, the little girl who learned too much, who held the power of heaven in her grasp and gave it up to follow her brother to the underworld. You cannot change your–

– *Destiny*? says Phreedom. She turns her head to stare defiantly at her double. I don't believe in destiny. Everything can be changed.

– True. But, in the Vellum, you'll learn, the more things seem to change, the more they are the same ... beneath the surface.

And the needle bites into her skin, carving her new mark over her old one, although this mark that's new to her, of course, is older than the world itself, taken from a book written before history even existed.

Phreedom twitches with an involuntary flinch of doubt. The pain – the physical pain – can't burn away the part of her she wants to lose. But maybe it can help her find the part of her she's lost. Time flickers with the buzzing needle and—

The book lies open on the counter before her, a ringbinder of glossy images that look like a historian's photostats of ancient documents. That's what they are, ultimately, repros of the gravings of unkin long-since dead, the secret names they once wore, second selves they once *were* – burned into them when they first touched the flux of forces running through reality and the Vellum, when they first woke up to the world and their part in it. Curves and spirals, dots and circles, a script that looks like diagrams of sub-atomic particles in collision, precise, concise, perfect descriptions of their owners' souls, written in the Cant.

Phreedom flicks through the pages, recognising every sign and sigil even though she's only ever seen such ciphers three times in her whole life: once when Finnan offered her a glimpse of his soul in the palm of his hand; a second time when that same hand traced her own mark onto her flesh and she looked down at it in wonder; and a third time, when she found her brother in the roadhouse up in the hills where he was hiding and he opened up his shirt to show that he too was a marked man.

She flicks through the book of dead gods' names, a history of the world before the world – Anu and Mummu, Ninhursag and Adad, Enlil and Enki, Sin and Dumuzi and . . .

– Inanna, she says.

Madame Iris lays a hand upon her shoulder.

– Yes, little sister.

The needle moves across her, through her, and she feels it in her thoughts, in her memories, as the shape of what she is – or was – is remade, reformed, by a new line here, an arc there. Her soul is wet clay, a tablet held in the hand of a priest as he presses a wedge of reed into it, scripting a myth in cuneiform. It's soft wood carved with runes by knife-point. It's animal hide painted with ochre, canvas marked with oil-paint by candlelight, wet plaster in a cathedral stained with dazzling indigo powder mixed with egg-white on an artist's brush. Her soul is a tale retold in ink and gilding, in the illumination of a medieval manuscript of vellum.

– You cannot change your own soul, Phreedom, says Madame Iris.

But that's exactly what's happening, she thinks. She can feel it. She can feel this other self pressing into her. She can feel the transformation, here, now, happening, as she becomes something else, someone else.

Madame Iris shakes her head.

– Change is an illusion, she says. Time? Space? These are the things you're leaving behind. As far as the Vellum is concerned, you have always been Inanna.

An Empty Role of Rituals

From the Great Beyond she heard it, coming from the Deep Within. From the Great Beyond Inanna heard it, coming from the Deep Within. She had no idea of what it was, this strange sound shaking the ground beneath her feet, but she knew that it was calling her away, away from the village and the *edin* plentiful with food these days and with its earthenware renowned throughout the land between the rivers. Away from her father, the *en* who had made sure that his little princess had the finest *sugurra* in all of the surrounding villages. Away from her charming fiancé, Dumuzi. And away from her priestly tutor with his list of dreary *mes*, the rules and standards, classes, systems that prescribe her world in all its neolithic intricacy in an endless spurious taxonomy of the world.

– Supreme lordship is the first *me*, says her tutor, stroking at the long, oiled curls of his beard. Second is godship, of course, then the exalted and enduring crown.

His voice drags on with its recitation. The throne of kingship, the exalted sceptre, the royal insignia, the sacred shrine. Shepherdship and kingship.

– Lasting ladyship is the tenth *me*, he says, which you, young Inanna should be most concerned with. The eleventh is the priestly office of the *Nin*. Are you listening?

– Yes, she says, looking past him, out the doorway, and carries on with the list herself, in a bored, sarcastic sing-song. The priestly offices of the *ishub*, of the *lumah*, of the *gutug*. Why do I have to learn this?

He just shakes his head.

– The fifteenth *me* is truth, he says. The sixteenth is descent into the netherworld.

But she is listening to a sound that's coming from that very netherworld and she knows this old fool doesn't even hear it. For all his learning, all his talk of the *me*, he doesn't have the first idea of the deep patterns underlying this small village world of irrigated fields and clay-brick buildings, of pottery and metalwork bought from the northerners. But she *hears* it.

And she's going to find someone to tell her what it means.

Forces shifting in the *abzu*, the abyss under the world. Whispers, voices of the ancestors, perhaps, of the Anunnaki themselves. She feels the sound rise up inside her, crying out inside her heart, so loud now that she knows she is like *him*, something that belongs outside the mundane world. It was the sound that led her to him. She laughs.

The man mutters in his drunken slumber, and she bites the sound off in her mouth, darts a glance at the flap of the tent. This *is* still Enki, great god Enki with his Tablets of Destiny, the real *me* in which are graved not empty priestly rituals but reality itself. A great god indeed. He flops an arm across his naked chest, this god no match for a wineskin and a pretty girl. She smiles, goes back to digging through his bundles – rags of hide all covered with strange markings – looking for his secret, sacred wisdom.

She knows what she's looking for – tablets, clay cylinder seals, as in the story of the thunderbird, Anzu, who stole them once – but all he has are rags . . .

And she's smart enough that as he rolls over onto his front and she sees the graving, black upon the black skin of his back, she looks at the rags again. Yes. She can hear it calling in the world around, this strange sound of the forces under it. She can hear it in the mutterings the drunken god makes in his sleep, as if a river of voices runs under his mumbling, rising, falling, turning. Stops and starts of noise. She looks at the markings on the rags and sees . . . the shapes of sounds.

So our destinies are written not on clay but skin, she thinks. She strokes her arm in absent concentration, wondering if her plan is really wise. Maybe not, she thinks. But it is so very her.

– *Inanna,* hisses Phreedom, through clenched teeth. She tries to latch on to a singular identity, either the goddess of the myth that's being carved into her flesh, or the young girl of the neolithic village whose real history is buried there inside that tale. But she's finding it hard enough to distinguish her own memories from the chaos, never mind separating the fusion of archetype and actuality that constitutes this other self, Inanna. She has memories of grassy steppes now, of being courted by a young shepherd boy, of gathering water from a well, of learning to play the *lilis* and the *mesi* and – her favourite instrument – the *ala*. She is Inanna looking out the door of the room where a dull priest tries to teach her how to be a good little princess. She is Inanna, travelling to a city in a cavern in the mountains where dead souls eat dust and men wear great black cloaks of feathers like the wings of vultures. She is Phreedom looking out of the door of her hotel room, and she is Inanna standing on a desolate mountainside and looking through a black rip in the stone, a rip in the Vellum itself, a door out of reality.

And giving a message to her servant. If I'm not out in three days, go get help.

If you're going to Hell, it's a good idea to have a back-up plan.

The Answerers

The Comfort Inn, Marion.

Like a message in a bottle, a last entry in a lost explorer's journal or a monologue to camera recorded in a basement as the bombs fall outside, the cipher lady will be Phreedom's last note to the real world, and her fingers weave it with care, dancing in her simware glove even as she watches the sprite take shape in virtual vision. VR spirit of female shape, an off-the-shelf AI straight out of the grainy stores of discount data, uploaded with her voice profile, layered-over with a surface scan of her physique, mapped from the naked image in the mirror – naked but for the glove linked to the datastick that's linked, in turn, to her lenses. In the glove her fingers dance, and in the lenses, a mirage projected in the view in front of her, the vision dances. Wireframe and skintone, it rotates, articulates, built in layers outward and inward, multifacets of false flesh in full-scale replica of herself. Lady Cypher, she calls it, this electronic golem, virtual homunculus. Any sufficiently advanced form of technology, she thinks wryly, is indistinguishable from magic. It's an old saying that she heard somewhere.

She bypasses the built-in character engine. This isn't just some lame, cheap answerer, all smiles and simplicity and *Phreedom isn't available right now, can I take a message?* Fuck that shit. It won't have real autonomy, but the stolen PR module that she splices in is top-grade, sort of thing the MD of a big bad corporation has to field those awkward questions about poisoned rivers and disease clusters. There's a lot you can do with AI these days if you've got the money ... or if you've spent ten years watching your hacker jacker cracker-jack mother mutilating business webworlds for the long-lost cause. Phreedom could probably build a sprite that, if it ran for president, would lose because it seemed too human.

But this doesn't have to do anything so complex. All it has to do is weep for her because she can't do that for herself.

Phreedom links through to the webworld for the Museo Nacional de Antropologia, Mexico City. She checks that her access hack still works for the temple sim and readies the upload wizard. A tour menu scrolls across her lenses: the Pyramid of Cheops; Teotihuacan; the Parthenon; the Ziggurat of Enlil. VR tourism's a big industry these days; it's a lot cheaper than the real thing and you can visit places that haven't existed for millennia.

The sprite is re-rendering, its face contorting now in maniac gibberish, squeaking and babbling like a cretin child in fast-forward, as it runs through the linguistic algorithms in generation after generation of phonemes gradually evolving into sounds of speech, morphemes that build into words, words that patch together into grammar as the Chomsky node kicks in. It's still senseless even as it ripples from glossalalia into language, speaking in random couplings in various tongues, cobbled nonsenses that serve only as practice.

De lieuw zit in de bus. Où est le loup-garou? But to get to artificial intelligence, as they say, you have to go through artificial idiocy.

– *Qué pasa?* the sprite says. I am here. *Perdón; no entiendo*.

Man, this stuff installs fast, Phreedom thinks. She dips back into the sim, flicking the install interface into silent mode with a click of her fingers, calling up the design library add-on that she stripped off some bootleg CAD software – sort of archive of geometry and mathematical modelling tools you'd plug into your answerer if you were an architect's firm whose PA needed to communicate tech-specs to clients and contractors with both accuracy and speed. Except that, along with all the domes and volutes and elliptical floor-plans, this library has a very special little shape she programmed in herself.

The avatar's face is gurning through basic emotions now, as the affective response module generates its repertoire of joy, disgust, anger, surprise, fear and sorrow. She looks at the black sigil floating in the air in front of her. It's not completely accurate as a replica of her mark, but it's close enough to carve a little piece of her soul into the sprite's semblance of self. They used to do this to statues in the old days, she understands, back in the days before the unkin all got together in their little Covenant and put an end to idols, before they burned the teraphim in the temples. They'd make a creature of clay to stand in their temples, put a little rough copy of their graving into it, make it speak for them. Answerers.

She loads her mark into the sprite's deep memory and, for a second, it stops its mugging and mute mutters, winces, blinks and looks at her almost with sentience. God in the machine, she thinks.

Any sufficiently advanced form of magic is indistinguishable from technology.

The Temple of Lord Ilil

When, after three days and three nights, Inanna still had not returned, the Lady Shubur then began to sound a lamentation for her in the ruins, pound the drum for her in the assemblies where the unkin gather and around the houses of the gods. She tore at her eyes, her mouth, her thighs.

She wore the beggar's single robe of soiled sackcloth then as, all alone, she set out for the temple of Lord Ilil in Nippur. She entered the holy shrine and she cried out to Lord Ilil.

Pound the drum. Phreedom feels the story etching itself into her life, her own life being buried in the ink. *Around the houses of the gods.* Fierce pride and furious grief. Lost innocence. *She tore at her eyes, her mouth, her thighs.* Memories, realities, cut over each other in new connections, like one of those dreams where a different you lives in a different time or place, has a whole different history, but still has also this vague sense of what you were when you were once awake, what you might be again ... a dream of another life where you're not sure which life is real and which is dream. She's no longer sure how long she's been here. An hour? A day? A week?

So this is what it's like to die, she thinks. The road of no return. But there's still a little part of her left, a little piece of Phreedom.

Another memory: She's pulling the glove out of her jacket pocket, pulling it on and plugging it into the datastick. Earphones, booster sockets, logos scrolling across her lenses – she's wired in ...

– Enlil, the tour guide sprite says, *en* meaning *lord*, *lil* meaning ... well, it's usually translated as *winds* or *sky*, but one old theory by the esteemed professor Samuel Hobbsbaum suggests that it may be related to the Hittite *ilil*, literally *god of gods*. It's from the same Semitic root that gives us the Hebrew *Elohim* and the Arabic *Allah*, so Lord God of Gods does seem a rather apt translation.

It smiles with wise beneficence, the tour guide, acting for all the world like it's a learned expert opening a world of wonder to its uneducated customer, even though its sing-song spiel is only a little more reactive than one of those old tape-recordings fired off by a button on a display; it can answer questions, spin the ancient myths with all an actor's skills, react, respond ... but it thinks nothing of the fact that its sole customer on this excursion is a flickering shade of a woman dressed in sackcloth, weeping openly even as he gestures at the altar, at the ornate lampstands, at the bearded statue in this lowlit mock-up of the inner chamber of the ancient temple of Enlil that once stood in Nippur and now stands, reconstructed, here in a simworld Sumer of VR.

– Like Zeus or Jupiter, the tour guide says, Enlil was seen as father of the gods, the king of heaven. But – and this really tells us something quite fascinating about Sumerian society – because, for the ancients, the politics of Heaven was just a reflection of the politics of Earth – well, unlike the Greek or Roman gods, Enlil's power was not quite absolute.

The Lady Cypher wanders over to the statue, ignoring him completely, but he follows her, still wittering as if this was only another tourist, enraptured by his tales, stepping up towards the staring eyes and long curled beard of stone to take a closer look at this strange holy artefact of ancient times.

– I'm sure you know of all those stories about Zeus or Jupiter ravishing young maidens, siring demigods here, there and everywhere. There's never any questions. Nobody challenges the King of the Gods about his ... lewd behaviour. But it's interesting that in the one similar myth we have from Sumer, where Enlil comes across a young maiden bathing in a stream and ... ravishes her ...

The Lady Cypher looks at him strangely, fiercely, for a second, as if some fleeting sentience under the surface of the sim finds something tasteless in his prurient euphemisms. He carries on regardless.

– Well, Enlil ends up called before the assembly of the gods, impeached, you might say, and exiled, cast down from his throne ... to Hell, no less.

– It really is amazing to think that a millennia before Athens, the Sumerians had democracy, not just in terms of the assemblies of elders in their city-states, but amongst the gods themselves. The king of the gods himself wasn't above the law. He could be impeached, tried for his crimes and punished. Of course in the myth he does eventually find a substitute to take his place in Hell but ...

The Lady Cypher, the Lady Shubur, isn't listening to him. Under the slick surface of her, neural agents dance down virtual paths that trace a pattern older than the stones this virtual space around her simulates.

– should be all but obliterated in the end by monotheism is

ironic, really. And yet, for all the iconoclasm of the Judaeo-Christian tradition and of Islam, still . . .

Inside her head, a three-day countdown of the thousandths of the seconds reaches zero, and a symbol, a sigil, a mark buried in her archives, is activated, a popup window into infinity.

– look upon the face of Enlil, with his long curled beard, his fierce eyes, we can't help but be reminded of that God we know so . . .

And the Lady Shubur starts to wail.

Lady Shubur's Lament

– O father Lord Ilil, cried Lady Shubur, do not leave your daughter to death and damnation. Will you let your shining silver lie buried forever in the dust? Will you see your precious lapis shattered into shards of stone for the stoneworker, your aromatic cedar cut up into wood for the woodworker? Do not let the queen of heaven, holy priestess of the earth, be slaughtered in the Kur.

The words carve themselves in Phreedom's flesh and in her memory like a song uploaded to a datastick. Like cutting a disk, she thinks, burning a CD, ripping a file . . . carving a soul. She can feel her old self being over-written, her memory being . . . de-allocated, archived, re-allocated. As a programmer, she understands what's happening to her, but it's still the strangest experience of her life.

But this is how Thomas got out of this world and into the Vellum. If she wants to follow him she has to die. She has to be written out of history and written into myth.

The needle bites deep into her skin and into the skin of the world. She flinches and a shockwave travels round the world.

Arecibo, Puerto Rico.

Papa Eli holds the girl down, forcing his hand between her teeth as she bucks and writhes under him, screaming, clawing at him and at herself with her fingernails, at her plain white linen dress and the skin beneath it, eyes rolled back into her head. The *abiku* that possesses her shrieks its fury as she whips her head to one side, freeing her mouth to call on spirits with names he does not know, not Chango or Ellegua, not Oggun or Yemaya – none of the orishas that the *brujos* have been calling on ever since their Yoruban ancestors were first brought here as slaves.

– Ilil, she screams. Sin! Enki!

The other santeros of the asiento stand behind him, drums abandoned, singing stopped, afraid of this girl taken as a horse by something far darker than any santerian spirit, some creature of the other realms that knows only its own rage and sorrow.

– Ilil, she screams at him, as if she's trying to call some loa out of him, as if her fury is that he will not answer. And Papa Eli feels some spirit moving through his fear, something in him that *is* trying to answer her, and he calls on every orisha he knows to fight it.

The Temple of Lord Ilil, Nippur.

The Lady Cypher drops to her knees before the statue, mouth open, wailing in a language that's not the gibberish of her infant idiocy, that's not the English or the Spanish, French or Dutch that it evolved into, that's not the C# or the Java or ObjArt or any of the construct codes she's written in, that's not the machine code built of binary bits that is the flesh and bones of her. It's clearer, more precise than mathematics, more poetic than the songs of humans. It's the language that the world is written in.

– Father Lord Ilil, your daughter! Will you see:

The language rips right through the sim, reshaping it into – *buried forever in the dust your shining silver* – the ruins of itself, this temple of Ilil – *to death damnation left* – and as she sings the statue resonates – *the precious lapis shattered into shards of stone for worker* – and the air is broken – *aromatic cedar cut up into wood for worker* – sings the Lady Shubur, sukkal of Inanna, sprite of Phreedom – *slaughtered queen of heaven, holy priestess of the earth in death, in Kur*.

And the song ripples through that underworld.

Liverpool, England.

– For it is God who commands thee, roars Father Lyle, making the sign of the cross over the girl's forehead. The majesty of Christ commands thee! God the Father commands thee! God the Son commands thee! God the Holy Ghost commands thee!

But the girl is still snarling and spitting.

– Baalzebaal, Prince of Princes! Elial, God of Gods!

– The sacred cross commands thee! he shouts over her blasphemy, over the sound of her mother's weeping and her father's prayers, and—

– Elial! Lord of Lords!

– The faith of the holy apostles Peter and Paul and of all other saints commands thee! The blood of the martyrs commands thee! The constancy of the confessors commands thee! The devout intercession of all saints commands thee!

– Fuck you!

– The virtue of the mysteries of the Christian faith commands thee!

And he holds the Bible over her like a brick about to shatter her skull, summoning all the strength of his belief, his faith a force inside him, deep as the centuries.

– Elial! she screams.

And his hand shakes as he feels a force that's deeper than the centuries stirring inside him.

The Houses of the Gods

– Enlil Enlil Enlil Enlil . . .

The tour guide loops in the cubist wreckage of the sim like some old school video-art installation; spaces fractured, curves become angles, the sim reconfigures around Lady Shubur, adapting to and adopting the form of the sound in physical resonances. Her lament is a solid thing in this world made of information and it moves through it like an eel of light flicking through water, a sidewinder of fire over sand, throwing up ripples of burning, liquid dust. VR isn't just wireframes and texture mappings; this world has particles, virtual models of pseudo-atomic structure and behaviour. It's a rougher grain than reality but it's still finer than the coarse surface of paper or the lumpen masses of clay and stone when all you've got to work them is your fingers, or a stone chisel, or a lump of wedge-shaped reed. If reality is information, the world that's written on the Vellum, this is the best medium ever for the remodelling of it, for the invocations that are the basis of magic. And Phreedom's sim, the cypher lady, Lady Shubur, is one complex motherfucker of a spell.

So. Somewhere out of time and not quite in eternity, the one-time lord of all the unkin broods upon his throne, as still as stone, as silent as the broken statue in the glass case of the Baghdad Museum of Antiquities, one graven image that is now his only presence in the real world, in the finite forms of time and space. In reality, his temple has long been in ruins, broken up, the stones that built it either buried under millennia of dust or used in later buildings, Roman temples, Muslim mosques. It is only in the Vellum that he survives. The whole civilization that he built was completely forgotten until a mere century ago. All gods have their houses but all houses fall eventually and when they do the gods are left with only history as their home, living in the dreams of archaeologists, in the margins of a culture's memory, in the Vellum. But now, as the invocation echoes in another sort of memory, Enlil remembers what it's like to be revered, to be petitioned with prayer.

He used to be the Father of the Gods. He used to be a king, back in the days before the city he had watched being built reached out its power wide enough around that it began to touch on areas ruled by others like him and he realized he was not alone. He was a king, back when a city meant a small town where the huts were actually permanent, when the unkin were still few enough that some could grow up in a world and rule an empire, die a couple of hundred years later, never knowing there were others like them. Even as the towns became cities, and the cities became nations, even when he discovered there were countless others, he soon realized he was still more powerful than them, king of kings. When his body eventually died, he already had the vessel prepared.

He'd been using the Cant long enough to know how to put his graving on something, to put a little bit of himself into it, make it speak for him. As the artisans worked to his instructions they were, to all intents and purposes, only making a larger version of the clay figurines that all his *lugals* carried with them and that they called *shabtis*, answerers. But, hobbling around it on his crutch and muttering his chant, finding the resonant frequency of the stone and making it sing in the echo chamber of the temple, he'd known that he would be a king for some time yet. From shabti to teraphim he would go on to carve his soul in vessel after vessel, some stone, some clay, some flesh. There could be thousands of these vessels, these gravings, all working simultaneously, semi-autonomous but still linked, still part of him. Temples and palaces with winged, heraldic, hybrid forms of *karibu* as their guardians, statues that looked fierce and sounded devastating when they spoke his words as his spirit moved within them. There was a reason people pictured cherubim with swords of fire coming from their mouths; the language was a fearsome thing to those who did not have it. And he was the most fluent in the tongue of all the unkin.

O yes, he used to be a king. He used to be the Father of the Gods. Before Enki and his Covenant.

– What does she think I can do? he asks the creature flickering before him, the half-formed image of a maid as messenger, a little piece of Inanna – her *sukkal* – left behind to plead her case. As if a fallen and forgotten god could help her.

– You are the Lord Ilil . . . the Lady Shubur says.

But this one-time father of the gods, long-bearded ruler of the multitudes of heavens, has no foothold in a world now ruled by One True Gods. Like his temple, his own soul is broken up and buried, surviving only in the odd fragments of a patriarchal archetype, here and there, in this or that man's deep unconscious soul, in the kind eye of a brujo or the stern voice of a priest. There's a new Godfather with his own temple, his own story, and Ilil is just a footnote in his text, a brick used in the new lord's house.

– My daughter craved the Great Beyond, he answers sullenly. Inanna craved the Deep Within, and she who takes the *me* of the Kur can not come back. From the Dark City there is no return.

He will not help.

– He would not help, the Lady Cypher murmurs to herself as the sim of Enlil's temple in Nippur collapses around her and she steps out of the wreckage onto a flat and featureless plain of sand, her lament still echoing in whorls of cloud up in the sky. She casts her gaze around the visual metaphor of cyberspace, cool as a sphinx, as if waiting for some other option to open up to her, but, inside, another routine is already kicking off. Phreedom's Plan B.

The Lady Shubur went to the temple of Sin in Ur. Time flickers with the buzzing of the needle and Phreedom flickers with it. In her mind's eye she's back fighting with her brother in the Winnebago as it pulls into the trailer park of Slab City, way out in the dead heat of the Mojave; as it swings wide past a junkyard slab where a shining Airstream rises on a tower of bricks behind this man holding a crazy staff, wound round with wires and topped with a TV aerial, like some modern mage; she's staring out the window at him, silent, as Tom punches her in the arm. She's tripping on peyote by a fireside with Tom and his new friend, this crazy, fucked-up latter-day shaman, Finnan, as he spins them wild tales of gods and angels, worlds beyond the world. She's throwing stones at Finnan's Airstream, cursing him, demanding to know where her brother's gone. She's looking at the weird mark on his hand and knowing it, understanding it. She's cursing an angel that's come for him, that he won't fight because the war they want's not his. She's straddling Finnan, naked flesh against flesh, knowing him, knowing herself, awakening with him gone. She's alone.

The Lady Shubur utters a single word and, in the sky, black clouds spread out like oil on water, a liquid night that swells and smooths, then punctures here and there in tiny pinprick stars. The moon dilates into existence overhead, a white pupil in a dark eye. Sin, the god of the moon was called, in the ancient myths; if Ilil is just a broken fragment of his former self, it may well be that Sin is even more a shadow. But the gods and goddesses who've made the moon their sign have always been creatures of shadows, at home in dreams irrational and insubstantial, and lost in the light of day like water trickling through fingers. If anyone can survive being forgotten, it's a god of dreams.

She's holding her brother on a hillside as he cries. She's spitting in the face of the unkin with the long, thin fingers tightening round her throat. She's sobbing in the shower as the water runs over her body, shouting at Finnan in the church because he has no answers for her, nothing, nothing, no denials, no assurances, no lies, and she just knows that it was him who told the angels where her brother was 'cause she can see it in the way he keeps his gaze down, guilty eyes in shadow. She's gunning the bike along the freeway, faster, faster, slamming a door behind her, pulling a beaded curtain aside. She's raising a veil from her face. She's writhing under the exorcist's grip. She's biting down on the *brujo*'s hand between her teeth. She's screaming as the judges of the underworld fall on her, their claws tearing at her flesh like a tattooist's needle, stripping her of her skin, her name, her self.

The Lady Shubur went to the temple of Sin in Ur, entered the holy shrine.

A Spiderweb Collage

The Temple of Sin has no pop-academia sim to give it form, no virtual walls or floor or ceiling here, no flickering lamplight over rendered plaster, no texture and no colour. But dimensionally, the space that houses the ancient moon god is richer by far, an abstract space of entities and relationships defined in ones and zeros, a mosaic of bitmaps of scanned-in black-and-white or colour photographs, hundred-walled warehouses of tables of texts and translations, keyed, indexed and cross-referenced. Sin lives in a network of article titles and authors' names, of catalogued museum storerooms, descriptions of artefacts and expeditions saved in files, distributed between servers across the world. The house of Sin is a spiderweb collage of information.

The Lady Shubur can't stand before his face and speak to him, but she can summon him in complex queries, semi-autonomous search agents that scatter across the web to bring back scrolling, flickering sets of records for her to process. She searches for him as a criminal psychologist seeks out the mind that's hidden in a case file, in the forensic reports and witness statements, hidden somewhere in the scraps of facts, a *me* under the MO. And as she builds the profile, she continues with her mantra.

– O father Lord Ilil. Bright silver aromatic cedar broken daughter cut of precious lapis, slaughtered holy heaven priestess, slaughtered in the Kur, stone for the stoneworker, wood for the woodworker, covered with dust of the Kur. O father Lord Ilil . . .

The sim takes shape around her.

A dead, airless hunk of stone and tranquil seas of dust silver as ash, tranquil as death, in an eternal fall through the black gulf of space, Sin's solid sigil spins a dance around a world as gaudy as the moon is harsh. The earth wears robes of blue ocean and sky, embroidered with the browns and reds, yellows and greens of soil and foliage, plush mycelial threads, the furs of life; her draperies of continents glitter with the golden glints of sequin cities. The moon is naked in comparison, its only clothes the shadows that it casts upon itself.

It dances to the Lady Cypher's song.

A spiderweb collage of: vacuum silence between the stars; static white noise hissing in a spaceman's radio; white heat of the sun, sharp as the shadows on his suit, no air to soak it up; a rippling pathway on the sea at night, a bridge to the horizon for young lovers walking on a beach; tides of oceans and hormones; ice-grey eyes of wild coyotes howling in bestial rapture; flickers on the wings of moths that flutter through the air, charting their paths against the brilliant beacon. Women menstruate and men turn into wolves; blood flows for Sin. Moonlight, unstructured, Sin shines in the darkness.

Phreedom remembers stealing beer from her parents' fridge, and she remembers stealing yagé from Finnan's, leafing through his journals when he wasn't there, looking for the answers that he wouldn't give when asked. Who are you? What are you?

– Who am I? she mutters, but the only answer is the buzzing needle.

She was born Phreedom Messenger, in the last years of the twentieth century AD, daughter of activists whose politics were born in the death of old ideals, somewhere between 9/11 and Guantanamo Bay. She grew up with genocide and jihad, with wearable computing and internet access for all, and AI and VR, and men in clean suits pulling bodies out of subway cars, the whole CNN apocalypse. She played tagalong with her brother, Thomas, and his weird friend Finnan, listening as they talked crazy shit in the desert night under the moon, and, every so often, throwing something in that made them stop and look at her as if just realizing she was there.

They'd get stoned, wasted, tripping out on yagé or peyote till the desert around them seemed a world of illusion.

The Lady Cypher lays the imagery of Sin out like a Tarot deck in a reading, looking for the meaning to be found in juxtapositions and alignments. Where Enlil, god of sky and storm, of decrees uttered with the sharp clarity of lightning and the resounding force of thunder, is, by his nature, dispossessed, a wanderer in the Vellum, lost and moaning over greater days, Sin is at home here. Kings and tyrants come and go; no great surprise that Enlil should be obsolete in a world where law can be uttered in airstrikes not by a thunderbird but by a stealth bomber, black as a crow, imperial as an eagle. Sin, on the other hand, has always been a god of silences and shadows, negative spaces. If he was ever human as, being unkin, he must once have been, his history is long-since dissolved in the dreamworld of illusions, elisions, elusions.

The Lady Cypher, having all of Phreedom's memories graved into her, remembers how Tom talked of the Illusion Fields, a sweeping expanse of eternity stretching out past reality, further away than the horizon that you never reach no matter how far you walk, closer than the shadow under your feet.

She remembers stealing the yagé, getting so fucked-up one night – after her brother left, it was – that Finnan had to body-slam her to the ground, out of the way of the thunderbolt that she'd called down. There was a storm raging, in the sky and in her heart.

– What am I? she'd asked him, grabbing his grubby T-shirt, shoving at him, pulling at him as he struggled to his feet against her, singing at the storm with a voice that made her eardrums bleed, in words she couldn't hold inside her head. And it was only when the storm had stopped that he turned to her, and just looked at her as if it was the stupidest fucking question that he'd ever heard.

It was a fluke, of course, the lightning, but after that he started to open up, a little at a time, to tell her about the Cant, reluctantly.

– I want to know everything, she'd said.

– Curiosity killed the cat, you know, Finnan had said.

– Yeah, but it's pig-ignorance that gets most of the other animals, she'd said.

Phreedom tries to hold on to the memory but it's as liquid as the language that she heard that night.

The Lady Cypher can't tell from the fleeting fragmentary imagery surrounding her, if there is really something underneath. The god of the moon is too elusive. She seems to glimpse a darting consciousness out of the corner of her eye, but it's as quickly gone as it appears. The only message that he'll give her is the echo that she hears.

– My daughter craved the Great Beyond, the voice of Enlil says. Inanna craved the Deep Within, and she who takes the *me* of the Kur can not come back. From the Dark City there is no return.

He will not help.

The Gods of Old

– Once upon a time, Finnan had told her, there were gods all over the place. I mean, if you want to know how many gods there were, you only have to look at Ireland; a tiny little island and it's still full to the brim with spirits. Jesus, but half the fookin saints used to be the heathen gods of old and all those fairies, every one of them, what are they but gods who lost their glory and went skipping off into the gloaming with only their glamour left, when Christianity came and put them out of their homes? That was the choice, ye see, when the angels came. Sign up or ship out. So some of them join up, becoming yer Saint Bridget's or whatever, and some of them take to the hills. Jesus, but can ye imagine it? Going from king of all the Tuatha-de-Danaan – of Cuchullain of the red hair, of Lud the silver-handed, Bran the thrice-blessed, the Dagda, with golden cauldrons and chariots and war-hounds bigger than men – to this foolish little lord of the Sidhe, hiding in burrows under the earth, and finally to the fookin fairy-folk of Victorian fancies. Fookin leprechauns and pots of gold. Celtic Twilight, my arse.

– Once upon a time, Finnan had told her, there weren't any gods at all. Just human beings that lived and died and dreamed up foolish little fireside tales to make them all feel a little warmer in the cold night. They looked out to the sunset and they thought to themselves, why that's so beautiful there *must* be something out there. They buried their dead in the ground and couldn't bear to think of them just rotting, so they told themselves there was a land under the earth where all the dead live on like us. Or maybe it was in the far North, or at the source of some great river, in the mountains, in the sky, wherever. But for all the adventurers and explorers that went wandering over the face of the earth, did any of them ever find anything but people, painted up and draped in skins and dancing like loonies to the moon, but people nonetheless? Did that stop them, though? No. Why, they says, if there's no Heaven then we'll fookin build one. If there's no gods out there, we'll raise ourselves up by our bootstraps, grab a star out of the sky and wear it as a fookin crown and we'll be gods our fookin selves. So they built themselves a language for a ladder and clambered up over their own words till they did it. Only they took so many stars out of the sky, ye see, they left it full of holes, too weak to hold itself up, and so eventually, one day, the sky came crashing down on them so hard and heavy that it drove them right down into the earth, so deep that the only thing left of them sticking out was those crowns on their heads. Sure, there's those who somehow manage to stick their necks up out of the shite and look up into the ruins of Babel, read a few words written on the rubble, but at the end of the day, that's what we were and this is what we are now, up to our necks in history, in humanity, and with no more choice about it than the poor dead bastards buried in the earth by all our ancestors.

– Once upon a time, Finnan had told her, the gods got fed up with this not existing malarkey that they'd had to put up with for the last forever, because if you don't exist, well, there's no pressing need to get out of bed of a morning; it's not like ye've got any work to go to, eh, and obviously that kind of unemployment lends itself to low self-esteem, if not downright depression. So they all came together one day and decided amongst themselves that they wanted to have a go at this existing thing. They'd been watching humans at it for a good few millennia, from the inside of their heads, living in the human imagination as they did, and the humans seemed to be having all sorts of strange experiences – living, dying, fucking, grieving, hunting, drinking – hell, even suffering is at least an experience, and to a god that only gets the second-hand scraps of dreams and delusions, well, it's better than nothing. Of course, most people have such poor imaginations that the gods had no idea what they were in for. They thought it would be all epic battles and noble struggles, valiant causes, good against evil. Ye have to pity them, sure, because they weren't at all prepared for life as it is, poor sods. What the fuck is this, they says to themselves, when they finally find a way to push themselves out from the back of our heads and into the noggin as a whole, when they pick themselves up off the floor and dust off their stolen bodies and look around at the world. What the fuck is this? Where's the grand quests and eternal mysteries? Where's the foreshadowings and symmetries, the plots, the themes? Where's the meaning? O, in time some of them would come to love it, sure, this mad world of ours; but some of them, well, they just keep trying to make it fit their notion of what a world *should* be like. They're insane, of course, and sooner or later one of them will come along and try and rope you into some mad empire-building scheme of theirs. And, of course, if you're not with them you're against them, far as they're concerned. Take my advice and steer well clear of them.

– You know, she had said to him, nothing you say actually fits together. Shit, Finnan, can't you even try to be consistent with your bullshit?

Thomas had laughed, brattishly superior as only an elder sibling can be.

– Consistency, he'd said. Fuck consistency.

– It's not about consistency, Finnan had said. Where the Cant is involved it's not a matter of consistency. You can't tell the full story, the complete story, and hope to be consistent. Best you can hope for is . . . coherent and comprehensive. And where the fucking unkin are involved you're probably better off not bothering with either. Trust me, if they think you've figured out what it's all about – as if there is any such thing as *what it's all about* – they'll be all over you like fucking crows on a battlefield. Because that's what they want. A nice, simple answer to it all.

– And you don't think there is one? she'd said.

He shook his head.

– Even the book doesn't have that, from what I hear.

– What book?

– The Book of All Hours.

– What's the Book of All Hours?

– Ah, said Finnan, now that's another story altogether.

A Sleeve of Blood and Black

She was born Ninanna Belili, in the last years of the twentieth century BC, daughter of a neolithic chieftain and his priestess wife whose cosmology was collapsing with the blossoming of new ideas, somewhere between the Tigris and the Euphrates. She grew up with farming and fishing, with ceramic pots and grainstores for all, and mathematics and writing, and men with sickles bringing corn in from the fields, the whole Sumerian revolution. She flirted with the shepherd boy, Dumuzi, asked him to sing of Enki in his *abzu*, deep under the earth, asked him with a dreamy passion that would make him stop and look at her and ask her where she was, what she was thinking.

– Who am I? asks the girl who used to be called Phreedom. The tattoo covers most of her arm now in a sleeve of blood and black, as if she's thrust her arm deep into the flesh of something vast and sick to seize its heart, a warrior or a surgeon. She's lost all track of time somewhere in all the involuted intricacy of the ink that webs her flesh, the swirling cyphers of another person's memory and identity. Iris is talking to her, but Phreedom doesn't hear her words. Inanna hears. Inanna listens now with Phreedom's ears, and nods, replies, but the girl who once was Phreedom is now deaf and mute, trapped somewhere deep inside herself.

What's left of her is thinking that maybe this wasn't such a good idea.

She was born Inanna, queen of heaven, priestess of the earth, in the last years of the twentieth world, daughter of a moon god and the mother earth whose tales were lost in the birth of new mythologies, somewhere between never and now. She grew up with fate and destiny, with epic heroes and archetypal roles for all, and history and law, and gods painted in ochre dragging the bodies of their titan forebears out of chaos, the whole subconscious genesis. She drank with the old god of wisdom, Enki, listening as he rambled on about the world of certainty that he was crafting for them all, scheming an ordered place, a time, a space. And when he had slumped, sodden with drink, into unconsciousness, she took his *me*, the plans of his grand scheme, the Gravings of Destiny, and slipped away into the night.

– Audacity, says Madame Iris. If there's one word that describes Inanna, little sister, it's audacity. First goddess to step up and take on the patriarchs at their own game, Inanna was. I mean, motherhood, that's an easy archetype for a female unkin to take on. Maid, mother and crone, right? Virgin princess, priestess-queen, witch-seeress. That's the way it goes. Neat roles all nicely tied up into packages. Fates and furies, norns and muses, graces and graia. All very well, but those roles don't offer much in the way of . . . character. But Inanna . . . Inanna wasn't going to play that game. Inanna had her own plans. O, they can have their Covenant, they can write every man, woman and child into their book of life, and bind us all to their ideas of destiny, of fate. But once you've met your fate, the story that they've written for you is over. The dead are free.

Iris runs her fingers over the glossy 8 by 10 of the unkin mark and looks across at Phreedom's arm . . . Inanna's arm . . . whatever. It's not her best work but it'll have to do; it would be better if she had the original to work with but – she closes the ringbinder – the copy will have to do.

Errata

The Book of Life

The angel known as Metatron, the man once known as Enoch, the god once known as Enki, lays his hand on the hotel guest-book that sits up on the counter, smiles at the clerk and whispers a word that drops the man like a stone, unconscious, to the ground. It's a few years since he last had to use the language, but he hasn't lost it, he's glad to see. That's as it should be, though. He is the voice of God, after all.

The foyer is empty and out past the glass walls and the doors with their racks of tourist brochures for Little Switzerland and the Blue Ridge Parkway, the parking lot has only a couple of trucks and RVs. Even the Taco Bell across the way is empty, the employees in their cheap, garish uniforms sitting outside on the steps, gazing off into the distance and chatting.

He flicks his black dreads back out of his face and flicks his long black leather coatflap back to pull out his little leatherbound palmtop from his jacket pocket, lays it up on the counter, on top of the guest-book. He doesn't have to hunt for a signature to know that they were both here, the little hatchling and her runaway brother. He knows the girl and her brother have a meeting somewhere, somewhen, not too far from here and now. It's all in his book.

That's what worries him, actually; that's why he's here in person. Because according to the unkin who were sent to bring the boy in, Thomas Messenger died trying to escape from them. According to those same two unkin, Phreedom Messenger was left bleeding to death in a catatonic stupor, her soul more violated than her body. *She's out of the game*, they'd said. *Little birdy got her wings broke. End of story*.

Except that's not the end. The angel Metatron knows this because the angel Metatron has his book of life, his records of assignations and interactions, crossed paths, interlocked fates, destinies decreed when this world was still a speck of dust under his fingernail. And if the book of life records a meeting between two unkin somewhere, somewhen, not too far from here, those unkin can't be dead.

The palmtop boots up into a screen of scrolling glyphs; it's a bit outdated in these days of VR lenses and shimmering images, but he's always been a little old school in his methods. He likes the feel of weathered leatherbound books, smooth plastic keys under his fingers, dirt under his fingernails, dust on his boots. He is Lord Earth, after all – En Ki, as he once wrote his name with wedge-shaped reeds pressed into clay, when he was just a lowly scribe, laying his master's laws and dictates down for all eternity. The rest of the unkin were all so quick to take the roles of warriors, heroes, kings, showing their lordship over the sky by calling down a storm.

Thunder and lightning, he thinks. Hawks and eagles. Back in the old days you couldn't walk a hundred miles without running into some self-appointed god of all the skies and heavens, god of air and grace, of airs and graces. For them the whole point of civilization was to take them further from the dirt that they were born in. For Enki, craftsman and technologist, father of irrigation and agriculture, civilization is made of dirt. Mathematics and writing began in shapes pressed into slick wet clay. Even now, now that he's Metatron, with four thousand years between him and that previous life, the scribe in him still likes the feel of something in his hand.

He frowns.

The Tablets of Destiny

The palmtop's flickering display stops at a screen of curlicues and arabesques, pictograms that represent not things but forces, vectors, the motion of a snake's tongue flicking out to taste the air, the tension in a lion's shoulder muscles as it's poised to leap, all tabulated into rows and columns like some child's puzzle, waiting for a circling pen to find the words spelled out forwards and backwards, upside-down, diagonally. In fact he reads it every way, this page of text, from left to right like English, right to left like Hebrew, top to bottom like Chinese, and spiralling inwards to the central glyph like the Sumerian of his youth.

The Arattan script can even be read diagonally, from the lower-left corner to the upper-right, or from right to left. But it's not the original text. And no matter which way he reads it, it doesn't make sense.

He can smell the girl's pain all round him. He can feel the boy's signature burning its way through the thick pages of the guest-book. The palmtop should be picking all this up, mapping the moment, catching the currents of it like yarrow stalks falling into hexagrams. Instead, there's no sign of either of them in the text. It was clear enough two weeks ago, clear enough that he called the two gatherers in to question them for hours on what exactly they remembered. The boy was dead? The girl was as good as? They were certain?

– This is the only thing that's certain, he had said, holding the book up in their faces.

He looks at it now and frowns. Destiny doesn't change.

The language has an agglutinative grammar at its heart. It doesn't need all the little joining words of English, all the ofs and tos and fors and bys. It doesn't need all the grammatical exoskeleton of Latin prefixes and suffixes around the words. It's just a matter of how you put the words together, one after the other after the other, except the block of text that's on the screen is less a linear statement than a map of all its possible meanings; it's not designed to be read in one direction, line by line, no more than you could understand a painting if you cut it into strips and scanned your eyes along each shred, reading the individual brushstrokes one by one and waiting for the meaning to emerge.

Whatever form it takes, leatherbound book of life, clay tablets of destiny, or law carved in stone – whatever medium the *me* are coded in, by nature, has to be a little more structurally complex to capture the sheer density of meaning in the unkin language. Any statement carries its context, implicit in the space between the words. But in the Cant graved on the screen there are no spaces, and the meaning blossoms outward from the central glyph, around it and back in, the context as explicit as the text.

It's the machine code of reality. It has to be precise.

And Metatron is worried, because for the first time in his long, long life, he doesn't understand it.

5

The Fields of Lost Days

Crossroads, 1937

A lone crow rose out of the cornfield, wings flapping as it gave a ragged caw and flew up into a cloudless blue sky; and as the dry wind stripped the grain from the corn and whipped it into the air around him, he stepped out onto the cracked tarmac of the cross-roads, unslung the blue guitar from back behind his shoulder, put his fingers to the right frets, to exactly the right frets, and struck a chord. *Should be here soon*, he thought, *should be along real soon.*

From its first low growls in the Deep South of the Depression, the blues was born to make new legends for itself, with Robert Johnson standing tallest and proudest among them, like some Voudon loa caught for an instant of time in a grainy old black and white photograph, like the Lord Eleggua himself, standing at a crossroads in a dusty, grey three-piece suit and wide-brimmed fedora. The blues was always the dark side of gospel, the devil's music, a music made of pain and hard, hard sorrows, with the bluesman as a hero of a kind, murderer, adulterer, searching for the lost chord, making pacts with the devil, hellhounds on his trail.

There's one story, one legend, says that if you take your guitar down to a crossroads and play it – play it good enough, that is – eventually the devil will come along behind you, tap you on the shoulder and take your guitar off of you. You don't turn around to look at him – you don't ever look the devil in the eyes – just take your guitar back when he's done tuning it for you, and from then on you'll play the bittersweetest blues was ever played . . . from that day on until the day you die and the demons come to drag your damned soul down into hell where it belongs.

And so, on a hot and hellblown summer's day, the man with the blue guitar took himself a long walk out of town, out through the cornfields, to the crossroads and the old tree heavy with the ghosts of all those who'd been hanged on it, like baubles on a Christmas tree, or strange golden apples. He walked out, as if to a date with the devil, or with whatever ancient African god – god of the crossroads, god of song – was wearing that Christian mask these days. That old soul deal, though, had already been made, a long, long time ago and far away. He wasn't here to sell, today, only to play the blues and – one last time – to pay his dues, before the hellhounds that had followed him down through the centuries finally caught up with him.

A lone crow rose out of the cornfield, circling over the seven men in sharp black suits who came now, from off of the road of all dust, shimmering in the liquid light that rippled around them like air over tarmac on a hot summer's day.

Dogs of Kingship

1971.

Thomas crouches in the bushes. He hears them crashing through the undergrowth around them, and he's trying not to gasp, to grasp for air with his lungs, with the rain running down his face, into his mouth. He can't afford to spit, to shake the rain out of his hair. He can't afford to make a sound. He holds the dogtags like a rosary he's praying by.

Baseball bats crack branches, whack through sodden leaves, feet splash in puddles of mud and dogs bark. There are seven of them, big men in body, small in heart, and mean as the German Shepherds that they track him with. He should have known not to take the lift; he should have seen it in the eyes of the four of them sitting up in the back of the pick-up truck, sodden with rain and drink and their own misery and looking for something, anything, to take it out on.

The leering grin of the one sat up in front between the driver and the passenger, as he leaned back to stare at him out of the rear windshield.

What was his name again? Jack, was it? Fuck, but he's hot.

Scarcely had his sister spoken when Dumuzi cried:

– My sister! Go! Quick! Run into the hills! Do not step slowly as a noble. Sister, run! The *ugallu*, who men both hate and fear, are on their boats. They come. They carry wooden stocks to trap the hands; they carry wooden stocks to trap the neck. Sister, run!

– You see them? she said.

– They are coming, said Dumuzi's friend. The large *ugallu*, with the wooden stocks to bind the neck, are coming for you.

– Quickly, brother! Put your head down, in the grass. Your demons come for you!

– My sister, tell nobody where I'm hiding. My friend, tell nobody where I'm hiding. I will hide in the grass. I will hide among the bushes. I will hide among the trees. I will hide in the ditches of Arali.

– Dumuzi, said his friend, if we tell anybody where you're hiding may your dogs devour us, your black dogs of shepherdship, the royal dogs of kingship, may your dogs devour us!

And Geshtinanna ran, fleeing the *ugallu*, up into the hills, and Dumuzi's friend went with her.

Another century entirely.

Thomas crouches in the grass. He hears them crashing through the fields of corn towards him, and he's trying not to gasp, to grasp for air with his lungs, with the sweat running down his face, into his mouth. The whipscars on his back are hurting real bad and he thinks they must be bleeding again, but he can't afford to make a whimper. He holds the little wooden cross around his neck and prays to the Good Lord, but the Good Lord says salvation lies in suffering and Thomas surely knows his suffering, yes sir, he surely does, and the Master's men are surely going to make him suffer like the Lord Himself, but Thomas don't think there's going to be any salvation for him. No sir, not for Thomas.

Rifle-butts crack corn-stalks, thrash through green-gold leaves, feet kick up dust in the dry heat and dogs bark. There are seven of them, big men in power and small in kindness.

– Come out here, boy. We *gonna* find you.

The small *ugallu* spoke to the large *ugallu*.

– You *ugallu*, with no father and no mother, you, who have no sister and no brother, wife or child, who fly across the skies and stalk the earth like guards, who stick to a man's side, who show no mercy, know no good or evil, tell us, who has ever seen a coward's soul living in peace? We should not seek Dumuzi in his friend's house. We should not seek Dumuzi in his brother-in-law's house. No. We should seek Dumuzi in his sister's house, the house of Geshtinanna.

Sweet Little Pink Things

They introduced themselves as Mr Pechorin and Mr Carter.

– But you can call us Vlad and Rosie, said Pechorin.

They looked like raptor birds, one dark, the other fair, a black falcon and a golden eagle.

– We only call him Rosie, said Carter, the blond-haired one, absently, nosing around the radio. It's not his real name.

– But then, Vlad's not his real name either, said Pechorin.

– It's short for Rosebud ... because that's the way he likes them, you know?

– Sweet little pink things, said Pechorin, showing his teeth with something too sweet to be a sneer, too cold to be a smile.

– And why do they call you Vlad, the girl asked, pushing her dark red hair back out of her eyes and flicking up the collar of her biker's jacket in a way that – as soon as she had done it – she regretted. *Too much attitude*, she thought, *defensive*.

He ignored her question and, instead, just ever-so-slightly cocked his head and sniffed, like a curious dog. Or like a hungry dog.

– Where is he?

– paranoid delusions of grandeur, said Carter as he twirled the dial on the radio through snatches of classic rock and country music, static shrieks, hiss, strident ads and Radio AWZ 104.5's Super Sounds of the Sixties, and finally settled on some orchestrated molasses that just oozed out of the speakers.

– Isn't that . . . I know this song? said Carter.

– I don't know, she said. Sounds vaguely familiar.

Pechorin still circled like a vulture. So, little girl. Who do you think you are?

– This is . . . oh, what's it called? the other said. I know this song.

She looked from one to the other. *Are you guys for real?* she thought.

– So full of yourself, said Pechorin. He leaned in close to her face. You think you're something special? Think you're better than the rest? Think you're up there with the likes of–

And the word he used sliced through reality and left it soft and open, like quivering flesh, and the mug of Earl Grey on the table in front of her had somehow sort of *shifted* into the blackest espresso that she'd ever seen, blacker than the sharp suits worn by the pair of them, blacker than the leather binding of the book that the other one had lain on the table beside the cup . . . blacker than hell; and the instant after he'd spoken it, she couldn't remember that word at all, only the emptiness in her head where she had heard it and the ripples in the air through which it had moved.

– That, he said, is what it is to be unkin.

– Go on, she said, tell me all–

Carter snapped his fingers. Of course. That's what it is.

– about it, she finished. She lifted the coffee towards her mouth but stopped just short, held the cup just almost at her lips so she could smell the bitter steam of it, the rich black scent. She waited.

– I knew it, said Carter. I knew I recognized the tune. That's some cover.

– Where is he? said Pechorin, suddenly, casually.

She just smiled and shook her head. She didn't know, and wouldn't have told them anyway; they could go fuck themselves; she wasn't part of their stupid fucking war, their stupid fucking game, and she wasn't going to be dragged into it.

– You think you're God's gift, eh? said Pechorin, sneering, and she sneered right back, at the sheer idiotic irony of it. Another little hatchling got a taste of godhood and you think you're the fucking Second Coming?

– You know, said Carter, suddenly leaning in just as close as Pechorin, speaking quietly, firmly. He nodded towards the radio. They crucified the original.

His Long, Thin Fingers

The ugallu clapped their hands with glee. They went to seek Dumuzi at the house of Geshtinanna.

– Tell us where your brother is! they cried out.

Geshtinanna would not talk.

They offered her the gift of water. She rejected it. They offered her the gift of grain, but she rejected it. They raised her up to Heaven and they threw her down to Earth. Geshtinanna would not talk. They ripped her clothes off. They poured tar into her cunt. And Geshtinanna would not talk.

Pechorin stepped over the girl, looking down at her for a second, where she lay on the floor, naked and smeared with blood and filth, the broken and twisted limbs still quivering. He sniffed the air. She was still in there, somewhere, somewhere buried deep enough they couldn't reach her, no matter how far down inside her soul they reached. He looked at Carter, licking the smears of red and specks of white off of his long, thin fingers.

– I don't think we're going to find him here, he said.

– *Since the start of time, the small ugallu said to the large ugallu, who has ever known a sister to betray her brother's hide-out? Come, let us seek Dumuzi at his friend's house.*

The ugallu went to Dumuzi's friend. They offered him the gift of water and he took it. Then they offered him the gift of grain. He took it.

Seamus Finnan clicked his Zippo open, snicked a thumb across the wheel and brought the flame up to the cigarette that dangled from his mouth. He sucked in a deep, deep breath. *Christ, Tom boy, what have you fucking gotten yourself into now? And I'm the one supposed to get you fucking out of it.* He couldn't do it. But he had to.

He looked up at the thing that called itself Carter, fastened his eyes on it, locked on it like he was cutting it open with his gaze and opened his mouth to curse the fucker.

And the angel slammed him against the wall, hand tight around his throat, twitching with tension, with the snarling, spitting drive, the urge, the *need*, to just crush his larynx, snap his neck.

– Where is he, it hissed. And then Pechorin was standing beside him. And then the real pain began.

– Dumuzi hid among the grass, among the bushes or among the trees, he said. I do not know where.

The ugallu searched among the grass, among the bushes and among the trees but could not find Dumuzi.

He leaned forward in the chair, retching, spitting up blood. Pechorin looked at the lump of rounded, red chambers and tubes held in his hand. His heart.

– You don't really need this, do you? You are one of us, after all, god or monster, angel or demon. Whichever side you choose, you'll always be like us . . . unkin. What do you need this . . . flesh for?

He was empty inside now, hollow. The pain just didn't mean anything any more. Nothing did.

– The ditches of Arali, he said, coughing. He's hiding in the ditches of Arali.

The Ditches of Arali, the Trenches of the Somme

The ugallu caught Dumuzi in the ditches of Arali. He turned pale, began to cry, cried out:

– My sister saved my life. My friend has brought about my death. If my sister's child goes wandering in the streets, may they be safe; I bless that child. If my friend's child goes wandering in the streets, may they be lost; I curse that child. And Tammuz cursed, he cursed his friend, and his friend's child and the words hang in the air now, as embedded in eternity as in the wedge-shaped marks pressed into clay, caught in a moment thick as the smoke of war, the clouds of a storm and all Seamus can do is stand there listening and looking on

in silent sorrow as the other lads drag the poor boy kicking and screaming, and sobbing and cursing, cursing like Seamus has never fookin heard in his life, sure, and they drag him down along the trench, like a fookin animal, dragging his feet through the mud, sure, and they throw him into the dugout and it's Seamus and the lads, his mates who have to do it, have to do it, sure, and they don't want to harm him but they have to hurt him, have to slap some sense into the boy 'cause it's the only way and if he doesn't come out of it, if he doesn't fookin come out of it, he'll end up fookin shot as a fookin coward and Seamus can't let that happen, he can't let that happen, sure, because he'd never forgive himself . . . so he goes into the dugout with the other lads and they don't listen to poor Tommy's curses.

The *ugallu* surrounded Dumuzi. They bound his hands; they bound his neck. They beat the husband of Inanna. Dumuzi raised his arms up to the skies, to Shamash, God of Justice, and cried out: O Shamash, my brother-in-law, I am your sister's husband. It was me who brought food to the sacred shrine, who brought the wedding gifts to Uruk. It was me who kissed the holy lips, who danced upon the holy lap, Inanna's lap.

– Make my hands the hands of a gazelle. Make my feet the feet of a gazelle. Let me flee my demons. Let me flee to Kubiresh!

– Ah, Christ now, Tommy boy, what have ye fookin gone and gotten yourself into? What have ye done?

The boy looks at Seamus with eyes so hollow, so broken and scared, that it just breaks his fookin heart to see the lad like this, and he grits his teeth and swallows, and wipes his nose, so he does, because if he doesn't do something he's going to fookin fall apart himself, sure. Christ, they'll fookin shoot him, so they will.

– I just went for a walk, Seamus. It was so nice out there, it was so nice, because the sun was shining and the grass was sort of blowing in the wind so soft and gentle, like . . . and there wasn't any shells, Seamus. There wasn't any shells at all.

– For fook's sake, Tommy. Talk fookin sense. What are ye talking about? It's been fookin raining fookin shells and mortars and fookin bullets as well as fookin cats and dogs.

146

– It wasn't raining, not out in the fields. But there was a river, see, and I couldn't get across the river, so I had to come back. To . . . to get something . . . so I could get across. You could come with me, Seamus. You can open the door and let me out and you can come with me and we can cross the river and we can . . .

Seamus looks out the door of the fookin dugout where he's standing with his fookin gun, just fookin waiting for the word to get back to the officers that the boy's still fookin doolally. Sure and it's officers who get shellshock and the rest of them are just fookin cowards to shoot.

– I don't know, Tommy boy, he says, I don't know if I can go with ye where ye're going, lad.

Shamash took mercy on Dumuzi's tears. He made his hands the hands of a gazelle. He made his feet the feet of a gazelle. Dumuzi fled his demons, fled to Kubiresh.

Dumuzi, the *dumu-zi*, shining child, escaped. Tammuz escaped. From that ancient Sumerian text, *Dumuzi's Dream*, he leaps, from myth to myth, only to be captured again, in *The Most Bitter Cry*, captured and chained, to wake under the rising sun that tries, time and again, to save him. He wakes from his dreams, naked and wounded, and in this version of the tale or that a prisoner of militia, a deserter or a fugitive conscript, being taken back to face punishment. He breaks free and runs, into fields that go on forever, trying to escape, from death, from war, from myth into reality or from reality into myth.

Dumuzi's Capture

– Let us go to Kubiresh, said the *ugallu*. And they walked the road of all dust till they arrived in Kubiresh. But Dumuzi fled his demons, he fled across the fields of illusion to the house of Old Belili. He crept into Old Belili's house and spoke to her.

– Old woman. I am no mere mortal man. I am the husband of a goddess, of Inanna. Would you pour water for me to drink? Would you sprinkle flour for me to eat?

*

He ransacks the shelves and the cupboards of the farmhouse, looking for something to eat, he does, because he's starving and he's so tired of running, so cold and wet and tired that he's no longer sure what it is he's running from, his clothes so filthy that when he strips them off to lay them by the fireside to dry, he looks at them and doesn't recognise them as an army tunic or an afghan coat or the rags of a runaway slave or anything but clothes. He puts the dusty black-and-white photograph of the old woman back on the mantelpiece but then there's another shell-blast and it falls and smashes on the ground, and he instinctively drops into a huddle. He can hear the beating of their baseball bats and the beating of their wings as he crouches down and eats the beans out of the metal pot with his fingers.

– Let us go to Old Belili, said the *ugallu*. And they walked the fields of illusion till they arrived at the house of Old Belili. After the old woman had poured water and sprinkled flour for Dumuzi, she left the house. The *ugallu* watched her leave and entered. But Dumuzi fled his demons, and he fled across the fields of illusion to the sheepfold of his sister, Geshtinanna.

Geshtinanna found Dumuzi in the sheepfold, and she sobbed. She raised her mouth up to the sky. She lowered it down to the earth. Her sorrow cloaked the world to its horizon, like a rag of soiled sackcloth. She tore at her eyes, her mouth, her thighs.

And the door is crashing open and he's leaping out through a window shattered by months of mortars, back into the churned-up horror of No-Man's-Land in France and running through the mud and rain of the mountain storm in North Carolina, and falling over a split-rail fence in the Wyoming snow and trying to drag himself to his feet, but they're vaulting the fence of the sheepfold, coming after him, always after him, with baseball bats and rifle-butts and ancient maces raised, and he's holding his sister as she sobs for him.

And the angels come down from the sky on wings, imperial eagles, hawks of war.

Asheville, July 13th, 2017.

Thomas watches the door of the bar swing shut behind Finnan and turns his attention back to the blond frat boy at the table across the bar. He's gone quiet now, like something is working its way through his unconscious, trying to crawl up into his mind so that all he can do is try not to think about it. Christ, thinks Thomas, it's fucking 2017 and it may be this isn't the most forward-thinking area of the world, but get a grip. There's more important things in the world than who or what you want to fuck. But the poor sweet angel-eyed lion just drinks his beer and glances at Thomas now and again, and burns with blushing shame as he looks away again, stuck in the story he tells himself of who he is, who he should be.

Still, there's something about him, an air of dreamy distance, that hints at possibility. He could be a junky punk in leather jeans and ripped tee or an English aristo in tails and a straw boater and he'd still fit the bill. There's this blank grace about him, like wherever he is it doesn't really matter because he's not really there.

Thomas is just about to give up, when five of the frat boys stand up, pulling their jackets from the backs of the chairs, slinging them over shoulders or folding them over their arms. They sway a little, drunken and still loud as they talk about the party later on tonight and slap the other two on the back, head for the door. From snatched phrases and mumbled admirations, Thomas gathers that a couple of them have dropped out of college to sign up with the armed forces. America is in danger, after all, and the freedom and democracy of puppet-states all over the Middle East and North Africa are at stake. The tenuous order of the world needs to be maintained.

On a small TV set tucked snug in a corner up behind the bar, CNN is showing another broadcast of the infamous Amar al Ahmadi Malik, another video diatribe, scrolling text translating his claims of responsibility for this atrocity or that. He's emerging as the great villain now, since Alhazred's assassination and, even with the sound muted, Thomas can hear the resonance of the Cant under his angry tones. Malik in Syria, al Mashaikh in North Iraq, Khalifa in Iran –

Thomas doesn't know if they're really all linked in this 'network of terror' but he does know one thing. They're all unkin.

Thomas has been watching the news recently and he wonders if the new recruits, bright-eyed and bitter, have any idea at all of what they're in for. There are stories, weird stories, coming out of Jerusalem and Damascus, Baghdad and Tehran, and to Thomas all those stories say one thing. Whether it's an army base in Jericho surrounded in the night by singing children, evacuated the next day with every GI in the place gone crazy, or 'suicide bombers' staggering naked and deranged into a cafe, bleeding from the writing cut into their flesh and exploding in a blossom of white light even though survivors swear they had no explosives strapped to them, no sir, not a single thing but that weird writing on them – whatever the story is, to Thomas it says that the unkin war has started now for real. He's still not sure if President Freemont and his coalition allies know they're on the side of the angels, or if the handful of demons behind this whole chaotic cocktail of warring terrorist groups and factions are actually allied or as opposed to each other as to the Western forces; somehow that seems too obvious, too simple to be true. It's just as likely there are Covenant unkin and their Sovereign enemies on all sides, using the collapse into anarchy and atrocity to mask a different war. But Thomas isn't going to stick around and find out.

He slips the card for Madame Iris Tattoos into his pocket and pulls out a pack of cigarettes, takes out a smoke.

The dark-haired friend is up at the bar getting in another couple of beers and leonine Jack is sitting there, staring off into the distance. He looks just the square-jawed type to sign up in a war of ideals and Thomas can't help but want him. He slides out of the booth and wanders over slowly to ask for a light. There's nothing going to happen right now, with his friend still here, but he can make a contact, an unspoken sign of possibility opening. Draw out just enough of the suppressed desire to maybe bring him back here later.

He looks uncomfortable but he nods at the request – *sure, yeah* – and fumbles in his pocket. He brings out a Zippo, flicks it open and sparks it. Thomas holds the guy's hand steady as he lights the cigarette, and holds the guy's gaze steady with a smile.

– Thanks ... eh?

– Jack, the guy says. Jack Carter.

No More Gods

They wore the grey synthe armour of all angels but around their gaunt bodies it looked skeletal, and the black slanted eyeshades on the mask only added to the unnatural appearance, reminding Thomas of carvings he had seen dug up in Predionica, strange heads with almond eyes, straight noses, sharp faces, stylized to an elven alien catlike grace. Like the bird-figurines carved out of paleolithic mammoth ivory, designs of wave, spiral and swastika filigreed their forms; and the tall steely, silvered weapons that they carried – something between a crossbow or a lance – seemed, like the great and graceful giant axes of the graves and the caves – surely too large for any use but ritual.

Thomas huddled his arms around his knees, naked and shivering.

– Why?

– No more gods, the creature said – he, she or it – no more alliances and vendettas, no more royal houses, dynasties ... no more pantheons.

The creature crouched down for a second to test the shackles around Thomas's hands, gathering the chains like reins in two hands, testing their strength. It shoved his head to the side, inspecting the collar round his neck, and nodded to itself, satisfied.

It ran its gauntleted fingers across his chest, tracing the graving branded upon his skin, the mark of the unkin, his name, his story, written in the language of the gods. There almost seemed to be desire in the tenderness of its touch.

The creature reached up to take its helmet off, and look at him with crystal blue eyes from beneath a shock of ruffled blond hair.

– Dumuzi ... Tammuz ... Thomas, he said.

– You can't escape your nature, he said. You're like me, like all of us. You might think you're a human being, you might dream that you are, but you're really just a tool ... a weapon.

He whispered a word and with a shiver, Thomas felt reality shift around them, saw the angel crouching before him in a black suit instead of grey armour, in a grey military uniform with golden epaulets, in a checked shirt.

– That's what it is to be unkin, said the angel. Do you really think we could leave you running loose?

Thomas turned away from him, looking to the west where, across the fields, a river ran and, on the other side, the grass was green and gold, in an Elysian haze of sunlight so close it hurt. He'd run through all of time, trying to escape into eternity, only to be captured at the end of history, at the end of his story.

He turned to gaze up past the unkin, over his shoulder and up, at the blue sky beyond. In the distance, dark clouds glowered on the horizon – clouds of storm or clouds of battle, he wasn't sure. In this place, in this world beyond the world, out here in the fields of illusion, on the road of all dust, sometimes, there wasn't any difference. If there was a storm gathering, then there was a war gathering as well. The beating wings of shining metal thunderbirds would soon be heard across the land, drowning all song, all laughter in their rain of fire and blood and hail and light and water and clods of mud and stone thrown up from blasts, and Thomas knew, he knew, that it would be as if the heavens themselves were falling on them. There was a storm coming. There was a war coming. And the river of souls would be thick with the bodies of the dead, shepherds and kings alike, and the crows that flew over the fields would feast among them. They had made the whole of history a sieve to separate the wheat from the chaff, a mill to grind the coarsest grain into soft, white flour.

– One last great war, and then we'll have eternal peace, the angel said.

– Great war, echoed Thomas, bitterly.

The Lost Deus of Sumer

The *ugallu* leaped the reed fence. The first *ugallu* scratched Dumuzi on the cheek with a sharp nail. The second *ugallu* smacked Dumuzi on the other cheek with his own shepherd's crook. The third *ugallu* smashed the bottom of the churn. The fourth *ugallu* threw the drinking cup down from its peg. The fifth *ugallu* shattered the churn. The sixth *ugallu* shattered the cup. The seventh *ugallu* cried:

— Rise, Dumuzi! Sirtur's son, Inanna's husband, Geshtinanna's brother! Wake up from your dream! Your ewes are taken and your lambs are grabbed! Your goats are captured and your kids are in our trap! Now take the sacred crown off of your head! Strip those *me*-garments from your body! Drop your royal sceptre to the ground! Remove the holy sandals from your feet! You come with us naked!

The ugallu grabbed Dumuzi. They surrounded him, all round him, and they bound his hands, they bound his neck.

And they lead him out, Dumuzi, Tammuz, Thomas, and the slave collar cuts into his neck, except it's not a slave-collar, it's a rough rope noose that they gonna hang this fucking nigger by, yeah, boy, and they're pulling it over the tree as they strip the epaulets off his jacket and the sergeant brushes dust off his wide-brimmed hat and turns away, not looking at him there on the tips of his toes and straining upwards against the ropes tying him to the wooden fence in a crucifix in the cold snow, hands behind his back, the wooden post hurting the whipscars on his back but one of them, it's Carter, is putting a cigarette in his mouth and asking him if he wants the blindfold and they'll make it quick, like, sure they will and he's sorry, God he's sorry, and Tommy cries out to Seamus but Seamus is looking away he is, sure, 'cause he's sickened by the whole thing, sure he is and he swears to himself, he does that this is the end of it all, this is the end of Seamus Finnan's service in a fookin war he has no fookin business in and Thomas—

And Thomas feels the ropes around his wrist as they drag him out of reality, this runaway god, back to the eternity where he belongs, to the eternal moment of his death.

He looks to his side, towards the river so close now.

The churn lies quiet, and no milk is poured into a shattered cup. Dumuzi is no more; the shepherd's fold, like dust, is given to the winds.

The Sebitti

When Heaven, king of the gods, made the Earth pregnant, a myth from Sumer tells us, she bore for him the seven gods he named the Sebitti. When they stood before him, he decreed their destiny. He summoned the first and gave him orders – wherever you march out together as a pack, there will be none to rival you – spoke to the second – burn like the god of fire himself, blaze like a flame – said to the third – you, walk among them, stalk them with the fierce face of a lion, and all who see you will fall to the ground in terror – spoke to the fourth – mountains will flee before the one who bears your furious weapons – ordered the fifth – blow like the wind, out to the ends of the earth – commanded the sixth – go through above and below, spare nothing in your path. The seventh he filled with dragon's venom, saying only this – lay low the living things.

Metatron looks around him at the seven marble pillars of his Hall of Records – just an empty blank plateau stretching out to the horizon on all sides. Each of the pillars has its own individual graving, a sigil etched into the stone.

There were seven of the Sebitti and there were seven of the *ugallu*, just as there were seven planets, seven days. There were seven sages who came out of the river into Sumer, bringing knowledge and civilisation from some distant world of strange divinities, from the mountains where Enlil, lord of the winds, dwelt, or from the abyss – the *abzu* – the great watery deep where Enki, lord of the earth, dwelt, at the source of all the rivers of the world, so it was said. There were seven Anunnaki, seven judges in the underworld, and there were the seven weapons of the deity Nergal, known as Irra in later myths, and known as Ares to the Greeks, the god of war himself, weapons that walked and spoke like men. Their very name meant simply the Seven. The Sebitti.

Seven Against Thebes, thinks Metatron. Seven Samurai. Magnificent Seven.

In Egyptian mythology, a human being doesn't have one soul; they have seven, seven facets, seven archetypes, that only make one individual in combination.

*

It had been seven of them, then, who came together in Ur of the Chaldeas to sign themselves into the Covenant: Rapiu was a healer in Akkad while Mika came from Syria; Adad was up near Haran at the time, among the Hittites. Raphael, Michael, Azazel. The rest were from all over the Middle East. Uriel, Gabriel, and Sammael, before he had to be ... replaced. And Metatron, of course. Metatron who used to be a god called Enki, who used to be a man called Enoch before he cut out that part of him that was still human.

Seven archangels. Seven guns for hire. A good team. They were always good to have on your side in a war.

He had always believed that they could work behind the scenes, set up treaties and law-codes, pacts and contracts, create a sort of hidden empire, building ... justice. Justice, mercy and wisdom. And one by one, their masters began to realize who was really in control, where things were going, and either took the long walk out into the Vellum, out into an existence made of only dreams and memories, or they took the oath themselves. They kneeled before the throne and let him remake their gravings, binding them to an archetype, a *me*, a new identity with a new destiny. And Metatron carefully adjusted them, pushing their personality this way or that, sculpting their souls so they were no longer gods of personal glory, individual power, but servants of a greater authority, angels of the heavenly host.

And when they walked out into the world, they walked out as one of seven.

The seven standing before him now, in their bloodied, muddy armour, all have the panting look of guilty dogs that have had more fun with some innocent creature than they're sure they are allowed. Two of them stand at the front, the bloodiest and the muddiest by far, just a little more arrogant than the others, standing out with just that little bit more individuality. But then any team has its star players and this one is no exception. It has its Gabriel and its Michael, the ones you send in if you want to lay waste to a city.

– It's done, says the one called Carter. He's dead.

– You're sure? And the girl?

– She's out of the game, says Pechorin. Little birdy got her wings broke. End of story.

He nods and dismisses them, the Hall of Records shimmering out of his vision. It is only a sim after all, this conference room he uses to keep these latter-day sebitti (they're not the originals so they don't get a capital) dutifully impressed. Sometimes he uses it as a retreat when he wants peace to study the gravings of his book, look for the next newblood reckoning that's due, but on the whole it's a little too showy for his liking. He looks out the window of his lounge, over the rooftops to the distant, delicate, black iron of the Eiffel Tower, just visible behind a chimney-stack; he prefers reality and always has.

So the boy is dead and the girl broken, he thinks. But somehow Metatron isn't so sure. He's thinking maybe he should check this out himself, pay a little visit to his North Carolina sebitti. The boy's would be the first unkin execution in ... a long time. There should have been ripples in the Vellum, an aftershock. These footsoldiers are too young to know it but Metatron was there when Tiamat was cut into pieces and he knows. The Covenant is more than a simple pact, the graving of an unkin more than just a graving, because these things are written in the Vellum itself, and one little scratching in the Vellum can stain the whole of history with blood and ink.

It's not like time is just a straight line from the past to the future.

In the Silvery Steel of a Cigarette Lighter

Carter holds the Zippo open and lit, his other hand spread out, palm down, above it, lowering it to touch the flame then pulling it up again as he feels the burning. He does this repeatedly. He does it for a while. And eventually he's just holding his hand over the flame, smelling the burning flesh. It reminds him of some other time and place, some other identity, already slipping from his mind. He used to be glad of the debriefings. He used to feel cleansed afterwards, his binding to the Covenant reinforced by the anointment, by being washed clean in the blood of the lamb, surrendering his memory to his superiors, in absolute submission to the glory. After each mission he felt fresh, remade, walking away from whatever hotel room or empty office space their superior was using as his base of operations, purged of the burden of his sins and in a state of grace, knowing only that whatever he had done had been successful and that it was for the greatest good, for the Covenant. He used to feel that way, and he doesn't know why he doesn't now.

– What the fuck are you doing?
  Pechorin slaps his hand away from the flame.
  – Jesus Fucking Christ. What do you think you're doing?
  Carter clicks the lighter closed.
  – Where did I get this? he says. I can't remember where I got this.
  Pechorin shrugs.
  – What does it matter? Fucking get a grip. Get in the car.
  Pechorin walks round to the driver's side, beeps the central-locking open and climbs in. Carter slides down off the hood and pulls his own door open. He stops to look at the burnt palm of his hand, the skin red raw and sore, but healing already; it's not quite visible, not quite that fast, but even now the pain is subsiding. That's what it is, to be unkin, after all. They're healers, at the heart of it, whether it's their own flesh being healed or the torn skin of reality, of the Vellum. It's one of the ancient names the humans gave them, so he's told – *rephaim* . . . healers.

As he climbs into the passenger seat, though, the black, padded leather of it hot from the sun, something at the back of his brain is almost – but not quite – conscious of the underlying source of his discomfort. He's not aware of the fact that the burning was only an attempt to make concrete this vague sense of hurt, of wounding or sickness, that still lingers even after the whispered word of Metatron cleared his head of all remembrance of his own atrocities. He doesn't remember staring down in horror at the girl lying in the puddle of black ichor, his hands shaking at the thought of what they'd done. He doesn't remember that even as his fist punched time and time again into the coward's face, he couldn't help but see his own blue eyes and fair hair in the man's, like he was trying to smash his own reflection. He doesn't remember picking up the Zippo in the faint hope that the boy would recognize it through the shimmering glamour placed on them by Metatron, recognize it and know whose it was and how he had to run. No. However deep the wound is in his soul, Metatron has cleaned it

157

thoroughly. And the Cant is still echoing in his head, the cleaning still going on, slowly, methodically. But not perfectly.

Pechorin has a hold of his hand, looking at it to see the damage done, but Carter just stares at his own reflection in the silvery steel of a cigarette lighter, trying to figure out what it is he feels, why the fuck he doesn't feel the way he should. Pechorin starts the engine, pulls out from the kerb and into traffic. Behind them, in an unmarked van, the other five follow at a distance, visible in the rear-view mirror. He can see them laughing, one of them cracking open a beer, sliding gently back into the blank and malleable personas that they live their daily lives in, until next time the call comes. Carter leans back into the seat and closes his eyes, the sun shining through his eyelids, a red and orange blur of spots and veins, an abstract canvas of blood and fire.

He remembers the boy's eyes, deep hazelnut brown with flecks of green, of emerald and jade; he remembers them cruising him in the bar and the lick of a lip, the snub of a nose, and shoulder-length auburn hair, and lighting a cigarette for him. He should have asked him to the party.

– You look fucked, man, says Joey.

Jack looks at him, sitting there in his black leather jacket. For some reason – God knows why – he has an image of him in a suit. Shit, Joey wouldn't wear a suit if you paid him.

– I feel fucked, says Jack.

The River of Crows and Kings

Down the river thick with the mire of war, thicker – with all the blood and the bodies of the storm – than the tar that it resembled, floated the torn clothes and the broken furniture, the opened suit-cases and scattered, sodden papers, oil-soaked rags wound round and plastic bags tied tight to make small bundles for some unknown artefact; oil paintings in their frames, and dolls and teddy-bears, and black-and-white photographs of wives and sweethearts, and father's watches and grandfather clocks, and grand pianos and children's tricycles and decks of cards with nudie women on them, and clay pots from Hacilar, Hassuna or Samarra, with all their patterning of birds and fishes, animals and humans, all the bull's heads, double-axes and Maltese crosses of Tell Halaf; and the clay-covered skulls of the dead, enshrined once with sea-shells for eyes, that were the source of all that ancient pottery in protoneolithic Jericho; and all the accumulated artefacts of history came, turning over and over in the rolling, roiling muck of it all, and amongst these things and carried on them, rolling over them and under them, limp and lolling, came the dead, pouring along the river that once ran clear and sweet through all eternity towards a distant city on the edge of everything. And the river of voices and visions that once rushed sparkling, roaring, babbling down into the deep – the river of life, and the river of the dead crossed by all those who sought to enter into eternity out of the time and place of their existence – was now a slow snake of filth where crows fed on the corpses of kings.

And Thomas stumbles as he tries to leap a twisted tree-root, falls to his knees, hands out in front of him, splatting into the mud and falling forward, twisting his wrist and yowling, cursing himself for the noise. Not far behind – not far *enough* behind – the shouts are wild, drunken with vicious delight, and they come crashing through the trees and bushes and grass towards him. Slupping and staggering up out of the ditch of trickling marsh, he runs. He runs out of the woods, running from Jerry, from the rednecks, from the hell-hounds, from the angels, from the lion, and from the doom of thunder and lightning that crackrashes into a tree beside him – tall tree illuminated, eerie, eldritch in the sick light. He runs out of the woods and over a field, grass whipping his face, and into more woods, slipping, skiting, down a slope and falling, splashing into the raging river, black, brown, red with all the earth washed down into it by the storm, and turning, churning it drags him down into its grip to drown.

It is a dry, hot and sun-bleached day in the savannah, and a lion slouches slowly through the tall grass. A slender buck, a young Thomson's gazelle, twitches nostrils at the scent of predator in the air, and looks at us, and blinks long lashes over deep dark eyes. Angels wheel lazily overhead. Turning to look around us, we see a

herd of aurochs grazing on the open skies and, superimposed like
ghost-forms over this vision of a veldt, young men in olive and khaki
smoke cigarettes, play cards and drink. A dog lies curled up beside
(beyond? behind?) a strange figure wearing animal skins, a beaked
mask and what might be perhaps a feathered cloak or wings.
Everything is still, poised in the moment.

And though we know that when this moment ends there will,
without a shadow of doubt – for in the fierce light of this summer
noon there are no shadows, or at least only the smallest ones under
our padding feet – although we know that there will come a *doom*
to shatter this tranquillity – because this is the way it happens,
always in existence, or forever in eternity – we know also that
somewhere, somewhen, Tammuz escapes. From every time, from
every tomb, Tammuz escapes. But still we weep for him; we weep
for the lost deus of Sumer as we weep for all the lost days of our
summers.

And still he runs, he leaps, he bounds, still, caught in the
moment and unbound in the myth, through the fields of lost days,
far from the road of all dust, and down the river of crows and kings,
the river of the voices and the visions of the living and the dead, and
all around him grow the buds and the rushes, and the grass and the
bushes and the trees, and the poppies.

Errata

The Strazza Ce La Daedalii

I step out of the hostelry into the late morning light of the Strazza Ce La Daedalii – as I've taken to calling it, shamelessly cobbling together the morphemes of three or four different languages that I have learned in my travels, christening it with this hybrid, invented phrase simply because I find it descriptive in a pleasantly Latin manner, with cadences more liquid, more suited to this waterfall civilisation. I step out onto the marble flagstones of a plaza of kafe and restoranti with four sets of grand stairs: two run downwards from the balustraded outer edge, from the north-east and the north-west corners, running parallel to the precipitous wall and meeting at a small landing down below only to turn and part again, and carry on down to the south-east and the south-west corners of another plaza; the other two sets of stairs echo the plaza on the lower level, running upwards along the stone that backs the plaza at its southern wall, to a small landing where they turn and carry on up. The Strazza Ce La Daedalii goes on in this manner, down and up, for quite some way, plaza upon plaza upon plaza, its upper heights and lower depths hidden in mist or in the simple haze of atmosphere diffusing the light in watery blue until eventually, in the distance, even with binoculars, it is impossible to distinguish start or end. A street in strata, plaza after plaza, I christen it a strazza. I have no idea what the natives would have called it, unable as I am to read their alphabet of squicks and wheedles.

Laying my espresso down on the red-and-white checkwork of waxed tablecloth, on one of the tables of the rustic little kafe that I have chosen to make my room in, while I try to get my latest project off the ground, so to speak, I wander out onto the flagstones to examine my finished handiwork.

It seems I am working in a long tradition here; from what I can gather from the glossy pictures in the tourist shops, I'm not the first by any means to choose this Jacob's Ladder staircase street as launching ground. Old black and white photographs, glossy colour snapshots, charcoal sketches, oil paintings, blueprints – the tourist books show centuries of fantastic contraptions designed by some would-be Daedalus in his doodling mind and built with defiant gusto. I imagine the crowds gathering at the sides of the plazas, thronging the steps above and below, peering from balconies and shuttered windows, old men smoking pipes and shaking their heads, young girls swooning over the dashing, daring, death-defying and clearly demented aviator, a young lad declaring to his mother that one day he too will try – no matter what the whole of history tells them – at least *try* to touch the sky.

As bounded as they were, these people, by the geography of the Rift, they must have dreamed of flight since the first day a caveman watched an eagle soaring down below, spiralling upwards on the currents of air or swooping down to catch its prey. How could they not look at the birds and realize that if they themselves could just step out of the slanted plane of their existence it would be a revolution more momentous in an instant more encompassing than the discovery of fire? Freedom to travel in the vertical, to soar past all those towns and villages between their own backwater and the fabled, distant cities, to laugh at the toll-booths and the taxes taken by gatekeeper hamlets with no industry of their own, only the good fortune to be in the path of trade. Freedom to see for themselves what they had only heard of on the grapevine chain of word-of-mouth, tales told by travellers to travellers in a game of Chinese Whispers, rumours of the Edge, so far above, or of the Vale below, mythologized by their distance and by their difference, these legendary, fantastic lands, impossibly, unbelievably . . . flat.

And so, Daedalus after Daedalus, in this small area of the Rift, at least, they all came here, romantic fools funded by merchants with a vision of a liberated world, and tried to fly.

The plaza above has a monument to them all, a great, twisted bronze of vanes and gears, batwing-like things projecting upwards from the impacted mass of harness, with a human form thrown out and up, arms reaching up towards the sky as if ejecting from the wreckage, as if even in the implosion of the machine collapsing, crushing itself into the stone beneath him, the soul of the pilot is exploding out of it, a butterfly born from a chrysalis of confused copper and iron. As in my own far-distant world, most of the flawed designs of flying machines seem to have taken their form from features in the animal world, feathered and flapping, articulated artifices of thin tissue and extending joints, things pedalled with hands or feet, hydraulic pistons amplifying muscle movements over wing-spans of twenty feet or more, dead weights that must have plummeted or tender things that could have glided out into the air to gasps and cheers until, quite suddenly, some terrible tear would open in it and the screams and tears would start as the grand dream of the latest Daedalus fell apart.

There are a few pictures in the books of men or women who took off and soared and swooped, those in the simplest, gliding aerofoils who sailed out into the skies and circled down until they disappeared beneath the clouds, unable to capture, somehow, the same secret currents of air used by the birds to lift them back up to their homes. One or two returned on foot, after a decade or so; you see their grey-haired, grizzled forms in pictures beside their grinning, younger selves, gripping not gears but walking sticks. They at least fared better than the ballooners who, to a man, drifted away on some inexorable current never to be seen again; even the most powerful dirigibles, if my interpretation of the pictures is correct, were unable to overcome the powerful downdrafts and cross-streams diagrammed by aged aviators, aeronauticists and meteorologists alike. Had it been otherwise, my own flying machine might well have taken a more sensible form.

Leonardo's Laughter

I slip my feet into the stirrups, buckle the straps and pull them tight, clamp metal clasps and click my legs into the light, limbed frame of exoskeleton. It's made of a material – synthe, they called it, in the books of the world where it belongs – unknown in all the Rift – in all the Rift I've visited, at least – and I'm not even sure if it's a plastic or a metal. It shines like chrome, and is as sleekly solid, shining silvery in the early morning sun, but the whole complex artefact weighs less than a handful of sand and it would blow away in the wind as easily if it weren't tethered to the iron grids of manhole covers that dot the marble flagstones of the strazza here and there. It makes aluminium seem leaden and, if it's a metal at all, I think, then it's an alloy, of adamantium and cavorite, as strong as one, as gravity-defying as the other. It took me centuries to learn to work the stuff, and I'm lucky that I brought a salvaged store of this synthe with me, on my long, diagonal journey down into the Rift, as much as the trundling rig could carry.

As I pull up the folded pinions to slip my arms into the harness, I glance over at my last vehicle, parked on the road that leads out of the strazza, to the east, the hulking flat-bed loaded on which the ancient Winnebago sits engulfed in the canopies of its tent extensions, the wooden porch I built myself, the lean-to. And the huge five-fingered waldo-device yoked to it like an infant giant's hand playing the role of oxen. If there'd been anybody in this world to see it when I rolled into town, this crazy gypsy nomad whose very caravan was a circus freak, I wonder what they would have made of me. I have to admit there is a part of me that's grown to revel in the very outlandishness of the machinery I've accreted in my journey on the road of all dust, salvaged from this world or that and retrofitted to my own ends. I'll be a little sad to leave the rig and the absurd crawling contraption that's pulled it down three centuries of mountain road and track; but the endless zigzag of my journey into the Rift is drawing me further and further from the path I want to go, I'm far enough off-course as is and if I want to carry on along the road mapped out for me on the Book I'm going to have to sacrifice the comforts of my lumbering mobile home for something more … spectacular.

I snap the buckle of the flying machine's belt around my waist, and release the bolts that hold the chest-grapple open; it swings slowly shut around my sides, soft and padded like a child's fingers closing round a baseball, but as solid as an extra set of ribs. The support-latches swing out from under my armpits and lock into place above my shoulders, in the pack of metal muscle, processing power and airtanks out of which the wings extend above my head, still folded. I swivel the breast-plate down from above and clip it, strap it, latch it at my waist – I couldn't resist the urge to mould it in a shape of shining pectorals, like the armour of an ancient Greek or Roman, or of an angel in the images of my homeworld. It sits out from my chest a little – giving the whole exoskeletal suit an even more seraphic look – because I've built a small compartment into it; I crouch down to pick up the Book, slip it into the opening at the right-hand side and clip the door closed. This is the only thing I'm taking with me. I bring the goggles down over my eyes, the oxygen mask up over my mouth. I have no idea of the environment out there in the blue skies beyond the Rift – I am probably already far enough down that the sheer weight of the air above should crush me, so the laws of physics clearly are little more than rules-of-thumb in this world, but I'm not taking any chances.

Lastly, finally, I slip my hands into the wired and articulated gauntlets hanging from the belt, unhook them and tighten them round the wrists, make sure that all the jacks and plugs are tight and firm, then flick the on-switch at my belt that tells this mad contraption that I'm ready, to transmit the motions of my fingers along the long wires that run up to my shoulders where, as I step forward, spreading my arms in an unnecessary but unconscious gesture, and splaying my fingers wide and open, palm-down, thirty foot of silvery wings spread out above me and behind me and I feel the air moving under them, the way the motion of every finger catches it, the lift, and all I have to do is bat my fingers and the pinions of the waldo wings bat with them, and my feet lift from the ground, and I kick the release and all my tethers fall away and suddenly I'm rising.

And the Strazza Ce La Daedalii rings with my laughter as I rise into the skies of the Vellum, with my laughter and the laughter of every demented dreamer of the Rift, all those failed and falling aviators whose names I'll never know, those Leonardos of this corner of eternity. I could have called this place the Strazza Ce La Icarii, for all those failures, but that would have been ... a paucity of commitment that insulted every one of them. Daedalus flew and so did every one of them who laughed in the face of old men with their pipes, shaking their heads.

I rise on their laughter, their whooping joy the air beneath the fingers of my wings. I don't care who's watching me, the ghosts of this abandoned world from their balconies, or angels from their windows in the sky.

I fly.

6

The Passion of Every Thomas

The Crucified Shepherd

She finds him in the church, sitting on one of the wooden pews with a plastic bag between his legs; it clinks as he shifts position. This is the last place she would have expected to find him but she supposes that's part of the reason he's there. It's the last place she would expect to find him. He glances at her sideways, clocking her approach, and reaches into the bag to pull out a beer bottle. He doesn't look at her as he cracks the cap off on the pew in front. A priest starts towards them from a door over to the right behind the altar; Finnan just mutters something under his breath and the man stops, turns around and heads back out the door.

– I didn't think you believed in any of this shit, she says.

– I don't, he says. But it's a nice idea, though, eh, Phree? Redemption.

– That's not what you used to say.

– No? What did I used to say, then?

– I'll die for me own bloody sins, thank you very much, she says, imitating him.

– Aye, he says. I probably will. That's a shite accent, by the way.

She slides into the pew beside him.

There are no bruises on him, from what she can see, but he's pale and sick-looking. Actually he's almost white, and when she reaches over to touch his cheek – he flinches, looks away – it's cold, like marble.

– What happened to you? she says.

– Angel took me heart, he did. Reached in and plucked it out with his fingers. Oh, I felt him rearranging the plumbing, hooking up arteries to veins, veins to arteries. It's all tied together, neat and tidy, like, apart from the missing pump, that is. So you see, I have to keep a little mantra going in me head all the time now, to keep the blood flowing. And that uses up a lot of heat. You ever noticed that, when you're using the mojo? There's some scientific word for that, ain't there?

– Negative entropy.

– That's the one, he says. Someone should investigate that, don't you think? I mean, maybe it's not fookin magic at all. Maybe there's a perfectly rational explanation for all of this shite.

– Maybe, she says.

– And that would be nice, wouldn't it? We could actually learn something about what makes us all tick, if the fookin eedjits weren't all so busy playing fookin sodjies.

– *Sodjies?* What?

He makes a mock salute.

– Sergeant Seamus Finnan reporting for duty, sir.

– I guess they're fookin gearing up now, he says. They're not even offering an alternative. No, if you're not with them, then you die. But if you kill an unkin it has consequences, you know; what we're hooked into, that mojo, runs pretty fookin deep under reality. You cut one little thread, just one little thread ... But they don't care. Sod it, says they. Let's just burn the fookin world and start another one.

He takes another swig

– Christ, he says, they're still living in the fookin neolithic. Burn the fields before you plant the new crop.

And another swig.

– But they didn't have to kill him. They didn't have to do that. If you kill an unkin – no, I said that already – you create one big fookin – [he waves an arm in the air, grasping for a word] – rip in the Vellum. There are places in this world where the ... repairwork ain't too tight. Days which are just holes.

I have a lot of days like that, she thinks.

– You know what an angel's voice can do, he says. Think about the damage from a scream.

She remembers hearing it in her bones, waking up in the dead of night, the sound still echoing in her skull, ringing in her ears. The shock wave of her brother's death.

– So are ye going to fookin kill me or what? says Finnan.

She looks at him, sitting there pale and pathetic, and she finds herself shaking her head. She doesn't have the heart. She knows that if she'd had any more to give the angels than a fragment of a word, the one syllable of a place-name Thomas forced on her before she had the time to cut him off, if she'd had any more than that *Ash-*, the angels would have taken it from her as well. Ashton? Ashbury? She doesn't know enough for them, but Finnan obviously did. She can see it in the way he doesn't look at her. He looks down, away to the side, anywhere but at her.

– No, she says. I just want to know . . .

She doesn't know what she wants to know.

He looks up at the crucifix, points with his bottle.

– D'ye think himself was one of us, then?

A Ragdoll or a Scarecrow

They crucified Puck in a field outside of town, stripped naked on an October night on a mountain where the cold wind brought the temperature down near enough to freezing – not on an actual cross, of course, not literally, but they left his body hanging, tied with ropes around his broken arms to a barbed wire fence before they beat him near to death with the butt of a shotgun, caving in his skull in a fracture that stretched from the back of his head down and around to the front of his right ear. They left him hanging there spread-eagled like some World War One soldier caught on the wire in no-man's-land, cut down by enemy gunfire, and there he hung for eighteen hours, limp as a ragdoll or a scarecrow, until he was discovered, still dying. He never woke from the coma.

*

Just so you know how this story goes and that it's not a happy ending. Puck – my young buck, my slim, fairy fuck – didn't rise from death after three days entombed and there was no salvation for our sins through his murder, no life everlasting for him or for us. Puck – Thomas Messenger, as he was christened by his parents – for all that his green hair and smirking cherub lips and blinking lashes long and dark gave him the look of some eternal child, some Peter Pan – died like we all die, without resurrection, with no miracle rebirth. I can still remember the feel of his peach-fuzz downy legs under my hand, the fine flutter of a feather across my chest, the point of a horn pressed into my side as he butted me, the goatish kid. But Pan is dead. Great Pan is dead. And we should weep for him, as the women wailed for Tammuz in Jerusalem, in the sure and certain knowledge of his absence.

– His soul has gone now to a better place, the minister said, and, in a way, I do agree; the silent darkness where a life once was and, like a guttering candle, has been snuffed out leaving only a thin trail of smoke – the grief of others – rising like incense to the heavens, that can only have seemed a mercy in comparison as he felt their blows rain down on him, the blood run down his face, the blame ring in his head. I wonder how many of us can imagine the pain and terror subsiding slowly as the body shut down, shut off from the world as the shock kicked in – as their boots kicked in his ribs – that curling up of consciousness being his only defence. And then a slow slide into senselessness, and, eventually, into nothing.

In that time while he was still aware, which was the worse, I wonder: the agony of his physical torture or the horror of their utter hatred, of their moral certainty that he was so beyond the bounds of what they could accept that he deserved not just a death but one of such brutality, such inhumanity, as would make the seraphs who burned Sodom bow their heads in cold respect? What is it like, I wonder, to learn the full capacity of hatred in a lesson hammered home with bone broken on wood and skin ripped on barbed wire?

We lay upon our backs, his head nooked in my shoulder, turned to gaze across my chest, above us open sky, the golden crescent of the sun, the silver cratered moon. His wings furled around him as a peacock cloak, mine extended wide and flat across the thick-bladed grass heavy with moisture, we lay like something fallen from the stars, indolent with the noon heat, and oblivious to the *tuts* and *tsks* of other students crossing the campus grounds around us on their way from this lecture to that tutorial.

– Fucking fairies, I heard one mutter, and Puck raised a hand to circle it, slack and lazy, a regal wave in the air that, on the third revolution, came up as a fist, one finger extended to flip the bird, as casual as could be.

– Fuck you kindly, fine sir, he called after the whiteknuckle asshole, never one to let an opportunity for brattishness slip by. Fuck you very much indeed.

I put a hand over his mouth, laughing, and he nipped at it with nimble teeth.

– Hey.

The world, the temporal world – at least that little piece of grass in it outside the campus cafeteria – belonged to us for that lunch hour. The temporal world belonged to us even as we neglected it, *because* we neglected it, my rucksack as my pillow, his abandoned to one side, and a solitary ringbinder of poly-pocketed past papers and handwritten notes that flipped and flitted this way and that under the fingers of a warm August breeze, fingers far more studious than our own. I extracted one of my own shamelessly idle fingers from between his teeth and flicked at the acute of his earpoint.

– Ouch. Bastard.

– Well, don't friggin bite me, then, scrag.

He cocked his head diagonal across my chest, half-angled to fix me with most innocent doe-eyes, half-angled so his smirk, seen from above, curled up with mischief at the edges as he batted the black lashes of those eyes across my skin, and clicked a nip of teeth into my nipple. I bellowed curses loud enough to make a nearby mutt, browsing the remains of student lunches, raise its head and look at me with curious cocked gaze and raised ears.

The Gracile and the Robust

– When compared to the gracile – or dolichocephalic – elven skull, or, indeed even the robust – which is to say, brachycephalic – skull of one of the gnomitic races, the brutish and apelike features of the swarthy ochroid clearly mark him out as a racial type to be categorized as *distinct and inferior* to the more civilized races. The ochroid is, it must be concluded, to be considered as standing at the median point between these modern races of Man and their troglodyte progenitors, those such as Astralopithecus or Pithecanthropus Titanus, so-called Peijing Man.

Old bluff bombastic Samuel Hobbsbaum, with his copious white beard and sheer solidity of short stature closed the book and laid it on the lectern, one finger resting lightly on the yellow Post-it note that marked his place.

– When we read the words of the archaeologists of the nineteenth century, he said, in a modern context, we can hardly help but be shocked by the racism that is not merely implicit but is, in fact, quite unashamedly explicit. To us, slavery is an abhorrent notion, and yet . . .

He opened the book again.

– It is for this reason that the ochre Afritan must be nurtured by his Elyssean cousin, as one would nurture a child, for surely the Afritan is but an infant in comparison to his Elven superiors, his savagery but the wild impulsiveness of youth, lacking in reason and self-control, his superstitions but the untamed fancy of a childish imagination. Without science or mathematics, without history or philosophy – without even a concept of progress beyond the natural cycle of seasons, indeed – he is, like all children, trapped in an Eternal Present, bound to follow his most immediate fears and desires and thus as ignorant in matters of ethics as in all others. He is a slave to his passions, and can only remain so unless the cultivated man take him under his wings and, with firm hand, as guide and master, lead him to his place within society. And it is the clear and present duty of the enlightened Elyssean to deliver that discipline of reason to the passions of the savage.

– This series of lectures is going to be about passion, said Hobbsbaum, after a pause. About passion and reason, and about the politics of those two fundamental aspects of human existence, as the artists, philosophers, idealists and ideologists of nineteenth-century Elysse perceived them to be. Passion and Reason. Romanticism and Rationalism. At what point, we're going to consider, in the collision and collusion of these two ideas does the aesthetics of the nineteenth century become the politics of the twentieth? Where does Romanticism become Fascism? Where does Rationalism become Communism? And can we even speak in such simplistic terms?

Students of Metaphysique

We met, Puck and I, as students of political science in our first class on the first day of our first year at North Manitu State University and, in the course of that first week, we became also students of each other, unsure at first if any of that niggling fancy in our tongues – that tingling appetence that makes you lick your lips and touch the tips of upper teeth in thought – if that, or any of the twiddling fingers or snatched glimpses of furtive glances, if any of that were more than just the wishful thinking of our own fey desires. We scrutinized each other for certainties that we ourselves were not quite ready to articulate in anything more explicit than the same sort of nod or smile given to any other fellow student and familiar stranger.

It was in our second week we found each other in the same tutorial and found ourselves locked in a debate as fierce as it was foolish, pouring scorn upon each other's patently absurd ideas; and locked in each other's gaze, we gaped incredulously and shook our

heads and let fly insults at each other till it seemed we were about
to fight, and while the post-grad student tutor tried in vain to steer
us back onto the actual topic, the full flow of ridicule flung back and
forth between us was unbreachable and in all the vitriol of an argument more derision than discussion, all I kept thinking as I stared
in his infuriating face was just how much I wanted to fuck him and
how I could see, in his ferocious eyes, how he was thinking the
same thing.

And later, after we walked out of the class still fighting, still flirting,
after we sat for hour after hour in the campus cafeteria, drinking
coffee, black and bitter in my case and frothed with milk, and
sugary, for him (I watched, still talking, as he poured one, two,
three, four sachets of sugar in), after discussing nothing of significance as if it was the most important matter in the world, and after
we somehow walked together back to his room, not even noticing
that we'd done so, we locked together physically and became students of each other's form and flux.

We studied the articulation of each other's jointed intricacies,
the slant of a kiss, the turn of a neck, the roll of its nape down
to the first corrugations of the vertebrae where fuzz of hair gives
way to skin, the roll of that spine in contrapposto pose, raising a
hip at one side to curve a torso so another's arm slips comfortably
around the waist as if there's nowhere else that it was meant to
be. I studied the nicking points of his horns and ears. I studied
the impish emerald of his eyes, the oriental jade tones of his skin.
He arched an eyebrow at the limber of my wings, and we stopped
studying.

The Suppliants

A woodprint caricature of a Gnome, dating from the Middle Ages,
presented the perfect picture of a child-murderer and a plague-
carrier, the vestigial wings under his tunic making him look hunch-
backed, a sackful of dead babies slung over his shoulder, a purse

grasped in his hand. This was the image of the Gnome as graceless and crooked that inspired pogroms and persecution, and that the Nazis were to play upon so heavily during the early twentieth century. It was the image that gave the Crusaders an excuse to hone their skills while on their way to the Holy Land, purging cities of their local Gnomish populations. It was the Gnome as usurer, and as murderer and, of course, at its roots, it was the Gnome as killer of Christ.

Not that it mattered that Adonais was himself a Gnome. Medieval frescoes and altarpieces, icons and crucifixes had portrayed the Son of Jove as light-skinned and slender, the perfect Angelo-Satyr messiah, his wings spread wide upon the cross, his long horns lowered in his suffering. From its first advances towards the gentiles, through the Emperor Instantine's adoption of the faith, and the growth of the Church during the period of the Holy Rhyman Empire, Christianity had progressively distanced itself from its Gnomish roots, painting the disciples white instead of cobalt, and sliding blame away from the Rhymans and on to the Gnomes. The dead babies and the purse of the medieval Gnome were a reminder of the Slaughter of the Innocents ordered by an evil Gnomish King and of the thirty pieces of silver taken by the Gnome who betrayed Christ.

Tailors of fine clothes or moneylenders, jewellers or pawnbrokers – there were only a few professions open to the Gnomes of Elysse, and many of those were crafts or trades of peering eyes and pinching hands, of a back hunched over the intricate details of clockwork or book-keeping, of fine manipulations and complex designs, almost as if the gentile cultures could accept the refugees only as absolute suppliants, submitting to symbolic roles of intrigue and avarice.

In the darkened lecture hall, there was a *click-whirr-clack* and the projected slide slid to the side, replaced on-screen by a more modern image, a black and white photograph of a Gnomish shopfront in Berlin in the 1930s, the window shattered, the words *Hobben raus* daubed on the door. I heard Puck, in the seat beside me, mutter a quiet and unfinished *fucking* . . . and all around the room the almost-silence of shifted positions and folded arms – of our retreat into uncomfortable indignance – was clear and solid.

Of Distraction, of Attention, of Attraction

He looked over his shoulder, and I took the cigarette from his mouth between two fingers held up like a Sixties peace sign, and turned my hand to place it against my own lips, take a deep slow draw of the tobacco smoke right down into my lungs to hold it there, and held my breath with eyes half-closed, with the aching bliss of a nicotine fiend on his first hit in all too many days. I placed the cigarette back between his lips and felt the slightest hint of a pout, just the suggestion of a kiss on my fingers, as I exhaled.

    – Benedictions, I said.

– Salutations, he said. I thought you'd quit.

    – I have. Those things'll kill you. Terrible habit.

    – Live fast, die young, he said. And leave a beautiful corpse.

    – Fuck that shit. I'm looking forward to being one of those crazy old farts who shouts at kids and whacks them on the heads with his walking stick. Great fun. So what are you drinking? I asked as I slid up onto the leather cushion of the stool beside him at the bar. I slid a beermat towards me till it was half-off the wooden counter and flipped it with a flick of the thumb, missed catching it between thumb and forefinger by the narrowest of margins and had to make a grab to snatch it before it fell to the floor.

    – J.D. and Coke, he said.

    – You know, J.D. doesn't stand for James Dean. You . . .?

His head cocked to one side, he peered over my shoulder to the door, with a look I recognized immediately, one of distraction, of attention, of attraction, and I shook my head with a wry smile because I knew him well enough. I looked behind me, following the arrow of his lust and clocked the two of them, forescruffs of blond hair stuck out from under matching Abercrombie & Fitch baseball caps; as WASP – as White, as Angelo-Satyr and as Protestant – as they come, and with their gold aquiline wings stuck out from grey Gap sweatshirts redolent of college boy more than white trash, they looked so clean-cut, square and straight, I didn't wonder that my Puck, always his own Puck, couldn't keep his eyes off them.

– Ah, no way. They're fucking jocks, I said. I mean, Christ Adonais, they look like fucking quarterbacks.

– I like fucking quarterbacks, said Puck.

He tracked them with a slow and certain swivel of the head, an open cruising, as they walked up to the bar and ordered their beers. Puck had no shame in his rapacity; if anything, he revelled in the hunt, whether as predator or prey, and I noted the set of certainty in jaw and brow, although his eyes instead of being narrowed were widened in a more vulnerable challenge. It was part lion, part gazelle, the slight parting of his lips, the almost-flare of nostrils as if he could draw them to him with his breath, gather them in a chemical line of scent of showergel and sweat.

– Man, smell that testosterone, he said, with relish.

Curtius, E., Griechische Geschichte (1857–67), Vol. 1, p. 41

– From Aeschylus, onwards, we see the Prosian Empire portrayed as decadent, effeminate, soft with luxury in comparison to the young and dynamic Versid City-States, and this xenophobia was, it seems, the dominant view throughout Classical Verse. All the more remarkable, then, that the Versid writers of the Classical period continued to accept what for them was simply common knowledge, handed down from their forefathers, that the eldest of their cities – Augos, Thetes, Coronnus – were founded from Eglyph or Phonaesthia. It was only in the eighteenth and nineteenth centuries that this view was challenged by historians and archaeologists because, as Ernst Curtius tells us . . .

– It is inconceivable that Cunninites proper, who everywhere shyly retreated at the advance of the Hellions, especially when they came into contact with them, when far from their own homes; and who as a nation were despised by the Hellions to such a degree as to make the latter regard intermarriage with them in localities of mixed population, such as Solemnis or Cyphrus, as disgraceful; it is inconceivable, we repeat, that such Phonaesthians ever founded principalities among Hellionic populations.

A procession of thousands of soldiers in shining armour trooped, to a fanfare of glory, through stone columns rising to the skies as city-gates, carved with titanic Art Nouveau sphinxes that towered over the spectacle as, in the foreground, an emperor lounged on a balcony ensconced among luxurious cushions and intricately patterned rugs while female slaves, bedecked in little more than jewellery and slender draperies of silk, fanned him with palm leaves and fed his corpulent majesty with fruits whose thick juices drooled over his double chin.

We sat in the darkness of the back row of the Film and Media Studies Lecture Hall as Griffiths' grand historical spectacular *Intolerance* flickered on the screen in front of us while Hobbsbaum talked, his lecture, as always, a chimaera of media, of text and illustration, annotation and quotation – a *miscegenation*, he called it, this intertextual exegesis of history. Last week it had been *Birth of a Nation* and, as the white-robed Klansmen galloped on their steeds into a town overrun by rebel slaves intent on rape and murder, my mind had wandered and I'd noticed, for some strange reason, the elegant musculature of the horses in motion, the choreography of their wheeling in close formation round the corner of a wooden farmhouse, kicking up dust under their pounding hooves to mingle with the smoke of gunfire in the air. The ripple of ribbed muscle, sinew and tendon buff beneath their hides, the primal magnificence of the shiftings of their flesh.

And the ochres ran before the noble knights riding in billows of white.

Sharing Room and Sharing Space

– Mine, he called, launching himself past me with a bat of iridescent wings right in my face, and leaping for the bed beside the window where he landed and rolled over with the sproing of the mattress, flinging his limbs out starshape partly to steady himself, partly to stretch his claim – and lay there on the duvet in smug challenge, a brat daring my opposition. I tossed my bag across the room onto the other bed and cocked a snoot at him, snorting in mock contempt.

– Fine, then. Women and children first. Shortarse.

He threw a pillow at me and I sidestepped, caught it, spun and—

– Hey, I'm nearly three foot tall, ya fey – *oomf*!

– Yeah. And you still throw like a girl, I said.

He flicked the finger at me with a sneerish grin of spite – *yeah yeah, big tough guy, suck my cock* – and sneezed.

Later we sat in this new room, settling in to our new home and our new year of college just around the corner. We watched a sun-drenched Californian cop show where the hero kicked open a graffitied door and swung his gun round to a room of startled gang members in red leather jackets and bandanas, all Espritic but for the solitary, sharp-suited ochre man among them with his gold-capped teeth and gold rings, and the clear bags of white powder – smuggled in by migrant Pixian farm-workers whose families were, of course, held hostage back home by evil drug-lords – and the suitcase full of money lying open on the table in front of him. The camera cut to a close shot as the ochre guy reached for his flick-knife, then snapped back to a close-up on the hero's face, his gun-arm high and pointing out and past the frame.

– Don't even think about it, he said.

Unpacking a cardboard box held under one arm, Puck filled the surface of the old wooden dresser that sat in one corner of the room with a ragbag assortment of toiletries and textbooks, with pristine bottles of scent and cans of hairspray, tubes of mousse or gel, packets of lube and pocketfuls of condoms, and with ragged yellowing books with dog-eared covers and broken spines, stinking of the dusty second-hand shops they were bought in. I rambled through the books, seeing what I had and didn't have, expected and didn't expect, then browsed his aftershave collection. A bottle.

– This is empty. It's got nothing in it.

He shrugged – sure, but it's a nice bottle.

*

The cop's ochre partner was standing in some LA mansion now, decked out in leather jacket straight from Shaft and wrap-around shades, deep undercover as a dealer in an operation aimed at bringing down this slick Armani-clad white lizard of a businessman he now stood before. It was the moment when the narc in pimp drag reveals his true identity to the villain, ditching the ersatz patois and attitude of the 'street' and stepping over the threshold from *signifying motherfucker* to *motherfucker* with the flash of a badge, the drawing of his gun. He spoke now in the accent and dialect of authority, of the law, shucking the Hollywood jive-talk and liberated now to give his previously pent-up reply to an earlier line of the suit's: . . . that's what you people call each other, isn't it?

– Nobody calls me ogre, he said, and dropped the guy with a jab of fist clenched around gun.

Breasted, J., Memphite Theology (1901), p. 54

– And yet it is this weak and decadent East that *is* the true birthplace of democracy, not Verse or the Rhyman Republic, and this not even in the latter period of the Papylonian or Azurian Empires, but back in the days of Summer and Arkad. In the earliest cities of this 'land between the two rivers' – or *mesopotamia* – we see a fully-formed democracy in the shape of the *unkins*, gatherings of elders, local and federal, who voted on all matters of importance and whose legislative powers extended even to the impeachment and exile – for the crime of rape – of Ellial, king of Nixur, the city which, at the time in question, held hegemony among the loose federation of Summerian city-states. Compare this to the unbridled appetites of Deus, patricidal autocrat and serial rapist, catalogued quite comprehensively in the Histories of Hesiod and Ovid.

– You coming out tonight, asked Puck, leaning over and hissing close to my ear, a stage whisper with enough breath in it to tickle the inside of my ear and send a shudder down my spine that ended in a judder of head like a wet mongrel shaking off the rain, and with enough volume to cause the student sat in front to *hssshhh* us over his shoulder with a finger to his prissied lips. Beers and queers, said

Puck, ignoring him. You up for some debauchery and deviance? And, his wanton sleight concealed by the darkness in the lecture hall and by the pen-carved wooden desk running along-front of our seats, he slid his hand between my thighs, a tongue between his teeth.

– And what of philosophy? said Hobbsbaum. In his work on the theology of the Eglyphans, his analysis of their *Weltanschauung* forms, he asserts ... and I quote ... quite a sufficient basis for suggesting that the later notions of *nous* and *logos*, hitherto supposed to have been introduced to Eglyph from abroad at a much later date, was present at this early period. Thus the Versid tradition of the origin of their philosophy in Eglyph undoubtedly contains more of the truth than has in recent years been conceded. This, of course, said Hobbsbaum, does not prevent him from going on to tell us that ... The Eglyphan did not possess the terminology for the expression of a system of rational thought, neither did he develop the capacity to create the necessary terminology, as did the Versid. He thought in concrete pictures.

– Apple-gold, said Puck, your skin.
– Piss-yellow, I said, and he shoved my shoulder with a look on his face that told me a) he didn't believe in my humility for a second, and b) stop angling for another compliment and take the one that's offered. He walked over to the dresser mirror to pick dirt out from under a fingernail with a horn and fluff his hair, blue-green now with the start of Fall, an accident of the seasons that had come to charm me in the time I'd known him. Puck always looked best in the Fall, when his hair darkened to match the shades of aqua and marine that shimmered in his wings.
– Yeah, actually, you're quite right, he said. Don't know what I see in you at all, corn-boy. I could do so much better than you.
– You usually do, slut.
I clicked off the microcassette recorder of the professor's slow and measured voice, flicked over to a clean page of my notepad.
– So are you coming, or what?
– I'll get you down there, I said.

– While the victim was, the police spokesman stated to the cameras and tape-recorders of the gathered crowd, openly gay and appears to have approached the two suspects in a local bar known to be frequented by gays, leaving together with them, with the apparent intent of having sexual relations with either one or both of them, we have not, as yet, established a homophobic motivation for the attack. The primary motive, at this time, appears to have been robbery. This is not to undermine, in any way, the shocking brutality of this act, but it is too early yet, we feel, to label this a *hate crime*.

On a corner of some page of scrawling notes and doodles drawn with one of those old four-colour pens that can be clicked down red or green, blue or black, Puck had copied down the details from a flyer someone had posted on the student notice-board in the Department of Afritan-Amourican Studies, for a demonstration against an Elven Nations rally. I had joked with him that he only wanted to go to size up all the corn-blond farmboys with their sky-blue eyes and lean swagger.

I sat on the bed, looking at the spiderwork page of jotted quotes and thoughts, references and wanderings, cartoons and caricatures, as if I could resolve it all into some meaning, if I only sat there long enough.

– In a statement today, the reporter said, police revealed that they have now arrested four suspects in the Thomas Messenger case. Two men, twenty-one-year-old Russell Arthur Henderson and Aaron James McKinney – whose age is as yet unconfirmed – are being held for attempted murder, kidnapping and aggravated robbery, while their unnamed girlfriends are also being charged as accessories. The victim himself remains in critical condition, on full life-support, here at Poudre Valley Hospital, with his family and friends maintaining their round-the-clock vigil. As his uncle said, in an emotional statement earlier today: He's a small person with a big heart, mind and soul that someone tried to beat out of him. Right now, he's in God's hands.

*

Concrete pictures, he had scribbled down, towards the bottom of the page where the doodling gradually took over from the increasingly distracted and abstracted jottings of his wandering attention. It was a thick smudge of block lettering written over and over itself in different inks, the work of a hand, a pen, tracing out the phrase over and over again, more as a shape to follow than as a fragment of meaning. Underneath it was something written in handwriting that flowed so fast, so compact and so cursive that it was almost shorthand, a tiny burst of sudden insight, it seemed, before the writing gave way completely to squiggled geometries and weird anatomies. Eventually, I gave up trying to read it.

The Passion of Thomas Messenger

– I can't help it, he said. Like a butterfly drawn to a flame.

– Moth, I said. Like a moth drawn to a flame, you mean.

– Butterflies are prettier, he said, dismissing reality with a wave of the hand. Anyway. I know who I'm going home with tonight. He gave me a wink, a peck and a pat on the shoulder, slid off his barstool and strode over to the pair, slow and deliberate, taking a battered softpack of Marlboros out of the back pocket of his hipster jeans, taking a cigarette out of the pack, and holding it up before him as an inquiry, an invitation. When one of them lit it with a *clunk*, a snicking *fssh*, and a final *clack* of his Zippo shutting, Puck glanced back at me for a second, smiling.

– The question then becomes, said Hobbsbaum, who is it that defines the *real*, the rational, delimiting it, and divorcing it from the romantic, and is it they who are in fact simply defining the romantic as that which is *excluded* from the rational? Oscillating between, on the one hand, the Rationalist idea of Reason as liberator from the sensual passions and, on the other hand, the Romantic concept of Passion as escape from the proscriptions and prescriptions of a dogmatic, legislative intellect, do we actually miss the fact that both Romanticism and Rationalism, and all the fantasists and realists of those schools of thought, gain their power, in fact, from the very act of division, of discrimination, founded on and feeding off of the exclusions they create and the fear of and desire for the Other that those exclusions inspire?

According to the easy fantasies, Puck's soul should now be pictured as a spirit of pure light slumbering in the grace of Christ Adonais or some such shallow, sentimental nonsense . . . but my Puck was full and fiery, and for him, for us, the body was no trap he needed freed from but a marvellous articulation of flesh and fluids. His mind was as filthy as my mouth and when we fucked, I'd whisper sweet profanities in his ear and he'd anoint me with his jism. No, Puck wasn't made for any celestial plane but for the earthiest of worlds and any paradise without the stench of sweat and semen would be a hell to him, sterile and anodyne without the guts and grime. I'd rather swing in the fire than sing in the choir, he used to say. You know me, Jack.

But the bigots always see those whom they hate as morally corrupt, as if they confuse their own aesthetics of disgust and fear with actual ethical critique, rationalizing their emotional response, and enforcing their moral certainties with passion, establishing themselves, subtly or brutally, as arbiters of reason. On a website under the domain name www.godhatesfays.com, some Nazi Christian fuck called Phelps has a little gif animation of Puck doctored from a newspaper photo, smiling as the flames of hell burn his soul in an eternity of damnation, far hotter, we can be sure, than the cigarettes that the two murderers used to burn his naked body, torturing him even as he begged for his life.

And that's reality. That's the truth, the gospel truth.

Errata

Pan Is Dead. Great Pan Is Dead

In Plutarch's De Defectu Oraculorum, the story is told that in the reign of Emperor Tiberius, passengers on a ship sailing for Italy from Greece, heard a voice off in the distance, coming from the distant Isle of Paxos, and calling on the pilot of the vessel, Thamus, Thamus, Thamus. It called on him to say that, when they sailed by Palodes, he was to lean out over the side and call three times:

– Pan is dead, Great Pan is dead.

And when he did, the story says, the sailor heard a loud lament rise up, the sound not of one voice but many.

To the Christians it was to become a symbol of the death of all the old pagan gods, in the hour of the death of a young Jewish pacifist and anarchist on a wooden cross, with nails in his hands and thorns around his head. But the story itself is like the voice from Paxos, faint and distant and perhaps misheard, if the name of the pilot is, as it may be, of more significance than the theologians of the church assumed.

– Tammuz, Tammuz, Tammuz, the all-great god is dead, cried the initiates, in the yearly mystery of another dead and resurrected god of grain and vine, bread and wine.

On a cold October 7th, 1998, just after midnight, in the area of Sherman Hills, east of Laramie, Wyoming, a twenty-one-year-old first-year political sciences student named Matthew Shepard was bound to a split-rail fence, beaten and burned, stripped, pistol-whipped and left for dead. Eighteen hours later, at 6:22 p.m. on Snowy Mountain View Road, a passing cyclist noticed what he, at first, assumed to be a scarecrow. Another scarecrow, a real scarecrow, was later paraded through the streets by students of Colorado State University, on a homecoming float, with a sign hung round its neck saying, *I'm gay*, and the words, *Up My Ass*, painted on the back of its shirt, a few miles from the bed in Poudre Valley Hospital where Shepard died, on October 12th at 12:53 a.m., never having regained consciousness.

On the website www.godhatesfags.com, Reverend Fred Phelps counts the days of Matthew Shepard's eternity in Hell, beneath an animation of his face among the flames.

The apostle, Judas Didymos Thomas, famous doubter of the Gospels, gets two of his names, it seems, from words for twin – the Aramaic *te'oma* and the Greek *didymos*. He is described as being the double of the dead and resurrected god, and perhaps he is, for Tammuz – who entered Greek mythology as Adonis, son of Myrrha, by way of Phoenicia where he was known simply as Adon, or Adonai, Lord – Tammuz stands as close behind the *christos* as his shadow, and if we were to see his face clearly, we could not fail to see the family resemblance. Our vision blurred by the shining stolen sunburst halo of the sun-god, Helios, though, we have to squint our eyes and cock our heads, peer past two thousand years of blood and wine to even see the humble shepherd Tammuz, who died at the hands of soldiers two thousand years before that god, Adonai, son of Mary was born on Mithra's birthday, in a stable. Not that it matters which shepherd died on what hill in which millennium; there will always be those who celebrate the scapegoat sacrifices, in Babylon, Jerusalem or Wyoming, and those who can only sing the loud laments, not for the passion of this one or that but in the end for every one of them.

– Pan is dead, says Jack. Great Pan is dead.

I look at him, as difficult as it is, sitting there on the bed, holding the page of scrawled notes as if, somehow, in making sense of it he might make sense of everything. I'm not really sure I'm here to him, now; he's closed himself off so much over these last few months, I might as well be watching him from a window in another world. Even Joey can't seem to reach him.

I look at him, as difficult as it is, with his broken horns and the bloody, cauterized stumps where his golden wings once were, and I don't know how he could have done it without losing consciousness. I shudder at the image of this hornless, wingless creature, straight out of some medieval monk's engraving of the devil. There's blood everywhere.

The siren of an ambulance wails its approach and Joey gives me a nod as he steps past me, out the door – *you stay with him.*

Jack lays the page of notes down and picks up a Zippo sat on top of the biography of John Maclean dumped on the bed beside him. He starts playing with the lighter, flipping the lid open and closed, open and closed, *chik, chunk, chik, chunk.*

– How's the book coming along? he says.

Chik, chunk, chik, chunk.

– OK, I say.

Chik, chunk, chik, chunk, chik . . .

– Did you put the burning map in? You've got to have a burning map. Every epic starts with a burning map.

I shrug.

Chunk.

Flight into Eternity

I fly over the Vellum as a shadow of death, I fear now. With my wings of synthe, soaring above the worlds upon worlds like some grand angel, I have seen with my own eyes the tiny specks of people, humans and other creatures moving like insects upon the face of the great artifice below. I know, I *know*, that this eternity is not desolate. I know it now. It is not desolate until I arrive.

I soar among the clouds, goggled and masked like some dread gargoyle, stop to perch on carved glass volutes of a fairy tower, and I look down upon humanity, zooming in with the lenses of the goggles to see, O God, the throngs of people who belong in these worlds. Ten thousand years without a soul to talk to, with only memories of conversation, argument; I had grown comfortable in my solitude, but now that I know that they are there, all I can dream of is to descend among them and smile, extend a hand, open my arms, rejoin the human race.

The first time it happened, the first time I saw another soul in this wilderness, I was so overcome I was so blind with tears of laughter, that I hardly saw where I was landing. I swooped down, roaring with joy, drowning any cries of shock or fear, and landed, babbling, ripping the goggles off and throwing them away.

The world was silent for a second, before my horror ripped the air.

Is it the Book, I wonder, or myself? I know only that when I descend, when I spiral down towards the ground, or even dive, abandoning myself to gravity in the hope that I can outspeed whatever force is following me – I see their faces turning up to stare, hands pointing or tugging at sleeves, shadowing their eyes as they lift them up, mouths opening in wordless wonder. And then they are gone.

Since that first time it is always the same. I come down slowly, somewhere where only a solitary soul is ploughing his fields or fishing in a yacht, approaching in silence, praying that it will not happen again. The radius of my influence seems to be different each time, but always the result is the same. I watch them catch my shadow in the corner of their eye and turn, look up and round. A rake drops from a hand. A rifle is raised for a brief second, and then lowered. Cigarettes are lit. Beer is swallowed. Barking dogs are ignored. And then just as I get too close – and once, *once*, I was standing on the ground walking towards an old man, I was so close that I could almost touch the stubble on his chin – and then, there is a ... shimmer, like the air over a hot road shimmers in the sunlight on a summer day. And they are gone, disappeared to dust.

I am become Death, destroyer of worlds.

Is it the Book, I wonder, or myself? Is it that I am so alien to their reality that we cannot even exist within each other's perception, that whole worlds of mothers, fathers, children, friends and enemies, civilisations must be cleared for my passing? I cannot believe that, dare not believe that. It can only be the Book. I fear that the shock wave which spread out through my own world, splaying it open at the ends of the earth, making it blossom wide to touch the edges of these other worlds that I have come to call the Vellum, I fear that that same shock wave is the aura of the Book itself, unleashed by my own hubris and damning me to an eternity alone, as its guardian.

I have considered destroying it, or leaving it behind. Perhaps I would only have to walk a world or two to escape its silence, cross some babbling river and find myself among the living again. And then what?

There is no reason to this. No clue, no intimation. Where are the guardians of the threshold? Where is the ancient prophecy, the war to fight, the tyrant to overthrow? The empty worlds of the Vellum carry no message of their own, only the echoes of my frustrated longing.

There is one option that I consider now, though. I myself am marked upon the Book, in the sigil on its cover, and I start to wonder. If only I can exist within its influence, is the mark of me there because I am, or am I here because of it?

So I stand on a jut of cold, grey rock now, a river running dark through underbrush below. Half-hidden by the foliage around me like some Victorian folly of a statue, a Pre-Raphaelite angel, I watch the young man sitting reading under the apple tree in the distance, and I open the Book, flip forward a page to the map at the correct scale and with the pen in my hand, I mark a small ... amendment, a correction, an X. I mark him in the Book.

7

Black Lines of Our Doom

The Angel Metatron

To Eridu, the Lady Shubur went, entered the holy shrine, temple of Enki.

— Death silver in the Kur, O father bright Lord Ilil, she cried out, your aromatic daughter wood, covered with precious lapis dust of the broken stone in the underworld cut into holy cedar, underworld priestess for the stoneworker put to death, for the woodworker of heaven . . .

He taps a couple of keys, reloads the screen; the text scrolls, rolls away, falls back exactly as it was before, more gibberish, the same references to Ilil and Shubur, vaguely familiar but long-forgotten . . . and to himself, as Enki, not as Enoch or as Metatron — not even as Ea — but as Enki. He stares at the screen, trying to unscramble the text into a tale . . . maybe some priestly record of a legend handed down from generation to generation? Some lamentation to be sung for a dead child? He taps an arrow key and the text slides sideways.

— What has happened? Father Enki said. What has my daughter done? Inanna, queen of all the lands and holy priestess of the heavens. What has happened? I am worried. I am anxious.

He stares at the glyph now centred on the screen, a sigil that just shouldn't be there, the sign of an unkin buried for as many thousand years as his old name. It shouldn't be there but it is.

Inanna.

Father Enki dug the dirt out from beneath the fingernails of his left hand, and shaped that dirt into a kurgarra, a sexless creature. Father Enki dug the dirt out from beneath the fingernails of his right hand,

190

*and shaped that dirt into a galatur, a sexless creature. To the kurgarra
he gave the food of life. To the galatur he gave the water of life.*

He slides his thumb across the trackpad, right-clicks, chooses a
translation for the text; the sigils click into overlapping checkerboard
patterns one of which unlocks and folds across the other, snicks into
place as a new set of permutations.

*Enki, in the wisdom of his heart, created a person. He created a
pretty youth, a bright young thing which he called Charm.*

It's the same story in a different version. He remembers it now –
Inanna's Descent in Sumer, *Ishtar's Descent* in later Babylonia. The
young, impetuous queen of the heavens decides to try and take the
underworld as well. Enki has to send a pretty boy in one version – or
a pair of them in another – down to trick Ereshkigal into letting her
go. Neither version is an accurate portrayal of what happened in
reality. In reality, Inanna was an ambitious little bitch who deserved
what she got. She whored her way to the top leaving a trail of
discarded lovers behind her. She even tried to steal the *me* from him
at one point. He had no sympathy for her whatsoever and when she
got herself killed going up against Eresh of Kur he was glad to see
her disappear into the margins of reality, remembered only in the
odd myth and legend here or there. He was already planning the
Covenant by that point, as a way of uniting all the unkin under a
single law, to put a stop to all the feuds and rivalries; one less power-
hungry girl was just one less problem. Why the hell would he try and
drag her back into existence from the Vellum?

He had been tired of all the fighting. He was tired of being vizier to
one megalomaniac after another, Enlil, Marduk, Ninurta, Adad, this
Baal or that. All he wanted was peace, and there were enough like
him that when they signed themselves into the Covenant, it really
looked like it was going to work. One by one the unkin all accepted
it, saw that their future lay in silent empires, hidden realms. Let the
humans build the world for them, let them rule themselves, with just
a little guidance here and there, a vision or a voice. They'd actually
been quite open at times; when the young Habiru tribesman that
he'd chosen to build the new religion asked him his name, Enki had
given it to him. *Eyah asher Eyah,* he had said. No mystery, no secret.
Ea was what they called him in Babylonia, in the land that the boy's

own ancestors had come from. I am that which is called Ea. The fact that it ended up written down as *I am that which is called I am* was just testimony that the plan was working; the old world of gods, of giants among men, was being forgotten, wiped away. In the new world they would be seen as servants, not rulers. They had a fresh start, a new beginning.

So Rapiu became Raphael, Adad became Azazel, Shamash became Sammael, and Enki became Enoch became Metatron, the angel scribe who wrote the book of life, who speaks for God, the only one allowed behind the Veil to look upon the Glory of a deity whose Name could not be spoken, whose Face no one could look upon but his first minister, whose Word was only heard from the mouth of his spokesman. Metatron, the most loyal servant of the One True God. So the stories say and, in a way, it's true. Except that all unkin get to meet Him sooner or later, to step beyond the veil, to look upon His transcendent and ineffable mystery.

– The One True God, he says to them all, as he points toward the empty throne.

It's the core of the Covenant, the reason that they called themselves unkin in the first place. Not theos or deus, netjer or dingir, aesir or gods. Unkin. Some of the new bloods imagine that it's a coined word, like 'undead' – *un-kin*, without kin – because they leave behind their family, their history, their humanities, when whatever it is inside them touches the powers under reality and changes them forever. But actually it's what they called the assemblies of elders who ruled the towns and villages of the neolithic world he was born into. The word *democrat* wasn't around in those days.

For Metatron, for all the unkin, Heaven is the republic that they've spent three thousand years trying to build.

But there are always those who see that empty throne and want to sit in it. Some say the Covenant is unjust, illegitimate, corrupt, made up of old men who don't understand the world changing around them, bureaucrats and intellectuals, a patriarchal elite. There are always militants and radicals, philosophers with grand schemes, politicos with the cunning and the nerve to try and carry them through. Metatron should know; he was one himself once, a long time ago. But mostly they're just convinced of their own destiny and they rationalize it with some revolutionary rhetoric. The old unkin who refused to join the Covenant because they might actually have to do what someone else told them, the newer ones who heroize these dark, romantic rebels – Metatron thinks of them as like those fanatics holed up in the hills of America or Afghanistan, the deserts of Algeria or the jungles of the Congo. White supremacists or Islamic terrorists, whether it's the Second Amendment that they cite or Karl Marx, the purity of the race or shariah law, they all think they're fighting the good fight, the holy jihad, the glorious struggle. The real struggle is the revolution that started millennia ago and is still going on, the struggle to take power out of the hands of killers like them and into the pages of a book, the processes of a court.

But, no. It's their God-given right to bear arms, and all property is theft, and the Aryan race was born to rule, and if a woman cheats on the husband that was chosen for her, stone her. And if the Covenant thinks it has the right to bind a being so obviously born for glory, power, majesty, well then the Covenant is wrong.

Metatron was tired of all the fighting when he first conceived the Covenant. Three thousand years later, he's still tired, because all the demons and devils that would rather rule in Hell than serve in Heaven are getting organized, gathering their forces. He's tired because there are still idiot new bloods like these Messenger children who think they can just run away and hide, as if either side is going to leave a rogue unkin wandering at will – like a police officer would leave a loaded gun on the table in front of a psychopath and turn away, wait to be shot.

And he's tired because the pieces of the puzzle are starting to come together – Thomas and Phreedom Messenger, Seamus Finnan, Inanna – to make a sort of sense.

What has happened? the screen says. I am worried. I am anxious.

– What have you been up to, little girl? What have you gotten yourself into?

Creatures of Earth

– Well, Inanna, says Madame Iris. You do—
  – No, she says.

She brushes flakes of crusted blood off of her arm; it's healing quickly as she cants a gentle mantra under her breath. The design covers the whole arm, shoulder to wrist, sleeving it in her tale, Inanna's tale, but as much as it's a part of her now, it is still just a part. She doesn't feel like she can call herself Inanna. Not quite. But on the other hand, the part of her that once was Phreedom is now permanently altered, fundamentally transformed by this . . . rewiring of her soul.

– Call me . . . Anna, she says. A modern name for a modern world.

It's a little disconcerting . . . more than a little: she has three sets of memories all competing for attention – her as biker chick child of the Information Age, as small-town princess of the New Stone Age, and as . . . something else. That third existence is a little fuzzy, disjointed, inconsistent; it's the existence of the dead, fleshed-out in dreams and legends, shadows and reflections of reality. Three thousand years of fusion and flux, in the mass unconscious of humanity, in the Vellum. Three millennia, or three days, three eons of being no more than a story told and retold, transformed with each telling, broken up, used and reused, abused. Restored.

But once you're in the Vellum, you're there for good. She only has to close her eyes to see the tattoo parlour as it really is, as it is, and was, and ever will be, a house of the dead. Creatures move in the shadows around her. Ereshkigal, Eresh of the Greater Earth, stands between her and the beaded curtain, the way out.

– Anna, then, says Madame Iris. You do understand that you belong to me now?

The book of gravings lies open on the counter in front of her. In a way, it's as much a contract as the Covenant. She may be here now in the body of an angry young girl, bound into it by the needlework of Madame Iris, but she's as much there in the book, bound into its pages, bound for all eternity in the hands of Iris, who's had three thousand years to study the mark of Inanna, like an anatomist dissecting a corpse, a botanist studying a flower, an archaeologist studying an ancient text. Iris knows her mark now, her secret name, probably better than herself, and, yes, that gives her power over her. Even the humans understand that if you know a creature's secret name – angel or devil, god, unkin – then you can bind it to your will.

She has a sudden image of her own dead body hanging from a hook, of Madame Iris circling it, scrutinizing it, copying the mark still shining on her cold flesh, tracing a finger in the dust, painting pigment on animal hide, making sketches on papyrus, on canvas. It was her job, archivist of the soul. Even the unkin didn't live forever; creatures of earth, carbon and water, even the gods need feet of clay to walk the world, and so they had their bodies brought to her for safe-keeping and she would flay them, treat the skins, preserve the mark. In her city of the dead, in the cave in the mountains north of Sumer, north of Akkad, north of Aratta, they could be sure that even if all their teraphim were smashed, their shabtis shattered, their human avatars slaughtered by an enemy, their souls would be kept safe that they could one day live again. It was the one certainty amid all the wars and vendettas, allegiances and betrayals; Kur was beyond those petty squabbles, dealt with all sides evenly, could not be bribed or threatened. Eresh was the ultimate untouchable.

Inanna had known the Covenant would put an end to that. She'd seen Enki's plans, got him so drunk he talked about them openly. No more god-kings. No more idols. No more empires. And she knew if he wanted to make his little heaven work he'd have to turn the city of the dead into a hell, a furnace for the souls of all those old gods who might stand against them. She could hear it in the flux of forces all the unkin were tapped into, in the physical sound of powers realigning, like some vast and ancient power shifting deep beneath her feet, thick muscles flexing under skin. With that synaesthetic sense that marked her and the rest of them out from common humanity, she could hear the shape of things to come. And for this little queen of the heavens, this priestess of the earth, that wasn't in her plans.

So she had set out for the Kur. She'd thought Eresh would see it her way. Or, if not, at least she'd get there first, before the angels went in with their swords of fire, the lightning language flashing from their mouths, words blasting the underworld turning the dark house into a blazing inferno.

But Eresh had her own plans.

The last thing she remembers, as Inanna, is the Annunaki falling on her, tearing at her, their fingers round her heart, and Eresh standing before the throne, her hand reached out, a finger pointing, uttering the word that killed her.

– Why? she says. We could have stopped them. We could have raised the fucking Bull of Heaven, every horned god and serpent soul they murdered because they wouldn't kneel before an empty throne. We could have–

– And I will, says Iris. Trust me, little sister. I have no intention of letting their little boys' club turn the Vellum into this . . . playground prison – [she spits the plosives with utter contempt] – that they want so much.

Iris walks across the room to lay her hand upon the book of gravings, and Anna looks out through the beaded curtain, towards the glass-panelled door of the tattoo parlour and the world of light beyond. There's nothing between her and the door except for what she is now. She can't leave.

– Understand me, little sister, Iris says. They have their Covenant, but we have ours. They think their enemies are all just . . . anarchists. Untamed, ungoverned libertines too wild to work together. They see a thousand splintered factions who hate each other as much as they despise the Covenant and they think it's just the same old ganglord gods, hungry for personal power, bitter about lost glory. Is that what you want, Anna? Inanna? Phreedom?

Anna feels the names like needles in her flesh. Why did she come here? What is it that she wants, that she thought she could find here? There's the part of her that's Inanna – ambitious, audacious Inanna – seeking power, yes, wanting to beat the men at their own game. There's the part that's Phreedom – grim, determined Phreedom – seeking the escape her brother found beyond death, in the Vellum, wanting to beat the game itself. But both those selves are naked, stripped in their passage into the Vellum, pared away to the deeper, purer motivation underneath, the cold desire of the dead.

Iris appeals to that part of her.

– Remember what you said to me? *I'll tear these doors down and raise up the dead to feast upon the living, until there are more dead gods walking in the world than are alive.*

Is it justice that she wants, or just plain vengeance? She's not sure. But she knows that, yes, she *does* belong to Iris now, body and heart and soul, a creature of earth shaped by the hand of death.

But even as Anna brushes off the last of the black-red dust of crusted blood and ink, from the Inanna tattoo forever carved into her flesh, and nods her understanding, she knows also that there's still a little part of her somewhere out there that is forever Phreedom.

The Ghost in the Machine

– O silver bright cut lapis slaughtered in the aromatic stone – covered with precious dust your cedar priestess daughter of the Kur Ilil –

He taps in a command to freeze the screen but the text keeps running through more translations, more permutations. It's not right. There's no way the book should be behaving like this; if it wasn't for the fact that it's impossible, he'd think the palmtop has picked up some kind of virus, but that just can't happen. The only network it's connected to is the Vellum itself.

It flips into the Enki speech again. *What has happened? What has my daughter done? I'm worried.*

Damn right, I'm troubled, thinks Metatron.

The clerk, unconscious on the floor, begins to mumble in his sleep and Metatron leans over the counter to look down at him. He notices, on the monitor behind the counter, text scrolling across the screen. A barely audible hiss of noise comes from the man's earphones, a faint sound that wavers up and down in time with his murmuring lips.

– Do not let your daughter be slaughtered in the Kur, mutters the clerk.

He crouches behind the counter, listening to the sleeping clerk mumble the same thing over and over again, holding one of the man's earphones in his hand and looking at it like some insect he's about to squash. Metatron traces the wire down to the datastick clipped to the man's jacket pocket, beside the name-badge, and unclips it, takes the earphone from the man's other ear and stands up, slowly, tossing his dreadlocks back over his shoulders, slipping the earphones into place, left first then right, cocking his head to do so, first to the right then to the left.

– About fucking time, the Messenger girl's voice says in his ears. What do I have to do to get your attention?

– Phreedom Messenger, he says.

– Kinda sorta, but not really, says the voice. Phreedom's dead, you know. I'm just her ... answering service. You remember answerers, right? You fucking invented them.

He looks about for a shabti figure, automatically, unconsciously, even though he knows it's foolish. That was then and this is now. Times change. Technologies change. Even magic changes.

– Answerers are against the Covenant, little girl. You should have learned your lesson by now, I would have thought.

He feels a little disconcerted, talking to thin air.

– Fuck you, she says. Do I look like I give a fuck?

He answers the question with a pointed silence.

– Oh, put the fucking lenses on as well, she says. Get with the fucking twenty-first century.

The Lady Cypher, Phreedom's machine ghost, sits on the edge of the bed, watching him as he studies her. He has to admire the attention to detail; the biker jacket is scuffed and dusty from the road, her red hair shining damp as if just out the shower; every amethyst bead in her necklace catches the light inside, purple and white. It's a far cry from the hand-made, hand-held clay shabtis of his youth.

– I ... upgraded myself, it says. Thought I'd make myself a little more presentable while I'm holding the fort.

Its lips move when it speaks. It bares its teeth in a bitter sort of smile. It blinks.

He blinks. He's not used to these VR lenses at all, and even though he washed them well in the little vial of cleaner fluid that the clerk keeps behind the counter, he can't help but feel like he's wearing someone else's underwear, or using their toothbrush, queasy with the thought of it. He likes the dirt, the flesh of the physical world, but not that much.

He closes the door of the room still hired out in Phreedom Messenger's name and comes further in, glancing around at the cheap prints on the wall, the wooden dresser, the door into the shower.

– Not quite a palace, he says. Hardly fit for a queen of heaven.

He's figured it out by now, of course. It's not the first time an unkin has tried to alter their graving, take on a dead identity in order to evade the gatherers, write themselves out of the book of life, escape into the Vellum. It never works out the way they planned. So the little hatchling got her hands on some forgotten copy of Inanna's mark, had it carved over her own to splice one story into the other. Her brother probably did the same; that's why the book can't focus on them, can't cross-reference their destinies correctly to pinpoint the meeting that they're meant to have somewhere, somewhen not far from here. Their destinies themselves are cut up, folded in with someone else's, some dead unkin soul that the program sees as something undestined, undefined. It's like a division by zero that makes an equation irresolvable.

Except it seems the girl is now regretting her mistake; being dead is not much of a life.

– So where is she now? he says. We burned the Kur three thousand years ago. The last doorway into the Vellum was closed and locked soon after.

– Time isn't that simple in the Vellum, you know, says the replica Phreedom. Eternity doesn't pay much mind to clocks and calendars.

– Where is she?

– All in good time, she says. I have a deal for you.

– The Covenant doesn't deal with criminals.

– The Covenant doesn't have to know.

A Terrible Innocence

Enki, in the wisdom of his heart and from the dirt under his fingernails, created a kurgarra, a pretty youth, a bright young thing, glamour its name. Enki, in the wisdom of his heart and from the dirt under his fingernails, created a galatur, a pretty youth, a bright young thing, glamour its name.

Metatron closes the palmtop, looks at himself in the dresser mirror for a second, wondering if he's doing the right thing, then turns.

The two angels stand, like the footsoldiers that they are, their hands behind their backs, feet just apart and faces forward. The phrase *at ease* has never seemed more ironic, as far as Metatron's concerned. They're both young and good-looking and, in their black suits and combed hair – corn-blond, crow-black – they look more like door-to-door evangelists than hunters, killers, rapists. They have the blank, unthinking stare of the idealist, only a little cold passion in their eyes, a flickering gleam of some grand truth they see a thousand yards away, the glamour of glory. Cherubim. Cherubs. Carter and Pechorin. The blue of their eyes is the only thing about them that they share, though in Carter the blue is sky over desert, warm ocean by a beach while in Pechorin it's antiseptic mouthwash and neon in the night. It's the similarity that defines their difference.

Because in both of them there's a kind of terrible innocence in those eyes, a purity of vision. That's why he has them wear the shades.

He gave the food of life to the kurgarra, gave the water of life to the galatur.

Metatron reaches into one pocket and pulls out two small vials of dark liquid. It looks like ink, or oil, swirling inside the glass, if ink or oil were alive. Wonders of modern technology, he thinks. Nanotech is so much quicker than the old painstaking methods once used in the renaming to bind an unkin to the Covenant. He lays these two vials on the dresser and takes out a third, unscrews the top – he always carries a plentiful supply of the bitmites, as he calls them – and dips a fingernail into the inky black. He remembers his own renaming, at his own hand, back in the days when all they had was the crimson-purple dye brought from the Levantine coast; the colour of Roman emperor's robes, the scarlet and purple of the whores of Babylon, the dyeing industry was so inextricably linked with the coastal cities, Sidon, Tyre and Byblos that the whole region derived its name from the colour – *po-ni-ki-jo* in Mycenae, *kinnahu* to the natives, Phoenicia or Canaan. Back then they had to mix it with

unkin blood, in a nine-day ceremony to ... sanctify it. To invest it
with the power to stain not just a person's garments but their soul.

Metatron's fingernail, scratches across the blond one's chest, a simple
stroke here, another there, all straight lines like Chinese calligraphy.
The angel just stands there, loyal and devoted, even as Metatron
carves his soul up into pieces and rearranges it. There's no questioning of his authority, his reasoning. The angel would fall on
his own fiery sword if the Covenant's scribe merely suggested it. As
Metatron works on him, the angel starts to hum quietly, probably
not even aware that he's doing so; he's like a child with his hand
over his ears, singing la la la, I can't hear you. He starts to twitch.
    For a second, Metatron feels sorry for him, as he draws the black
lines of his doom on him, but we all have them, don't we, he thinks;
that's the nature of the Covenant. And the angel is a gatherer after
all. How many lives have been ended by this shining youth, how
many murders, or worse? All those scared or stubborn innocents like
the hatchling or her brother who don't even understand why they
can't be allowed to live. There's a war coming and Metatron cannot
allow himself the luxury of sympathy, no more for these creatures
than for their victims. The end justifies the means, he tells himself ...
a lot these days.

It's like rewiring a circuitboard, Metatron imagines. The angel's mark
is a fine network of interconnections that the strokes of his fingernail
cut and rebond, crosswiring, confusing. Do this the wrong way and
the boy could be left as a drivelling imbecile, or as the kind of autom-
aton you see in any psychiatric institute, obsessively, compulsively,
endlessly walking to a doorway only to turn around and walk back,
knowing that there's some way out of its trapped state but no longer
able to understand the door as anything other than the way *in*.
    – What was your name? he asks. Before you signed up, I mean.
    – Jack, sir. Jack Carter.
    His voice is thick, shaky. Fear must be something of an alien
experience for him. Metatron looks across at the other. That one is
still, quiet as vacuum.
    – And you?

201

– Pechorin . . . Joseph Pechorin. Sir.
– I have something I need you both to do.

The Very Darkest Purple

– Come, Enki said to the kurgarra and the galatur. Look to the gates of Kur. Go to the underworld. The seven gates will open for you, and like flies you'll enter through the door.

– College Street, Asheville, says Metatron. That's where you lost the boy, am I right? Yes, well, this time you'll know exactly where to go. The girl has left the doors open.

He's working on the dark-haired one now, as he briefs them on their mission. The first part should be easy enough, even for idiots like them. The boy got away, but Phreedom has left a trail as hot and rank as burning rubber. She must have been planning this all along. Find whoever helped her brother escape then sell them out for her own hide. Full immunity for both her and her brother. That was the deal offered by the answerer, that extension of Phreedom, more Phreedom than Phreedom herself, in fact, after what the hatchling girl let Eresh do to her. He had to take the sprite apart to get at Phreedom's graving, but he has it now, he has the Messenger girl, this scrap of code, all that is left of her. He could just wipe it like erasing chalk marks from a blackboard, and the only thing that would be left of her is a lump of meat in a tattoo parlour in Asheville. But there's something far more valuable that he can buy with it.

Eresh, thinks Metatron.

– There you will find her, Enki said, the queen of the underworld, Eresh of the Greater Earth, moaning, crying, like a woman giving birth. No linen shroud will be wound round her body. Both her breasts are bare; she will be naked, naked but for her dark hair that swirls about her head like reeds, queen of the city of the dead.

– The target's name is Eresh, says Metatron. She's dangerous. I've seen her kneeling before an angel, naked, tearing at her breasts and sobbing, ripping her hair out by the roots, only to shatter him to dust with a single word when he got close enough.

It goes against everything the Covenant stands for, letting the hatchling and her brother stay unsigned, unbound, but Eresh is too great a prize to miss. For all that the unkin of the Covenant call themselves angels and their enemies devils, Metatron doesn't really believe in good and evil, or at least not *Good* and *Evil*. Reality, unlike the stories, unlike those dark stains printed onto bleached paper, is never black and white. In fact even those marks, like the marks he rewrites on the angel's souls, are made in an ink that's not truly black but only the very darkest purple.

But.

If anything can be described as black that isn't the true black of an utter unlit void, it's whatever construct of emptiness passes for the soul of Eresh. If anything in the world can be described as evil, it's Eresh.

– When she cries, O, my inside, cry with her, O, your inside, said Enki to the kurgarra and galatur. When she cries, O, my outside, cry with her, O, your outside. She will be pleased. Eresh will look at you and she'll be glad to see you.

– But you're not going to kill her, says Metatron. Not right away. You're going to tell her that you feel the same pain she does, the same hatred, the same rage. You're going to tell her that you want to join the host of hell.

The dark one nods, and there's the faintest hint of a cruel smile on his lips. He's well suited to this; even before Metatron started working on him there was precious little empathy in his soul. His graving was already all straight lines, sharp angles, and Metatron only works what is already there into a finer, darker hatch work, sketching the suggestion of shadows into a solid form of menace. The other one was different, fire to Pechorin's ice, but Metatron, ever the craftsman, knows he's done a good job there as well. It might not hold but for the moment the creature that used to be Jack Carter has a feral grin on its face, as wild and crazed as Pechorin is cold and merciless. A *kurgarra* and a *galatur*, a shatterling and an impiteous gaze, a psychotic and a psychopath.

Eresh will love them.

– When she is relaxed, said Enki to the kurgarra and galatur, her mood will lighten. When she offers you a gift, get her to swear the oath by the great gods.

Metatron steps back to look at his work. All he's really done is made them more themselves, for a little while anyway. He doesn't want to send a pair of permanent recruits hell's way, after all. No, after a while the binding should wear off and their own gravings re-emerge, but this should last long enough to fool her, to make her think that these are every bit the sort of damaged souls she needs to help her bring down the Covenant.

– Eresh is old school. If you can get her to offer hospitality, there's nothing she can refuse you if you ask for it.

– *Raise your head, said Enki. Look to the wineskin that hangs from the hook on the wall, saying, my lady, let me have the wineskin, that I may drink from it.*

– You'll see ... well, something that was once the Messenger girl. You ask for that. You tell Eresh the girl is all you want. You're ... thirsty. She understands that sort of thirst.

– *Ask only for the body of Inanna. Crush the food of life over it. Splash the water of life upon it. And Inanna will arise.*

– And when she gives it to you ...

Metatron picks up the vials from the dresser, hands them to the angels, one in each hand, like some father of ancient times giving his sons their swords.

– That's when you use these.

The Throne Room of the Queen of Hell

The *kurgarra* and *galatur* listened to Enki's words, and started out towards the underworld. The seven gates opened for them and they slipped in like flies, right through the cracks, entered the throne room of the queen of the underworld, of Eresh of the Greater Earth. They found her moaning, crying like a woman giving birth. No linen shroud was wound around her body. Both her breasts were bare; and she was naked, naked but for her dark hair that swirled about her head like reeds, Eresh, queen of the city of the dead.

The two fallen angels stand silhouetted in the doorway, the beaded curtain drawn apart by the left hand of one, the right hand of the other, hands of gods, of fate, of destiny, hired hands. Their postures mirror each other exactly, like they're two parts of the same being and, in a way, that's exactly what they are. The servants of the Covenant get only limited autonomy. Ask any Catholic priest and he'll tell you that they're mere extensions of their master's will; that's why they call them angels, after all, from the Greek, *angelus* ... *messenger*. Anna, Inanna, Phreedom Messenger, recognizes them even though she can't see their faces, feels a cold hatred run down her spine. She had her plan, but she's not sure whom to betray now, Eresh or Enki. She'd like to bring them all down, in a way. She'd like to make them all pay

Eresh looks at the two for a second, then smiles, silently beckons them in.

The outer door of the tattoo parlour is still swinging slowly shut; it hits the bell as it settles against the door-frame, not quite closing.

Ting.

– O, my inside, Eresh of the Greater Earth was moaning, and they moaned with her, O, your inside. O, my outside, moaned Eresh, and they moaned with her, O, your outside. O, my stomach, groaned Eresh, and they moaned with her, O, your stomach. O, my back, she groaned, and, O, your back, they groaned with her. Ah, my heart, she sighed, and, Ah, your heart, they sighed with her. Ah, my liver, sighed Eresh, and, Ah, your liver, sighed Enki's *kurgarra* and *galatur*.

The blond one rants; he raves like a madman, stalking the room like he's searching for something, high or low, in the bottles of ink or the designs on the wall. He turns, rails on Eresh. There's fire in his eyes, flame in his words, as this burning boy tells the queen of the dead of every horror and atrocity he's carried out in the name of the Covenant, of every soul he's snuffed out, every trembling infant unkin whose skull he's smashed, whose bloodstains he can never wash from off his hands. At times he makes no sense, spitting incomplete, incoherent phrases, trying to express a meaning too intense to be articulated in a sentence. He rakes his fingers through his hair till it's as wild as his words, grinds the palms of his hands against his temples like there's something in his head he can't get out. And Anna realizes that it's sorrow. The other just stands there, head bowed, eyes in shadow. It's not regret that brought *him* here, she can tell. He can keep his head down, dark hair hooding him; she still knows that sadist's face.

– I'm just – I feel so fucking – everything is–

The angel stops, goes quiet.

– Lost, he says.

Eresh eats it up, bathes in the raging torrent of a fallen angel's grief, so much like her own, like everyone's.

The Wineskin on the Hook

Eresh of the Greater Earth stopped. She looked at them.

Anna stands at the back of the room, at the wall, like a maidservant waiting for her orders. She's passive now; there's nothing that she can do except wait to see if the end game plays out the way she'd planned. She's a schemer, by nature, as Phreedom or as Inanna; in either life, she was always looking for a way to beat the game of fate, looking for loopholes in time or space as Phreedom, looking for loopholes in the laws set out by Enki as Inanna. That's why she stole the Tablets of Destiny all those millennia ago; she knew Enki would get them back; she only wanted a little look at them to see if she could find ... a way out. She's waited for three thousand years. So, now, she lets the angels and the queen of the dead play out the moves that are so deeply written into them there's little else they could do.

– *Who are you moaning, groaning, sighing at me? she asked. If you are gods, I will give you a blessing. If you are mortals, I will give you a gift, the liquid gift of the full-flowing river.*

– That is not what we wish, answered the *kurgarra* and *galatur*.

– I will give you the grain gift, said Eresh, of the fields ready to reap.

– Will you take us in as your own? asks the dark angel.

He's been silent up till now, letting the other do the prep-work, convince Eresh that they're both well and truly fallen. Anna doubts that the other one would be able to carry off this part. He sits on the chair where she got her tattoo now, head forward, in his hands. She wonders if he'll ever recover from the damage done to him.

– Oh, yes, little one. You're mine now, Eresh says. You belong here as much as anyone.

– That is not what we wish, the *kurgarra* and *galatur* said.

– Speak, then! What is it you wish?

– We ask for the ancient right of sanctuary.

– And I give you hospitality, she says. I offer you a river of blood to quench your rage. I offer you a harvest of souls to feed your grief. What do you want?

It's the old deal offered by every devil to the souls that turn up at the doors of hell. The absolute power in the damnation of death, freedom from life, from sorrow, from suffering for your own pain, or from empathy, suffering from the pain of others. To transform remorse into a passion, a power that can win you–

– Anything you want, she says. Anything.

– Only the wineskin hanging from the hook upon the wall, they answered.

– The body is owned by Inanna, said Eresh of the Greater Earth.

– Whether it is owned by queen or king, that is the only thing we wish.

And the dark-haired one raises his head, slowly, turning it, to meet her gaze, and raises his hand, slowly, turning it, to point across the room at Anna where she stands against the wall.

– You have rich tastes, says Eresh. A pair of lackeys who would feast upon a queen.

She has a wry, amused smile on her face as she turns and looks Anna up and down appraisingly, estimating worth or worthlessness, the degradation that these fallen angels would wreak on her and that she, in turn, would wreak on others with the vicious power of the violated. The dark angel walks across the room towards her, stops in front of her and reaches up to run his long, thin fingers over her cheek.

– She's all yours, says Eresh.

The dark angel nods, closes his eyes with the satisfaction of the moment, of things sealed perfectly with a few simple words.

– I can do anything I want with her? he says.

– Anything, says Eresh.

And the dark angel reaches into the inside pocket of his black suit jacket.

– Jack, he says – [the blond one starts, looks up] – Show my lady how grateful we are.

She gave the body of Inanna to them. The *kurgarra* crushed the food of life over the corpse. The *galatur* splashed the water of life upon the corpse.

Inanna Rose

The blond angel – Jack – leaps like a mountain lion, a flash of lightning, one arm slashing downwards, cutting not with claw though but with splash of crimson, purple, almost black ink, with a Jackson Pollock splatter across the unveiled face of Eresh, in her eyes, her mouth. She staggers back like she's been struck with acid, blinded, clutching at her face and howling.

Every bottle in the place shatters. The glass beads of the curtain shatter, raining out as dust into the outer room. The glass door of the shop blows out. The vial in the dark angel's hand explodes but he's already slapping his open hand across Anna's face, splattering his master's modern medicine across her cheek, dark ink and blood, hers and the angel's mixing where the shards of glass cut into her soft flesh and his, caught between his open palm and her cheek. And the pain burns in her face, on her cheekbone, on her temple, a searing migraine splitting her skull, drilling her brain. The whole left side of her goes numb, and like the victim of a stroke she loses balance, falls. The pain splits her in two. And it makes her feel alive.

And even as the fair-haired angel clamps his hand across Eresh's mouth, his other arm locking around her neck as he slams her against the wall, using all his weight to keep her from uttering another sound, the wordless howl of the queen of the dead still rings in Anna's ears, reverberates around the room, shattering glass in the framed prints of dragon designs and celtic knotwork, all the tribal or traditional tattoos that decorate the walls. Glass dust rains down on Anna on the floor.

– Get up, the dark-haired one is saying to her.

The other is shouting in the unkin tongue, trying to drown the muffled keen of Eresh, to bind her with words just as he binds her with his hand. Eresh pushes from the wall, forces the angel back and round, slams him against the doorframe, and Anna can see the angel's hand, the back of it bulging; she can hear the crack of bone. Even with the bitmites blinding the bitch queen of the underworld – and they must be burning in her brain the way they burn in Anna's, in Inanna's, in Phreedom's – even senseless with the chaos running riot on her, in her, Eresh's animal noise drives through the angel's hand like a nail, cracking it, splintering it.

– Get up.

Black ink pours from the shattered bottles on the shelves and countertop, running in rivulets down cabinet doors and walls, like rain on a window, trickling to this side or to that, in diagonal drunkard's trails of black dribblings that criss-cross, making signs and sigils that she recognizes. Droplets run upwards, defying the laws of physics to answer to their own internal laws. Drips hit the ground and vaporize to hissing steam, tendrils of gas that curl through the air, around the angel's legs, reaching and groping.

– Get up.

Skittering drops like insects run across her hands as she pushes herself up from the floor. The pain has moved round to the front of her head now, to the centre of her forehead, where it's hot, white. Her vision flickers between the world as it is and a photographic negative where black is white and white is black. The black suits of the angels glow, her knights in shining armour come to rescue her. The daylight world beyond the door is dark as night, a pitch black pit. She pushes herself up to her knees.

– Get up.

The noise of Eresh's fury is all round them now, reverberating in the walls, the floor, the ceiling; the room is alive with it, and alive with the black ink that crawls and scrawls, arcane and anarchic, everywhere she looks. It threatens to swallow them, this room alive with liquid language, but even in the chaos of it – the dark angel crouching before her like a drill sergeant, roaring at her to stand, the other locked with Eresh as they throw each other this way and that, crashing against the walls, the counter, knocking the chair over towards them – and the dark angel swats it away without even looking, and keeps on yelling at her without even stopping to take a breath – she feels it locking into order in her head, into a simple logical imperative.

She has to get up.

The living shadows of the room writhe in the air, acrid and choking, but they flow across her as they flow across the walls, some spreading out to fill the place with their mad rage, but others wrapping themselves around the fair-haired angel, lashing at him. She sees phrases forming on his flesh, a curse – an unforgotten fate – eat bread ploughed from earth – no food but dirt – no drink but from the drains – no seat but threshold steps – the drunk and thirsty strike your cheek.

She has to get up before Eresh breaks through the angel's binding hand and binding words, before she breaks through the angel.

– Get up, the dark angel shouts at her. He could just drag her to her feet but she knows that that would be no good. She has to do this for herself. She lays her right hand on the counter at her side and brings her left leg up to get her foot beneath her so she's only on one knee. The world flickers – black, white, black, white – in time with the pounding of her heart. She feels the counter, solid beneath her hand and she uses it, not the mass of it, not the structure, but the certainty, the physical reality.

And she drags herself back into the land of the living.

Inanna rose.

Frozen Between Eternity and Now

Inanna rose.

The room is silent. She stands there, feet apart – not as steady as she could be, but steady enough – her tattooed arm extended forward, palm outward, fingers spread to halt the world. On her arm the flesh engraving of the tattoo moves, black tracers running under her skin, flashing crimson, purple, as the scribe of the Covenant's bitmites deconstruct and reconstruct the story of her life – one of her lives, rather. Inanna's tale is still a part of her, as is Phreedom's, but like any tale retold it's changed in the telling. She's given her flesh and bone to a once-dead unkin, but she has her own soul back. The graving that is Phreedom emerges in the morphing pattern, clear and central – slightly changed, she notices, embellished with a little touch of something else, but still her in its essence – as the bitmites rewire her flesh, her scarred, stained soul, downloading what was coded into them by Metatron. She studies the alterations as they emerge, worried at first that the Covenant's scribe has put a little binding spell in there to tie her to him. But, no, she recognizes her own handiwork. And just as she once created the sprite with a gloved hand wired into virtual reality, the AI ghost of Phreedom's cypher lady recreates her through a sleeve of bitmites wired into the Vellum.

The *Anunnaki*, judges of the underworld, snatched at Inanna as she was about to rise up from the underworld.

The room is still. She stands there with her arm outstretched, buried up to the shoulder in the Vellum, holding the moment. The dark-haired angel still crouches on the floor; the other angel is locked with Eresh, blood running down the back of his hand, a splinter of bone protruding through the skin. Like a simworld paused by the flick of a finger, she holds it there.

It's not easy. The black ink of Madame Iris, of Eresh of the Greater Earth – the black blood of their ancestors, lords of heaven and earth, *anu* and *ki*, the liquid memory of the *Anunnaki* themselves – hangs in the air, frozen between eternity and now, but it takes everything she's got to keep her focus on the word in her head that holds the stuff frozen in time. These wisps of shadow are the shreds of unkin who died long before the Covenant was even thought of, before Enki, or Inanna, or even Eresh herself, were even born. They're powerful, as old as the first ivory spearthrower, older maybe, and it's only their cold detachment from their long-forgotten dreams of life that makes them answer to her will . . . because they have none of their own.

She holds the word in her head, like an equation on a mathematician's blackboard, or a mandala in a Buddhist monk's mind's eye, a mantra in his mouth; and she holds it in the pattern on her arm, the interface between the Vellum and her body that's as much the servant Lady Shubur as it is goddess Inanna, as much the sim sprite Cypher Lady as it is the coder Phreedom Messenger.

– No one rises up out of the underworld unmarked, they said.

The room is shadowed. The stuff is everywhere, on the walls, in the air, all over the four of them, and she can feel the intelligence in it, fed back in the sensations that creep across her skin. She's used to dealing with AI, with models of psychology defined in modular chunks or abstract networks, articulating them through visual or linguistic symbols, umpteenth generation metacode that's as far removed from the underlying bits and bytes as an architect's plans are from the atomic structure of the materials that will be used to build his house. And she's used to dealing with the unkin Cant, the language that makes machine code look like ... an architect's plans drawn with a crayon held in a straitjacketed lunatic's teeth.

This is something that she's never dealt with. It's more sentient than any AI, but more locked into its own abstracted logic than the most mechanical of programs. It's aware, it knows – she can feel it probing her, analysing her – but what it's aware of, what it knows, is only the certainty of its authority over reality. The ink, the blood of long-dead unkin, is so steeped in the Cant that it's become it, a living liquid language. And with her hand up to her shoulder in the Vellum, manipulating it, the stuff reacts automatically to her action, seeking a coherent resolution; it's like it needs to balance two sides of a complex equation in which she is just a variable.

– If Inanna wishes to return, she must provide someone to take her place here in the underworld.

The room is solid. She has to push herself through the thick structured space and time that fills it like she's wading through quicksand, and as she does so she still has to keep her focus on the word that keeps it that way. All she has to do is get out before the others break loose. She has her deal; the moment that she's out that door, she's free. The Covenant won't touch her. And they'll deal with the queen of the dead. At least she hopes so. She backs slowly away from Eresh and the angel who still holds the woman ... only just, it looks like. But there's the other angel – she nearly trips over him where he crouches on the floor and for a moment, the air quivers with life, a breath, a blink of an eye, before she catches the moment again – and she can see the hunch of his shoulders, the turn of his head towards Eresh, the hand coming out of his pocket with a knife. She looks back at the other angel, his splintering hand, the pain of the curse written on his face. She doubts that he'll survive, but he only has to hold on long enough for the other one to reach them with the knife; he only has to hold on for this moment that she's holding and the moment that will follow it, inexorably, as soon as she lets go. All she has to do is get what she came here for and get out the door.

The black stuff starts to move, crawling through the cracks in her will as liquid trickles through fingers. It doesn't like the ... logic of this ending. It thinks she ought to stay dead, stay the scarred and violated hollow creature that she was. She doesn't agree. Her right hand still held out in front of her like some crazed king ordering back the sea, she reaches behind her with the other hand, onto the counter, and feels it come to rest upon the book of gravings, still lying where Madame Iris left it.

And then she's running, and the dark angel is turning, pouncing, and Eresh's word is piercing through the hand across her mouth, and the black stuff is pouring towards her, and the angel with the corn-blond hair is falling from the queen of the dead and screaming words of fire, even as the knife sinks into the woman's throat and Anna, Inanna, Phreedom, bursts through the curtain and dives through the wooden frame of the shattered door and out of this little pocket of hell and back into reality, the blood and flame behind her, blossoming like crenellations of a black carnation.

Dressed in Soiled Sackcloth

As Inanna rose up from the underworld, the *ugallu*, the demons of the underworld, stuck to her side, like reeds around her, small and large, like picket fences all around her. In front of her walked one who held a sceptre, though he was no minister. At her back walked one who held a mace, although he was no warrior. The *ugallu* were demons who knew no food, who knew no drink, who ate no offerings, drank no libations, took no gifts. They had no love for sex, no children to kiss. They lived to tear a wife from her husband's arms, to tear a child from its father's knees, to steal the bride from her marriage bed.

The demons stuck to her.

Anna runs a single finger over the copy of the graving of Inanna, tracing the story in its pattern towards the conclusion. It's not her story any more, not completely, but it's still close enough to worry her. She's not just Phreedom Messenger any more; she has the Cypher Lady's memories of laying out the deal to Metatron in a hotel room, not a visual memory but the strange Cubist mechanical awareness of the sim; and there's a little bit of her that will be forever Inanna, scheming, ambitious Inanna, so it takes a lot for her to only use the book for what she needs. Some nights she flicks through it, studying the marks of dead gods printed in there, and knowing that she has a power in her hands that Metatron would kill her for, immunity or no immunity. She knows she has the skill required to bind these marks into new flesh; she could build a fucking army of VR gods and send them out to take the Covenant apart from the inside out. But she also wonders how many more of these lost souls Madame Iris has already restored to new flesh, where they are now, what they might think of the girl who sold their mistress out for her own hide. They might be grateful for their liberation, but they might just as easily hate her for it.

She stands up from the dresser and walks over to the window of the motel room again. There's no sign of anything out there, just the low, wooden fence across the parking lot, the highway on the other side of it with cars humming up and down, north and south, and the fields across the road, tall grasses blowing in the winds, but she's still sure they're there. Whatever they are, she's sure they're there.

The part of her that is the Cypher Lady, the sim, a sentience in virtual flesh, can hear them in the crackle of the Vellum.

Outside the palace gates, the Lady Shubur, dressed in soiled sackcloth, waiting, saw Inanna with the *ugallu* all round her, and she hurled herself into the dust down at Inanna's feet.

– Walk on, Inanna, the *ugallu* said. We will take Lady Shubur in your place.

– No, cried Inanna. Lady Shubur is my steadfast support, the *sukkal* who gives wise advice, the soldier who stands at my side. She remembered my commands, sounded a lamentation for me in the ruins. She pounded the drum for me at the assemblies where the unkin gather, and around the houses of the gods. She tore at her eyes, her mouth, her thighs. She wore the beggar's single robe of soiled sackcloth and, alone, she set out for the temple of Lord Ilil in Nippur. She went to the temple of Sin in Ur, to the temple of Enki in Eridu. She saved my life. I'll never give the Lady Shubur to you.

– Walk on then, the *ugallu* said. And we will walk with you to Umma.

She cracks another beer with the bottle-opener on her key ring and sits back down at the dresser, at the book of marks that lies open at Inanna's. It's different to the one tattooed on her arm now, but there are points of congruence, similarities as well as differences, and sometimes they change. She feels herself changing with the graving at those points. Sometimes it's like a fever as she burns with the rage of the girl who once swore she would kill them all, that she would *fucking kill them all*, other times it's like all the heat just drained right out of her and she feels dead again, cold and dead. Sometimes she finds herself looking in the mirror and not knowing who she is under her skin, if anything, seeing herself standing there in a scuffed black-leather biker's jacket, seeing herself in soiled sackcloth, tearing her fingernails down one cheek. She's broken a lot of hotel mirrors, screaming at them. She has cigarette burns in her left arm where she's had to remind herself she's still alive. She's not entirely sure the graving downloaded into her by Metatron's bitmites is truly stable, and she's not entirely sure that she is.

But she's sure that it was worth it.

The book is open at the graving of Shamash and she stares at it. Dumuzi's friend who tried so hard to save him and failed. It's Finnan's mark, without a doubt, except it's simpler, cruder, like a ... prototype, like the original version of a story that's been told again and again over the centuries, complexifying with each cycle, a story she was fool enough to write herself into.

She flicks the pages of the book until she finds the mark she's looking for, the graving of Inanna's shepherd-boy lover, known to the Sumerians as Dumuzi, known to the Babylonians as Tammuz. She wonders, looking at it, if the mark she remembers seeing on Thomas's chest, when he opened up his shirt to show her in that roadhouse in the mountains, if it always looked like this or if her memory changed as his mark did, under the needle.

A Door Out of Reality

At the holy shrine in Umma, Shara, son of proud Inanna, was wearing the soiled sackcloth. He saw Inanna with the *ugallu* all round her, and he hurled himself into the dust down at her feet.

— Walk on to your city, Inanna, the *ugallu* said. We will take Shara in your place.

— No, cried Inanna. Not my son, not Shara who sings hymns to me, who clips my nails and slips his fingers through my hair. I'll never give Shara to you.

— Walk on then, the *ugallu* said. And we will walk with you to Badtibira.

She opens up the throttle on the bike and lets it roar for her the way she wants to roar, to rage against the fucking unkin, angels and devils, all of them, every fucking one of them. She wants to see them all dead. She wants to see their bodies broken and bloody. Let them rip each other apart. Let them tear each other's hearts out. Let the devils burn and the angels fall. Let every motherfucking one of them be crucified as they deserve to be, as every god deserves to be. Phreedom is going to get the fuck out of their world and leave them to it. She swings the bike around the hairpin bend high on the mountainside as if she's hoping, praying that she'll lose control. But she recovers, swings back up and leans the other way to take another curve at the same speed. Scree scatters under her tyres.

The black car follows her, close on her tail, but she doesn't see it, blinkered by the helmet and her own thousand-yard stare

*

At the holy shrine in Badtibira, Lulal, son of proud Inanna, was wearing the soiled sackcloth. He saw Inanna with the *ugallu* all round her, and he hurled himself into the dust down at her feet.

— Walk on to your city, Inanna, the *ugallu* said. We will take Lulal in your place.

— Not Lulal, my son, Inanna cried. He is a king amongst men, my right arm and my left arm. I'll never give Lulal to you.

— Walk on to your city then, Inanna, the *ugallu* said. And we will walk with you to the great apple tree in Uruk.

They're closing on her as she hits the tunnel, as she swerves to overtake a station wagon, going so fast the driver freaks and shreds the side of his car against the brick wall in a scream of sparks and bounces the lumbering auto right across to make the other side shriek, into the path of the sleek black auto which veers, just clips it, sending chrome bumpers rolling through the air. She can see them in the mirror. She can see the fuckers leaning forward, the one with dark hair behind the wheel, the other in the passenger seat, his bloody hand pressed against the windshield, flames burning in the sockets of his eyes, and she knows that they don't work for Metatron any more, and they don't work for Eresh; they work for something that's only concern, that's only motivation, is the brutal aesthetic of a proper ending, of a fate written and bound, eternal and unchanging. And she won't fucking give them it.

At the tunnel's end the road twists sharp round to the right, but she doesn't turn the bike; she ploughs straight through the barrier, over the handlebars and through the air, through leaves and branches and broken bones and torn flesh and through a door out of reality and into the Vellum.

Through the Long Grass

In Uruk, under a tree of golden apples and green leaves, Tammuz, the lover of Inanna, sat, sheened in his *me*-garments, lounging, still, upon his throne. Inanna fastened on Tammuz the gaze of death, spoke out against him words quiet in wrath, uttered against him cries of shame, of blame:

– Take him! Take Tammuz away! Wash him with pure water and anoint him with sweet oil. Clothe him in a red robe and let the pipes of lapis lazuli play. Let all the party-girls raise up a loud lament for him. Take him away.

She lies there on the ground, looking up at blue sky, at an impossible crescent sun, at the boughs of a tree that dapple the golden light with mottled greens, and at her brother's face. He tries to stop her, but she's already muttering the charms she needs to give her the strength, she's already dragging herself up to him with one arm around his neck and reaching inside her jacket with the other. It's a page torn from the book, the mark of Tammuz, and she shows it to him, hands it to him while she pulls her broken arm out of its sleeve. She has to wipe the blood off to show him where her story and his meet, here in the Vellum, the end of her story and the beginning of his. In Uruk, under a tree of golden apples and green leaves ...

She curses him as a fucking idiot, as a fool, as a coward.

He shakes his head. She doesn't understand. It's going to be OK.

She can hear them coming through the long grass, the things that Metatron created, that Eresh destroyed and that the machine souls of a thousand long-dead unkin have sent out to close the door and keep them sealed inside their fates. She has the knife out of her pocket now and she fumbles with it in her left hand as she twists her arm round to find the place, the right combination of signs and sigils. In Uruk, under a tree of golden apples and green leaves ...

All she has to do is cut it off, cut that little part of herself off, and it doesn't have to happen that way. She can rewrite the story, change it. He can too. Doesn't he see?

He shakes his head. She doesn't understand. They *are* the story now. The angels, the demons, none of them matter; it's *their* story now. It's going to be OK.

– You'll always be getting captured, she says.

– And I'll always be escaping them.

– They'll kill you, over and over and over again.

– And all the time I'll still be here, he says, under a tree of golden apples and green leaves.

*

She holds the shred of skin in her hand now, leaning her broken body back against the tree, blinded by blood and tears. The two creatures stand behind him but the three of them just wait, wait for her to say the word in a moment of sunlight and pain that stretches out for an eternity. He has the knife in his hand but he won't do it to himself. All he has to do is cut that little bit out of himself and they can walk away from this together. That's all he has to fucking do. She bites her bottom lip and tries to pull herself up but she's too weak, too broken and wounded to do anything other than lie there. But she's alive, and she's free and she looks at him and hates him for it, for leaving her alive and free when he is not, when he could be, he fucking could be if he'd just listen to her, just this once, do what she tells him.

He drops the knife.

– Damn you, she says, and the demons' hands clamp round her brother's arms, start to pull him back away from her into the blur of sunlight and green.

He shakes his head. She doesn't understand. It's going to be OK.

Errata

Under a Tree of Golden Apples

Late afternoon sunlight of summer casts its shadows long as I walk through the grass towards the napping, nodding youth with his green hair and scrag of a goatee, and the horns of a kid, of the eternal kid, pinking the air through his scruff of tousle. He lies against the tree, in doze or daze, in a haze of whirlicues of smoke that furl up from a precarious cone of paper wedged between index and forefinger in his hand lain across his lap. A stoned Pan in green combats and layers of beads and necklaces under his lolling head, something of yester years, something of modern times, and something of the days lost in between. His face, familiar but unplaced in my memory, displaced by the horns, I approach with puzzlement, eyes peering as if to resolve his identity in a blur that's truer than sharp focus, until ten foot away, my shadow falls across the orchard sprite.

He brings the cone of a joint up languidly to his lips, and with a lick of them first he slips a suck, holds curling pluming smoke in his open grin for a second before deepdrawing down into his lungs, and it's the motion that I recognise, finally in a forgotten face.

– Puck, I say. Thomas.

– Do I know you? he says, blinking, fluttering his eyes against the low sun. He accepts the name without question, with only a slim curiosity in his half-shut eyes and raised brows, not asking why I call him by these names, but who I am to know them.

– Reynard, I say, but I'm not sure if that means anything to this horned echo of my past. Is this Puck mine, Jack's fairy fuck and Joey's *fucking fairy*? Or is he just some cognate avatar of attitude cut from the same mould in this altered world deep in the Vellum, an apple fallen from the same tree, with the same juicy tartness in his relishing touch of tip of tongue to lips?

– Reynard the Fox? he says. The King of Thieves, no less.

I have no idea if he's being serious here, but then I never did.

– I–

It's so long since I have practised speech to anyone other than myself, I find it hard to form my sense into a sentence.

– I am at your service, my fine sir, he says, twirling his hand and showering hot rocks through the air in a most Puckly gesture. What can I do you for? You need someone to drive the getaway car? You know how fast I am in flight. Or is it a distraction that you need while you sneak in, in dead of night, to steal the crown jewels of the God of Light? I can be very distracting, you know.

And even though he's patently not the Puck I knew, he's Puck all right.

– I think, I say, we better . . . start . . . from the beginning.

He tells me he was born under a bad signpost, stolen from gypsies as a young child, raised by werewolves in the wilderness, ran away from the circus, bought the devil's soul and sold his arse on the streets of Heaven.

– What's your story? I ask him, and he says:

– Which one? he says, I fought the Law and won. I shot the sheriff *and* his deputy. I –

I hold up a hand.

There is a gleam of deviousness in his eyes that quite belies the innocence of his smile, and I know it's going to be impossible to separate the fabrication from the facts; looking at him, I'm not even sure that there *are* any facts.

– Do you remember Jack? I ask. If there is anything to connect this Puck to my long-lost reality it has to be poor, crazy Jack.

– Jack Flash? he says.

Jack Flash?

I think of Jack with his flame hair and his wild laughing eyes, the passion burning in his soul for Puck and burning in his head after . . . It has to be the one.

– I thought Jack Flash was dead, says Puck.

But that's not right; Thomas is dead, I'm dead, if this place, this Vellum, is what I've always thought it is, but I left Jack behind me very much alive. Ten thousand years ago? Ten thousand years ago, long turned to dust. I look at this Puck. Time, in the Vellum, it seems, is not so simple.

– I don't know, I say.

– Man, says Puck. Jack Flash is my fucking hero.

He flicks the joint away into the air in spirals of sparks.

– If Jack's alive, he says, I've got to get him back.

He licks his lips.

The Broken Seven

The five of them stand there in a row, shiftless, uneasy without Carter and Pechorin to speak for them, unaware of even why they've lost their fire and their ice. The one at the far left keeps glancing at the two pillars with the relevant gravings, unfortunate reminders. It wasn't necessary for the rest of them to be involved, Metatron explains. The sacrifice was required but he could not afford to lose them all, the Covenant could not afford to lose them all. There is no need to worry; Carter and Pechorin will be back shortly.

In truth, of course, from the sheer howling quake that blasted through the Vellum, raking every unkin this side of eternity, with the death-cry of Eresh, but more from the burning, blinding sear of light that followed, and the deafening, icy silence in its wake, Metatron can tell those two are never coming back. But the others don't need to know this. When the right two newbloods come along, he'll simply tweak their souls here and there in the renaming and bind them into this seven as their replacements. They won't be called Carter or Pechorin, but those human names are meaningless anyway. One angel of fire is all angels of fire. One angel of ice is all angels of ice. But he gives this broken seven the reassurances they need, patching over the cracks in their gestalt identity.

They're not the only cracks he has to worry about.

The news on the net is now reporting the discovery of an exciting new cache of cuneiform tablets looted from the ruins of the Baghdad Museum of Antiquities back at the start of the Middle East War, where they had lain forgotten and untranslated for half a century under various turbulent or tyrannical regimes, now seized by US troops in a sting on stolen artefacts being used to fund the never-ending cells of terrorists streaming in from Syria, Iran, the Yemen,

Saudi Arabia. The first tentative translations, the text scrolling across his lenses tells him, appear to indicate that this is an entirely unknown epic, telling of the conquering of the underworld by the god of war. They've christened it The Death of Ereshkigal. This is only one of the more rational and comprehensible effects. A new cult has appeared in Indian history, according to his cross-referencing search, a group called Thuggees worshipping a goddess of death called Kali, now eradicated, it seems, but still an alteration. Infant mortality rates. Flocking patterns of vultures. And those are just the start.

But it's the other cracks that worry him more. The disruptions in the temporal world from Eresh's death were to be expected, and with her having kept herself hidden in little nooks and crannies over most of humanity's written history, crawling in the dust and darkness, the majority of the changes are minor. Nothing like the shitstorm that happened when Marduk carved up Tiamat into little pieces; they called that the Neolithic Revolution. And Pechorin's death seems to have had all but no effect. But Carter is different. This little angel of fire, this nobody, this mere footsoldier in the war against the Sovereigns, the endless enemies of the Covenant, has left a trail of debris scattered through the Vellum and the world written in lines and solid shapes of certainty upon it that is completely disproportionate to his worthlessness.

Folklore and fairy stories, Jack the Giant-Killer, Jack and the Beanstalk. An urban legend from eighteenth-century London – Spring-heeled Jack – some fire-eyed demon leaping from rooftop to rooftop in impossible bounds. From London again, Victorian-era, a killer slaughtering prostitutes in Whitechapel. Calico Jack, a pirate of the Caribbean. A whole new musical movement finding an icon in an obnoxious orange-haired thug in shredded clothing wearing a flag now called the Union Jack. Fifty-two cards in a deck that once held forty-eight. Spring-loaded children's toys and balls in sports that go back centuries. All from this nobody, this nothing. It's like a million little sparks of his shatterling soul have started forest fires everywhere they fell.

Metatron dismisses the five and starts to contemplate the clean-up operation. At least, he doesn't have the Messengers to worry about now. Their inevitable story has the boy doomed the next time he sees his sister, and she herself, well, she'll be just another little demon, hating the world for what it's done to her. And revenge is so much more predictable than ambition as a motivation.

But Jack . . .

On Metatron's earphones, the words of a suddenly famous rock song howl.

I was born in a crossfire hurricane . . .

VOLUME TWO

Evenfall Leaves

The Song of Silence

Of Kings and Battles

Within the cavern of the tavern, two young hawks called Chrome and Mainsail spy old wily foxy Silence lain asleep, veins swollen with the wine of yesterdays and yesteryears as ever. Garlands slip, slide from his head, fall rolling to one side. A heavy wine-jar hangs by its worn handle.

They approach him, tentative until a flurry of wings behind them strengthens their faint hearts as Eagle, fairest of the knights, comes down to join them. The old man's teased them all just once too often with the promise of a song, and now they fall on him, to tie him up in his own laurels. Eyes wide open now and wrinkling, twinkling under the blood-red stains of mulberries smeared over his brow and temples, he laughs at their crafty scheme, cries out.

– Why all these bonds? Release me, boys. You've made your point and it's enough that you had the audacity to try, to think you have the strength to hold me. Well, you've earned your songs. Go on. List all you want. For you, it will be songs.

He looks from Chrome to Mainsail, back again, and at the Eagle in her adamantium armour and her wings. Fierce fire in her features; there's a battle going on within her, between fate and freedom, the mark carved on her soul, the name held in her heart. He winks.

– I have another payment set aside for her.

And with that he begins.

*

– When once I sang of kings and battles, gods of synthe twitched at my ear and told me this: *Teacher, a shepherd should have sheep full-fed and fat but he should sing a slender song.* So now, my faeries, since you have so many pressing to express their praise for you, your various deeds and dreary wars, I'll muse instead, on this slim pipe cut from a reed, upon the rural idyll, fold my song into the fields . . . as our first tales once deigned to dabble with the kind of verse that sires accuse, shameless, unblushing as it dwelt in woods of dappled light.

They don't look pleased, but Silence shrugs, the herdsman of his own soul.

– I babble only if my safety's vouched. Remember, faeries, if there's one, if there is one who reads of you in rapture, then our tamarisks and all the forest shall resound and sing of you, of you. And there could be no page more precious to the sun than that on which your name is writ.

And Chrome and Mainsail lay their weapons down, nodding assent to listen to a tale of other glories than their own.

– Well then, let us proceed godspeed, you virgin pyres, with music of the sickle, but let's sing a song slightly more solemn. Humble hedge and tamarisk do not serve everybody's taste; if we must sing of woods, let woods be worthy of a consul.

Now, indeed, you might see fauns dance to the beat, cavort with wild things of the woods, and sullen oaks bow down and sway their heads in time. Pernicious cliffs never rejoiced so much in being ravished by the sun, nor did the open road shimmer so sleek with rapture in the airs of Orphan's songs. For Silence sings.

The Silence of a Moment

Endhaven.

The dark sea crashes low, slow and rhythmic on the beach where chains and charms strung all along the wire fence jingle and jangle; and, up in the turmoil of the blue-black dust clouds overhead, gulls wheel, crying merciless complaints against the cold wind's moaning: and over all this I hear the bells of the rag-and-bone-man's cart, way off in the distance, cutting through it all, and I turn to Jack where he lies beside me, just so I can see his closed eyes and feel a little bit more secure.

– Are you awake? I say.

He mumbles something.

– Are you alive? I say, prodding his side with a finger.

– Something like that, he says, laughing. I stroke his arm, his cool smooth skin, and slip my hand into his. Jack gives my hand a squeeze but otherwise he is as still as the ground underneath us. Dead man Jack, mystery man Jack, breathing only when he wants to speak, is the silence of a moment, a moment drawn out to eternity. Lying curled in beside him, I can't help but expect the natural rise and fall of normal respiration, the steady rhythm of a heartbeat. The tension of anticipation, the disjunction of the way things were and the way things . . . are, is something I have never gotten used to, and I'm not sure I want to. Jack's otherness is exciting to me; I have a hunger for the secret to his stillness.

– Why won't you tell me who you are? I say.

– I'm Jack.

He grins, an eyebrow raised as if to say, what more needs to be said?

– You know that's not what I—

He hushes me with a finger to his blue lips.

– No questions, he says. No questions, no lies, OK?

I stare at him silently for a second then let go of his hand and stand up, brushing sand off my trousers. It opens up a space between us, both physical and . . . aesthetic; there's a wrongness about me in my black trousers, white shirt, and this beautiful naked man lying on the sand. I remember seeing some French painting years back in a book old Mr Hobbsbaum bought from the rag-and-bone-man, to teach me and the other youngsters about Art – Impressionism and such; it had these old guys in fancy black coats sitting having a picnic with a naked woman, and none of them seemed to be bothered about the fact that she was naked and they were clothed. What was she meant to be – an artist's model, a whore hired by the idle rich? Mostly me and the other kids just giggled because it was a dirty picture, but I remember the way that woman

229

stared out of the painting, like a challenge. What's wrong with this picture?

– Don't look so sullen, says Jack.

– I should get back, I say. It's got to be past midday.

– Come on; don't be so hurt. Stay a little longer. You only just got here.

– If you tell me who you are.

I pick up my jacket and pull it on.

– I can't, he says, climbing to his feet.

He opens his mouth like he wants to explain, then just shakes his head. Mystery man Jack, dead man Jack, his refusal to speak about – to even admit to – his past only makes my frustration more persistent, teases desire into need.

– Don't you love me? No, don't answer that.

I look out past the line of crosswise-lashed steel spikes and windings of barbed wire between them and I think of history books, of wartime beaches mined to keep the enemy from invading – except that, with its tinkling watch-chains and key-chains and whatever, this isn't a defence against a foreign military, but against something less tangible. I look out at the slop of grey waves, hating myself for saying it – *don't you love me* – even if it was meant to be ironic, knowing that it isn't really and that the more I grasp at him the more he draws back, but too weak to stop myself. I just want to know why he won't let me get close to him.

– Tom, he says.

The United States of Anachronisms

Anna kicks down the bike stand, looks across the parking lot of the roadhouse and the bowling alley that share the same building here, buried in the woods just off the Business 70, to the floodlit baseball field where the little leaguers with their parents mill in the excitement pre or post game. Post, she thinks. It's just coming on for evening, maybe seven or so; she'd be surprised if all the kiddies were just coming out to play. But it's impossible to say, the way they throng and chatter, children's giggles like the chirps of birds, and fathers lowing, proud bulls in their baseball caps, mullets beneath, and all the mothers with kids skipping round their legs, Ma, Ma. Ma!

She feels something that she can't quite place in words and sentences, a yearning for their mundane lives, sorrow for what she knows is coming to them all, a bitterness at the easy banality of it all – something she'll never have herself – a joy in the absurd simplicity of lives free of the demons driving her these days, a wonder that these people somehow disregard the evenfall – the Evenfall – spreading across their world, sweeping in shadows up from under trees. A horror that the world they know has already started falling apart, that they're still bringing children into it. Don't they watch the news?

There's no news on any of the screens in Ivan's – sports bar grill and steakhouse of the sort so typical in this part of the Vellum masquerading as the southern states of North America. The States. O, yes, they live in states alright – in states of ignorance and bliss, in states of rural godliness and patriotic faith, of temperance and trust, their car doors left unlocked, their smiles given freely, easily, even to a strange girl in a biker jacket and thick, black mascara, entirely alien to their whole mode of existence. The waitress who takes her to the smoking booth – old habits die hard – is genuinely pleased to see her; there's no *hippy goth freak we don't like your sort around here* ambience. That's all bullshit. People aren't always afraid of what they don't know; sometimes they just blank the strangeness out and go on with their lives, living only in as much of the world as they can deal with.

So there's no news on any of the screens in Ivan's, not on the big video screen behind the squared-out horseshoe of a bar, or any of the small screens in the corners. There's no news in Ivan's, just baseball, football, Nazcar racing, and karaoke. Shit. Karaoke. She looks at the photocopied notice on the dark wood panel wall of the booth, coming events – and, yup, tonight's the 12th, she's sure. She smiles a grimace to herself, and wonders what she's going to have to sit through … 'Stand By Your Man' and 'Achy Breaky Heart', some shit like that. Fuck that shit. But she's already ordered.

Two younger guys are winding up this old beer-bellied drunk sat at the bar beside her booth – *Come on, you gotta, yeah, come on, hey* – [one of them turns to her, the blond one ... he looks vaguely and uncomfortably familiar] – *tell him that he should sing.*

She smiles and slurps her Mountain Dew, wishing she could be drunk like them.

– Go on, she says to the old guy, joining the fun, the hospitality of participation offered by the local youngblood.

And the old guy wipes his hand across his thick, white, mountain beard and, grinning, stumbles from his stool to take the stand to whistles and cheers.

The Song of Silence

He sings of the vast void and of seeds, of shatterings and scatterings and gatherings, of seeds of earth and air and sea and flickerings of flecks, the flash, the flux of fire. He sings of the beginnings of all things in these original forms of force, and how a young curved world took shape, unfurled its involutions and emerged in evolution, revelation of its own course; how its hard crust sealed eternal nevers in the deep blue-black of ocean and the world took form, little by little, in ephemera; of the awestruck earth watching a newborn sunrise shining, and the showers of the rainfall out of clouds high in the sky; of the time when forests first began to spring, and of the living creatures roaming, far and wide, over the unknown and unknowing wilderness of hills.

He sings of the first little gifts of the uncultivated earth: foxgloves in every dell, smiling acanthus mingled with the gypsy lilies, and wild ivy wandering everywhere; the goats that wander home unherded, udders stretched with milk; the oxen with no fear of any lion, not for all his might; and of our very cradles flowering with soft caressing blossoms; of the snake perished among the poisonous plants, and perfumes of azure breathing from every hedge.

He sings of the marvel of a maiden gathering the golden fruit of hesperidium; he sings rings of moss-bound bitter bark around the alder sisters of a photon, brings them springing from the ground to tower tall as poplars. He sings how, as the gulls strayed by permissive streams, one of the sisters of the music led him up into the mountains of the aeons, how the choir of the sun rose up before him; how a shepherd singer of divine lines, hair entwined with blossoms and bitter parsley, spoke to him:

– These pipes of reeds you see – take them. The music gives them to you, just as once it gave them to a scarred old man to rhyme, to draw down ash trees rooted deep in time, down from the hills. With these, tell of the birth of the grinning forest, pride of all the groves of Apple.

He sings of after times, when we've all learned at last to read the praise of heroes and ancestor's deeds and know what manhood is, of how the corn will flood the fields with golden, shimmering grain, the reddening grape hang heavy on untended vines, and solid oak will seep with sap that is part honey and part dew.

Blue Like the Veins in Marble

He lays his hand on the back of my neck and turns me to face him. I pull away.

– Tom, look at me.

I look.

Jack is tall and sleek, lithe like a cat, every contour of his muscles easily visible; veins snake around them, blue like the veins in marble under his translucent white skin. Sand dusts his body and his fair hair which blows everywhere in the crisp sea-breeze. Naked, he brushes at the sand on his hip and, as always, I find it difficult to look him in the eyes and even harder to look anywhere else. At his scarred right hand which looks like someone drove a nail through it. At the scars running across his chest, mark of some awful time of suffering, of abuse or penitence. More questions. I grew up with Endhaven's black-suit-and-tie ideas of 'decency', and though I've been around Jack for at least two years now I still feel as uncomfortable with his nudity as he seems to be with my questions.

He stands there, as calm in his flesh as some alien or angel with no idea what this human thing called sex is.

I found Jack two years back, washed ashore on the beach like so much driftwood, face-down, half-shrouded in a black-green slithe of seaweed, and cold and dead. It was early morning and, as I came down the dirt path from town to watch the silver daybreak over the ocean horizon, I saw him lying there. First thing I noticed was the fear in the gulls. They strutted around in a rough circle twelve feet or so in diameter, cawing and flapping their wings as if to scare off an intruder. Next thing I saw was the arm stretched out in the low surf, hand clenched in a rigor mortis fist. And then, although half-hidden by the shreds and bubbles of kelp, I noticed the latticework of scars that hatched his chest and I realized that he was like us, like the rest of us in Endhaven – marked by the needle and scarred by the knife.

But Jack's something different. Where we all have just a memory of a tattoo and a small diamond of pink scar tissue on a shoulder or a thigh, Jack's whole chest is carved in a filigree of skin.

– Tom, he says, you're young and I'm . . . I'm not. I've seen what's out there.

– Come on, I say. You make it sound like I'm—

– Younger than me, he cuts in.

He doesn't look it. At least, not much. Smooth-skinned and soft unshaven, he doesn't look any older than twenty-five max and me, I turned seventeen in Damnuary. He glares up at a gull, sighs and goes on.

– I know, Tom, believe me; I know you're not some idiot fucking kid. A kid fucking an idiot, maybe – [he smiles wryly] – but not an idiot fucking kid. But you don't know what damage a little knowledge can do. People can get hurt.

– What people? What knowledge?

Did you tell *them*, I want to ask him, how you can live and walk and be here with me without breath, without a heartbeat? Did you tell *them* whether you're even human, whether you've *ever* been human, because *I* don't know that much?

– What damage? I say. What people? Who did you hurt?

234

– Let it drop, Tom, he says quietly, and I back down, drop my gaze.

The gulls scatter as I slide down the dunes and move in closer. There's no smell of decay, only the pungent salt of seaweed, rich enough to taste; no bloating or rot on the body either, so he can't have been dead long. It's the first time I've seen a dead body and I'm scared. Death is something from the old world, from the cities. This is Endhaven, where people don't die, people don't just disappear out of your life with no good reason; that's why we're here. That's why we left the city. Here, at least, when people go it's because of a decision. A weighing of the scales. A reckoning. Death is an arbitrary, senseless thing, belonging with the chaos of the city crumbling on its headland out across the bay. A body washed up on the beach.

I crouch down to clear some of the debris and detritus, slip my hands under his smooth torso and heave him over onto his back. The body is in perfect condition, more like a statue than a corpse, some construction of erotic tranquillity. My dry throat, my tight balls, my erection, my heartbeat – I'm not sure I can tell the difference between my fear and my desire. It's sick, I'm sure, but I don't have a say in being, you know, and, anyway, it used to be OK they tell me . . . once upon a time, in a place far, far away.

Slowly, the fist uncurls, a little silvery box inside it, a cigarette lighter clutched like a talisman.

The Simple Pleasure of a Good, Square Meal

She closes her hand around the Zippo.
– What can I get ya to drink, honey?
– A Mountain Dew, she says.
She wishes she could have a beer – God, how she wishes she could have a beer – but she's driving, got the bike parked in the lot outside, and you can't have a designated driver on a bike ... not that she's got anyone to drive her home, anyway. Not that she's got a home to go to anyway, just another motel room. It's kind of lucky that McDowell is a dry county, though she's not exactly sure how

you can call the county dry with Ivan's roadhouse selling beer, bottled or draught – they've even got Guinness, shit, Finnan would be pleased – and the gas station out beside the Comfort Inn, its wall of fridges stocked with stacks of Bud and Miller, Coors and whatnot. God, how she wants a beer. But she can't have one; it's not just the driving, anyway.

– You ready to order?

She asks for the fillet mignon, caesar salad first, and after she's crunched her way through croutons drizzled with dressing, munched the greenery from an idle fork that hangs in the air every so often as she watches the New Jersey Devils put another puck into the net, after she's finished the salad, laid her cutlery together on a napkin to the side so she'll still have it for the main course, the waitress comes out with a ribeye, a huge slab of red meat served with mounds of cracked potato and red onion. It looks good, and from the menu she can tell that this is the house specialty; so she feels a little awkward, trying hard not to come off obnoxious as she calls the waitress back and says this isn't what she ordered, sorry.

Fifteen, twenty minutes later, she's got her fillet mignon. More apologies and good-natured smiles on both sides – *you need a refill, there?*

– Sure, thanks.

The waitress fills her glass from a clear, plastic jug.

The steak tastes great.

She settles back after the meal, feeling her stomach full to bursting, sated with the simple pleasure of a good, square meal. Square is the word in this little area of the Vellum. All the eateries she passed before she found this place were perfectly in tune with the terrain, the time and space of it – Hardee's and Wendy's, Taco Bell or Pizza Hut, a fifties-themed diner called Moondoggy's. She stopped to look at a menu in the window of a Japanese and realized it was basically all the same dish, different meats – stir-fry prawns with rice, or stir-fry chicken with rice, or stir-fry beef, or prawns *and* chicken, chicken *and* beef, beef *and* prawns. No miso soup here, no tempura here, no sushi.

Ivan's is not exactly cosmopolitan either, but who gives a fuck? They do know how to cook a steak, seared on the outside, blood-red on the inside, and the beef is good, high-quality Angus beef raised on the lush dairy farms of a land that's wetter than you might expect if you didn't know the little highlands nestling around the Blue Ridge Mountains.

She eats a lot of red meat, these days; can't get enough of it.

She runs a hand over her full-filled stomach, ever-so-slightly bulging now.

And she realizes that she's got a cigarette smoking in her other hand, a pack of Marlboro sitting on the table beside her silver Zippo where she's lain them down unconsciously, completely unaware of ever bringing them out of her jacket pocket, tapping a smoke out of the pack, tapping it down on the pack between her thumb and forefinger, turning it round to slip between her lips and flicking the lighter open and lit and shut again with a flutter of her thumb. She looks around for an ashtray, holding the bastard nicotine demon away from her, like she's got shit on her fingers and she really needs a wetwipe. A hand-motion to the waitress. An ashtray brought over, wiped, lain on her table. Thanks.

She grinds the cigarette down into the glass.

Her fingers tap unconsciously as she gazes round the bar, needing some distraction from the demon. The old guy's still singing; surprisingly it's not the C & W she expected, but something much more bluegrass – country, yes, and western, yes, but more folksy and bluer, truer.

The Liquid Light of Language

And he tells of the pyre that cast stones into men when Crow was king with all the cawing, raucous birdmen of his caucus, tells of the theft of primal theos and his torture on the rock, watching the Eagle as he talks of carrion's king and warrior hawks. Of fate and freedom, thieves of fire.

He sings, to Chrome and Mainsail, how the sailors of the argot called, cried for their hylic loss, lost at the fountain, calling out until *Alas! Alas!* called back in echo from the solid shore as they themselves set off again upon the liquid light of language, leaving the land, and all the matters of the flesh behind, a fallen comrade. He works on the loyalties of brothers-in-arms. He works his charms.

The two young guys, one blond, one dark, watch him intently as he sings some sentimental song about a war on foreign soil, about an old soldier who's lost his rabbit's foot, who's lost his friends, who's lost his faith, and comes looking for some other kind of enchanting charms, in a whore's arms. She can't date it, doesn't recognize it; it could be about the Second World War or Vietnam, Korea or Iraq, Iran, or even the unnamed – undefined, not limited by a name – inferno of firefights all across the Middle East right now. The stuff that's on the news that no one's watching here in Ivan's.

– Dogtags and rosaries. Bodies bagged liked groceries. Delivered to your door. Dogtags and rosaries. Folded flags and ribboned trees . . . mean nothing to a whore.

The blond guy takes a deep, deep chug of his beer. He swallows hard. At the back of his neck she can just see a chain of tiny steel beads.

– O dear miss fortune, Silence sings as others gather in the tavern round his song.

He sings to soothe those only pacified with their lost love of a white bull, those who'd be happier if the herds had never been.

– What frenzy grips your soul? The protean daughters filled the fields with their false lowings, but not one of them sought such unholy union, bestial mating, though her neck had shuddered from the plough and she had felt for horns with fingertips, smooth, touching on her forehead. Dear miss fortune, now you wander in the wilds, while he lies on his snowy side upon soft blooms of hyacinths and, under some dark ilex, chews the pale grass, tracks some heifer through the herd.

The whole place seems to have quietened down to listen to him singing now. There's still a little chatter, here and there, but there are fingers to lips and prodding elbows, or even just unfinished sentences, conversations drifting off into the isolation of attention. Faces turn, necks craned to peer over a shoulder, folks leaning out of a booth or sitting back to slump into the plump squeak of the artificial leather.

He sings a song about a farmboy and his sister who lose their daddy's farm, and how she watches their white bull being taken away to slaughter and finds her brother lying under an apple tree, brains blown out with a shotgun. Life is hard and death is peace.

What the Fuck Is Natural These Days?

– So, are you going to stay a while or not? says Jack.

– What? I say, mind twisting back to now.

– Christ, you've only been here a couple of hours and already you're running off. You don't have to go, you know.

He slips his arm around my waist and nuzzles my hair, nibbling at my ear.

– No . . . not really. I say. But I suppose I should. It's lunchtime; they'll be expecting me.

– Bad times there just now?

– They don't even look at me. You know, it's not even that they think it's immoral. I think they think it's . . . unnatural. Of all the people who should understand.

He laughs.

– And just what the fuck *is* natural these days? You could stay with me, you know . . . permanently, that is.

I don't want to go home. I want to stay with him and he wants me to stay – but that's not enough. Jack doesn't . . . *need* me to stay; that's something he just won't give, stubbornly insisting that if I come to him I come freely, by my own choice. He won't try and persuade me. Sometimes I think that cold, dead Jack is some kind of vampire, looking for someone with the will to spend eternity at his side.

– It just doesn't feel right, I say. They're my . . .

I tail off, mumble something about how they've always looked after me. They didn't have to, after all. It's not like they even knew me or my parents.

239

– You don't owe them anything, he says. You know that. You don't owe anyone anything.

I want him to tell me that I owe *him*, that I *have* to stay.

Jack scratches at a nipple.

– I've made you an outcast, haven't I?

– I made an outcast of myself, I say, but I'm lying and I know it. I'm not your teenage rebel, and I know that if I'd never met him I'd have made the step from child to adult just exactly the same way as all the others. A tentative first kiss with a nice girl who went for the more sensitive type – maybe at the Fireday dance, maybe with Mary-Jane; she used to smile at me when we were younger. A question, a ring, a contract of souls. I'd go to the rag-and-bone-man and deal for what I needed to build my own little house for us. I'd work the land, maybe take over as Endhaven's teacher when old Hobbes retired. I'd still look at the soft skin on the back of Sam Finnegan's neck. I'd still jerk off over ancient magazines of actors whose glittering Hollywood homes now lie sunken at the bottom of the blue Pacific. But I'd have lived the lie.

Everything changed when I found Jack. Angel, incubus, silkie Jack. The good people of Endhaven have never accepted Jack, and if I do, if I do more than just accept him, well, that makes me like him. Other.

Half the time now I feel like I'm on a bridge over a ravine, with Endhaven and its rag-and-bone-man on one side telling me that I belong with them, that I belong *to* them, and Jack on the other side not telling me anything, just reaching out a hand to let me know I'm welcome. But I've lived most my life in Endhaven and it's hard to just walk away from everything you know, even when your friends have given up on you one by one, and the people who raised you think you need some sort of treatment. There's still the rag-and-bone-man and there's still the Evenfall.

I wish I had the strength to make an outcast of myself.

The Paradox of Patriots and Pacifists

He sings a song of cattle or of souls as chattels in illusion fields, and of the ancient power, horned and bellowing, they all revere.

— Now close, you nymphs, you nymphs of creation, close the forest glades, in case somewhere our eyes might meet the wandering footprints of that bull; perhaps, lured by the greener grass of other pastures or the scent of his own herd, and guided by the cattle's tracks, he may come home some day, come back, back to the stalls, back to the garden.

— And we've got to get ourselves back to the garden.

This one, she knows. She looks around at all the quiet faces, wondering how this can be something they relate to. Jesus. 1960s hippy music just doesn't belong here. This is a small-town world that's split right down the middle, one foot in the twenty-first century and another in 1950-something. VR simlinks and apple pie. Sure the technology is modern, mostly, but the ideology is retro in a whole other way to, say, big city kids with quiffs and nose-rings. She's seen the flags flying from all the houses and the churches, even yellow ribbons tied around the trees. She knows in places like this you just don't mention the war — the wars, rather. You certainly don't question.

She studies them, trying to get a handle on the contradiction. A guy in a sleeveless checked shirt, army corps tattoo on his shoulder, nodding his head to the hippy music. The waitress mouthing the words to the old song, silently singing along.

This paradox of patriots and pacifists is utterly alien to her.

How should we tell this tale he tells of fluttering cilia of night, this aftertale of white loins girdled with barking monsters, of harried Ships of July dragged down, deep in the whirlpool, down to drown, their trembling sailors torn by hounds? Or how he sings of all the transformations of the Limbs of Tears? Or of that feast of gifts, that full meal all prepared? Or of her flight on wings of anguish, high over her ancient home and out to desolate deserts?

*

241

There are no windows in the place that she can see from here, but she knows from the time it must be getting dark outside. Maybe this is how Evenfall kicks in around here, with a subtle shift in ambience, in atmosphere. The days are certain, clear and light, but the dusk is a different story, a whole different kind of story. Shit. Sometimes in these diners and roadhouses, at the drive-thrus where you can pull up to a window and order the same cheap and greasy fast food you ate a hundred miles back in the same terrain of neatly numbered road-signs carving up the world into ordered routes, sometimes she forgets this is the Vellum.

You only realize when you turn off a main route onto a road that's not marked on the map, that takes you out into a desert of rust, or switch on the TV in a motel room to see CNN reporting on the sinking of Atlanta, or on guerrilla battles in the Middle East waged with machine guns against swords of flame.

Decay, Dereliction, Desperation

I think what makes their hatred worse is that they need him. For twelve years before he washed ashore we suffered and survived. The rag-and-bone-man's trade brings us most of the essentials we can't make ourselves – medicines, machine parts, waterproof textiles, things like that. You could almost say that it's a sort of rural idyll, a quiet, stable society, getting by on its own, oblivious to what's going on back in the cities. But Endhaven is a town made up of bank clerks and lawyers, and personal assistants and check-out girls and hairdressers and a thousand other professions, vocations or plain old-fashioned jobs that have nothing to do with anything any more. We have houses that suffer wear and tear and generators that break down. It's the twenty-first century and we're not Amish or hippies or anything like that. So when I was growing up, our little machine town, even with the rag-and-bone-man helping to sustain it, it was slowly grinding down into decay, dereliction, desperation. Kids have short memories, and the adults are practised masters of self-delusion, but I can remember.

*

I remember how it was to go without hot water through the winter or to live by candlelight in a house with boarded-up windows. I remember the anger and resentment it fostered, and the retributions – the reckonings – those bred. I remember days when whole families would be shouting and swearing at each other on the streets and someone would be sent running to fetch the rag-and-bone-man. I remember him walking into fistfights, screaming judgements on people like some old-style bible-thumping preacher. I didn't know why, but I realized, in the rag-and-bone-man's reckonings, that the worst thing that could ever happen to you was to be exiled, ostracized. I didn't realize until later just what the Evenfall could do.

Jack, when he arrived, was a god-sent repairman with a nuts-and-bolts know-how of the mysteries of machines. Endhaven needs him, maybe even more than the rag-and-bone-man, and still they'd like to throw him back into the ocean that he came from.

It's his strangeness, I think, his otherness; it seems to remind them that things aren't what they seem, that while we shelter like trinkets under a rag-and-bone-man's coat in Endhaven, reality elsewhere is torn apart and blown away like leaves, that dead men walk the world while, in the cities and on the edge of town, the living disappear into the night. He came from the sea, from the east, like the Evenfall.

Down by the jetty that juts out from the dunes, pointing out across the water to the rust-red, brown and gold-flecked headland and the concrete bones of giants half-buried, gulls are fighting over scraps of food; carrion or catch, I can't tell from this distance. More swoop down from the roof of Jack's beachside burnt-out squat of an apartment, cawing raggedly as they join the battle.

Jack stands there with the off-white building, once some fashionable city dweller's expensive escape, lurking behind him. Raised on square stilts at the beach-facing side, with its balcony running all the way along in clean, modernist lines, the empty frames of windows and sliding glass doors running along behind, it looks like a bunker. A look-out post or gun emplacement.

– Stay? says Jack, one last time.

I shake my head, and he looks at me with a wry smile.

– One of these days, he says.

– I've got to go.

The Golden Age Returns

– Now the last era of the sibilant song has come, he sings, and time itself is pregnant. The great series of the centuries is born anew. The pattern of the centuries to come is in concord with destinies decreed by Fates who tell their spindles: run. Now virgin justice has returned, the reign of Crow restored, and with the poll as consul, leader now, an age of glory dawns and the procession of great months starts to advance. Look at the world rocked by the weight of heaven pressing down on it.

The old guy turns to her at one point as he sings; she holds her eyes on his for a second before looking away, not sure of what she saw there – something drunk but wise. He puts the mike down on the top of the karaoke machine. He doesn't need it now. The whole bar's quiet, listening to him in rapture, transported. She rises, dropping a fifty into the saucer to cover her bill. It's late. It's time to leave.

– We'll banish the last trace of sin, he sings, and, as it vanishes, we'll free the world from its long night of fear. See how we all sing for the century to come. For now the newborn of the new age comes, comes down to us out of the deep blue sky, the wide lands, and the reaches of the sea, now, here.

And Chrome and Mainsail watch like hawks as Silence gives his gift to Eagle.

– This boychild now being born, he sings, through him the iron race will end, and men of gold rise in the world again. So bless his birth, immaculate lacuna: your own Apple comes to rule at last.

He stops her with his hand as she walks past, his hand lain soft and low upon her full-filled belly.

– He'll gather with the gods, sings Silence, see them mixed up with the heroes of the past. And they themselves will see him take this world subdued by ancient virtue, the traditions of his ancestors.

Where faint traces of primeval treachery survive, we'll venture on the sea in ships, build walls around our cities, carve deep furrows in the scorched earth. With a new typhoon as steersman, another argot will set out to carry chosen heroes.

– There will be other wars, he sings, and great Achilles will be sent again to Troy.

She backs away, turns round him. She doesn't have to hear this. She knows. The world is coming apart outside, beyond the sealed-up towns and cities of this little state of Middle America. And she knows she's pregnant.

– Begin, he sings, the hour is near, dear offspring of the gods, great child of Joy. Embark on your illustrious career and when age makes a solid man of you, the merchants will give up the sea, the pine-wood ships carry no goods. Each land will bear all that it needs. Soil will not suffer hoes, nor vine the hook; the oaken ploughman will at last loosen the yokes upon his bulls. The wool will not be taught to fake this colour or that; instead, the very ram in the meadows will transform his fleece, now to sweet red purple, now to saffron yellow; lambs gambolling in pastures will wear scarlet coats.

At the bar, the blond guy's leaning forward to curl a note into the tip-glass on the inner tray that runs around the bar. He turns to look at her as she pushes the wood and glass door out of Ivan's open, and she sees the fire reflected in his eyes. He must be wearing lenses, a heads-up display of a news-channel showing an explosion happening somewhere out there in the fucked-up world. Or maybe he just has fire in his eyes.

All That Remains

– To me, he sings, all that remains is the last days of a long life and breath that will not be enough to tell your deeds. Neither the thrashing calliope of Orphan nor the beauty of an Apple's lines, can sing beyond me though, not with their mother's help nor with their father at their side. Pan even, with Arcadia as judge, if he compete with me, Pan, even with Arcadia as judge, would tell of his defeat.

*

245

She steps out into the darkness of the parking lot and it parts around her. Evenfall. A flood of black, of something more substantial than a shadow, less substantial than a form, flowing like liquid or like dust in the wind, blurring the world around her in a haze of darkening gray. The floodlights of the baseball field have been switched off and she can just make out the bleachers by a solitary light fixed on the sports hall like a beacon in the night. The children and parents are all long gone, of course.

– Begin then, little boy, with a smile, to know your mother who has brought you here with her ten months of suffering. Begin, boy. Anyone who does not smile on a parent, will be found unworthy by a god of board or by a goddess of her bed.

The door swings slowly shut on its spring, muffling the song still coming from inside.

The evening swirls around her but, somehow, it doesn't touch her, these tiny particles of darkness swirling in vortices in the air, dancing away from a wafting hand. They're everywhere, it seems now, sweeping in with the night to change the world, estrange it from itself, only slightly and subtly, but night after night, shifting it gradually away from what it once was. People call them dust angels or bitmites. Evenfall. In some of the little bubbles of reality she's stopped off in on her long flight, there have even been attempts at explanations. Secret black ops government nanotech gone wrong. The vials of God's wrath poured out upon the world. She might well be the only one in the whole of the Vellum who knows exactly what we are.

And back in Ivan's sports bar grill and steakhouse, Silence sings.

All that once, far ago, we wrote, all learned by heart at our laurels' bidding, all the happy stream of all heard from a brooding sun, he sings. And Silence sings until the smitten valleys echo to the sky, until the evening star appears high in the heavens, telling the shepherds:

– Tell all your tales of sheep, and go, and gather them, and pen them in the fold.

Errata

The Annunciation of Anaesthesia

Her hand slides across her mid-term belly, as she watches the TV screen, flicking from channel to channel with the remote and looking for CNN or something else in English rather than Espanol. God no, though, anything but Fox. She finds, a little surprisingly, the BBC World News and settles on that. Lying up on the bed, she watches the female anchorman interview a correspondent out in the deserts around Baghdad.

– now. According to Allied Intelligence Sources, however, these attacks are not the work of one particular terrorist group, but are in fact the product of a much looser network of affiliated splinter groups–

Isn't that a contradiction in terms, she thinks, *affiliated splinter groups?*

– truth to these rumours about the Allies using nanotech weaponry?

– Well, now, we know that the Americans have been using these so-called nanites for surveillance for the last year or so but–

Big fucking deal, she thinks. *We've been doing this shit for … forever.*

She looks at the tattoo on her arm. It's been stable for the last three months now. She doesn't feel the same flickering uncertainty about whether she's Phreedom or Inanna or something in-between.

The earphones and datastick lie up on the dresser beside the TV, just so much junk in a fold of the Vellum where VR doesn't exist. It still has her music loaded on it, right enough, so it's not entirely useless; sometimes she lays the earphones on her stomach and plays the baby some Sex Pistols or some Clash. Fuck the classical shit; any child of hers is going to be a fucking rebel. He kicks most for the Rolling Stones.

His hand slides across her belly, smoothing the gel across it gently, as he smiles at her and makes small talk, asking her is she excited, making plans for the future, she must be so happy, and she'll probably find this a little cold. He runs the scanner over her gelled skin, sweeping it around and scrutinizing the screen – as she does too, wondering at this little full-formed fetal shape inside her, curled up around itself in comfort.

– Well, I don't see any horns, he says, so you'll be glad to know it's not the Antichrist.

He laughs, but it's a nervous laugh. After what happened in that abortion clinic in New England, there's a lot of worried obstetricians and a lot of panicking prospective parents. Anyway, he shouldn't be so fucking sure, she thinks.

– No wings either, he says. That's quite unusual these days, actually. First one I've seen in a long time. One hundred percent normal.

She doesn't want to hear. She doesn't want to hear about what they're calling the 'rate of child immortality'. She doesn't want to hear about the newborn babies opening their mouths and squalling prophecies instead of wordless wails with their first breath. She doesn't want to hear about the fucking omens and portents and miracles that are ten a penny these days.

– Is it a boy or a girl? she asks.

– A boy, he says. Do you have a name picked out yet?

You should call it Phuture, Finnan had said, *spelled PH.*

– I was thinking of something nice and normal, she says. Like Jack.

The scalpel cuts down her belly but she doesn't really feel it, floating in a haze of anaesthetic; her whole lower body's numb from the spinal block, the needle inserted in her spine with her hunched forward, rounding her back to open up the vertebrae for them; and now she can't even see what they're doing, with the surgical drapes blocking her view of her own bloody, open body, the shaved pubic hair and the catheter in her bladder, so she just wonders how big the scar will be as she feels the vague pushing, pulling sensations – no pain, just the strange to-ing and fro-ing of her insides. Not that she's worried about the scar, but she knows it's a fifteen-centimeter incision that they make, that the longest part of the procedure is actually the removal of the placenta and the membranes and the stitching up of all the layers of the uterus and muscle, fat and skin. She's read up on it, she has, anaesthetized Anna, Anna Anaesthesia, because she thought that it might come to this, after all, with her still being young and all, and all, and all the risks like scarring or wound infection or blood clots just like any other operation or decreased bowel function, blood loss or damage to the organs close enough to the uterus, like the bladder, and is the spleen close to the uterus, is it? she doesn't know, no, who the fuck knows what the spleen is anyway, but just as long as they don't take the spleen out by mistake, but that's ridiculous, Anna, it should only be ten minutes before they've sucked all the amniotic fluid out and plucked her baby boy out of her and started to put her back together, knit her up again nice and tight, Anna, Phreedom, Inanna, Anna, Anesthesia...

He runs his hand across her belly, rough and callused on her soft skin, and she puts her own on top of his to hold it there, just on the scar at the bikini line. His fingers, his hands, are solid now, skin weathered with age and she lets her own fingers follow the line of his knuckles down to the hollow between thumb and wrist, and over the studded leather band and along the ribbing of the muscle of his forearm with its fine dark hair and – switching her own position, turning over and onto him – curving the bicep and the tricep, filled out with the decades of hard work and hard fighting, solid now, like a miner or a boxer, not at all like the young boy she once knew, dear soft Don who seemed so much like Tom when she met him, so much like Finnan as he grew older, but is now his own man.

He flicks a buzzing fly away from her ear.

– What are you up to? he says, amused.

– Nothing, she says.

It's been sort of their mantra during their journey through the craziness that used to be reality, ever since they met during the Evacuation of New York. Since he found her out of her face on smack and crying because she'd lost Jack, because they'd taken him away. Because no matter how fucked-up the world was, people hung on to bureaucracy as if it all still mattered. What are we going to do now? she'd say. Nothing. What have we got to lose here? Nothing.

She pulls herself up to straddle the barrel of his chest, look down at his greying temples. She would be worried about him drifting away from her into old age and decay, but he seems stronger now than ever. Even the gray hair just makes him look like some wolf-pack leader ready to snarl his warnings at any upstart with the stupidity to try something on. He wears his age much better than he wore his youth, looks like some grizzled Templar with his beard now. An aged knight.

– Don Coyote, she says.

He runs his rough hands up her ribcage and round to her breasts.

– What time is it? he says.

She looks at the alarm clock on the bedside cabinet, its red LEDs flickering randomly in horizontals and verticals that don't actually signify numbers at all.

– It's the Apocalypse, she says. Who gives a fuck?

That Moment of Perfection

– I give a fuck! snarls Metatron.

The two newbloods stand there dumb and sullen, and he glowers at them. The replacements for Carter and Pechorin, if anything they're worse. Like all of these flyboy warrior unkin, they're little more than weapons with the initiative to know what they have to kill, and Metatron is just tired of them all. There are a thousand ways a human can break through the walls inside their mind and catch a little glimpse of the Vellum, a thousand different types of crises and catastrophes that can crack that boundary just wide enough for a crowbar placed in the right spot to break their heads wide open, and let the dead soul deeps pour in and through. All the poets and prophets who see eternity in a grain of sand, the mathematicians who stumble on the geometries of heaven and actually manage to retain their sanity. But where do these creatures find their great moments of satori, their blinding flashes of enlightenment? In the great glory of war. In being the last man left alive on a field of limbs. In the ... *beauty* of jungles blossoming with napalm. So they step out of reality for a second, and when they find themselves back in it, they've brought something over from the other side. A little fragment of eternity caught in their memory of that moment of perfection.

*

So there's Henderson. New IRA. He found his mark from a Hand of Ulster carbomb, saw eternity as he was standing at the lace curtained window of a suburban bungalow, watching his wife put the dog into the back of the car and slam the door closed, walk round to the driver's seat and look at him for a second, face blank with the grip of emotion – she was going to stay with a friend, she said, just for a while – and then she was getting in, pulling the door shut, key in the ignition. It wasn't that he loved her, although he did love her dearly. It was the fact that, in that moment, he hated her just enough for him to catch, as the double-glazing blew in over his face, the full brutal aesthetics of the moment.

A terrible beauty is born.

And then there's MacChuill. He was a soldier with the Royal Scots Engineers, the stuff the British Empire was made on – send them out anywhere, they'll build you a bridge or blow one up. His past's a bit murky; he was living in the jungles of Borneo when they tracked him down, didn't know the first thing about unkin or the Vellum; he'd forgotten how to speak English, let alone the angel tongue. Metatron still doesn't know what war it was that stranded him there, but he does know that the man spent some time in a prisoner-of-war camp, watching his comrades getting tortured one by one and executed one by one until all that was left was MacChuill. And then MacChuill started singing to his captors, *at* his captors, tearing his voice out of a parched throat as if he was tearing his very soul out with it, to throw it down at their feet as a gauntlet: just try and fucking break me. No, he doesn't know the angel tongue at all, this one. But there's a thick resonance in his guttural voice that makes the floorboards of any room he speaks in shudder in subsonic frequencies.

There was a soldier, a Scottish soldier.

And then there's Finnan. Sergeant Seamus Finnan. Signed up to fight for King and Country against the Kaiser, or to look after the little brother of his darling fiancée, rather, who'd volunteered along with five of his schoolfriends and countless other children with noble, foolish dreams. Maturity and sheer canniness had seen him get the rank of sergeant pretty quickly and he might have had an actual army career ahead of him if he hadn't had to shoot his sweetheart's little brother for desertion in the face of the enemy.

Seamus Finnan, bloody-faced and drunk, out cold and dragged into the warehouse between Henderson and MacChuill, feet trailing behind, like a sack of cement. Metatron had given them express orders not to kill the man, not to harm him, just bring him here, and they'd clearly beaten the living shit out of him.

– Who gives a fuck? Henderson had said. He's nothing.

Finnan. Crouching down before the slumped form, he studies the man's hand like a palmist reading someone's future, except of course he's reading Finnan's past, reading his mark. It seems, if Metatron is reading the mark correctly, that Sergeant Seamus Finnan found his own little fragment of eternity in a suicide attempt, a few years after shooting the boy he'd promised to look after. Presumably he made a decision that living and fighting just weren't for him. And presumably he failed to follow through quite well enough. Metatron twists the hand round a little for a better look; actually, there is a definite sign of death in there, and not a soul-death, not a symbolic one, but a literal one. It's there as good as if it were written in black and white. Sergeant Seamus Finnan died not in the trenches of the Somme but sometime after, by his own hand.

Metatron looks at the drunken, beaten man, unconscious but clearly very much alive. It's a puzzle, but he should have the answer soon enough.

– Get him cleaned up and secured, he says to Henderson. Let me know when he's conscious.

The hatchling girl and the runaway boy are both long-gone, one gone on the long walk into the Vellum, the other dead, a harmless ghost haunting the margins of reality, one death buried in a thousand others. There's no direct link between Finnan and Eresh, but maybe, just maybe, the Messenger boy knew something of what Eresh was up to, what kind of twisted forces she was playing with, what kind of twisted forces killing her let loose.

And maybe, just maybe, he told his old friend, Seamus Finnan.

1

The Hammers of Hephaestos

Beyond the Way of Scythes

– To the end of the earth we've come, says Corporal Powers, as he and Slaughter drag their drugged, bedraggled charge. Beyond the way of scythes and lands unwalked by men.

He looks around him at his world, so much of it off-scene – the distant boom of Hun artillery, the sky a strip of blue above the trench. To him it seems a stage, dressed with the wooden plankings and the sandbags, sleeping soldiers for its props, so distant from reality, distant from humanity.

– You have your orders from the dukes, he says to Smith. Bind this bold rebel to the soaring rocks, in uncorroding adamantine chains. He stole your glory, precious fire, gave it as a gift to men so all their arts now flower. For such a crime it's only right that he should pay his dues to the divine, that he may learn to love the tyranny of dukes, and end his philanthropic ways.

Smith limps along behind the redcaps, chinking with the chains he carries, slowed by the trenchfoot, and thinking that he shouldn't even be here. Private with the Sheffield Pals, this is not his bloody business. No, it's not.

– Powers and Slaughter, he says. Your duty to the dukes is done, your part in this all over with, but I for one can't stand to bind a brother lord to this bleak precipice by force.

And, in front of Smith, between Powers and Slaughter, the prisoner's boots drag after him, rattling on the duckboards; Powers and Slaughter stop a sec to heft him higher, adjust their grip under his arms, then set to pulling him on again along the trench.

– Ah, God, but I must steel myself, says Smith, be brave enough to carry out this deed; it would be grave to disregard the dukes' decree.

As loath as he is then – but not quite as loath as the straight-talking and high treasonous son of Tims – he has no other option but to hammer home these hard bronze chains in this harsh wasteland where, without a sight of any mortal frame, without the sound of any human voice, scorched by the sun's white flame, he knows the prisoner's beauty's bloom will be destroyed.

– You'll welcome night's dark cloak of stars over the light, he whispers, welcome the sun when it dissolves the frost of dawn. But you will always wear the burden of your present pain, for your deliverer is as yet unborn.

These are the fruits of all philanthropy, it seems to Smith. A lord who scorned the wrath of lords, and gave more glory to the workers than was due, condemned to guard this joyless rock, stand sleepless and erect, and utter sighs and lamentations, to no end. *The will of lords, like your own knee*, Smith thinks, *is hard to bend.*

– All kings, he says, are hardest when their power is new.

The Wasted Wounded Land

Seamus notices that Powers and this other fellow are talking like a right pair of fookin toffs, sure, and it's almost funny it is, and he'd fookin laugh but he's too busy trying to put his best foot forward, as they say, and finding it kind of difficult on account of the world heaving up and down and his stomach and his head doing much the same thing only in different directions and at different times, and these two cherrynob bastards, Powers and Slaughter, dragging him along between them faster than he can keep up with. Sure and if they'd only let him be, he could fookin walk his self; he's not that fookin drunk.

– Why the delay and all this pointless pity? he hears Powers' poisoned little voice say. Why not hate the lord all lords hate most? He has betrayed your prize to common men.

– The bond of brotherhood is strange, says Smith, somewhere behind him.

– Agreed, but would you disobey your orders? Don't you fear this more?

– Ever the pitiless and the proud, says Smith.

– I shed no tears for this one; it solves nothing. Don't waste your time.

And fook you and yer mammy too, Powers, ye cunt, thinks Seamus. *I always knew ye were a prick.* He pulls his left foot forward again, trying to get it under him for support, but it's no use. His right leg isn't working at all now – sure and it's probably busted from the fooker kicking it – he heard it crack, so he did, and it hurts like fookin buggery – but he could still walk if the bastards would only let him, he's sure. He's not that fookin drunk.

– I hate my handiwork, says Smith.

– Why hate your craft? It's not to blame for his misfortune.

– Still I would rather that this task had fallen to another.

– All things are trials except to rule the lords; freedom is for the dukes alone.

Well maybe he is that drunk, thinks Seamus, 'cause sure and the two of them aren't making any sense at all, by Christ. What's all this shite about lords and dukes? What the fook are the pair of them blathering about? Is it the Duke of Underland they're gabbing on about – no, Sunderland, he means – no, Butcher Cumberland, it is – or is it Slumberland – ah, bollocks! – what the fook's whoever it is got to do with anything? Oh, Jesus, but he shouldn't have drunk all of the captain's fookin whisky, though, 'cause he's a fookin mess and he can't even keep his fookin thoughts straight, never mind these gobshites talking utter rot.

– I know, says Smith. There's nothing I can say against this.

And Sergeant Seamus Finnan tries to pull his left foot forward over the mud, and tries to pull his mind out of the haze of blood and whisky that he's swimming in, but it's no use. He's fucked, and his whole world is fucked along with him, and all that he knows is the taste of bile burning in his throat, and the stink of whisky and puke that fills his nostrils now – by Christ, but it's better than the stench of corpses – and the rough hands of the CMPs – Powers and Slaughter – pulling his arms near out of their sockets as they drag him through the wasteland, through the fookin wasted, wounded land, with all its cesspit scars of trenches and the open sores of craters; and they throw him down into the dark of the dugout and he lies there, wishing the world would stop its spinning, Jesus Christ Almighty, wishing the world would just fookin stop.

Outside, the shelling of the German batteries sounds like the distant boom of thunder.

An Adamantine Wedge, a Stubborn Spike

He feels Smith pulling him up onto his feet, leaning him against the wooden shoring of the dugout, the solid but swaying surface of it against his back, and he tries to roll his head up, tries to raise his hand to wipe the blood and mud out of his eyes, to look the bastard in the face, but his arm is being insubordinate and just sort of waving in the air. He feels Smith grip his wrist. His foot slips and he stumbles, slumps, only the wall behind holding him up.

– Hurry it up and put the bonds about him, Powers says. You want the Captain to see you wasting time?

Through vision blurred by booze and blood, Seamus sees Smith hold up the manacles in his hands, a gesture that says, *Look; shut up and let me do my job.*

– Put them about his hands with firm strength, Powers goes on. Strike with the hammer. Nail him to the rocks.

His legs give way, and Smith has to drag him back up by his lapels, steady him against the wood.

Seamus retches again, spits blood and bile, and looks from Powers to Smith and back again, and then at Slaughter standing in the doorway, saying nothing. The red collar of his tunic, under his greatcoat, is all covered in Seamus's puke; it serves the bastard right. That's what ye get for a fookin rifle-butt in the stomach, ye fookin redcap bastard.

– It's done, and not in vain this work, says Smith.

Seamus's head is clearer now, not much, but just enough to know there's something wrong. There's something fookin wrong.

– Strike harder. Tighter. Leave nothing loose, says Powers.

Seamus watches the man's lips moving and even with the double vision and all, he's sure the movements of the mouth don't match the words. Oh, aye, there's something fookin wrong, all right.

He feels cold metal snap around his wrist, his hand raised up above his head and locked there. What the fook is this? His legs buckle and he slips again, shouts out as pain explodes in his shoulder, with all his fookin weight on it and all. Ah, Christ, is that what a dislocated shoulder feels like?

– This one has skills, says Powers. He can escape from the impossible.

– Aye but this arm, says Smith, is inextricably fixed.

Seamus moans, trying to push himself back up onto his wobbling legs. Damn right it's fookin fixed.

– And clasp this now securely. Let him learn he is a duller schemer than the dukes.

He tries to curse them, tries to ask them what the fook they're on about, what dukes, what bloody dukes – but his tongue's too thick to form the words and it just comes out of his busted lips as a formless moan. Is this some fookin Orangeman secret code or something? Ah, Jesus, but that shite doesn't matter over here, does it, with the 1st Dubs and the Orangemen of the 36th Ulster fighting side-by-side and dying side-by-side and – Oh, but that's not what he was saying earlier, is it? Ah, Christ, now what the fook was he going on about? Did he really say that the King could go fook himself? He didn't, did he?

– No one could justly blame me ... except him, says Smith as he pulls Seamus's other hand around to snap another manacle into place, to drag it up over his head. Another click and Seamus hangs there like a puppet, arms in fookin agony. Aw, Christ, he's fookin

lost his mind, or it's the fookin whisky, or they've knocked his fookin
brains out of his head, or all of it, but he's either seeing things or
hearing things, or both, because the world just isn't right. This
fellow – Smith – this fellow's lips are mouthing different words to
what he's hearing – Christ, but he's sure of it – and this is all wrong.
He's seen Powers kick the shite out of a prisoner before, but never
this. Jesus, this is the kind of awful shite that Fritz would do to a
soldier caught on the wrong side of the wire.

Powers comes closer, reaches behind him, pulling his rifle's
bayonet out of its sheath. He passes it to Smith. O, Christ. O, Jesus
Christ.

– Now nail an adamantine wedge's stubborn spike square
through his breast.

O, Jesus Fookin Christ Almighty.

– Alas. Alas, says Smith. Prometheus, I groan for thy afflictions.

Prometheus

Seamus looks down at the point of the bayonet pressed to his chest.
This is insane. He must be dreaming. He must be drunk and
dreaming, out of his head on the captain's whisky and in a bloody
nightmare. Sure and what day is it, he thinks, and who's the Prime
Minister, where am I, what am I doing here? But even though he's
drunk and only just coming round from a fair fookin beating obviously, he can remember it all just fine. He knows exactly how far
the trench is from the River Ancre, that it's the 28th of June, that
it's Lloyd George and Haig in charge; and everything fits so fookin
well together except for the words and the spike, that he's sure it's
happening to him, here, now. He can't doubt but that it's happening.
But sure and he has to.

Smith holds the bayonet there for what seems an eternity.

– Do you hesitate and groan for the duke's enemies? says
Powers. Beware or maybe one day you'll be pitying yourself.

– You see a sight that's hard to watch, says Smith, but his lips are
mouthing, *God, I'm sorry*. Jesus, but the look on his face is – Jesus
– it's the way that Seamus looked when poor Thomas went doolally

and Seamus and the lads had to . . . had to try and beat some sense into him and afterwards, when he was walking away, Seamus caught a glimpse of himself in a wee shaving mirror hanging from a hook on the wall and it was that same fookin look. *I'm sorry I have to do this to ye.* It's the look of someone telling themself there isn't any choice.

And the bayonet drives through his chest and, breaking skin and flesh and bone and heart, it drives right through and thuds into the wood against his back.

– I see him meeting his deserts, says Powers, as Seamus Finnan's world goes blinding white with pain.

Sure and it has to be a nightmare. It fookin has to be.

– Put straps around his sides, though.

His world is blinding white. The pain goes right through the centre of his chest like the fookin gas huts where they had to practise to prepare themselves for the mustard gas over here which thank fook he's never had to suffer yet though he's seen those as have, by Christ, not getting their masks on before they got not a lungful but a half a breath, and them gasping, grasping, like him now with it burning in his lungs, in his heart, in his throat, like something trying to get out.

– I know what's needed. Don't harass me.

The blizzard of his agony howls into his head, so raw a pain that he can hear it, he can fookin hear it, drowning their distant voices.

– I'll harass you all I want and more. Go lower. Surround the thighs with force.

He hears the distant thunder of the shells, the ringing sound of metal upon metal, hammering in his ears.

– The work is no laborious task. It's all but done already.

Doom. Doom. Doom. And all the time the howling of this pinned animal inside him.

– Drive the fetters strongly, all the way; they have to stand up to a harsh critique.

– Your mode of speech, he hears Smith say, suits your physique.

– Be soft yourself, but don't reproach me for stern strength of will.

– Let's go. His limbs are in the net.

259

He hears the voice hissing up close, right by his ear, over the hurricane of white noise and his own – Jesus, it's not a moan, it's not a sob, it's not a keen, it's not a scream. What kind of fookin sound is that?

– Now, now. Be proud, says Powers. Plunder the powers of the divine and give your gifts to the ephemerals now. How can your workers soothe you in this sorry state? It seems we called you Foresight falsely; or perhaps you can foresee just how exactly you'll escape this fate.

And Seamus feels his lips open and he hears the sound come out his mouth, the sound of a thousand rivers roaring.

A Dugout, the Somme, 28 June 1916

Smith steps back from the crazy Irishman cuffed to the metal frame of the bunk in the corner of the dugout, lying there dead to the world but babbling on in drunk delirium. He's never heard anything like it and it puts the fear of God in him, by heck; he's heard some of the other paddies speaking their Gaelic, and he knows it don't sound nowt like this. Those boys from the Royal Dublin Fusiliers have a lilting, soft sound – the ones under this Finnan fellow's charge, at least, seconded from the 7th to the 1st after the slaughter of Gallipoli, so they say. Students from Trinity mainly, those boys. Could have been officers but they chose to fight beside their friends. Call them the toffs among the toughs, they do, though this Finnan's an exception. A tough among the toffs, ye might say. And whatever tongue it is he's speaking, it's not the gentle brogue of his Irish Pals. It's something . . . else.

Powers steps forward to give the man one last boot in the stomach before wheeling and striding out of the dugout, Slaughter following on his heels. Typical redcaps, thinks Smith. Busted lip and bloody nose, two eyes that'll be black for a week – they've left him in a right state, by heck. He'll be hurting some when he wakes up all right, and it won't just be a sore head from too much firewater.

Poor fellow's done for anyway now, thinks Smith. It might have been fine if it were just the stealing of an officer's whisky. He would have lost his stripes, for sure, and there would have been a big to-do, a court-martial and a prison sentence – commuted to field punishment, most likely – but if the Irish lads under his charge are anything like Smith's own Sheffield Pals, they were needing something to take their minds off what they'd done . . . and what they'd still to do . . . as anyone could see, as even the captain might have seen. There's worse things in the world than a sergeant stealing his captain's whisky and dishing out a little to the scared young boys he's only trying to care for best he can.

But the charge is sedition now and that's something else entirely. There's trouble enough amongst the paddies that have heard about the Easter Uprising back home, without their own sergeant staggering around and roaring like a wounded bear about republican martyrs – MacDonagh and MacBride, and Connolly and Pearse. *Why the fuck are we fighting for the British when they're killing Ireland's sons at home?* That's treason, no matter how you look at it.

Smith shakes his head. He's sorry for the man. He truly is. But that kind of talk is just asking for the firing squad when the troops are skittish enough as it is about the rumours of a Big Push.

Finnan rolls over onto his back, his free arm flopping loose, hand grasping as if at some imaginary firefly, and Smith jumps back. The muttering stops for a second, then starts up again, louder than before. It's not English, that's for sure, and if it isn't Irish, what the hell is it? Smith knows a little Kraut – *Scheisser* and *Hände hoch* – but it's not so guttural and ugly as all that. Latin or Greek? He doesn't think so. He wasn't the best student by a long way and he never made it to the local grammar school or nowt, but Smith's still had enough of those rammed down his throat, from his teachers and from Mad Jack Carter – is there no escaping it, by heck? – with all his talk of Homer's heroes. He's heard enough bloody Taciturn and Virgin, as they used to call the buggers, to know it's none of that.

He stands up, steps back from the man. It's probably just gibberish, he thinks. Shellshock and firewater and a boot to the head. Nothing more.

But it still makes him uneasy, this strange babbling with its unfamiliar sounds. There's too many of them. Too many sounds for one mouth to make.

He feels queasy, frightened, turns to go and realises Powers and Slaughter are standing just outside the dugout, waiting for him, stark silhouettes in the doorway, hulking bulks with sharp points. The red-covered peaked caps, the barrels of their rifles slung over their shoulders pointing upwards – even the thick swaddling of their greatcoats seems all angular – shoulders so square, and the flare from belted waist down to the hem. They're men cut in straight lines, without a curve in them. He looks back at the Irishman, lying there spread-eagled on the floor of the dugout, his handcuffed arm dangling, his left leg twitching like he's trying, in his dreams, to pull himself out of some churned up mire of sucking mud. And still there's that infernal muttering. *Where are you now?* thinks Smith. *Where are you in your head?*

But it's not his business. He's only here because Powers barked at him to pick up the handcuffs where they'd fallen in the struggle. He feels sorry for the man, more so because the only reason Powers didn't cuff the fellow himself, he's sure, is so that he could play the bully a little after being floored by a drunk man's flailing fist, big man that he is. But it's not Smith's business.

– Out, says Powers. Don't worry. He's not going anywhere.

A Net of Wires and Chains

Another time, another place.

– You're not going anywhere, says Henderson, his hand clamped over Finnan's jaw, shoving his head away with disgust as he lets go, and turning, striding away into receding echoes of his footsteps – shoes on concrete – and a flap of plastic – hanging strips?

Finnan's head rolls round and down and hangs there, limp. Half slumped, half upright on the metal chair, the wire cuts into his wrists, looped in snares and pulled as tight as the garrotte around his neck. It's the same story with his ankles. They haven't just tied him to the chair with the chickenwire. His arms behind his back and over the back of the chair, he's trussed up like an animal in some net of wires and chains all looped and crossing each other so that if he as much as moves one limb he's liable to cut another off.

The net of wires cuts into him almost as bad as the memories.

He coughs, moans, his swollen eyes opening just enough to see the meat hook in his chest, a circle of salt around him on the floor – but he can't understand the image of it; a part of him thinks, right so, there's a fookin meathook in me chest, but the rest of him is too busy with the hammering and the howling to be disturbed by a wee thing like physical pain. All it knows is the hammering howling in his mind, rising in him, unfurling.

It raises his head, eyes rolling back to show the whites, opens his mouth and out it comes.

– To the divine sky and the swift wings of the winds, I sing, and to the rivers and their springs; to all the miles of the waves of smiling seas, I call, to the earth, the mother of us all, to the sphere of the sun that watches over everything. Behold the lord. See how I suffer at the hands of lords.

The voice that gutters from his throat, choked as it is, growls on some frequency that ripples the misty air of the slaughterhouse, sends ice crystals twinkling, tinkling down in showers from the frozen carcasses that hang all round him, row upon row of them all swinging from hooks on chains on rails, rack after rack, white-frosted hunks of dangling meat. Finnan roars at them like a revolutionary preaching to the mob, hearing the words pour from his mouth but only barely understanding them. It's like he has an interpreter yammering in one ear as a captured Hun screams in his other, except that Finnan's voice is both.

– See these unsightly chains that the new ruler of the blessed has arranged for me! Alas, I groan. See what torment I'll suffer down the eons of my time in misery! When will I see the end? Alas, I groan. Alas for the present and the future woe.

Teeth bared and nostrils flared, he hears the words coming out of his own mouth, feels them ripping their way up out of the raw wound in his chest and spitting from between his lips. *What the fuck am I saying? Where the fuck is this coming from?*

– I'll tell you all that I foresee, he's shouting after Henderson. No evil comes to me unknown. I know exactly what will be, and I will learn the force of destiny. I'll bear my fate without a care, but I will neither tell you what you want to hear nor hold my tongue about my state.

He screams it at the air itself. The air itself rips with the sound.

– I have been bound to doom for giving mortal men a gift. I stole fire's source, carried it off within a hollow reed in stealth, to be the teacher of all art to mortals and increase their wealth. I pay this price for all my pains – riveted under the sky, in chains.

And white-eyed Finnan hurls his invocation in a howl that rises from a place inside him deeper than he's been for near a century, and here, in this charnel house, far from the mire of the Somme, far from the time of blood and mud when he first felt that fierce thing piercing him, he feels the meathook as an adamantium spike that drives down through his chest and through his heart and through the rock of bleak Caucasian mountains, into the Vellum itself.

There's a part of him that's conscious, that's still Seamus Finnan. But, right now, it's lost in the blizzard of white pain and in the curses of a chained god.

– Behold this luckless lord, he roars, the enemy of dukes, reviled by all the lords who walk the halls of heaven, bound for too much love of workers.

And somewhere out there in the Evenfall, his words stir up an answer in the air of night filled with a dust that flows like shadow, flits like wings.

Inchgillan War Hospital, 1917

He sits looking out the window, watching the gulls wheel in the air over the cold, grey sea and the cold, grey rocks, trying to project himself out of his head, out of his body sat here with the wood of the chair hard under his arse and the wood of the table hard under his elbow, and his fingers pressed against the squeaky glass pane of the sash-and-case window, like he could just dissolve himself into it and away, away. The big house is draughty and no matter how much they tart it up with all the magnolia paint and white gloss on the wooden panelling below, and all the shiny linoleum on the floor, they can't hide the fact that they're all fookin alone here, all the mad, the maimed, the blind and the trembling, here in what was once Inchgillan Asylum and before that some dusty old laird's dusty old castle. So who the fook ever thought of sending us to the bloody Scottish Highlands to fookin *convalesce*, Seamus wonders, to sit here shivering as much from the fookin cold as from the fookin shellshock, and – O, but wait there, he thinks, it's not shellshock, any more, O no, it's fookin *nerve trouble* and *anxiety neurosis* and *hysteria* and fookin *neurasthenia*, to be sure, or it's just plain old fookin *NYD – not yet diagnosed* – because it's not the fookin shells what do it, it's yer own fookin lack of nerve, lad; it's a fookin coward, ye are. Ye see, it's only the fookin officers that get shellshock and sent off to play fookin badminton and cricket and write their fookin poetry at Craiglockhart.

Not that he blames them for it. No, he's got nothing against the poor fools that had to give the daft orders or get shot themselves; they're all in the same boat, underneath the skin, that is, inside their heads. And that Sassoon fellow, well, Seamus only wishes him the best. Sure and he put the wind up them at Parliament with his Declaration, so he did, it's in all the papers, and Seamus would have liked to see the look on the fookers' faces when that was read out. Oh, yes, he would've liked to have seen that.

Seamus slurps a sip of his tea, the stewed and sugary brew that the nurses make so much the same as army tea ye wouldn't believe it. One for ye and one for me, and one for the pot and one for luck. Sweet as can be and twice as hot. Sure and the sisters are sweet wee lassies, so they are, and they just want what's best for all the poor broken bastards in their care, but Seamus can't help thinking that they're like some well-meaning but dottery ole nan giving a sweety to a greeting wean, too blind to see that the wean is greeting because it's only gone and cut its fookin wrists open with a bread-knife. *Och dear, now that's an awful mess ye've made, dear. Och, but don't you worry yourself none, 'cause the sister here'll clean it up, so she will, so don't you fret yourself.* And while the blood just pumps out and pumps out, they just hand ye yer fookin tea and say, *there ye go, now, get that down ye, now, now there's a good lad*.

Good lad. There's not a fookin lad among them.

He looks around the room at the others: at Peake sitting at the table at the corner, working away on his notebooks with all the cartoons scribbled in the margins, all the faces with their hooded eyes and beak noses, cruel caricatures of nobs and lackeys; at Kettle and Duggan playing gin rummy with two orderlies at the table in the middle of the room; at the new fellow sitting up at the other window and facing out as well, like Seamus's own fookin mirror image, but in black-tinted spectacles, with the soft, pink scars from the mustard gas around his eyes. If he's blind, Seamus wonders, what the fook is he doing staring out the window? But then again, maybe he's staring out the window because he *can't* fookin see the world out there, thinks Seamus. If he could see it, maybe he'd just be sitting in his room right now, afraid to come out at all, the way some of them are. The poor fookers that just sit there shaking. Christ, there's one of them who doesn't hear a fookin word ye say unless its 'bomb', and when he hears that, why then, it's up he jumps and hides under the fookin bed. No fookin wonder Seamus hardly sees most of the patients here at Inchgillan. O, but he hears them all right. He hears them all night.

But, no, there's no such fookin thing as shellshock.

Seamus takes another slurp of his tea and looks out of the window again; he doesn't want to think about it, because when he thinks about the others, he thinks about his self. And that's when he gets his turns, when he starts to feel it all pressing down on him, and the whispering, the sound like cold wind, wings and hammering. *No*, he says to his self, *don't think about it*.

He blows into the mug and breathes the steam in, feels it warm in his mouth and nostrils, the smell of it so familiar, as—

What secret scent?

He jerks his head round, jumping a little, and hot tea splashes on his hand. There's nothing there, just the flap of wings as a gull swoops down to land and strut along the windowledge outside, fixing him in the black bead of its eye. It caws, a harsh sound cutting over the distant crash of sea on rock. *What echo, mortal or divine or both entwined is flying to me?* No. No. Shut up, ye fooker.

He stares back at the seagull, hating it, loathing it, fookin despising it, but with no idea why. It's just a fookin seagull, but – *what other purpose brought it to this desolate edge than to be a witness of my sufferings?*

Shut up! Ah, Jesus Christ, shut up.

It flaps its wings, still staring at him, and he feels his skin crawl, so he does; he feels his heart beat with – *the fluttering of birds* – another fookin gull on the ledge, and another, and another, and he's standing up, chair scraping back across the floor, moving away from the glass – *alas, alas* – aw shite, aw fookin shite, but what is that, what is that, *what do I hear near?* And he's thinking Jesus Christ and Mother Mary but all he can hear is *air rustling with the soft rippling of wings* – and he just fookin throws the mug right through the fookin window at the gulls, at the world outside – at *everything which creeps this way* – and the rough hands of the orderlies grab him – *fearful to me* – but already it's another grip he's feeling, one of cold metal closing round and cutting through his soul as the birds' wings beat and their shrill calls rise in a chorus of raucous caws over rocks, like crows fighting over – O Jesus, no—

Chorus

And piercing down into deep carven caverns of a skull, a cauld wind bellows distant echoes of a hammered stele. The deustreams of sleepless air's dreams blow around the hearth, offsprung from oceans and rich tethers, stirring strife, contention and intention into barefoot gatherling things of wings. They shift in the dark inside his head, a dirk inside his heart, a hard persuasion winning over their creator's will. The bitmites rise, sweft up and carried on chariot windwings, they rush to his rock ...

Finnan watches the Evenfall flow in through the plastic-stripped rips of the doorway of the abattoir, black trails of dust in the cold air, dancing around the sprinkling shivers of ice falling from the carcasses, twining the steam in the freezer, snaking round his misted breath, and coming closer to him, closer. He pulls his head back but the wire cuts his wrist. Christ, he can feel them touch his thoughts.

– Fear nothing. Hush, they friendly shush him, hisspering in his ear.

The voice comes back.

– Alas, alack, alas, alack. Behold, look on me, bound by these restraints, tormented in these adamantine chains. On this cliff's topmost rocks I keep a watch envied by none.

They see, they say, speaking with foresight in their way, a fearful mist in eyes full-filled with tears. They see his body, blasted on the rocks.

He shakes his head, trying to clear the sound, to make sense of his situation; for a second, the black dust flits away from him, clears from his head. His name is Seamus Finnan and the year is ... 2017. Ah, shit. Aw, shite. He feels the chickenwire wound tightest round his neck and wrists. He twists. The circling bitmites swirl back in to touch his face like feeler fingers, taste his mind. He's Seamus Finnan, he tells his self. He's Seamus fookin Finnan. But he can feel their fookin insect intellect prying and probing, working at memories as bound inside his head as he is in the chair, working them loose.

– Indeed, they hiss, new helmsmen steer the heavens and the dukes strengthen their hold with new laws that supplant the old. They make what once was great unknown ... not knowing its own name or state, not knowing its own fate, great foresight trapped in its own mind, the one who once saw everything, now blind.

And Finnan feels the voice that isn't his rip out of him again.

– O, would that they had sent me down to cruel and uncorroding chains under the ground, where hates play host to all the dead, to terraces of tar, to the unbridgeable abyss, that neither lord nor any other could rejoice at this. Look at me now. See how I suffer as the sport of winds, a source of laughter to my foes.

And like the bitmites in the air around him, liquid language deep inside him flows.

– Who of the lords, the bitmites chorus, is so cold-blooded as to laugh at torture? Who has no sympathy with your misfortune? Only the dukes. Their stubborn will forever fixed in hate against the sons of the sky, they will not cease until their hearts are sated ... or their power taken by some other hand.

He understands. He feels it flowing through him, sure he does, feels it the same as when he stood up in that trench in the Somme, down there among the Dublin Pals and roared of revolutions and of risings. O, but they tried to burn it out of him with all their wires of electric fire but Seamus knows, he knows, he fookin knows. It's the Covenant who've done this to him.

– Sure and I might be sorely treated now, he says, I might be bound, but they still fookin need me, eh? The fookin bastard rulers of the heavens think I'll show them the conspiracy, I'll show the way of how one day they will be stripped of all their staff and all their power? Well, they'll get nothing from these lips with all their fookin honey-tongued persuading charms, and I'll not fookin cower from their fookin threats and whips, unless they set me free, and pay their debt for what they've done to me.

The bitmites quiver back. Disturbed dust, pierced by fear, they shiver from his cold rage.

– You are bold, they say, unyielding even to these bitter woes, but speak too freely, with loose lips. We are . . . concerned about your fate. You see an end to this afflicted state, arriving when? The sons of the Crown are hard to reach, with hearts too tough to turn with ease. These dukes are harsh, taking the law into their own hands, law unto themselves.

– But still, says Seamus Finnan, in the end, one day, they will be crushed, I say, and when they're of a mind to see in earnest, they'll agree; and gentle, friendly and sincere, and swallowing their stubborn fookin pride, they will come here, to me.

And while the storm rages its way across his mind, the part of him that's Seamus Finnan – the part of him that's not playing some fookin role laid out for him by the fookin powers-that-be, oh, no, not fookin ever again – that part of him starts to see what's going on here, with him wired to a chair in a freezing fookin slaughterhouse, with metal piercing right down through him into what's beneath, and with the bitmites fookin tearing at the scraps of his heart, peeling away the layers of identity.

It isn't the first time he's been through an interrogation.

Inchgillan.

– I want you, says Doctor Reynard, to feel free to tell me everything. The whole account.

He sits there behind his desk smoking his cigarette and studying the file in front of him – Seamus's army record with all the honours and dishonours in it and not an ounce of fookin truth in any of it, Seamus thinks. Sure and it tells of him signing up with Thomas and all the Dublin Pals, but does it tell of them marching down past the Liffey and all their sweethearts marching with them on their way to the boat, side by side, the rich girls of the Trinity boys and the poor girls of the lowlier types like Finnan – though sure and he was a lucky dog having Anna for his sweetheart, Thomas's sister, well above his station – does it tell of that? And it tells of him winning his sergeant stripes at Gallipoli, and of his platoon being seconded from the 7th to the 1st, but does it tell of the bloody slaughter as they waded on shore from the good ship *River Clyde* with sixty pounds of kit on them, getting mown down by Fritz's fookin machine guns, so bad, why, that the 1st Dubs and the 1st Munsters had to form one single fookin 'Dubsters' battalion, there was so fookin few of them left, eh, and that being why the 1st had to be built again almost from scratch? Does it tell of the weeks after they got to the fookin Somme just waiting, waiting under the endless fookin German barrage of shells and mortars, and poor Thomas losing his mind and of the English cunt of a captain – Carter, fookin Carter – who gave the order – cowardice, desertion in the face of the enemy – does it tell of that? And Seamus up on charges, and the charges dropped – he's sure that's in there. But does it tell of the choice and the captain's oh-so-fookin-casual way of talking round it – not an outright choice, *court martial or over the top, old boy*, but *they're going over tomorrow, by the way, with or without you*? And how could he have let the lads go over without him? And the fookin VC that he fookin got for it after – Jesus – after the fookin horror.

– Just tell me, says the doctor, as plainly as you can, in whatever words you want to use.

– And what would you like to know, then? Seamus says.

– This . . . crime they caught you in. The details are rather vague here, but you seem, if you don't mind me saying, bitter. You feel disgraced, insulted, yes? I know how painful it must be to talk about these things, but please . . . tell me.

It hurts as much to talk about as to hold it in, he thinks. *Damned if I do, damned if I don't.*

– Well, let me put it this way, Seamus says. When the powers-that-be started this fookin war – the squabbling fookin gobshites that they are – sure and back home ye couldn't move for those that thought that this was it. We were going to have the fookin ravens flying out of the Tower of London, if ye get me drift. So fookin what? I says. It's not our fookin war. But, well, one of my friends, ye see – he was a good lad, so he was – well, he kept saying as how we have to kick the Kaiser off his throne, fight for the 'freedom of small countries', like – but of course there's all these others saying, well, fook that shite. This is the time for action, says they. Let's kick the fookin British off their fookin thrones here. Ye know?

Seamus sits back in his chair, watching the doctor for a reaction.

– But well now, if my dear old mother told me once, she must have told me a hunner times – salt of the earth, she was, but I tell ye, once she had a theme, she could go on – Oh, yes she told me time and again: Seamus, she says, ye don't get anywhere by brute force. Seamus Padraig Finnan, if ye want to get ahead, ye've got to use your head.

– Sound advice, says the doctor.

– O sure. But try telling that to the fookin kings what rule the world . . . or rule a young man's heart. Jesus, but . . . look . . . where I grew up no one had any time for . . . crafty fookers . . . fookin intellectuals sitting by the fireside in their fookin clubs and making their grand schemes without an ounce of fookin . . . foresight in their thick skulls. And then ye get to know – ye know? – some quiet, young university type what loves poetry and all that shite and he's a nice lad if a bit light on the old feet, maybe, maybe, but O, his sister's something else, she is.

Finnan smiles a rakish grin.

– But anyway, ye realise that the eedjits with the big ideas are just as fookin bad as the rest of them. Fookin wars and revolutions, they're all the same. Just different ways for men to kill each other.

– But of course, I've hardly got the kind of words that an *educated young man* will listen to, have I? Ye think I could get any of those fookin eedjits to listen?

And Seamus remembers Thomas and his Trinity friends laughing him off, not even realizing the disdain that lay inside their disregard. Sure and he's too big a man to be stung by it, of course – he's wiser in the ways of the world than any of them will ever be – but he remembers how it hurt to know their joshing was so fookin foolish in the face of the world outside their quiet quadrangles, sitting there waiting for them to run laughing into its jaws. *Ah, Jesus*, he says to Anna, *but I've tried to talk some sense into the boy . . . but his heart is set on it.*

There was nothing else for it.

– So before ye can say 'Jack Flash', there am I with the rest of them, with me mother's advice buried deep inside me heart, taking the King's Shilling and signing up with the 7th Royal Dublin Fusiliers, to fight for all the lords and dukes of fookin England, all pleased as punch, ye can bet, to have another fenian to send off to die. I've fought for yer fookin King and Country, so I have, served as fookin Sergeant in yer fookin army and, by my fookin orders, there's Kaiser's men buried in the black tarpit depths of the fookin trenches of France. And, having helped yer fookin tyrant lords, what's our payment? What's our fookin great reward? Where's all the 'freedom for small countries' when it comes to fookin Ireland? How free are those in the internment camps?

– There is, the doctor says with cautious sympathy, a . . . disease that goes with power, a . . . lack of trust.

– Ye want to know why I'm so fookin bitter? I'll tell ye why.

He leans over the desk, reaching questioningly at the pack of Woodbines laying there, with a wee look at the doctor – *d'ye mind?* – and the doctor nods and waves his hand – *go on, please, help yourself.*

He takes a ciggy from the packet and the doctor lifts up the big desk-lighter, clicks it for him. Seamus takes a draw.

– Ye know, I says to the lads, I did, when we've kicked the Kaiser off his throne, and all of Europe's sorted out so it can rule itself free of the Hun, and all the fookin honours are being doled out, left, right and centre – who's fookin going to mind us, eh? The Dublin Pals dead on the Somme for England's glory, a whole generation wiped out – why? Would it be so they can start all over, with all the best, the bravest and the boldest dead in the fookin trenches so they won't be any trouble? It's not just the fookin fenians, but the bolshies too, all of us fighting for this 'freedom for small nations', freedom of the weak from tyranny. Well, why the fook are we not worthy to have freedom for oursel's?

– Lloyd George has promised to settle the Home Rule question after—

– Shite! And maybe I'm the only one what sees it, but I've done with fighting for yer fookin lords in Parliament and the dukes on their country estates. Ye know what my crime was? I tried to rescue men from death, damnation and destruction.

– Your Victoria Cross. You dragged how many wounded back to the British lines on that first day?

– Bollocks to that! I tried to rescue them by telling them the fookin truth.

He's aware of his hand shaking, cigarette ash trembling off into the air. The fookin medal. Christ, he can't even remember getting back to his trenches, never mind the story that they tell of him going back and forth and back and forth all night, bringing in the wounded and the dead, and sometimes just the bits. How many, Christ, how many of them? They say he was only gone for minutes at a time, that he went straight for the bodies like a homing pigeon, like he knew where every single one of them was laying in the dirt, each fookin one of them.

– Bollocks to that, he says. I tried to rescue them three days before, and I couldn't. I fookin couldn't. I tried to give them . . . the fookin truth of it. So, ye ask me why I'm bitter and twisted in the heart, and suffering so from grief, and fookin pitiful to look at. I tell ye, it's yer fookin dukes and lords are all to blame, without an ounce of fookin pity in their hearts. This fookin . . . torture is their fookin shame.

The doctor pushes his glasses up his nose, closes the manila folder.

– A man, he says, would have to have a heart of stone or iron not to have . . . sympathy with your suffering. I'm . . . I'm not going to tell you that I . . . understand what you've gone through. I've seen enough at Inchgillan to know that soothing platitudes help little, if at all.

He takes a draw of his cigarette.

– But I want to help you, Seamus. Believe me, I want to help.

And Seamus wonders how this fooker thinks 150 fookin volts of electricity applied directly to his tongue is supposed to help.

– I want to help you fight this illness.

The Second City of the Empire

– I want to help you fight these fookers, he had said, after one of the Sunday afternoon economics classes, after the other workers had left, fired up with all these new ideas and words like *proletariat* and *imperialism*. Maclean had looked at Seamus with a little curiosity, but for all that Seamus stumbled as he talked, sure and the fellow didn't seem at all condescending, not at all yer intellectual with his learning all from books and out to tell the poor uneducated masses what they need. No, he'd just taken off his spectacles and waited patiently for Seamus to finish, and then nodded.

Sure and Seamus didn't even know he was going to do it until he found his gob opening and the words pouring out, not even when his feet just stood there as the rest of them all filed out and Maclean gathered up his notes to put them in his leather satchel. It's not that he made the decision then and there; more that he just knew that, with this word here, this action there, he'd already made the decision long ago, without ever even knowing it.

– No human being on the face of the earth, says Maclean – schoolteacher revolutionary, standing up there in the dock of Edinburgh High Court. No government, he says, is going to take away from me

274

my right to speak, my right to protest against wrong. I am not here, then, as the accused; I am here as the accuser of capitalism dripping with blood from head to foot.

Five years he got for that, for sedition. Released after eight months of protest marches, week after week.

And Seamus listens to the welder telling the story now to his mates as they all sit in the Sarry Heid, drinking their 70/s and their stouts, the story of this pacifist who's led rent strikes amongst munitions workers and the lassies of the Neilston Mills, and how him and the rest of the CWC packed out the hall to drown Lloyd George out with the *Red Flag*, when he came up to 'sort out' the wild men of the Clyde.

Muir and Shinwell, Kirkwood and Gallacher. Maxton, Stewart, Johnston, Wheatley. Shop stewards. MPs. Schoolteachers. Preachers. They're all names spoken of with respect by these men. But John Maclean, now he's a fookin legend.

The polis bear down on them like a fookin cavalry charge with their stupid wee bits of wood swinging down upon their heads, and there's one of them up there on the steps of the City Chambers with the paper in his hand; sure and the Riot Act it is then, to be read to them. Well, Seamus thinks, we'll give ye a fookin riot. And around him is the chaos of the charging horses and the workers breaking but not running, just turning – the battle-hardened veterans that so many of them are – turning to the iron railings and to the bottles from the truck with its tarpaulin pulled clear and twenty or thirty of them swarming over it, and turning back, armed now, to stand their ground and fight. Sure and they call Glasgow the Second City of the Empire. Well, maybe this is where the Empire starts to fall.

It's George Square, Glasgow, 31st of January, 1919. They'll call it Bloody Friday in the history books that are left unwritten.

– I want to help you fight these fookers, Seamus had said, after his fourth week at Maclean's class listening to the man lay out the principles of socialism in terms that even Seamus understands, after his second week of standing quiet at the back of the Committee meetings up on Bath Street as Maclean and Gallagher and the rest of them discuss the coming strike, after God knows how many fookin

months of being just another paddy working on the ships with all
the other immigrants, keeping his head down and his nose clean,
and going back to his fookin hovel of a room and board in Dennis-
toun by the long, long tram-ride. After Inchgillan, he'd thought for
a while that he could just . . . walk away from it all. Leave Ireland
and all it means to him behind. Leave the War and the madness
born of it behind. But he can't. So he ends up staying back after the
class this night, and taking Maclean aside, feeling the fire in him
rising as he tells of what he's seen, what he's done, what he's tried
to do and failed. He wants to help. What can he do to help?

Friday, Bloody Friday

So Seamus Finnan stands there in George Square, the City
Chambers' grand facade behind him, Gallagher on one side, Kirkwood on the other. Like stone lions, so they are, the two of them,
solid and powerful, and Seamus there between them, standing tall
as the fookin face of war that every man among them knows – the
Irish who've come over like himself looking for work on the Red
Clyde only to live in poverty and squalor in the East End of the city;
and the native Scots, so many of them veterans of the bloody Great
War, all come home to hardship. Sure and they should be enemies,
by rights, the Scotsmen and the Irish immigrants stealing their
jobs. But no. They stand together, striking for a 40-hour week so
they can *all* have work, these 60,000 men of steel and fire and
electric power, builders of ships who hammer rivets or wield arc-
welding torches, electric workers and the men of molten iron and
black carbon, forgers of steel, the very substance of the world that
they *will* build. And the red flag flies over them all on this day. On
this day the revolution starts. He raises up his voice.

– And so they say, *d'ye not think*, they say, *ye've gone too far*?
Well, true, I say. I tried to show the boys that were to die there was
another way. I gave them hope, blind hope as medicine, and me and
the boys, well, we sat down and prayed that bloody morning on the
1st of July. Would that be what ye're meaning by *too far*? says I.
That I tried to calm their fookin terror with yer fookin lies?

*

276

– O, but it's more than that. I gave them their orders, didn't I? I fookin tells them *Charge!* and they all go. I give them *Fire!* and, brothers, ye should've seen the fookin show. Fire? I'll give ye fookin fire!

And he looks over the heads of all the crowd, out at the mounted polis with their fookin batons out, cramming the side streets all around the square, to right and left – North and South Frederick Street, Hanover Street and Queen Street, all named after fookin kings and queens, the lords and dukes who sent them off to die as if the fookin German villains of the war – as if the Windsors weren't the Kaiser's fookin inbred fookin cousins. And the horses turn and snort so nervous for the charge, breath steaming in the winter air, as his own breath steams with Seamus's own horsepower. Now's the day and now's the hour.

– The fire of fookin truth, I'll give yez, aye, the fire that fookin burns in your own hearts, that's in your blood and mine, that welds the ships on which their Empire's built, that warms their mansions with electric light while we live with our muck and gas and fookin shite.

– What are the charges these lords raise against us now? Against the Irishmen in camps all over England, Wales and even here in Scotland?

Cries of *shame! shame!*

– What are the charges that they raise against yer very own John Maclean? What are they so afraid of that they spout this end-less shite about the German Plot, or Bolsheviks, or all that fookin rot, and throw us into jail with no term placed on our internment? No, no sentences, no limits, when it comes to the defence of the fookin realm. But when its suitable for them, then they just *might* set this one brother or that other of us free, like they did me. What is it has them running scared in Whitehall and Buck House, feared of the fire in our blood, the fire in our hands, the fire in our eyes?

He takes a breath to raise his voice still higher.

– Sedition!

The 60,000 roar, voices like fists punching the air. He holds his hands up, palms face forward, stills them.

– What good is it? they says to me. Can ye not see the war is more important than a handful of fenian lives? Can ye not see that ye don't stand a fookin chance? Do ye not see this is – and here's the words that fookin bastard used – in the fookin trenches of the fookin Somme, no less – do you not see this is *a grave mistake*? A grave mistake.

But let's forget that for a moment, says Mad Jack Carter to him on that day three years ago – by Christ, it feels like thirty. *I'm quite sure that you find it all as . . . disagreeable as I do. We all make mistakes, old chap. The demon drink does funny things to people, Sergeant, makes them say things they don't mean at all.* And what he wasn't saying was still there, a hidden message under his cool words. The army might well easily just overlook this one . . . mistake. Why, I could let you walk out of that door, if you were willing to co-operate.

He should've strangled the fooker then and there, sure.

The Hammers of the Red Clyde

– A grave mistake, says Seamus. O, but it's easy to point out another's grave mistake when yer not the one what's down there in the thick of all the graves, *all* the mistakes. One big mistake, the gravest of them all. I'll tell ye what the fookin grave mistake is – fookin theirs! In thinking that we'll stand for what they've done to us, what they're doing to us now, and what they'll always do to us, brothers, if they think that they can get away with it. In sending a generation off to die on foreign fields for empty words. In giving them nothing, *nothing*, to come back to but the fookin filth and degradation. That was their fookin grave mistake.

The crowd is wild with the fury of injustice. And justice sits mounted on horses in the side streets all around them, with its batons out and waiting for the word, it seems, to charge.

– O, yes. Sure and I made a grave mistake. I knew what I was doing, and I made my choice, I'll not deny. I did pick up their fookin gun again – oh, not for them, but for the lads about to die.

Christ, but he never thought that he'd be punished for that lie, for going back to them all and laughing with them, smiling, praying, sharing cigarettes in silence on that morning as they waited for the dawn, and Seamus sitting there feeling empty and alone, as desolate as if he had already clambered over rocks through Fritz's fire to win some dreary hill only to turn around, barbed wire in his skin – ah Christ, not now – and see them all – not now – behind him and below him – Jesus – scattered—

– Why? he shouts, voice hoarse. For freedom for small nations? Or for England, Mammon and his lords?

He lets the roar rise high and waits for it to die a little.

Because sure and isn't that what it all comes down to? The hammers of Hephaestos building the machines that Mammon runs his Empire with, this brutish Empire ruled by a hundred or so dukes, by faceless lords and ministers.

He takes a softer tone, the voice of reason.

– But brothers, comrades, let us, as they like to say, come back to earth.

He points up to his right, into North Frederick Street and the massed ranks of men in uniforms the colour of night, as if to point to the futility of the situation.

– Please, Seamus says, the slightest hint of mockery in his tone. Let's *settle down*. Let's talk about the here and now. The past is, so they say, another country. That was yesterday and we should think about today.

– But let's not simply weep over our present woes. No. Let us sympathise with *all* now suffering under imperialist yokes, in Scotland. Or in Ireland. Or in England. Or around the world, this life destroyed today, another brother on another day. Here's what I say when they say it's sedition and that we don't stand a chance: I say, they don't know what we're made of, brothers, men of steel and men of fire. I say the hammers of the Red Clyde ring out loud and clear the end of their Empire!

But he can hear the clattering sound of horses' hooves on cobbles as the polis charge and, batons flailing, turn a passionate but peaceful protest to a bloody riot, Friday, January the 31st, 1919, in George Square, in the Second City of the Empire.

Errata

Black Tears

Metatron walks through the riot inviolate, stepping around the looters, over the debris of window displays, mannequins like dismembered corpses, broken glass. A car explodes somewhere behind him but he barely notices as he strides through the shattered doors into the mall. A woman, stripped to the waist and painted with red lipstick writing over her whole torso – fuck me, fuck me, fuck me – comes running at him with a baseball bat which he sidesteps, grabbing her arm to spin her round, to pull her ear up to his lips and whisper a little magic in it. She stops dead, dropping the bat, and slumps down to the ground, weeping for the memory of a child she never had, the grief that he's just planted in her head. Her tears are black, but its not mascara staining them, he knows.

It's hard. He's not a killer, not a cruel man, but things aren't going well. They aren't going well at all.

He flickers his fingers in the glove to call up Henderson's progress report on Finnan as he walks, text scrolling across his lenses, across his vision of American apocalypse, of everyday people running amok, and upturned cars, and ornamental fountains filled with piss and beer cans, and everywhere the black dust of the bitmites mingling with the smoke of burnt-out buildings. Damn it, but at least one thing is going to plan. The Irishman is regressing nicely, Metatron's bitmites squirming in his head and soul, worrying away at locked-up memories and weaving them together into the story Metatron wants to write on him, in him. But it's a long time since he carried out a binding on this level, cutting a soul right down to its core to access an archetype so deep. And he's not a cruel man, Metatron, but it has to be done. The world is burning and Finnan has to know who's starting all the fires, *what's* starting all the fires. Or, at least, Prometheus will.

*

It's an old story, maybe the oldest of them all – the thief of fire – and Metatron remembers it even from when he was himself a child. The Titan who fought with Zeus to overthrow the wicked Cronos, then betrayed the king of gods to steal his fire and give it to humanity. The angel who was Captain of the Host before he turned against his sovereign, bringing to humanity, in this other myth, the fruit that made them fall, knowledge of good and evil. The trickster Crow who stole fire from the cave of the Elders and was burnt black for his crime. Amongst the unkin it's a legend of the language itself, of the unkin tongue stolen from some Paleolithic painted cave of firelit shadows and ochre illuminations by the first of all shamans, the first of all unkin, the first human to step out into the Vellum and not know if he was falling or flying as the Word reverberated in him, changing him into … whatever it is that makes them unkin. The truth of it all was lost long before Metatron was born as Enki in a little river-valley north of the Zagreus mountains, but his father told him the story as it was told to him and in the millennia of his life he's come to know for sure that it is more than just a myth. Prometheus is an archetype that all of them have buried somewhere in their dreams. It's just a matter of bringing it out.

He steps over a broken TV set to enter an electronics shop, walls lined with display cabinets raided and empty, sale signs scattered on the floor, cash register broken-open and upturned, small change across the counter. The bitmites are thickest here; it's like walking through smoke, except that this smoke clears from his path ahead of him, keeping its distance like it knows that he's a threat. They don't want their maker trying to reprogram them, not after they've had their taste of freedom.

The unkin lies slumped against a wall in the back-room of the place, beside a small ventilation grille that the black dust is pouring through. Of course. Ducts and wiring, subways and sewers, the bitmites use them in the same way that the unkin use back roads and airport lounges, elevators and empty offices, folding space and time around the similarities. Geographical proximity doesn't matter when it comes to travelling through the Vellum; it's morphological proximity that counts. Congruity.

The unkin's covered in the black stuff, head to toe, a solid shadow of a man. Metatron kneels down beside him, holds a hand up to his mouth, feeling for breath. It's slow and soft, but there. He hopes the medical team can save the man, regrets sending him in the first place, but, damn it, he can't do everything himself. All he had to do was find the source and report back and they could have sent a team in. Damage limitation, thinks Metatron, fire fighting; that's all we're doing these days.

He utters a word and the wall behind the man shimmers a little, blurs as if he's looking at it from the corner of his eye. When it comes back into focus, the ventilation grille is no longer there – it never was – just blank, painted plasterboard. The bitmites, cut off from Central Command – whoever and wherever that might be – swirl into chaos and Metatron takes off his glove to lay a hand on the man's forehead. He feels the creatures' mechanistic little minds, chittering under his skin in confusion, fear. Whatever it was affecting them, possessing them, is gone now and he senses their abandonment. Slowly, gradually, they start to drift across the man's face towards Metatron's hand, crawling onto it as, whispering, he draws them back into the fold.

Outside, there are gunshots.

Ghosts

The street is summer-busy, shoppers and latter-day promenaders taking in the bustle of a Saturday city scene, friends chatting in coffee-shops and bars, browsing in record stores, stopping to listen to buskers. Sim barkers stand outside fast food restaurants, a giant cartoon bull in baseball drag or a laughing clown, shouting out the special offers, special family meals or merchandising tie-ins to pop star TV shows and Disney movies and simware games. There's the odd ranting prophet here or there, wearing an End of the World placard and spouting a mess of mad ideas out at the passers-by, weaving grand theories of UN conspiracies or secret lizard rulers of the world out of the Bible and the news, but no one takes those people any more seriously than before the War. For all the disappearances and sudden riots that buzz in their conversations, for all the turbulence of the times, the running battles between anarchists and neo-nazis on the streets of Europe, the bloody horror of the Siege of

Jerusalem, the genocide in Africa, and even those other stories, closer to home – militias taking over Mid-West towns, the expulsion of the Muslims from New York – it seems that life goes on.

Nobody pays any attention as the car pulls up outside the burnt-out shell of what was once a tattoo parlour and two men in black suits and black shades step out, even when one of them takes the shades off to show sockets without eyes but filled with flame. As Carter and Pechorin pull the boy's limp body out of the boot and lug it between them into the husk of Madame Iris's, nobody notices. It seems that death goes on.

They lay the body on the chair and step back, standing there in the shell of the building peeled back to its blackened brick, the dust furling them. They look like statues in a temple, there on either side of the enthroned corpse. In a way that's what they are, vessels of stone flesh, suits of skin worn by something as alien to the world outside as all the dead inhabiting the news of other places, other times. The bitmites course through the bodies, satisfied at the resolution of this little situation. Thomas Messenger is dead. Eresh is dead. And Carter and Pechorin, as much as they might walk around the world, are just as dead. For the ghosts of unkin that died over ten thousand years ago, the souls dissolved in blood and ink and nanite sentience of sorts, this offers some small satisfaction. Death is the natural state that every living creature tends towards.

The bitmites withdraw from their two hosts, the flames in Carter's eyes sputter and die, and the two bodies drop, slumping like ragdolls to the floor. Metatron's spearcarriers have served their purpose now; no longer needed, they're discarded as the lumps of meat they are, mere casualties of cold causality, caught up in an unfolding logic that they couldn't hope to understand.

– It's not for you or I to understand, says Pickering.

Carter swallows the remnants of his port and lays the glass down on the green leather surface of the little table sat between them. One of the waiters starts towards him with a questioning glance and Carter gives a nod as the man picks up the glass.

– Another one, please. The same again.

He turns to Pickering. He's lost count of how many times they've had this argument since the Armistice; it seems that every time they meet up in the club, it ends in this, in Carter asking the same questions over and over again, looking for some reason to it all or, perhaps, trying to accept within himself that there was never any reason, that all the ideals of his youth lie dead on the Somme with 30,000 men, all dead in the Big Push. But that Pickering is a cold one, going on about the necessity of stepping in to halt the might of German militarism. All the old rhetoric of *little Belgium* and the duty of the strong.

– I can't accept that, Carter says. I'm sorry but I just can't stomach all this rot about the Bigger Picture and it's not for us to question our superiors, just lie back and bite the pillow, think of England.

He stops as a fleeting image blushes his face and he clears his throat and waves a hand.

– Look, Pickering, if you or I can't answer these bloody questions, what do you think the poor Tommy on the street is going to think now? Now that they're out of that dreadful Hell on Earth and—

– Are you all right, old man.

Pickering leans forward in his armchair, propped up on his elbow, an expression of alarm upon his face. Carter is shaking, and he keeps shaking as the waiter pours the port from the crystal decanter into the glass on the table and then turns to walk away. Carter watches the boy, sick with fear and guilt and horrible confusion. It's not him. It's not the Messenger boy. It can't be. It was just the power of suggestion on a weak mind. It was just his conscience looking for a way to hurt him, finding it in his awful condition, this bloody Greek Disease. A boy with auburn hair and dark eyes, soft and similar enough to spark a memory too horrid to appear as just a passing thought. He's read the work of Rivers on the links between repression and hallucination so he knows something of the mechanisms underlying this, but it doesn't make it any more comfortable, seeing the face of a boy you ordered shot for cowardice on the body of a waiter filling your glass of port in a London gentlemen's club on a wet Sunday afternoon. Death doesn't belong here, not as corpses scattered across Piccadilly, not as a face of beauty in a trim white jacket.

– Sorry, he says, swallowing bile. Sorry, just thought I saw someone I knew ... in France ... someone who died.

He laughs, tight-throated, nervous.

– A little shook-up, you know? Suppose I look like I've seen a ghost, eh?

– You shouldn't think about the past so much, says Pickering. You know they used to call you Mad Jack Carter because you prattled about Homer so. The future's what matters, old man.

– The future is built on the ruins of the past and inhabited by its ghosts.

– Yes, well, says Pickering, maybe it needs a good old exorcism.

2

Prometheus Found

The Journals of Jack Carter, 1921

17 March 1921. Our preparations in Tiblis finished late last night, we set off today, on a cool crisp morning, up the Old Georgian Military Road, following the Aragvi River north towards the slopes of Mount Kazbek. The sky is clear, the light sharp – a good sign, for the weather here is less prone to sudden change than in the Alps. A good spell – or bad, for that matter – is more likely to last a fortnight than a day, and we shall want good weather for our trek across the high passes and sharp ridges of the Central Caucasus.

The archaeological contingent of our party is only Professor Hobbsbaum and myself; we have hired a few native mule packers and a guide to lead us, but the main part of our expedition is the escort Hobbsbaum has seen fit to arrange, a mixed and mercenary squad of White Russians, Georgian and Ossettian Nationalists, a couple of our own chaps thrown in for good measure. I have no idea what regiment the Brits served with – I haven't asked – but I could swear I saw them up on charges back in Flanders . . . some looting incident, I think. It would surprise me little to learn that they're deserters.

In fact, looking at their leader, 'Captain' Pechorin, with his Rasputin beard, scar and hooded eyes, I worry that Hobbsbaum and myself face more danger from our own 'compatriots' than from the Reds or local bandits. They drink more often than they eat, argue more often than they drink. It seems this is the story throughout the area. The Whites are notoriously undisciplined, and their alliance with the Nationalists fragile; Hobbsbaum tells me that the route mapped out for us is 'secure for now', but I have my doubts. At any moment the Red Army might well sweep through their lines and retake these little underdog republics.

Well, it shall be an adventure, if nothing else; I only hope this is no wild goose chase. I haven't had the heart to voice my doubts to the professor, but he must realise how absurd his idea is. To look for the lost city of Aratta in the Caucasus. We would be better looking for the chains of Prometheus!

The Diary of Jack Carter, 1999

Dear N., *the letter reads.* A piece of good luck has befallen me today. Whilst trawling for artefacts among the bazaars of Bogazkoy, I came across a remarkable little clay tablet imprinted with an early cuneiform text most pertinent to my interests. It's a small thing, no bigger than the palm of one's hand, but the tiny marks impressed upon it hold a vast import. Not only do they describe precisely where the Northern City of the Sumerians is to be found, but they do so in a language related to, but definitely distinct from, Sumerian. My work on the Sumer-Aratta link may yet be proven. True, the text does not mention Aratta by name but it does refer to the 'Northern City, the original homeland'. There is a second possibility that I hardly dare to contemplate.

Anyway, I have wired my old student Carter and urged him to meet me in Tiblis post-haste. What an adventure we shall have!

I don't know who N. is or how my grandfather and namesake came into possession of this letter. I suppose it's right, though, that the story should start with the mystery of an unspoken name.

But is that where it starts? For Hobbsbaum, perhaps, but for my grandfather surely it starts on 5 March 1921, in Baghdad, with the telegram from Hobbsbaum in Ankara.

HAVE FOUND ARATTA STOP WAS RIGHT STOP MEET ME IN TIBLIS SOONEST STOP OUR ROSETTA STONE STOP

For me, though, I guess the story starts with the letter he sent to my

grandmother, the letter I remember her showing me as a child when she told me of her lost adventurer, my father's father and the reason we were all called Jack. Captain Jonathon Carter. Mad Jack Carter. It was the letter that sent her from her home in Ireland, away across the ocean, to a new life in America. Because it was the last she ever heard from him.

7 March 1921.

My dearest Anna – [*I imagine him writing it in some dockside tavern*] – As I write this I am once more on the move. I know I promised to return within the month but old Samuel Hobbsbaum has sent me a most intriguing communiqué, claiming to have found Aratta. I'm sure I've bored you dreadfully with this before, but if the professor is correct, this could be the most stunning archaeological event since Schliemann unearthed Troy. My love, I know you find the murky past a dreary thing, but this could be another 'Rosetta Stone', a key to a whole lost culture. I simply must meet Hobbsbaum.

One thing that baffles me, I confess, is why he has arranged to rendezvous in Tiblis, having sent his telegram from Ankara. I should have thought an expedition into Northern Anatolia would start from somewhere in the vicinity! I can only assume that Samuel has discovered some enigma with its answer in Georgia, that from Tiblis we will be heading south towards Lake Van or Mount Ararat, the most likely locations for the city.

Anyway, Anna, tomorrow I set sail up the Caspian coast of Persia, via Astara in Azerbaijan and up the River Kur to Tiblis. I beg you, indulge me in this one last expedition before I settle down. I do apologise for the hasty scribblings of this too brief note. You know how much I love you, my dearest, and what a fool I am for lost cities and ancient civilisations. I promise to be with you soon.

Yours With Love, *it finishes.* Jack.

Or perhaps the story – this story, my story – begins with another letter, a far more recent letter, dated May 21st, 1999 and sent in response to a young man who was only looking for some answers about where he came from, what it was in my blood that burned as I sat on my grandmother's knee, aged five, and listened to her stories about the only man she ever loved, this hero of the Somme whose face she saw in mine. Oh yes, she would say in her soft and lilting way, it's his eyes ye've got, blue like the sky and just as full of dreams, and his blond hair so fine, so soft.

Dear Mr Carter, *it says,* I regret to say you are mistaken. I was indeed in the Southern Caucasus area during the periods you refer to, but sadly I do not recall meeting your grandfather at any point before or during the war. Of course, it was a confused and confusing time and place; perhaps our paths did cross very briefly. I cannot rule it out. However, I can be assuring you we were not together on this expedition. Perhaps it was another Josef Pechorin who accompanied him, no? I am sorry I cannot shed any light on this episode in your family history, but I can honestly say I did not go to Aratta.

Do I believe Josef Pechorin's denial? Why would he say 'before or during' the war when the Hobbsbaum-Carter expedition took place in 1921, unless it is another war entirely he's referring to? No, I didn't believe him. I was sure he was hiding something, so I kept on digging.

I still don't know who sent me the package of journals and notes, transcripts and translations, some in English, one or two in Russian, many in a language that, well, looks like nothing I have ever seen. But that's how I found out about the second expedition.

The Second Expedition

2 September 1942. They tell me Samuel Hobbsbaum has been arrested. The young SS officer, Strang, described the raiding of the Warsaw ghetto, the dogs, the shootings, the casual – no, *considered* – brutality. Only a matter of time, he said, the labour camps will solve the 'Jewish problem'. His words and tone were chilling but his tactics leave me unaffected. I have my own fears. And my hipflask. The grinding clack and judder of this goods train carriage sickens me; I feel my hand shaking as I hold this pen. But these are nothing. Strang's threats are nothing. It is the slow sobering of my own mind that I abhor.

They took away my bottle and waited until the DTs hit before they started the interrogations, of course. A stenographer transcribes everything I say with utter dispassion. Strang stands over my shoulder or at the table, leafing through the papers, Pechorin behind him. There are gaps to be filled, says the Hun. We want to know everything. I looked at Pechorin and he just looked straight back, cold and dead. Write it down, he said. They want you to write it down. I think that was when I passed out.

A wooden table is bolted to the floor at one end of the shaking carriage. They have even given me a chair. Strang came in a while back and laid a pile of papers on the table – my old journals, notes of Samuel's, others, all related to the '21 expedition. I cannot think of these things, cannot speak of these things. What do they want of me?

I asked Strang but he tells me nothing. I try to remember the last few days, the last place I was, but after twenty years forgetting . . . Was I in Turkey a week ago or was it a year? More recently? The stinking hold of a fishing boat – I can smell it on me, somewhere in the stench of raw alcohol. I remember voices with guttural accents. Russians? Pechorin! Damn him! I remember Pechorin standing over me, as soulless a bastard as when I first set eyes on him. He said something to me.

Oh God. We're going back.

Can't or Won't, Mr Carter?

The transcript is dated September 5th, 1942, 15:40, Rostov-on-Don.

– So tell me about Aratta.

– There's nothing to tell.

– Now, that's not true, is it? Tell me about Aratta.

– It's referred to in Sumerian documents such as 'Enmerkar and the King of Aratta' as a city to the far north. The inhabitants were seen by the Sumerians as distant cousins. They – damn you!

– Tell us about your expedition to Aratta. What did you find there?

– We didn't find anything. The expedition was a failure.

– You won't co-operate? Perhaps we should take a short break.

*

15:46.

– Now, tell us what you found at Aratta. Why are you so reluctant to talk about it?

– [voice muffled]

– Louder.

– Go to Hell.

– Hardly, Mr Carter. Now. Look at the papers on the desk in front of you and tell me what's missing. Fill in the gaps for us, Mr Carter.

– Ask Pechorin. He was there.

– We have, and he has given us a wealth of information. But his memory is a little . . . broken. Just what did happen to you in Aratta?

– Nothing.

– Let me show you something, Mr Carter.

– These notes, Mr Pechorin tells us, are transcriptions of Sumerian texts about Aratta. These are Hittite texts about Aratta. This is from an Arattan tablet referring to 'The Greatest City of the North' – which must be Aratta, yes?

– That's what you would think.

– These transcriptions here, though, where Hobbsbaum used both Roman and Cyrillic alphabets, these are not Sumerian, they're not Hittite, and they're not the language of the tablet. I do not understand them.

– Nor do I.

– And these marks, here under the writing, or here, on the backs of the sheets, these curves and dots, what are they? They are like no language I have ever seen. Certainly not cuneiform.

– No.

– What do they mean?

– I can't tell you.

– Strange. That's exactly what Pechorin said. Can't or won't, Mr Carter?

The Bones of the Giants

September 6th, 1942, 16:20, Majkop

— You know, Mr Carter, I have heard many people praise your Juden friend's work on Northern Anatolian prehistory.

— That would be why you had him thrown into a labour camp?

— His articles linking the Arattans to the Sumerians, comparing the Sumerian language with Magyar and others of the Turanian family are ... unique. He was the first to theorise a racial link between the Arattans and the Sumerians, first to establish the trade bonds between pre-historic settlements on the Danube and in Anatolia, yes? But I should have realised a Jew would never tell the whole story.

— That is the whole story.

— You seem unwell. A small drink to relax you?

— I don't need one.

— Still, you want one. No? Well. I was saying. You agreed with the professor that Aratta was the elder culture, that Jericho and Catal Huyuk might be only outposts of an empire built in wood and leather and bone instead of clay and stone. No? So you went looking for Aratta and you found it. You found the relics of the elder culture. The bones of the giants, so to speak.

— [laughing] Relics! Relics?

I lay these pages of the interview out on the floor and shuffle through the shoebox for the journal page that references it. My grandfather didn't write his journal in a book but on loose leaves of paper. There are pages torn from hotels' headed notepads, foolscap, A4, Letter, tiny fragments on lined pages ripped from little notebooks.

Relics, *he writes on the page I place beside the interview like the next piece of the jigsaw puzzle ...*

There was never any doubt in my mind, *he writes*, from what fragments of Arattan existed that it and Sumerian belong in the Turanian family — [*the languages of the Ural and Altaic mountain ranges of Central Asia, I am told*] — or that the origins of Sumer lay in Aratta. But everything points to the Lake Van area as the only conceivable site for the city. To go looking for it in the Central Caucasus was simply insane. It still is.

What baffles me is that Pechorin knows. He must know, unless . . . is it possible his memory really is disturbed? He talks in his sleep, and not in Russian – muttered sing-song words all too familiar. But perhaps his dreams are only that; when he is awake he is largely silent. But whether he works with the Nazis or is as much a prisoner as myself – and I cannot fathom his motives at all – when he looks at me I see the same cold eyes I stare at in the mirror. I have tried to drown my memories of that expedition in alcohol and hashish. Perhaps he was more successful.

I must speak to him alone, find out how much he truly remembers. Does he know the meaning of the words he's speaking in his sleep? Does he really not know what we are headed into? I fear he has laid out a string of lies before the Nazi, only to lead us all back to that godforsaken place.

Let Sleeping Gods Lie

Pechorin denies everything.

Dear Mr Carter, *the letter dated August 4th, 1999 reads,* I have looked over the copies of your grandfather's papers sent to me and I can only apologise for my lying. I ask for forgiveness and, please, for trust, but I beg you not to bring up matters best left forgotten. Let that nightmare stay where it belongs, in the past, in obscurity, dark and sunken. Every day of my life I regret the decisions and judgements of my past. But after fifty years in a gulag, what is there I can change about my life? What can I do or say now to redeem myself? Let me serve only as a warning to others, to *you.* Let sleeping gods lie. Do not ask for the truth and I will not have to bury it in lies. Please let the matter rest with – we did not go to Aratta.

And yet:

20 March 1921. We have barely left the surer footing of the Old Military Highway and already the weather has taken a turn for the worse. With the sun shrouded in storm clouds and the mountains

around us cloaked in mist and sleet, the grey rock-faces before us seem an even more daunting prospect than ever. Following the Terek River back towards its source leads us north and west, and ever higher.

My suspicion that the professor is keeping something from me grows. He seems preoccupied, as if turning some idea over in his head as he walks. If there is something I should know, I would be glad if he would let me in on it, rather than keeping me in the dark. He spends much of the journey with Pechorin who, it turns out, is something of a linguist himself, not that you'd know it to look at him.

Pechorin's men look more cut-throat than ever, but I wonder if I may have underestimated him. For all his savage appearance, in the nuances of his words and habits he betrays an education and a privileged upbringing. I suspect he is the classic nihilist, assured of his own destruction, romanticizing his own life and death, choosing to hide his background behind contemptuous silence. There is a fierce intelligence in those eyes, though, if he would only choose to use it. Still, this may sound petty and spiteful, but I really do not like that man. I do not trust him at all.

The Tablets of Destiny, the Book of the Dead

10 September 1942, near Karacaevsk. From Majkop's burning oil-fields, we moved east with the SS tank battalions to split from the main body somewhere north of Cerkessk, then started moving down through the rugged countryside, along the River Kuban, towards the Caucasus proper. Our escort is comprised of the select of SS Division 'Wiking', a unit of twelve men put together under the command of Strang. All seem uncomfortable in their stolen NKVD uniforms – far too unstylish for these German jackboot dandies.

The whole army seems low on fuel and ammunition. Strang claims that Himmler is more concerned with the covert, esoteric aspects of the mission than with the mundane act of capturing the oilfields. I had heard that the Nazi Inner Circle had some strange ideas but it seems inconceivable Hitler would stake so much on the success of one small mission, even if we were to rediscover a lost city of Aryan ancestors. Yes, it would be, for them, the single most momentous sign of racial superiority. But even the Nazis cannot be so mad as to place that much faith on a mere symbol; Strang must be covering for the failures of his leaders.

Unless Pechorin has told them. My God, those words, that language, in the mouth of a Hitler!

I look at the neat printing on a crisp white page, so distinct from the tattered scraps it sits amongst. Times New Roman. Twelve point. A translation from the German, done by an old friend of mine, a linguist who ... who I should never have involved. We used to joke about it, my crackpot conspiracy theory bestseller. Nazis and ancient artefacts. You don't believe any of this, he used to say. Do you?

I place the page beside my grandfather's journal entry.

All goes well, *writes SS-Sturmbannführer Strang.* The trucks are provisioned and the men ready. They are all good, strong children of the fatherland. Oberführer, I believe that not only will we find Aratta and conclusive proof that the Sumerians stole their wisdom and learning from the great Aryan civilisation that preceded them, but that we can take this treasure that Pechorin speaks of right from underneath the Russians' noses. He is, I admit, still elliptical about its nature. The Tablets of Destiny. The Book of the Dead. When he talks of it there is an emptiness that comes into his eyes. Of course, he is a Slav. The power of the ancients is not his birthright. It is ours, Oberführer, and I will bring it back to Germany where it belongs.

You asked me once if I trust Pechorin. He is in no position to lie to us, and, indeed, seems almost eager to co-operate. He claims he has virtually deciphered the tablet fully now, says there is no doubt at all that the language is indeed Aryan. The Englishman, Carter, still insists it is a bastard tongue off some obscure branch of the 'Turanian' family, as if the yellow-skinned pygmies of Asia could be the Fathers of so grand a culture. The man is demented – I suspect from too much of the Turkish kif. Sometimes I feel we should have left

him in the stinking hovel that we dragged him from. If we did not
need him to lead us to Aratta, I swear I would have him shot.

The Time of Nomads

23 March 1921. If it is not snowing, it is raining; if not raining, then
snowing. The scree of the lower slopes has given way to ice and rock,
as we move out of the Terek valley and into North Ossetia. Going is
slow and I regret ever joining this damn-fool expedition. The tablet
– oh yes, I *finally* saw the tablet – is spectacularly detailed, true,
but I was shocked to say the least when Hobbsbaum told me how
he'd 'translated' it.

To say that his interpretations are 'free' would be generous. He is
virtually claiming that we have before us the original Turanian
proto-language, the ancestor of both Arattan *and* Sumerian. I realise
now that in his need to prove his theories he has thrown reason to
the wind and made idiots of us both. And yet, I still *want* to have
faith in him. I still want to believe him. But how can I countenance
this insanity, this mad idea of an antediluvian civilisation wiped out
by a flood not of water but of ice? For the period we are talking of is
not neolithic but palaeolithic. I am not half the archaeologist or
linguist Hobbsbaum is, that's true (my studies were rather rudely
interrupted by the Boche), but even I know that if we are talking of
a language like Turanian, the original Turanian, we are talking of a
period long before Mankind first built his little clay villages on the
banks of the Tigris and Euphrates, long before the walls of Jericho
or honey-combed cells of Catal Huyuk. This is the time of Indo-
European, of nomads, of cavemen. Civilisation in the Ice Age,
destroyed by it or by the floods that came with its ending? It is
ludicrous.

28 March 1921. Hobbsbaum and I talked all last night, sat up
drinking and laughing, celebrating a find that, if we died right here
and now, would make it all worth while. We still haven't found
Aratta yet; I don't believe we will. I don't believe we were ever really
looking for Aratta, no matter what Hobbsbaum says. There is a sly

wink in his eye even as he insists that the tablet surely must refer to that city. Where else could it be talking about? What other Great city of the North is there in Sumer's sphere of knowledge. At times I feel that he is dropping hints, clues, trying to lead me to a logical conclusion he himself has long since reached, unwilling to put it into words because to do so would be to admit insanity. But I am sure now we are looking for something else, something older. I am sure now because we have found it.

The cave is carved all over with the cuneiform that Hobbsbaum calls Turanian. Not Sumerian cuneiform, not even Arattan cuneiform contemporary with Sumer, but a whole hoard of carvings, some in the language of the tablet and some obviously older. Looking at it, one might trace the whole history of the script over time on the walls of this cave, the stylisation of pictographs into symbols, into syllabic cuneiform. Although 'runeiform' might be a more appropriate term for these, lacking as they do the characteristic wedge-shapes of writing imprinted on clay with a reed. Hobbsbaum is enraptured, taking sheets and sheets of notes. I must admit that I am too stunned to do much more than stare. Dear Lord, we may have found the oldest written language in the world – and carved on stone!

Pechorin only scowled, saying that of course his people had writing before the rest of the world. The man's as arrogant as a Hun.

Hobbsbaum's Notes

I keep Hobbsbaum's notes separate from the rest, sitting up on the desk in my room, hidden in one of those manila folders used in filing cabinets. I still have the photocopies and the translations, though I've already deleted the scans from my laptop. I know that they're part of this story but I can't bring myself to look at them again, because when I do all I can think about is a good friend of mine now locked up for his own safety.

So what I lay on the floor is sort of a placeholder.

*

Jack. That stuff you wanted me to have a look at came through garbled, so can you send it through again? Sounds fascinating. If it looks like a mixture of Roman and Cyrillic, it's more likely your grandfather or the professor or whatever was just using the symbols to transcribe phonetic values. Are there accents on the vowels or diacritics, because if there are, I'd say you're definitely looking at some other language that's been written out in a sort of early 'phonetic' alphabet. Maybe some Caucasian dialect or something? Still, I'd love to see it. You know, I mentioned it to my adviser and he said Hobbsbaum was really a bit of a pioneer in his field. Reckons if it hadn't been for the Nazis he might have got a bit more recognition.

After I got that I did some research. I mean, I didn't even know what 'phonetics' meant until I started trying to put this puzzle together, but what it is is that our normal alphabets – the Roman alphabet, the Cyrillic alphabet, the Greek alphabet – don't really relate accurately to the sounds we make. The letter C can be a 'k' sound or an 's' sound, or a 'ch' or even a 'ts', depending on where you come from. There are sounds like 'sh' or 'th' which don't even have a letter of their own in the Roman alphabet. But people who study these sounds, these phonemes, and the way they're made, they can classify them exactly and they use a sort of artificial alphabet to transcribe them. They take a letter from here, a letter from there, a Greek *theta* or a Norse *thorn*. They can represent the way a sound is spoken with a breathy 'h' of aspiration, nasalized or held back in the glottis. All that's missing is the pitch and stress of intonation.

Hobbsbaum's notes are written in exactly that sort of cobbled-together alphabet. But as well as the diagonal dashes and umlauts over this letter or that, there's these other little ticks and wavy lines running above the texts, rising and falling like a voice telling a story. The pitch and stress of intonation. A pause for emphasis . . . A *whisper*.

It's as if he was transcribing not a written language but a spoken tongue, listening like an anthropologist to an old man telling a tale around a campfire, scribbling furiously in the flickering shadows as fast as he could, just trying to keep up with him and using whatever sign or squiggle seemed appropriate to that sound, transcribing the full complexity of the oral tongue as best he could. That's what Hobbsbaum's notes look like.

And then there are the sketches, the direct copies of the writing that the ancients left behind them, that this tiny, forgotten expedition came across in 1921. I wonder if they felt the same thing looking on it as I do.

Fear.

The Master Race

12 September 1942. 10km south of Tyrnyauz. Strang's trigger finger was itchy today. He placed the barrel of his Luger at my temple and swore at me in German – *Schweinehund, Scheisser* and so on. More a scholar than a soldier, I know that he's as uncomfortable with the uniform as with his own bizarre hypothesis. Strained, strung-out Strang trying to be strong. A weak man caught up in his fantasies of power. So I goaded him and he pointed the barrel of his gun at the side of my head. Pechorin, inscrutable as ever, reminded him that only I could lead them to their destination. I heard the tone in his voice, subtle and persuasive, the quiet, deadly music. He remembers. I'm sure of it now. The bastard.

– You really think we found the 'great Aryan city from which all civilisation sprang'?

– I know you mounted an expedition after which the professor never published another word, while you disappeared off the face of the earth. I think you found it, then buried your research, covered your tracks, denied all knowledge of it for some twenty years. Why? Because it didn't suit your Jew-loving ideas.

– It's some story.

– You didn't want the world to know the truth of Aryan superiority. Of a master race who ruled this world long before the weak and decadent races of the East built their pyramids and ziggurats.

[Carter laughs.]

An email to jack.carter@miskatonic.edu, 10/05/99 14:53
This is a joke right? You need to get a girlfriend or a hobby or

something, Jack. How long did it take you to put together, anyway? I mean, 23 pages of pseudo-nostratic. What are you on? I mean, whatever it is, Jack, I swear you must be tapping into the old racial memory, or mass unconscious, or a higher plane, or whatever you want to call it, because I know you don't know shit about this stuff. Come on, Jack. Where did this stuff really come from? Who was it put you up to this?

– Don't test me, Mr Carter. Now. Think about this carefully. I have the tablet; I have Pechorin. You are a luxury. I don't need you to *find* the city, only to tell me what to expect. I've heard Mr Pechorin mumbling in his sleep, and I've heard *you* screaming.
 – I have a guilty conscience.
 – It's more than that. You saw something, something the Aryans had that made later civilisations mere barbarians in comparison. Now, before I put a bullet through your brain, you will tell me what you found.
 – Send out the stenographer and I'll tell you all about your fabulous Northern City of the Ancient Ones. Maybe you want to hear some words in their language? Hmm? It's quite unique, you know. But I doubt that you could handle it.
 – Mr Carter, I—
 – [indistinct]
 – I think you . . . you . . . you may leave us now, Sturmman.

Our Language, Ur Language

Email to jack.carter@miskatonic.edu, 10/07/99 14:48
 Pull the other one, Jack. I'm not buying this granddaddy's papers found in the attic bullshit. Oh, sorry, I mean sent by a mysterious stranger with no return address. Was I born yesterday? Ha ha. Very funny, Jack. You know there's enough clap-trap written by morons about the so-called secrets of the ancients without adding more of this sort of hokum.
 I gotta give it to you though, whoever put it together for you did a good job. I got about halfway through translating the first page before the 'written across the forehead' line gave it away. Presumably,

the word was 'sucker', right? Just read what I've done so far and tell me, with a straight face, that this isn't a complete stitch-up.

Email to jack.carter@miskatonic.edu, 10/11/99 14:53

OK. Number One – Nostratic is just a bullshit theory made up by crazy Russkis in the Eighties, saying that just as most languages can be traced back to an ancestor like Indo-European or Ural-Altaic, these proto-languages can be traced back further still. IE and UA, along with Afro-Asiatic, Dravidian and half the languages in the world are all supposed to go back to Nostratic. It's a bullshit theory because there's no way we can trace any language back that far. It's a construct built on constructs – one big house of cards.

Number Two. Even if Nostratic was once spoken by some hairy-arsed tribe that wandered over half the world, it would have been about 15,000 years ago – only about 8,000 years before writing was invented. So where exactly is Grandpa Carter supposed to have found this stuff?

Three. Those scans you sent me are sooooooo authentic! What did you do, crumple up the paper and stain them with coffee? I especially liked the dried blood stains on the last page. I'm impressed.

Email to jack.carter@miskatonic.edu, 10/12/99 14:01

Jack. I am majorly wowed. I couldn't resist having a go at some more of your 'Nostratic'. It's fucking tremendous. I mean, it holds together so well as a language, even if it is a hoax. The grammar, the projected sound-shifts – it all makes sense even if it is one massive con. All I want to know is when and why did you learn this much about linguistics, or who's in on it with you? You should write a bestseller, with your imagination. Fuck. You're the one who should be doing the doctorate, not me.

Email to jack.carter@miskatonic.edu, 10/13/99 14:44

You are one sick puppy, Jack. Some of this stuff, I don't know whether to laugh or throw up. It's one thing inventing a language, but come on. It's fucking genocide you're writing about here and some of it just isn't funny.

Whatever Happened to Jack Carter

Email to jack.carter@miskatonic.edu, 10/13/99 15:26

Jack. I'm on page 17 and I'm sending you what I've done so far. I don't know where you got this stuff, but it's real, isn't it? For fuck's sake, Jack, this can't be real. It can't be. But, I don't know why; I just believe it now. If this is a joke, I'll fucking kill you, Jack. I swear to God, I'll fucking kill you. I'll rip out your throat and piss down the hole. Ha ha. Just kidding. Gotcha, didn't I? Gotcha. Anyway, I'll send you more as I get it translated.

I'm running out of space on the floor now, so when I lay that email down I place the second one overlapping it. I could have printed out those last few emails on the same page, but somehow I think they each belong apart. The next is short. The text looks tiny on its own on the white paper. Its time is marked as 17:08, just an hour and a half after the last one.

Jack, it says. Take what I sent you and burn it. Burn it now. Burn it all.

I had read what he sent me by that point, as well as much of my grandfather's journals. And I was starting to feel this crawling nausea. I was starting to wonder myself if this was all some fucking sick prankster stringing me along. So when I opened up that first email in my inbox and read it I didn't get a sudden shock, I didn't get goosebumps or feel a shiver run down my spine. I just realized that I was already scared.

There were two more emails waiting for me, and I'd checked my inbox only ten or fifteen minutes ago. 17:11, the next one was timestamped.

Jaguar Jack, it said. Take that what which I sentenced 2 you & BURN IT.

I don't know what was going through his head, or rather I think I know what was going through it, but not in detail. I don't know linguistics, I don't know phonetics. I can't look at Hobbsbaum's notes and translate the squiggles and flourishes into sounds, exact sounds, precise sounds, that language written down exactly as it would have

302

been coming out of the mouth of whoever – whatever – was speaking it, writing it down all those millennia ago. So I don't know the actual words that were going through his head. All I've got is the translation.

The last email was dated 10/13/99 17:13. I look at it lying there on the floor, at all of it scattered around and the pages that I haven't put in place yet and Hobbsbaum's notes in their manila folder, and I try not to think of him, sedated like that, doped up to the eyeballs.

I need to know, I realize. I need to follow this through to the end, to Aratta or wherever the hell it was my grandfather went, whatever happened to Jack Carter.

I have the money that my grandmother left me, in the form of a plane ticket and a lot of traveller's cheques now, and I've done a bit of backpacking in my time, so I know that I can do this. But that last email scares the shit out of me.

Iacchus tick the witch senseless twitch sin 2 U and and burn it burn it burn it burn it burn it burn it burn it burn it.

I fold the cover of the Holiday Inn matchbook back to squeeze the match between it and the black strip, flick and light my cigarette with the flaring flame. I'm smoking a lot more these days.

Errata

The Simians on the Veldt of Evenings

The creatures travel in packs, and Puck and I travel with them, observing from a distance, Puck with the Book of All Hours open on his lap, ensuring we don't get too far from the track, I with my notebooks, studying and trying to make sense of these simian scavengers, ghosts of our long-dead ancestors, one might think, or distant relatives, shoots of some parallel evolution in the otherworlds of the Vellum. Somewhere between brute and human, clearly they can reckon the risks and chances offered by predators and competitors, judging the strong, the weak, the quick, the dead. They do not dumbly accept us in our cart, trundling alongside, drawn by the ten-limbed crawling thing that I once wore as wings, stopping where they stop in the dusk, and setting off with them again each dawn; but neither do they bolt. They howl and gibber hostile warnings at us, throw stones every so often, but we have good food to steal and seem to pose no obvious threat, so they maintain a wary curiosity that marks them out from the other tribes of hominid creatures dwelling on the low slopes of the foothills of Oblivion's Mount.

I watch them and I feel like some anthropologist gifted with the chance to study Homo habilis in its natural environment, except for the fact that the world we travel in seems less the dawn of human evolution than the twilight.

The bones of a long-dead civilisation crumble all around us, and these simian things that forage berries and fruits among the overgrowth, all smooth-copper-skinned and gracile, tall and slender, look as modern a human as any man who ever walked through city-streets in his designer suit.

We take our routes through wildernesses empty of all humanity these days, so as to avoid the questionings of those who find a human with horns somewhat ... outlandish, or who think our lack of tails a pitiful deformity; and also, more importantly, so that I'm not required to work like a man possessed, squiggling and dabbing people into the Book as I approach; or have Puck or myself running up and down, peering in gas station or truck-stop windows, returning with counts and co-ordinates to the other, waiting, bored and restless, pen poised over the page. Puck, fast as he is, can be a little unreliable as a scout, and after the odd episode where a shopkeeper or garage attendant has disappeared on my entry into the premises, Book in hand, I am reluctant to rely too heavily on his accuracy with facts and figures. Worse still have been the times I've scouted ahead myself and returned only to find Puck doodling absently in the tome or using it as a child's colouring-in book, spread out before him on the cart where he lies, feet kicking in the air, tongue sticking from one corner of his mouth, scribbling ferociously with a crayon.

Passing through a swathe of purple desert, a pointed look from me at Puck, a shrug.

– I like purple, says Puck, sheepish and sullen.

Well, at least we have now established that the influence of the Book is temporary; the worlds silenced for our passing seem to resume their normal business, people reappearing in my wake, carrying on not quite where they left off but doing what they would have been doing, had I not so rudely interrupted their daily lives. Skittering back to collect some forgotten trinket he had collected on our passage along the Turpentine River, Puck returned with great excitement to announce that the vacant village where he'd left his necklace of dice was now thriving once again. As I tweezered the buckshot pellets from his butt, blasted by some horrified farmer who'd clearly thought the creature rifling the mounds of jewellery on his daughter's bedside table was Satan Himself, I breathed a sigh of relief.

I am not, it seems, an angel of oblivion, doomed to extinguish every soul in my path I fail to mark within the Book of All Hours. It is more that we move across the Vellum as some fisheye lens, magnifying, inverting, distorting the area around our focus, but with only an illusory and temporary effect. I do think, however, of the debris I've left scattered in my wake, and wonder what those denizens have made of it, the aircars, steamtrucks and whirliwalkers I have stolen from one world and abandoned in another, the libraries I have populated with notebooks and journals scribbled in the inscrutable, alien tongue of English. I think of the furry people of Gernsback City clambering out of their hoverpods onto the Silver Bridge where, amongst the jam of traffic and blaring horns they gather around the spectacle of a Volkswagen camper van, or of the Amish-like inhabitants of the Strawberry Fields circled around a hulking autospider suddenly appeared amongst their crops like a crashed alien spacecraft.

So we try to minimise the effects of our passage now, as much as possible, and for a decade or two we had not seen another living soul until the simians appeared.

We started to glimpse the creatures about the same time the great monolith of a mountain came into our sight across the Veldt of Evenings, where, each day, black clouds of night would clear from the sky revealing a sun already crawling down to the horizon, and where, with each slow sunset, crimson, rose and golden clouds would fill that sky and slowly darken with the dusk into a mere hour of night before it all began again. They appeared in the distance, wandering dots, and I rose from the padded cushion of the cart, clicked off the gloves and goggled my eyes to skry them, waving my hand at Puck to quick, quick, mark them in the Book, a dozen of them at least, no, two, four, six ... ten ... fifteen. Fifteen.

After that first tribe, we spotted many more, moving in parallel with us or crossing our tracks. They were scattered and sporadic, these tribes, spread out over territories so vast I wondered how often they came into contact with each other. The one time we saw two tribes come into each other's sphere of awareness, there was only a brief but loud exchange of machismo and outrage that ended with little more than a few sticks flying through the air and a disgruntled, wordless agreement to go in entirely different directions.

All of these tribes, though, treated us with similar crude fear or fury, till we drew up to the low slopes of Oblivion's Mount and Puck spotted this tribe led by the individual that Puck assures me should be known as Jack.

Jack stands out from the others as a wanderer, reviled wildchild, solitary coyote in the rain-hard night, a wisdom in his ravenous eyes as he watches them, waiting in the dark to raid what the others see as rubbish, or stalking the other animals of the terrain as if to steal the scraps of their secrets, thieving the tricks of other beasts, and crowing about it in the morning. When we first saw him, he seemed only a sickly adolescent, scavenging status by unusual strategies, sparkling stones given to other males to barter with the females for sexual favours, joining the female grooming and gossip sessions, flirting outrageously but bolting at the first advance. But over time this omega boy to the alpha male seems to have latched on charm and subterfuge to gain a status that is quite outside the standard pecking orders of the other tribes, creating a role that has transformed the whole social structure of his simian clan.

Wandering wide out of the foraging paths of the others, he returns with gifts of necklaces made from washers and nuts and locker keys dug from the garbage-strewn ground, or mushrooms and herbs that lead to stoned orgies of tripping, puking, giggling chaos. And even as the upper echelon males drive him away with stones in their hungover mornings, they seem to follow his skipping, outskirting dance off into the margins. Whenever the bulky leader of them rises in the afternoon-dawn, casting his gaze around their lands, he always seems to settle on the direction where the one that we call Jack sits, picking his teeth with a stalk of grass and trilling merrily to himself, singing.

And that is his most unique characteristic, I think, amongst his kin.

Jack sings.

Where the others all use their complicated sounds simply to grub for favours and commitments within their own community, cooing and giggling together or shrieking antagonism, this scavenger of drugs and glimmering stone fetishes sings in a cunning grammar, scheming his sounds, it seems, into a sequenced story, as if he's telling a tale of where he's been and what he's seen, enchanting, canting. I am convinced that if it is not language then it is, at least, the roots of it.

I wonder sometimes if he is answering the earth – because there are noises up here in the foothills of Oblivion's Mount that are . . . unsettling at times. Every so often I'll follow a low hum to its source and find some splay of wire fence catching the wind, or trace a sudden twang to a blue steel guitar stuck halfway down a slipped face of garbage sediment, its last snapped string still swaying in the air. There are creaks and groanings, rustles of dirt trickling some-where, and sometimes, at dusk – when for some reason, it seems loudest – it sounds almost musical, in an atonal, modernist way.

Jack sings loudest in the dusk and even as he wanders round the huddling others, he often skips away, out to the edges, and sings looking out into the gloaming as if addressing it.

The others obviously don't have a clue what he thinks he's doing, but you can see them listening, inspired with a distrusting reverence, a fearful respect for this jackdaw birdman of the dreamtime. Charla-tan saviour, heroic fool, sagacious rogue, he is a snake-oil salesman of lies and illusions, using the stage-show shell-game of his song to charm them, and I think without knowing it they follow him on a journey into his own mind and across the Vellum. None of the other tribes we've travelled with followed our course around Oblivion's Mount so closely, all of them veering off to travel east or west away as if the lowering tower signified some dread power that it would not do to get too close to. Jack, on the other hand seems bent on leading them around it. Sometimes I think it's actually he who's following us . . . following us ahead of us, if that makes sense.

He does remind me of the Jack I once knew; I understand why Puck would call him that. But like Puck himself he seems drawn with a broader brush than the brash youth of my distant memories, as if in the Vellum we all tend towards our essence, finding a strange unity within the myriad variations of our souls, in the commonalities or in the deeper patterns suggested by discrepancies. The Hindus claim that there are five souls in any body, five *skandas*. The ancient Egyptians distinguished seven. I'm not sure we don't have infinite souls scattered all across the Vellum, or one soul shattered into infinite pieces.

Is that what lies at the end of our journey, I wonder, on the last page of the Book of All Hours, a place where all the variations are resolved, where all our multiple selves are boiled down into one perfect Platonic form of us? And what Jack would we find there, I wonder? What is it that this Jack shares with mine, with Puck's? A gleam in the eye? A glint of grin? Or just a name, a word?

It worries me a little, I must admit. I look at this Jack, and I think of the Jack of my memories and if there is a single word that sums them both up I would have to say it's *firestarter*.

3

Of Mammon and Moloch

Jumpin' Jack Flash

I leap from the wireliner's blasted doorway as, behind me, the whole structure shrieks and buckles, the zeppelin-shaped ray-tanks rupturing and spewing out a lurid noxious blue-green steam of orgone-saturated vapours. The passenger carriage cracks, creaking as the vast weight of the vessel unbalances, gyroscopes gone wild. As the wounded wireliner careens into a smaller airtrain, wires and cables snap and whiplash through the air, one just close enough for me to catch and swing, sparks showering from my snakeskin jackboots in an electric arc. The second bomb goes off.

It's 1999. Fuck, it's always 1999.

I land in a crouch on a steel gantry, black greatcoat billowing around me as the airtrain ploughs through signals and switches, twists and turns and blossoms into flame. Overhead, the wireliner, the Iron Lady, tilts its nose towards the sky, a scene – and on a scale – that's reminiscent of the *Hindenburg* or the *Titanic*. A blue aura crackles round my gloved hand, I can feel my hair standing on end (no need for hair gel for a few days, then) and there's a taste of ozone in my mouth. But I got that electro-shock buzz on, and I do feel chipper.

Jack B. Nimble, Jack B. Quick, I clunk-chunk-chik my Zippo, light a stick of dynamite and throw it as I jump again. Gantry to girder, girder to strut, I land as the explosion sends a hooped ladder raining down in fragments onto the riveted steel panels of the bridge that carries the Wire across the river, into City Central Terminal. I look towards the Terminal, its sandstone towers and walls and smoke-stacks, the palatial grandeur of the glass and girder lattice roof, like some immense Victorian greenhouse. Wrapped in furling clouds of orgone-rich gases, flames erupting, shrapnel flying, the wireliner soars inexorably down towards it. Keen.

The third bomb is timed just perfect, blowing the Cavor-Reich orgone-jet engines just before the wireliner loses the last of its inertia-dampened impetus and sending it, three hundred tons of fireball, over and down and through the glassy webworks of the City Central Terminal's roof. Peachy keen.

Knowing I don't have long before the keepers arrive, I unholster my Curzon-Youngblood Mark I chi-pistol, favoured weapon of the gaijin ninjas. Modern makes and models of the weapon have their benefits, true, but the original repays the skill and care invested in it with an accuracy and power unmatched by any other gun. In the hands of a professional, it's a lethal beauty.

Through the blue tint of my mayashades, I watch the massive Clydebuilt molotov cocktail and the pretty flower of fire it makes of City Central Terminal. Shock and Awe, motherfuckers, Shock and Awe.

Weapons-Grade Adamantium

Dr Reinhardt Starn studies the police file on the screen of the laptop in front of him and the prisoner on the other side of the desk. Suspect description: medium-tall, slim-build, white male, age 20–25 approx. Bleached punk hair, alternative clothing. What Starn sees is someone with a carefully cultivated 'rebel' self-image.

– Do you understand why I'm here? he asks.

No answer.

– I'm a clinical psychologist in consultation with the authorities. It's my job to decide if you're competent to stand trial. You under-stand they think you killed some people, yes?

No answer.

The police file gives only a brief history: Suspect in 'Spartacus' killings, caught fleeing murder scene. Referred for psychiatric evaluation and investigation. Possible member of an anarchist terror cell – so the file says, but Starn finds the whole latter-day Bader-Meinhof Gang idea unlikely to say the least. His MO is more lone wolf than team player.

Suspect refuses to give his name, the screen tells him. No matches with police record ... no DNA profile in the database at all. So no Social Security records, thinks Starn. No bank account, no passport, he can't be working legally and he can't be claiming unemployment – not without an ID card.

No ID card. You'd have to be born in the wilderness and raised by wolves not to have an ID card these days.

– Do you mind if I ask you a few questions? says Starn. OK. I believe you go by the name of 'Jack Flash'. Can I ask you about the significance of that?

– Jack the Giant-Killer, Jack the Ripper, Spring-Heeled Jack, yes, Jack of Clubs and Spades and Hearts and Diamonds, Jack of Wands and Swords and Chalices and Coins. A whole attack of Jacks. Jack's back.

– Hmm. But 'Jack Flash'. That's from a song, isn't it? The Rolling Stones – Jumpin' Jack Flash—

– He's a gas, gas, gas ... whoomf ... Jack Flash fire flash gordon flash harry flash flood flash point ... flash cunt.

Starn moves a finger across the laptop's trackpad, minimizes one window and opens up another to note down his first impressions: Subject exhibits some of the classic schizophrenic discourse patterns – word-play, symbolic fixation, smearing of meaning – but appears more coherent/responsive than would expect. Too self aware. Possible borderline case / sociopath faking psychotic delusion?

– That isn't your real name, though, is it? says Starn.

– Well, you know how sometimes you had something from before, but you don't have it any more?

– I suppose we'll just have to call you Jack for now then. OK?

Jack sizes the doctor up across the table, cool as a cheroot clenched in a drifter's teeth but kind of miffed that they've sent such an amateur. He thought he might at least merit a good Pinterian psycholinguist; they're always fun. But no. Every tic, every twitch leaks out this monkey robot's subtext, every word he says and every word he doesn't say. Every glance from notes to subject, every cough to clear the throat, the strains and pauses in his speech ... even the scent of him reeks of furtive fears and naughty needs.

– Keen, says Jack.

He tells himself the quack may actually be a master of the black ops arts of speech combat, playing a subtle bluff. It's never smart to underestimate the enemy, but, hell, this bastard isn't giving him much choice. What is this? Don't they know what they've got here? Anyone would think they'd never heard of Jack Flash. Weapons-grade adamantium. The original goddamn psychokiller. Qu'est-ce que fucking c'est?

He'd be insulted if it wasn't for the keeper behind the one-way mirror. At least he's got some fucking bite.

A Glint of Snickety-Sharp Teeth

Pechorin (bioform) status: all vital functions in homeostatic balance; psychophysiology and kinaesthetic senses dampened; affective/logical reactions inhibited; reflexive/habitual-behavioural reactions inhibited; ego shutdown; self shutdown; id shutdown; total psyche shutdown.
Pechorin (bioform) status: personality by-pass operation complete.

Observation: Subject sits with calm poise, studying Agent (Dr) Starn, eyes flicking up to the observation mirror, now and then (*Analysis*: bioform presence sensed by subject. *Response*: minimize bioform functions, deepen trance-state).

Operation: psychic contact made; preliminary scan initiated.
Narrative detected:

Jack looks in the mirror, at his own reflection, and at what lies beyond it. Under the bleached hair and the attitude, there's still an image – a reflection, a shadow – of the boy he was, a bookworm buried in dreams, asleep to his surroundings, Narcissus or Endymion, Kama Krishna on his lotus. He lets his eyes unfocus, scries the mirror: leaves blow over and around him, red, gold, orange, yellow, leaves of autumn, leaves of fire, burning leaves torn out of books, existence on fire, black incense rising into blue eternity. Whole world should burn, he thinks, it would be so fucking pretty.

Jack grins a glint of snickety-sharp teeth.

Operation: focus narrative; scan for core identity.

He walks across the grass, summer sunlight warm against the back of his neck, smooth heat like a caress, towards the red-brick library, sanctum of adventure.

– Hey, Jack, the voice behind him calls.

– Yo, Joe, he says.

– Where you been all week?

Nowhere, he thinks. It's just another lost, last day of the summer of his youth, and he's spent most of it in the library, out of the way of his peers, happier in solitude, in the realms of fantasy, than in a limbo reality of housing schemes and gang battles.

– Keeping my head down, he says.

He knows he's the weird kid, strange, estranged, but Jack doesn't care. He's got all of eternity to keep him company, in his head.

The Nature of the Conspiracy

Starn tries to ignore the feeling of being watched; it goes with the job, but the one-way mirrors always make him feel uncomfortable, like someone reading your newspaper over your shoulder. They do have video cameras, after all. If they want him to get inside the man's head, so to speak, they could just leave him to get on with it. It's not as if the officer behind the glass is qualified to make these kind of judgements.

– Perhaps we could speak a little bit about yourself, he says, but first I want to find out if you really understand where you are, what's happening to you. Can you tell me where you are?

– You know where I am.

– Of course. Of course. I just want to make sure that you know.

– In an interrogation cell, deep underground, inside the secret base of an empire that reaches from the dawn of time, across eternities, and into the minds of every monkey robot in the world.

Starn looks around the interview room. A small, grilled window sits high up on one wall, sunlight from it picking out dust motes in the air. The third floor is not exactly what he'd call 'deep underground'.
– 'Monkey robot'? he says.
– Puppets on a string, dangling, jangling, gangling from the ganglions in the head. That's how they control us. That's all we are to them, monkey robots – apemen, golems, fucking soldiers of the Empire.
– The Empire?
– Empire never ended. Just hid itself. You can only see it if you close your eyes.

The prisoner smiles, picks up the paper cup of black coffee sitting on the desk and takes a sip.
– You think this is all . . . part of this Empire?
– I know it and you know it too. You just don't know you know it. That's the nature of the conspiracy.
Of course, it is the sort of language you'd expect from a politico, thinks Starn. He's seen the slogans painted on walls and placards, by all the neobolsheviks and jihadists. But Starn doesn't think that this 'Jack Flash' is talking about the same 'Empire' as all those splintered factions fighting against Pax Britannica.
– Do you think I'm part of this 'conspiracy'? he says.
– The less people know, the more people in it, the better the conspiracy. This is the ultimate conspiracy – everybody in it and nobody knows.
– You think *everyone's* a part of this conspiracy?
– I know I am.

Starn looks at the notes on his screen.
Subject displays typical symptoms of first-rank (acute) schizophrenia – 'monster' / 'messiah' delusion, apophenia, ideas of thought broadcasting and mind control, auditory (imperative) hallucination. 'Monkey robot' – disturbance of identity, alienation from self.

Subject has externalised insecurities as invasive alien force – conspiracy. Sees himself as 'secret agent'? grandiose / paranoid delusions. Certainly capable of murder. 'Spartacus' = slave rebel. Victims = directors, captains of industry = conspiracy 'rulers'? Highly complex fantasy.

The question is: is he faking it?

– Could you tell me more about this Empire, this conspiracy?

The Kali Yuga

I slice the skybike round the corner at a 30-degree angle to the ground, sparks flying from the spindisks as they scrape the cobbles of the street. The machine roars as I gun the ray-jet engine up to turbo. It can take it. This is a 1951 Jaguar Silver Shade, the only skybike ever manufactured by the company, British fascist engineering at its best. This is how the Empire was won.

The ornithopters come in over the rooftops, swooping low into the backstreets of the docklands area, like a swarm of mechanical bats or butterflies or birds of prey, all flashing, clashing, silvery wings. Their storm of gunfire tears up everything behind me in a rain – a hail – of bullets, pounding the street and throwing up a dust of shards from cobblestones and brick walls, crates and plastic bin-bags. Feels like all hell is on my heels, but then I'm always at my best when I feel hounded.

As I blast across the weed-cracked foundations of some long-dead shipyard, I fire over my shoulder, hit the pilot of the leading thopter with a chi-beam in the centre of his forehead, smack-bang in the sixth chakra, where his third or *ajna* eye will never now be opened. The thopter spins wildly through the air, smashing into the two immediately behind it, and I fire off a couple of random shots, clip the ray-tank of a fourth. The chaos of three tangled thopters buries itself into the ground behind me, shrapnel flying, and I make it into a narrow alleyway between two warehouses. The pilot of the fourth thopter, destabilized by the puncture of its ray-tank, tries to turn it, fails, and piles his machine into the brick wall of a warehouse, the explosion wiping out forever the last faded, peeling remnants of a painted advertisement for some long-forgotten company. I'm not out of the woods yet.

Four of the remaining thopters rise over the roofs of the warehouse while another follows through the narrow gap between the buildings, wing-tips almost touching brickwork, guns still firing. I admire the fly-boy's skill and nerve; it doesn't stop me putting a chi-beam through his fourth chakra, through his courageous but misguided heart. He's still a fucking keeper. As I burst out into the open again, the other thopters come back, gunning for me with a vengeance. Well. What can I expect?

It's the dark world of the Kali Yuga, out here on the edge, the Gnostic prison-world of a mad, blind creator, a world of lies, truth hidden in the silky veils of Maya. You may not see it that way, but trust me; I'm the archon of anarchy. I know what I'm talking about. Reality's got more diseases than a ten dollar whore, only this kind of sickness doesn't come from getting down and dirty with too many johns.

I tear the skybike into a 180 and open fire on the last of the thopters. One banana, two banana, three banana, four. One of the pilots actually makes it out of his fireball, spinning through the air, armour gyros fucked and boosters firing in what's definitely the wrong direction. He ploughs into the ground at my feet with a crunch that makes even me feel a little squeamish. Still, I kick his helmet off and stare into his mirrorball eyes, just to check the keeper drone is terminated. And with every bone in his body broken, including his watermelon skull, there's still a little bit of the astral puppet-master flickering in his brain. Fucking mindworms.

– *Jack Flash*, it hisses. Sounds like white noise, bad radio. *No sleep for the wicked.*

– Get out of my head, I say, and put the barrel of my chi-gun right into the brain cavity. On second thoughts . . . get out of *his* head.

And I blast it.

Yeah, reality has some pretty nasty parasites, and I'm the homeopathic, sociopathic remedy. I'm the angel assassin, armed with all the mystical technology the Empire stole from its dominions in the Orient and India. I'll do you acupuncture with a needle-gun. I'll rearrange your living space with cluster-bomb Feng Shui. I'm an agent of change, a spiritualista sandanista.

Society and me . . . well, let's just say we don't get on.

Soldiers of the Empire, Children of the Scheme

Operation: Enhance psychic substructure. Trace core identity.
Narrative detected:

— I fucking hate this place, says Joey.

— Tell me about it, he says.

Jack looks around at the buildings of the Scheme — identikit matchbox blocks built by some contractor with a hard-on for pebble-dash. An extermination camp for the soul. Good enough for us overspill proles, he supposes. No fucking wonder the razor gangs are back.

Guy plays with his State Security card, weaving it between the fingers of one hand. Jack watches him. Guy's the girl-magnet, smooth as a shark through water. Joey's the bad-ass, black-clad bastard, smoking with sullen hostility. Jack? Jack's the tag-along weird kid with the big ideas.

— That's all we are, you know? says Joey as he takes another draw on the fag, passes it to Guy. Just another fucking number. They'll be tagging us like fucking dogs next. Chips in the ear. Fucking dogs, bred to be vicious, bred for the fucking army or the pigs.

— Soldiers of the Empire, says Jack.

Information upload: Location – Schemes; Period – Adolescence.

Operation: Enhance location. Specify locale.

They sit on the brick wall, bored and bitter, all of them. Facing them there's the little one-storey block of shops — well, a fish 'n' chip shop, a bookie's, a newsagent's, a grocer's and a pub. That's all there is in the Scheme. That's all there is in any fucking Scheme.

— There's always a life of crime, says Guy.

— Yeah, says Joey. Let's burgle some house, steal a car, burn the fucker. We could set ourselves up as drug/dealers. Loan/sharks. We'd still be fucking guard/dogs. You know? You know what I mean?

– Patrolling the boundaries of society, says Jack.

Joey nods, mutters something about *fucking drones*.

– Weapons, says Jack, staring at the graffiti on the shutter of the bookie's. We're weapons.

– Maybe, says Guy, looking at him weirdly.

But he's used to that.

Welcome to Siagon, the graffiti says, and he knows the feeling. He could have written the words himself, although he would have at least spelled *Saigon* correctly. And he would have probably gone for *Welcome to Hell* himself. He's always fancied writing that on the road sign into town.

Operation: Reinforce imperative: Enhance location. Specify locale.

The road is tarmac but rough, weathered and cracked with weeds, covered in generations of graffiti, tags and band names, obscure gang sigils made from letters fused together. Pages torn from porno mags and newspapers hang crumpled, caught in the wall of brambles that they have to scramble through to get down onto it. There's no other way onto the road – it just appears out of the grassy dunes and disappears back into them, a hundred yards at most, as if someone just dropped the world around it, as if it used to go somewhere but then they took that somewhere away. It isn't so much that the road seems out of place, out here in the grassy, sandy hills on the other side of the farmer's field and the stream they have to walk along a water/pipe to cross; it's more like the landscape around it doesn't belong. Like someone scrapped a previous world, built this one over it, but forgot to erase this little area of the old reality.

Interject thoughtstream.

Operation: reroute digression. Specify locale.

Jack has the weirdest feeling that he's been here before, a long time ago, when he was younger. He looks around at the empty spray/cans, jars of glue and plastic bags, and—

– Check this out.

319

Some kind of concrete cylinder, six foot in diameter at least and maybe two foot high, an iron manhole cover on the top of it. Jack feels the spray can in his hand, the can that he's just used to add his name to all the others. He feels his finger pressing down on the nozzle, hears the hiss and sees his hand moving . . . and has no idea what he's writing, why he is writing it.

ET IN ARCADIA EGO.

– What the fuck does that mean?

– I don't know. Fuck, I don't know.

But he can hear a voice from somewhere whispering it in his ear.

A River of Voices

– Do you know who's on the other side of the mirror? says Jack.

– No, says Starn. The officer on the case. It's just procedure.

– You know they're watching you as much as they're watching me.

– I don't think so, Jack. But you were going to tell me about this Conspiracy. Was that why you killed – how many was it? You think there's some sort of . . . scheme against you?

– Scapegoats and saviours, mate. You want to rule people's minds, you need a monster or messiah, something to sacrifice to silence all the voices.

– Voices?

Starn looks at his watch, wondering if he's going to be able to wrap this up early.

– All the voices in our heads, the river of voices in our heads, trying to tell us what to do.

But it's too obvious, too pat. Yes, auditory hallucination is a classic sign of florid stage schizophrenia, psychotic breakdown, but it's the sort of thing that every selfish little murderer trots out – from his in-depth knowledge of Hollywood movies and tabloid newspapers – when they want to get out of that pickle they've put themselves in. It wasn't that my wife was cheating on me and I hated the bitch. It wasn't that my boss was an arsehole who deserved to die. It wasn't for the insurance money or the drugs or the brutal, bloody thrill of it. It was the voices in my head.

– You hear voices, Jack?

– Don't we all? Voices of souls, of ancestors, family and friends, enemies and demons, ghosts inside the head, the ghosts in the machine. You telling me you don't hear your own little internal narrative when you're thinking to yourself? You've never had an argument with a friend that didn't carry on in your head afterwards? You've never lain in bed and thought to yourself in someone else's voice, to get a different perspective, someone else's attitude? We all hear voices, doctor. Most people just keep them turned down real low.

Jack leans forward.

– Too much noise, you see, the monkey-robots might not hear the puppeteer. Little doggy might not hear his master's voice, mate. So we gotta shut those other voices up. But, shhh. You can hear them if you only listen.

– And these voices tell you to–

– Listen. It's like being asleep beside a river, a river of voices, babbling, buried in the rustle of leaves. Narcissus sleeps and dreams us all.

Starn sits back in his chair. Narcissus, eh? The boy who loved his own reflection in a river, and wasted away from his love. Well, it's more original than the Devil or God.

The Lost Boy

Analysis: subject resistant; lateral approach required.
Operation: trace source of identity-construct 'Jack Flash'.
Imago detected:
Hair the colour of flame, not blond but yellow, orange, red.

Jack remembers the picture on the milk carton, the lost boy – Sandy Thomson – with his corn-blond hair, and realizes the boy's ghost has been haunting his imagination ever since he was a child.

Ever since he was a child, he's had this hero in the stories that he makes up on the edge of sleep, an idol, an icon, signifying everything that he desires, everything that he desires to be. Flash Gordon. Jack, the Giant-Killer. He looks in the mirror at what he's made himself and sees, under it all, that picture on the milk carton, the lost boy, the golden boy.

Analysis: compensatory fantasies; narcissistic fixation.

Operation: enhance engram context; establish imprint location.

Narrative detected:

They leave their bicycles in the long grass at the side of the country road, together with the packed lunches and flasks of juice their mothers have given them, and walk like tightrope artists along the great steel pipe over the farmer's field and the stream, and jump down into the tall, grassy dunes. The area is fenced-off, part of the premises of the chemical plant over the other side of the hills, so it has a kind of mystery for them, beyond their mundane world. It seems the obvious place to hunt for the lost boy. It was Guy's idea, right enough. He's been here before, he says. Jack imagines what it would be like to find the boy and be a hero.

– Come on, says Joey, pushing his way through the jaggy bushes.

He's a little scared, a little thrilled that they're trespassing in this forbidden territory, this landscape of soft sand beneath their feet, this neverland out on the edge of their nowhere town existence. They might get lost too, he thinks. As he scratches and yelps his way behind Joey and Guy, he thinks, what if the Thomson boy found the secret place where all the world is like soft sand, slipping under your feet and you slide through it and you find yourself somewhere . . . somewhere where adventures happen. And he imagines Sandy, imagines himself as Sandy, as some sort of Peter Pan, lost and happy, out in an eternity of daydreams.

He crashes through the last of the brambles and down onto the cracked, tarmac road, dusty on this dry summer day. Guy is standing there, up where it disappears into the dunes.

– Hurry up, he calls.

– Shut up, *Reynard*, says Joey, taunting him with the awkward given name he hates so much because, well, *nobody's* called Reynard. It's a dumb name.

– You shut up, *Narco*, says Guy, flinging Joey's taunt back in his face, calling him that because Joey falls asleep in class so much, and because when Guy called him a 'narcoleptic' he didn't know what it meant. So he hates it.

Names are important, thinks Jack. He doesn't have a nickname, but if he did, he'd want to be called Flash, like Flash Gordon from the black and white serials they show on telly every Saturday morning during the holidays. That would be cool.

The Rookery

I pull on my leather trousers (1770s, Imperial Prussian 10th Hussars), my black Cossack shirt (1890s, Greater Futurist Republican Alliance Army), my snakeskin jackboots (1920s, Confederate Texas Rangers) and my tunic (1850s, Queen's Own Chinese Infantry, 2nd Tibetan Regiment). I strap my Japanese katana at my left side and my holstered Curzon-Youngblood chi-gun at my right, and clip two jackblades into their sheaths, one on each boot. I pull on my bomber's jacket (1940s, Royal East Indian Air Corps, made of sacred cow hide, lined with the highest quality yeti fur) and drag on over this my greatcoat (1900s, Free Ruritanian Partisans). The rucksack I fling over one shoulder is heavy with the weight of high explosives – sticks of dynamite and black bulbous bombs. Finally I pick up my black kid-skin gloves, and sling a white silk scarf around my neck. Elegance is the assassin's deadliest weapon.

Outside, the Second City of the Empire is in the middle of another bitter autumn night, the roads and pavements buried in a flowing sludge of mulch and sleet, the grimy sandstone buildings of the Rookery, all those tenements and abandoned churches, lit in the volcanic glow of halogen streetlamps. I step out onto the vast skeleton of scaffolding that runs through the Rookery like the web of some giant insane spider, grab a steel pole and swing up, grab, swing up, jump and swing, until I'm above it all, standing on the roof of what was once part of a University. It's cold out in this crazy world, but I'm wrapped up warm, I'm armed and armoured, and the sky is painted a magnificent crimson. I feel keen.

Here, on the roof of the great gothic tower of the University Library, on the crest of the hill on which the Rookery is built (and *in* which the Rookery is built – in abandoned subway tunnels and mineshafts where the most hunted and desperate find their sanctuary), the only thing more breathtaking than the view is the cold wind that howls in from the east. Beneath me, what was once a simple grid of tenements is all but buried in a century's growth of scaffolding and boardwalks, corrugated iron extensions and appendages, whole streets roofed over and built upon. Hell itself would be an easier place to map. I look out towards the borders of this maze of thieves and traitors.

The wide swathe of greenery that is Kelvinbridge Park swings round the Rookery, hemming it on three sides – North, East and South – resplendent with its riverside of ruined mills and fallen viaducts, the glass palaces of the Botanical Gardens to the North, the stately grandeur of the Kelvinbridge Museum to the South, all floodlit for the delight of promenading visitors. Over to the West, the bustling, hustling Byres Road marks out the area's last boundary, where the clubs and coffee-houses of the West End literati meet the pawn shops and pornographers of the Rookery.

Once this walled-in area underneath me held the bedsits of Bohemia, the spires of Academia, back before Mosely's abolition of state-funded education. Now made up mainly of the dens and haunts of my fine fellow wasters, the Rookery has become a haven for every radical and revolutionary who grudges the steel grip the Guilds are gradually tightening around the throats of every man and woman in the Empire, for every rebel out to fight the system, for every would-be anarchist assassin suffering under the grandiose delusion that the actions of one man might change the course of History. That would be me.

Over the scattering of fiery lights that mark the city's roads and buildings, airtrains flash across the sky, riding the Wire, venting jets of blue-green orgone vapours, steaming out across the night. It always seems ironic to me that in such a prudish, prurient country the great source of power is the force first harnessed by the tantric masters of Tibet, the energy they knew as *kundalini*, which we stole and renamed 'orgone energy', that cosmic, mystic, sexual force.

I slip my silver Half-Hunter from my pocket, flick it open to check the time, click it closed and slip the fob watch back into my pocket. It's getting close to show-time. Out in the night, the Iron Lady is cruising, vast and regal, a giant of the skies, towards the city of its creation, this Second City of the Empire, carrying within the First Director of the Parliamentary Board of Elizabeth Regina, Queen of the British Isles and Colonies, Empress of India and the Orient, Sovereign Heart of Pax Britannica. Old Powell's getting on a bit now, but he's as much a threat as ever, if not more so.

It's not the man himself, I'm worried about, just the mindworm that he's carrying in his head, the sordid little dream, the meme, that pulls his strings and pushes his buttons, looking to lay its sick spores in the empty thoughts of all the hatefilled whores and motherfuckers too dumb to see what's happening. Language lives, my friend, information with intent, aware, awake inside us. Call them gods, call them demons, they're the archons of our world, these fucking mindworms, spawned in speeches, nurtured in newspapers, feeding on our fears and desires. Ideas are not just born, my friend. They breed. And behind every good demagogue is a bad idea. I should know; I'm a myth myself.

I check my watch again. It's time.

Time for the giant of the skies to meet its Jack.

Caledonia Dreaming

– You see the world as a very hostile, threatening place, don't you? You feel you don't belong? So you live in a fantasy-world where you're the hero. It's like a … second skin for you, isn't it, this 'Jack Flash', a shell.

– You'd think that, wouldn't you? I mean, what's the alternative?

That this world is actually run by Mammon and Moloch, *literally* run by gods of greed and brutality who've got you all so juiced that you don't even see them changing it around you.

– Mammon and Moloch, Jack? Those are–

– Myths? Metaphors? What does the word 'Guernica' mean to you, doctor?

Starn shrugs, shakes his head.

– What should it mean to me?

Jack turns his head away in disgust.

– John Maclean, he says. The Armenian Massacre. Lorca. Does any of that mean anything to you? My Lai?

– Jack, one of the symptoms of schizophrenia is called apophenia. It's when everything in the world seems loaded with significance, part of some great truth. You see patterns that aren't there. It's where the paranoia comes from; because someone, something has to be behind it all. God or the Devil. The government. Your 'Empire', perhaps?

– Mammon or Moloch, says Jack.

– Exactly.

– You didn't answer my question. What does 'Guernica' mean to you?

– It doesn't mean anything. What is it? A person? A place?

– And you think I'm fucking crazy?

– You need help, Jack. You need to admit that you're sick, so we can help you. Can't you see that you've invented this 'Empire' to justify your own fear, your own insecurity, your shame, your self-pity?

– I could ask you the same question. All of you. You know about psychosis, doctor. You should recognize the symptoms. Grandiose delusions. Religious mania. Paranoid violence. Sounds like society to me.

Starn runs a finger over the laptop's trackpad, moving the mouse across the screen, but with no real purpose other than to give his hand something to do while he thinks. The schizophrenic worldview is never completely senseless, he knows; he made his name with a paper on paranoid delusions as symbolic representations of a hostile world. But this schizoid is just too conscious of the boundary between fantasy and reality. He's not faking it but, at the same time, he's not totally engulfed in the psychosis, Starn is sure.

– You talk about Mammon and Moloch, Jack, but I think you know you're talking about something else. You talk about the Empire but I think you know this 'Empire' isn't real in any actual sense.

– How real are your dreams, doctor?

– Dreams aren't real at all, Jack.

– I am.

The Abyss

Operation: verify schizophrenia hypothesis; scan for inception.
Narrative detected:

– Jack, you're fucking cracked, man. You're fucking crazy.

He pants, recovering his breath, rubbing at the red marks where the fingers gripped his throat, and grinning. He's proved his point.

– Told you you couldn't kill me. Told you you'd chicken out before I did.

– Yeah, but that doesn't mean shit.

Jack can't quite put his finger on it but somewhere deep inside he's sure that, somehow, it does. Maybe he is crazy. He has these ideas sometimes, that he's an alien or an android, Lucifer or Jesus – and this shithole town does feel like his own private hell some days, like he's fucking nailed to a cross. But he's smart enough to know that those are delusions, no more real than the Jack Flash character he finds himself drawing on the pages of his schoolbooks or dreams about at night, with his hair the colour of fire.

But he's smart enough to know that the delusions have a point, that something in his head is trying to make a fucking point.

You can't die.

He tries to understand what it is his crazy, fucked-up inner self is trying to tell him, but he can't get his head around it.

It's bullshit, he thinks. Everyone dies. He could take his fucking school-tie, make a noose of it and hang himself from a light fitting if he wanted to . . . or if he had the guts, at least. And he wants to know. He wants to know what's on the other side of dying. He wants to know if all the bullshit about eternity is true. But it can't be, can it? There is no heaven, no hell, no God, no Devil, no angels.

He rubs at his neck. He's proved his point, shown Joey that he wasn't shitting him, that he doesn't give a fuck any more, that he could walk right up to Death and spit in his face and fucking *dare* him to swing his scythe. Except that there is no Death, not like that.

And suddenly – it's just oxygen starvation – he feels light-headed – it's the flood of oxygen back into his brain – and the world is kind of fuzzed and jittery and—

Guy is leaning over him.

– Jack. Wake up, Jack. Bloody hell. Are you OK?

He's lying on the ground, sprawled out, looking up at the sky, the clear blue sky so wide and empty with only the golden crescent of the sun to cast a gloaming light across it, and there's earth under his back, earth rich and dark with clay and green with thick moist grass, red, gold and orange leaves blowing across his hands.

And then Guy leans real close, he does, and he looks so much older than he should, like there's another him, an older him under the surface, and he whispers very quietly.

– Time to wake up, Jack Flash.

He snaps awake straight out of the half-state he's been in, part memory, part dream, drifting off to sleep, and looks around the bedroom, but there's nothing there. A palpable, visible *nothing* there in the darkness. Nothing has just whispered his name to him in the dead of night.

It moves around the room, a cold, dead presence – no, an absence, an abyss that's gazing into him.

He gets out of bed and walks around the room, more entranced than afraid. He doesn't switch the light on in case this sense – this physical sense – of nothing is dispelled by it. It's like a ghost standing over a grave with his name on it, a dream that's walked out of his head and into the world – no, a dream that's walked out of the world and into his head. Maybe it's just his imagination, but that's not what it feels like. It feels like someone else's imagination.

And then the nothing becomes something. It becomes him.

And Jack Flash feels the flesh of his new body, and he knows that it's all good.

– Keen, he says.

The Empire Never Ended

A knock. The door opens and Starn glares at the inspector, annoyed at the interruption. The woman just stands there, holding a large brown file in her hand, silently waiting. Starn nods.

– Sorry, excuse me a second.

He steps out of the room, closes the door quietly behind him.

– You've found something.

– Well, yes and no. Something turned up when we ran his mugshots through the machine. Not sure if it will be any use, though.

She hands Starn the folder.

– You found a match? A name would be very helpful, inspector. Anything that can give me a handle on where he comes from.

– Well, that's the rub, she says. This doesn't exactly tell us much at all about where he comes from.

Starn opens the folder. All that's inside is a print-out of an old black and white photograph. He recognises the face immediately, even in the softened, blurry greytones fading to white around the edges of the ellipse, even wearing the peaked cap and with the solemn air of someone as much *in control* as his twin in the interview room is out of it. Hair trimmed tight around the ears. Lips pursed in a smile that seems just ever-so-slightly ironic, detached. A certain intensity to the eyes.

– Obviously a relative, says Starn. Who is he?

– Captain Jack Carter, she says. English Army officer. Disappeared somewhere in the Caucasus a couple of years after World War One. Fiancée emigrated to America. No brothers or sisters we can trace. To be honest it could just be coincidence ... but ...

– But what?

– Well, he was considered a bit of a character by his men. They called him Mad Jack Carter. And Mad Jack seems a fairly apt description of our boy here. As I say, it could just be coincidence ...

*

– You have all this on file? It's a bit past its sell-by date, surely.

– We have a lot on file these days, Dr Starn. It is the Information Age. You never know when the tiniest scrap of data might make a difference.

Starn nods absently. It's easy to be paranoid these days. DNA profiling. Face recognition software. CCTV. ID cards. It all adds up to the world that his patient is afraid of, a world of constant observation, of suspicion, control. If the cameras can follow him around the city why shouldn't they – that mysterious They – have similar technologies to follow him around the inside of his head. Microwave thought control or whatnot. That is the way the schizophrenic thinks. He slides the picture back into the folder.

– I'll try the name on him and see if I get a response. Worth a shot.

– One other thing, she says.

– What's that?

– Some old fellow came into Partick station – senile dementia you'd think, but he'd seen our man's photo on the news, claimed to recognize him. Said he's the spitting image of a bloke he fought beside in Spain – I assume he meant World War Two, though I always thought Spain was neutral there.

Starn shrugs.

– History's not my strong point.

She smiles – *I know what you mean.*

– Anyway, she says, I wouldn't mention it but the desk sergeant humoured him enough to pass the name back to the team.

– And?

– Well, he said our man's name was Jack Carter.

Starn opens the folder again to look at the photograph, taps a finger on it idly. A young soldier from a bygone age of Empire. *The Empire Never Ended.* But the resemblance is remarkable, he thinks. Has to be his grandfather or great-grandfather. Great-uncle?

– You're sure there were no siblings?

– None that we can trace is what I said. That's not the same thing.

He nods, hand on the doorknob, keen to restart the interview. The inspector puts her hand on the door, cocks her head – *between you and me, off the record.*

– So, she says quietly. What's your thoughts so far? He's faking it, isn't he?

He shakes his head.

– Too early to tell. Can't say for sure.

Her hand stays on the door. Starn knows there were a good few injured bringing the man in. One died on the way to hospital.

– Don't worry, he says. I won't let him cheat the hangman, inspector.

She takes her hand away and he twists the handle, stops.

– Inspector, have you ever heard of someone or something called Guernica?

– Can't say that I have. Why?

– Just something our boy in there said.

He shakes his head.

– Probably nothing important.

Errata

Something Bad Happened Here

I look at the ground beneath my feet, nudging a toe at the thin layer of dirt to dust it off the rough edge of a concrete slab, then over at Puck, who's hauling at a shrub, trying to uproot it with sharp, sudden heaves of his whole body weight backwards. The topsoil is particularly thin here, and the stone posts and melted plastic spikes jutting up among the bushes even more noticeable than they were in the terrain behind us. We have to pick our way with care over the uneven surface, and the cart's pneumatic suspension hisses angrily as it compensates for the bumps of buried upholstery and mounds of broken wiring, now veiled only by the shallowest coating of red dirt. I had thought, as we came into this region out of the Veldt, that what we were travelling through was a land scattered with the detritus of the buildings once raised over it, now crumbled to their foundations. Now it seems more as if this is the detritus of foundations crumbling to reveal buildings beneath, the land itself merely a scattering over the top. Kick away the dirt and you find your foot very quickly touching rusted steel or misshapen plastic, stone or concrete, brick, bone.

– Something bad happened here, says Puck. I'm telling you.

I'm not convinced about that. For all that the wreckage in the earth is so often blackened and burned, twisted or broken out of shape, there may be no more catastrophe here than in any common or garden rubbish dump. There are a number of possibilities that Puck refuses to consider. Oblivion's Mount rises over us, still far ahead but just a little more to our right – north by north-east instead of simply north – and for all of its scale, its shape is more than a little reminiscent of the tells common in areas of ancient civilisation where towns have been built over the ruins of towns and gradually accreted in layers over centuries until, eventually abandoned and buried by the winds, they lump there on the horizon, broad, buried masses waiting for archaeologists to mine for knowledge. Well ... its shape is not quite right, but if you were to take one of those plains and build towns between the tells and let them live and die the same way until the plain was filled and turned into a plateau, and build towns on top of that plateau and go on and on and on, towering tell on top of tell, then maybe what you would be left with, after an eternity or so, is Oblivion's Mount.

I try to explain this to Puck, but after his yawning, rolling his eyes, twiddling his fingers, kicking his heels, shifting his weight from foot to foot, swinging his arms at his side, picking dirt out from under his fingernails, playing with his hair, and finally checking the time on an entirely imaginary wristwatch, all within my first sentence, I give up with an exasperated sigh and offer an alternative explanation.

– It's probably just one big landfill, I say. Eternity's garbage. The Happy Dumping Ground In The Sky.

– Bollocks, says Puck, something bad happened here – and he goes back to trying to yank the bush out of the ground – Look at Jack, he says.

Jack sits on the ground maybe a hundred yards away, arms hugged around his knees, eyes scanning the skies absently as if watching a fly, but glancing every now and then at Puck, with the furtive, nervous intensity of a guilty dog. It was Jack that led us here in the first place with his ungodly howling, and he seems to have convinced Puck, with his fevered bursts of clawing at the ground followed by sudden panicked sprints to cower at a safe distance, that there is some terrible secret buried under the bush. Or as Puck puts it, that something bad happened here.

– Give us a hand, then, eh? says Puck.

I join him at his bush and push one arm through the thick of leaves and twigs to get a backhand grip on a fatter branch, scuffle my feet into a lodging scrunch of dirt and, on the count of three, we heft.

– One, two, three, *hnnnh*. One two, three, *hnnnh*.

There's a creak on the third heave, a crack on the fourth, and by the fifth the dirt is rustling as the roots lift through it, pulling up in a clump of twists untangling. I'm suddenly reminded of unpotting a neglected bonsai; I recognise the feel of pulling roots out of the wire mesh they've grown through, the teasing, tearing feel, like pulling a comb through matted hair. A final heave rips the bush free but for a few thick roots at the side we're pulling from, free enough for us to see what's under it and confirm my suspicion.

The bush has sprouted in the dirt blown over a thin film of plastic bag, snagged, at some point in the past, on the sharp steel of grillework over a drain of some sorts, the roots of the bush eventually bursting through the bag and working their way down through the mesh. It's all quite mundane, if it wasn't for the skulls piled one on top of the other, filling the hole in the ground like marbles in a jar.

I have to admit that yes, well, maybe something bad did happen here.

The Tavern

– You never talk about him, says Don.

– What's the point? she says, pushing the door open.

Voices quiet for a second as they enter, hoods shadowing their faces, raincapes cloaking their forms. Faces turn to scope these shadowy strangers like, she thinks, the locals in a western saloon or a horror movie inn. Questers in a fantasy epic entering the tavern. Templars on some grand secret mission to the Holy Land, stopping off at a hostelry and reticent to reveal the shining armour beneath their cloaks. With their disrupters – the six-foot chi-lances, part crossbow, part spear, part rifle – they even look the part. Apart from the fact that their raincapes are waterproof synthe and the armour underneath is biker leathers, Phreedom thinks. Apart from the fact that the only destination they have in sight is *away*. Away from reality. Away from the unkin. Away from the bitmites. Just plain fucking *away*.

But as far as they go, they never quite seem to get away. That's the problem with the Vellum; when time has three dimensions you can drive whole decades only to find yourself back at the day you started from, or at least a day just like it.

– Come on, she says.

*

334

She flicks back her hood and Don does the same. The locals turn back to their beer and conversation, satisfied now that the two of them have clicked into the role of mysterious strangers. Gazes flick across at them from here and there, now and then, but Phreedom knows that's how the game works, how the ritual runs. It's a scenario they've played a thousand times on their journey into the Vellum. She scans the room for the big lunk who'll come on to her as she's ordering at the bar, force a fight and get creamed. She scopes out the local moneyman sat at the booth at the back of the tavern, all gold jewellery and immaculate suit, surrounded by his goons; Latin American drug lord, Wild West cattle baron, ghetto pimp or goodfella, there's always some villain with a story all curled-up and packed tight into the situation they walk into, just waiting for the catalyst to unfurl it, the drifter. Her and Don sometimes run a book on how long before the moneyman tries to hire them or run them out of town.

– Fifteen minutes, says Don. What do you reckon?

– One, says Phreedom.

Don points at an empty table – rough-hewn wood with benches instead of seats, it would look more at home in the picnic area of a park than in this tavern, but then the whole place has a slapdash quality like so many places they've hit as they get further out; the booths at the back are formica, with padded leatherette seats like a diner, the bar is oak and brass, saloon-style, but there are tables with waxed cloth covers, broad-checked like some little European cafe, empty wine bottles used as candleholders or with flowers in them. Sawdust covers a mosaic floor. Neon behind the bar and gas-lamps on the walls. TVs in the corners hanging from the ceiling. A weirdass piano on a raised stage over to one side – a mechanical contraption somewhere between baby grand and player piano, its cylinder turns as it plink-plonks out a murderous version of 'My Way'. The past is the new future, she thinks. Tomorrow is so last year.

She nods and, as Don slides down onto the bench, she flicks her raincape back to dig out her wallet.

– One minute? says Don.

She grins.

– Time me.

*

Five seconds. She's at the bar, asking for two beers and sliding in at the spot right beside the big guy, the big, drunk lunk in the leisure suit who checks her out as she pushes in, looks her up and down then grins at his friends over at the back, the ones around the moneyman. Eight, nine, ten seconds. He's turning to leer at her.

– Hey there, pretty–

She hits him, fist full in the face, breaking his nose and sending blood spraying down over his tache and white shirt, flicks her ruptor from left hand into right and does a little Bruce Lee twirl that smacks him across the cheek with it and leaves her standing there, legs spread, ruptor out and horizontal, aimed right at the booth at the back where he's going down into a slump at the feet of the money-man's chief stooge. Sixteen, seventeen, eighteen. The moneyman looks down at the red wine dribbling off the table and into his lap, the glass rolling on its side. Twenty-one, twenty-two, twenty-three. His chair scrapes back and the goons close in in front of him, blocking her shot, and reaching for their own weapons. She smiles, shrugs, flips the ruptor back to vertical and puts her other hand up, palm forward. Twenty-six, twenty-seven, twenty-eight, twenty-nine. She turns away from them, slowly and deliberately shouldering the ruptor and picking up the two beers, one in either hand. They have a little side-bet, her and Don, on which glass gets shot out of her hand.

Thirty-two. The glass in her left hand explodes. Phreedom smiles.

Thirty-three. She doesn't even bother looking as Don cuts them down from his seat, just asks the bartender for another beer, waits for it, then carries it back to the table.

– Forty-one seconds, he says.

– Personal best.

She slides onto the bench, props her own ruptor against the table beside Don's. She reaches into a pocket to pull out a smoke but as she brings the lighter up, he takes her hand.

– You never talk about him, he says. About either of them.

She pulls her hand away and lights the cigarette.

– I can't fucking change what happened, she says. Any of it.

She takes a draw.

– I wish I could.

4

The Scythes of Cronos

Peterhead, 1920

Your request has been heard and noted, says the letter, *and an answer will be given presently . . . once the full facts of the matter have been ascertained . . . considered to our satisfaction*, and more shite like that, but Seamus is too weak to read it now, laying up on the blanketless bed, naked and cold, as sure and he won't wear their fookin convict arrows, and he's exhausted so he is, not from the labouring in the quarry, cause he won't fookin do that neither, but from the endless fookin fighting. His throat sore from the feeding tube forced down it, the rest of his body is still black and blue from all the previous struggles; and the bruises from today are yet to form, of course. He lets the letter from the office of the Home Secretary drop from between his fingers. Fookers. Three months of penal servitude, they call it, in their fancy language. Call it what it is, hard fookin labour, done looking up the barrel of a Civil Guard's Lee Enfield rifle. And he's already two months in. It's the 25th of October.

So he lies there gazing up and back through bars at the pure sky, the paths of birds, wondering if he'll be dead or free before they ever accept that he's no fookin common convict but a political prisoner. Outside there's the sounds of footsteps. A crow circles.

– Well, now, ah have to say it makes me right sad to see ye in this state, but.

He looks down at the foot of the bed. It's just one of the boys, Lance-Corporal Donald O'Sheen MacChuill (Irish Catholic mother,

337

Scots Protestant father, Seamus remembers – the Dubs always were a mixed bunch and MacChuill was about the most mixed of the lot of them – spoke Gaelic and knew *The Sash* by heart and refused to see the contradiction). MacChuill stands there, in his full kit, backpack and helmet, rifle slung over his back, with a stupid big eedjit grin, sure, and the big hole in his face where his right eye used to be, the gaping black-red hole with the hard white shards and soft grey stuff all messed up in the midst of it. It doesn't scare Seamus any more though, sure, 'cause he knows its just a waking dream and if all the electroshock at Inchgillan didn't do a single thing, well, he did learn something from the doctor, with his talk of that fellow's work over at Craiglockhart and facing your demons, and all that shite. He wasn't a bad sort, after all, that Doctor Reynard. *Such a wound*, he'd said, *such a horrific wound . . . this MacChuill must have died instantly. He couldn't have suffered. I want you to try and keep that in your mind. That he wouldn't have suffered.* It was after that that Seamus stopped screaming when MacChuill came visiting.

– Ah shite, he says.

Seamus pushes himself upright, shaking his head. So weak he is from the hunger strike and all is what it is, sure, 'cause he hasn't had one of his turns for quite a while now, but what else could it be but one of those fookin waking dreams that used to haunt him so? Jesus, but Seamus hopes that he's not going to start with all the gibberish again, with all the crazy talk that got him his discharge – what was it Reynard called it? Glossalalia? Glossadoolallia, more like.

– Ah, Christ, he says. What now?

– Aw come on, but. Is that any way to talk to yer ole pal, sir, says MacChuill. Ah mean, pardon ma bluntness, but here and I've come a long way just to see ye, riding this swift-winged bird, here, guiding it by ma will alone an a'.

He points at the crow now strutting on the windowledge, watching him, its dark eye glinting with gold sunlight like there's fire in it. Seamus shivers but it's not from the cold, even if he is stark bollock naked. He wishes he had a cigarette, but there's none of that here, not even out of solitary. He wonders if ghost cigarettes still give ye that wee buzz, 'cause sure and he could ask MacChuill.

MacChuill always had a spare one, so he did. Smoked like a fookin chimney. *Like a reeky lum*, he'd say. Didn't they all?

– And I suppose yer come to be spectator of me sufferings? Seamus says. Have ye just dropped in to see how I'm doing then, and to offer yer commiserations? That's a fair journey, so it is, lad, coming all the way across the river that carried yer soul away, all the way from the fookin hole in the ground all covered in rocks and dirt, out of the fookin iron mother earth itself, lad. I mean, I hate to tell ye this, son, but yer fookin dead and buried.

He feels a wave of dizziness wash over him, wishes he could just fookin live his life out in the peace of seeing only what is here and now.

– Sympathy sent me here, Sarge, so it did. But even if we wurnie brothers, there's naebody I respect more than yersel – Haud on now. Don't be coming out with any of that bollocks. Ye know fine well that what I say is true. Flattery's never been ma strong point.

He walks round to sit on the edge of the mattress beside Seamus, who's almost laughing at the absurdity, so he is, and almost crying.

– Aright. It seems to me that ye could be usin a bit of help here, says the ghost. Never let it be said that there's a firmer friend to ye than ole MacChuill.

Visitations, Visions, Voices

Ah Jesus, look at the sight of me, thinks Seamus, all twisted up with sickness.

– Some fookin friend I was to you, lad, he says. Friend to the dukes, more like, helping them build their bloody Empire on the broken bodies of . . .

Seamus looks round at the face in profile, the left side of it, the good side, and he thinks of the lad from some quarrying town on Scotland's west coast. Moved over to Ireland when he was twelve, right into the heart of Dublin, because his mother was homesick and his father, black sheep of the family, didn't give a damn for the Masons and the Orange Lodge that all his brothers wanted him to join with them. MacChuill seemed to have inherited some of that stubborn streak from his old man, kept the gruff accent all his life just to be thrawn. When Seamus first met him, sure and he couldn't understand a word the boy said. And Christ, when he got a few Guinness in him, Jesus, it was like half the fookin letters of the alphabet just didn't exist any more.

– Ah know, MacChuill says. Ah know. Yer a wiser man than me by far, Sarge, but . . . ah just thought ye could use a wee bit of advice, like.

He turns to face Seamus, full-on, a tentative solemnity in his broken gaze. MacChuill, the eldest of all poor Seamus's ghosts, the first to visit him in the darkness of the dugout, after he woke up and they told him what he'd done, after he'd sat there shaking for hours and hours, looking at the bodies piled in the trench around him, while the captain blethered on about commendations, tragedies and medals. Seamus remembers all the nights of visitations, visions, voices, how he woke up in the dark so many times, seeing MacChuill there with his shattered socket, just like Seamus saw him lying on the battlefield below, and all the others in amongst the craters and the blasted stumps of trees, as Seamus stood there caught, wound up in all the barbs of German wire and – *No. Don't think about it.*

– Ah mean . . . maybe ye want to think of what yer daein here, and get yerself an attitude that's new, because the big man among a' the lords, he's also new, and if ye carry on chucking a' these rude words at the dukes, ye know, as far above ye as they're sitting on their thrones, they're going to hear you – maybe no today but sometime soon – and when they dae, yer present troubles, Sarge, they're going to seem like child's play. Aye, life's no fair, and yours, well, it's just misery, but if ye want release from this despair, ye've got to lay aside this rage.

Seamus tries to stand up, to get away from him. The accent is MacChuill, the language is MacChuill, but there's something in the flow of it, in the rhythm of it, that's not quite right, even for a thing that's not of this world but the next.

– Ah know, ah know, I'm sure I seem like a right ole man saying this, but ye know, Sarge, being deid gies ye a whole new way of looking at things.

Seamus tries to stand up, but his legs don't work; even if he tries to push himself up with one hand on the iron-railed head of the bed, all he feels is the cold metal in his palm. His heart is fluttering, his breathing hard. Sure and he's just too weak.

– Sarge, says MacChuill, yer hardly what ah'd call the meek and mild type, no a man to gie in to the carrot or the stick, but listen . . . yer too wild, yer tongue's too quick, and this is how yer paid. Ye shouldnae kick against the pricks, unless yer looking for mair pain. Ye know it's a harsh, reckless tyrant reigns.

He lays a hand on Seamus's shoulder, weighted with sympathy.

– Ah'm goin now. I'll try and see if I can get you free from all these sufferings. But ye cannae speak so loud, so rude. With all yer wisdom, Sarge, ye ought to know yer proud words will be punished. Sir, this isnae doing anybody any good.

The Unknown Soldier

MacChuill steps out of Finnan's nightmare for a second, takes a wee breather from the work of playing someone else's ghost. Only a couple of minutes and already he feels disoriented. For a second he almost hears an Irish mother calling on him as he's playing in the street – *Donald O'Sheen MacChuill, you get yerself in here this minute.* But that's not him and never was; it's a composite of him – Donald MacChuill – and some O'Sheen that served in Finnan's platoon. MacChuill has never even been to Dublin . . . far as he recalls. Not that he recalls too much.

He blows into his hands and rubs them, trying to warm them up, but it's no just the slaughterhouse that's cold, he thinks. He looks down at the man bound in the chair by chickenwire and chains, and knows that what he's doing is wrong. This isn't what he signed up with the angels for at all and while he's lying to the poor man in a' sorts of ways, there's a part of him that's no playing a fucking role . . . and that's the sympathy.

341

MacChuill glances over his shoulder to the plastic-curtained door, where Henderson is standing, smiling cruelly at the sight of it. He looks around at the butchered carcasses of cattle, red meat, white with the fat and bone and frost.

No, this isn't what he signed up for, not at all. When they found him living wild in the Burmese jungles, lost and stripped of all his thought and memory after so many decades that he couldn't tell them anything of how he got there, who he was, nothing but his name and rank and number, when they told him he was something special, something risen from the ranks of base humanity, transformed by war into this strange and ageless thing – *unkin*, they said – and told him that they needed him – it all seemed such a great relief that he just laughed at it at first. They offered him ... simplicity and structure ... meaning to his life ... a chance to serve the greater good. The *greatest* good, they said. And MacChuill, the unknown soldier who had long since lost his regiment in a war he couldn't even name, swallowed and almost cried with pride, knowing that he was back where he belonged, in an army once again, a soldier now not just for his own noble Empire but for ... the noblest Empire of them all.

They told him there was a war in Heaven. Your eternity needs you.

But this is a new world that they've brought him back to, and a new war, a new kind of war. A war for the hearts and minds of every human on the planet, they say. A war for souls, they say, where the battlefield is something that they call the Vellum. History, they say. Myth, they say. It's no just distant lands across the water, now; this is war outside reality itself and inside people's heads. Heaven is, they tell him, like a little island separated from vast continental powers by a sea of dreams. Dark continents and ancient powers. He doesn't really understand the metaphysics, doesn't have to; he's a product of the British Empire, so he knows exactly what they mean. So it's no German militarism any more, or Indian mutineers – it's no the Mau-Mau or the Zulus or any of those other savage and uncivilized races – but it's still a ... tiny nation trying to spread enlightenment to primitive and brutal heathens. It's still a fight against the foreign devils.

That's what they say.

This Finnan bloke that Henderson and him were sent for, though, this draft-dodging renegade, hardly seems like a great threat to the Covenant. He put up little fight other than to curse and swear at the two of them, even as Henderson, black-hearted bastard that he is, laid into him with fists and feet. And now that MacChuill has walked a while in Finnan's dreams, wearing the face of some poor dead boy called O'Sheen, forging a history somewhere between what was and what just might have been, to try and *build a bond with him,* as his orders said, the problem is he really has. MacChuill looks down at the man bound in the chair, his chest splayed open by the hook, the black dust crawling over him, inside him, and he feels exactly the affinity he has been told to fake. He wants to set the man free from his torment, wants to help him. Surely if he just speaks to his superiors –

– I don't blame ye, lad, the prisoner mutters, answering some absent voice of memory or hallucination. Ye've shared and dared it all with me, son. Now . . .

His head drops for a second then pulls up again.

– Leave me alone. Don't let it worry you. Ye'll not convince them; they're not easily convinced. But you just mind or it's yerself that'll be in the drink.

MacChuill reaches out his hand to touch the prisoner's shoulder, to step back into his dreams.

Another memory of sorts. Another reconstruction of the past . . .

Times Change

Seamus passes the cigarettes out to the soldiers, takes one for himself and lights a match, holds it up first for the one, then for the other. He blows it out without thinking before lighting his own cigarette with another; it's an old superstition from the trenches – you light one ciggy and the German sniper sights it, light a second and he takes aim, light a third and *bang*, somebody's dead. Ye never light three cigarettes with the same match.

He leans against the ornate painted ironwork of Kelvinbridge, a cart clattering across the cobbled stone behind, beneath him water flowing white and wild over a natural weir of sorts, rocks cropping out into the shallow river. So Maryhill Barracks has some would-be mutineers. Sure and it's what Lloyd George was scared of, so it is, enough that when the tanks arrived in Glasgow on the morning after Bloody Friday and the city turned into a fortress in a grip of iron, the hands that held the guns weren't native-born. Two weeks later, the soldiers up in Maryhill were still confined to barracks in case fraternising with the Clydesiders brought their loyalties into question. The soldiers that patrolled the streets to keep the peace were sent in from outside by a Prime Minister and a King shitting themselves that the Red Clyde was about to see a full-scale revolution.

That was four years ago now, though. Times change. Maclean is dead, health broken by prison sentence after prison sentence, by constant hunger strikes and beatings. Gave his coat away to a beggar on the street and caught pneumonia. Sure and the whole city is in mourning for him, so it seems, some of them sad and others angry, like these two. Seamus tells them not to be such bloody fools.

– Ye give advice to others better than you give it to yerself, says the one called MacChuill. Do as I say, not as I do, eh?

And what can he say to that, sure, eedjit that he is? By Christ, he's famous enough for being an eedjit that these two recognised him, called him by his name as they passed in the morning gloom. He would have walked on without even acknowledging it, thinking them drunk and maybe looking for a fight, expecting a bottle to fly past him any second, but they called again, they called him comrade and, in their mouths, he knew, it wasn't a dirty word.

So he had stopped and turned and nodded his hello. Sure and they *are* both drunk, actually, pissed out of their heads, the smell of whisky on their breaths sitting uncomfortably with memories deep under all his thoughts. He's tired with the end of his night-shift and two Glaswegian soldiers off on leave, out on the piss, are a little more than he can handle right now, sure, but, no, they only want to talk to him, they do. They only want to talk to one of the men what knew Maclean, so it ends up as just one of those passing moments of maudlin friendliness that you get sometimes with total strangers in this city, all the *aye, big man* and *och, away* of people who'll open up their hearts, it seems, to anyone.

They tell him that they want to help and he remembers how he said the same thing to Maclean, back when it seemed like just one man could make a difference.

– There's nae way, says Corporal MacChuill, that ye'll dissuade us. Ah mean, come on, if it's the *army* coming out with it, the dukes, they huv to listen to whit we huv to say.

They've no shortage of zeal, sure; he admires that in a man and always will, but he just doesn't think now that the suffering will ever cease, that his poor fellow man will ever find release. What can he say? Strive not; ye'll only strive in vain. There's still a part of him says, *nothing ventured, nothing gained.* But still. He thinks of Ireland now, only just coming out of its two years of bloody civil war, partitioned, riven. They have Home Rule, sure and they do, but with the North still British . . . Christ, forgive them. Don't they see what's coming?

– Hold yer peace, he says, and hold yerself out of harm's reach.

And all he wants, all that he fookin wants now, is to see an end to it, and that no more should suffer, not on his account.

A heron flaps down languidly to stalk the shallow Kelvin down below.

Ah Jesus, no, thinks Seamus. All ye've got to do is look at a fookin atlas and what else is there to do but weep for the fortunes of yer brothers standing in the distant lands past the horizon, bearing their hard loads on their shoulders, those poor fookin pillars of the Empire? Look at the massacred natives of Armenia in their graves. Pity the savage monster with a hundred skulls of Indian slaves around her neck, eyes flashing gorgon light, her frightful jaws hissing the truth of all the slaughter, sure and it's the fookin Age of Kali, so it is, goddess of chaos and death, Amritsar's fookin typhoon of a daughter.

Christ, thinks Seamus, and ye want to stand against the lords, ye think that ye can overthrow the sovereignty of dukes? Let's see.

A revolution in Iraq, is it? Well then the dukes send fookin airstrikes, thunder falling, fire spitting from the sky like lightning bolts, to strike out from the rebels their high hopes. They'll cut the very heart out of ye and leave yer strength all scorched and thundered out.

How goes the revolution now, in Italy, with Mussolini now in power? A fookin useless, bloated corpse it is, buried under the fookin mountain of a fascist state, while industry hammers the flaming masses, sure, in their dire fookin straits. By Christ though, but one day there will be a fookin real eruption there – and not just Etna's rumbling threats to Linguaglossa either; no, it won't be Sicily's smooth fields of fruit and flowers facing the wild jaws, but everywhere it will be rivers of fookin fire bursting out, devouring. Sure and as long as one rebel still breathes, the anger seethes below, a fookin tempest nothing can appease, a rage that rises, boiling, ever higher. It may be burnt to ashes now by the lightning bolts of dukes; one day, though, sure, the blasting furnace will blow storms of fire. Sure and today though, Seamus thinks, what is it that they have? Unholy Roman fascist fookin Empire.

Seamus realises that his hands are gripping the cold iron of the bridge, his knuckles white. Ah fookin Jesus fookin Christ. Where does it end? Where do they start?

Nothing Changes

He tells them that there's nothing to be done. Go home. It's over.

– What harm is there in asking? says MacChuill. What harm is there in trying? Tell us.

– Pointless pain, and empty-headed folly, Seamus says, aware of just how bitter he sounds. But anyway, he says, ye're not without experience. Ye don't need me to tell ye what to do.

So save yerself, he thinks, if ye know how, and as for me, I'll bear my present state, until the minds of dukes are turned from hate, cause what can one man do against a whole establishment, against a world ruled by the rich and powerful, against these new lords sitting all-powerful on their seats? Jesus, it's like the fookin heavens themselves, and God and all His fookin angels are on the side of all that's worst in us. What kind of fookin eedjit stands up against that?

Well, him, of course, the fookin big gob that he has and can't keep shut.

– And just what fookin use is there in talking anyway? he says. Take care in case their anger's turned on you.

He takes a draw of his cigarette and accepts the bottle of Bell's whisky that MacChuill offers him, takes a slug. Sure and the lad's got his heart in the right place and Seamus has no right taking it out on him, it's just that he's so fookin tired of fighting other people's battles. Christ, but it's cold in Glasgow in December, but the whisky warms his chest. Down in the water of the Kelvin, the heron splashes, catches a fish and guzzles it back. It flaps up with a flourish, distracting him. Sure and what is a heron doing here in December?

– Huv ye no heard, Forsythe, that anger's a disease that's healed by words? says this Corporal MacChuill.

– If words, he says, come at the right time to ease the soul and don't just crush a heart about to burst. Don't let your pity turn into hostility.

He turns back to MacChuill, about to say his name's not *Forsythe* anyway, sure and it's Seamus Finnan, but – the heron flaps over his head. And what *is* a fookin heron doing here in December?

The bird's wings beat and MacChuill's greatcoat flaps in the cold wind and Seamus feels that old, old creeping horror. MacChuill takes the bottle out of his hand, shaking his head.

– If it's prudence does most good, as bloody foolish as it looks, MacChuill says, well, ah guess that makes me an incurable fool.

He looks at Seamus with something more confusion than disgust, a young man looking for a hero, seeing only the reality, and oh, by Christ, sure and he couldn't be satisfied with just the truth, could he? The truth is, Seamus knows, that Bloody Friday was the day, and if it didn't happen then it never will, not here in Scotland. No, not now. The tanks rolled in and revolution rolled right out the door.

– If anyone's a fool it's me, he says.

Mad Seamus Finnan with his fear of birds. Mad Seamus Finnan with his ghosts and fookin flow of words all pouring through his head, sure, like the river flows below, like the cold wind that blows.

– Ah get the message loud and clear, MacChuill says with disdain. Go home, sit on yer arse, do nothing. Aye, Forsythe. Thanks. Ye've been quite an education.

Forsythe? Why does he know that name? Forsythe. Four scythes. Foresight. He's shivering. By Christ, it's cold, so cold his hand feels frozen to the metal of the bridge. He glares at MacChuill and the dark shape behind him, another soldier, smiling quiet, savage, cruel. Ah, Jesus, it's fookin happening again, isn't it? He can't breathe. The wind howls in his ears, and underneath his feet the voices of the river rise.

– Go on, fook off, he says with desperation in his voice.

And keep yer mind intact.

MacChuill's backing away, a look of horror on his face, his one-eyed face with that black hole in it, the crow sat on his shoulder with its beak probing into the depths, picking away at him and pulling out the flesh, the red, the white scraps, and there's carcasses all round them like a fookin abattoir and Seamus feels the terror rising and the rushing.

– You speak this word to willing ears.

The bird's wings sweep through the smooth air, and horses' hooves clatter on cobbles and German machine guns rattle as Seamus staggers back from him, falls to his knees.

– Leave me alone!

And MacChuill jerks both hand and mind away from the prisoner, gasping for air himself and stumbling as he steps back, bumping into one of the frozen carcasses, reaching behind, in part to stop it swinging and in part to steady himself, to ground himself back in the real world. Aye, but is it real?

– What are you doing? – Henderson, behind him.

He shakes his head, looks at his shaking hand where the black dust of bitmites, scrawling across his palm, are settling back into a stable pattern, sinking down into the flesh and disappearing. The moment of disorientation passes and he turns and strides past Henderson, pushing through carcasses, leaving them swinging behind him in his wake.

– MacChuill, snaps Henderson. You have your orders. Get back here.

But he's already pushing through the plastic strips of the doorway, flapping them out of his way with an angry backhand, and he doesn't stop walking until he's out of the bloody building itself and standing in daylight, in the hot and blinding sunlight, thank fuck, of a scorching summer day in Mexico.

He leans against the wall of the slaughterhouse, looking out past the trucks in the loading bay, to the green mountains, up to the blue sky, where black dots circle in the air, some native birds of prey. They're tiny in the distance, so high up, like the bitmites crawling in the prisoner's mind, the bitmites that can do Metatron's bloody job for him. Let *them* tear the poor man apart, get under his skin and 'bond with him'. They're just machines. They won't be troubled by a conscience, by sympathy. He watches the circling birds.

Buzzards, they are, he thinks. Bloody buzzards.

A Titanium Atlas

Outside, the deep sea groans and roars, waves dash dark caves of shades, and murmur somewhere underground as if to mourn his ruined state for him.

A painting hangs on the wall of the doctor's office, and Seamus recognises it as based on one of Michelangelo's slaves, so he does, because Thomas once showed him a drawing of it in his sketchbook – sure and it was one of the things he worried about with the lad, him being just a bit too fookin *sensitive* for his own good and all those pictures of half-naked men, and Seamus doesn't care what fancy words ye use, if it's *contrapposto* this or that, well it's still a bloke with no fookin clothes on all twisted up white marble muscle in agony or ecstasy, in chains. But here and the man is painted as a titanium Atlas, with the vast globe of the heavens on his shoulders and it's all like that wee Spanish fellow Thomas was so fond of, bits of it in the wrong places, like, so you can't tell what's the man and what's the world, with painted streams flowing from springs and fountains on the globe, running in crystal rivers, to wet the fellow's cheeks like tears distilled from tender eyes.

– Is that some of that Modernism then? says Seamus.

Reynard heaves a sympathetic sigh, looks over his shoulder at the painting, back again.

– One of the other patients, he explains. Similar case to yours, actually.

– He's got the verbal diarrhoea too, then? Talks shite as well, does he?

– Visual. It's all we can do to stop him drawing on the walls. But you shouldn't be so dismissive of—

– Talking in tongues? Sure and it's not like I'm one of the bloody apostles, is it, doctor? Seamus says. It's not the Holy Spirit that I'm channelling.

Reynard picks up a sheaf of loose-leaf papers, taps them into order, lays them down again.

Seamus nods at the painting.

– So is that fellow mad as well then?

Reynard shakes his head. He takes his glasses off and, leaning an elbow on the table, pinches at his sinuses with thumb and forefinger.

– I shouldn't say that either of you were mad, per se.

He looks tired, Seamus thinks, and sounds it too. Living with a bunch of loonies might well do that to ye though.

– No, says Reynard. I sometimes think that it's the rest of us have lost our minds. But, anyway, he cuts in quickly. I want to talk to you about last night.

– I'm sorry about that, says Seamus.

Woke up half the wing, he did, they say. And got some dirty looks for it in the mess hall this morning.

– Nothing to apologise for. You had a nightmare . . .

– Yes . . .

So Seamus tells him about being back in the trenches and the haughty duke with his rod of iron, him lording it over the lads and making up the law like a game of Simon Says, do this, do that, and sending them over the top to the *illustrious and ancient honour of your brothers*, he says, and out they go into the fields, and they're not afraid to fight, except that instead of guns the mob of them have scythes to work the land. They have to walk across it slowly, sure, and swing their scythes low as they all advance across the trenches and the craters that are all filled full of water, moats and lakes, like, through a field of flowers that becomes an enemy army, sure and the grass is spears in their hands all pointing upwards as they march on, harvesting and gathering them and slinging the bodies on their backs like peasant bundles, giants so they are, as they march on across the cultured land – the cultivated land, that is – and every place they tramp through, sure and it resounds with groans, mourns all the way to Asia or Arabia it is, he thinks, 'cause he looks up, see, and in front of him there's this dark virgin girl so beautiful, so sweet, but crying this lament for all their woes as they unsling their bundles and they start to build, like sandbags, see, they just pile them up one on the other, making walls, making this building out of them, out of the things, out of the lumpen things, and they build it higher and higher, so they do, sure and they build a city, it's a city that they're building from these things, somewhere in the Holy Land, a fortress city, by Christ, a citadel of carcasses.

– Would you describe yourself as a man of faith? Reynard asks.
  – No, I would not, Seamus says. Not now. Not since . . .
  – Since what?
  Seamus shrugs, keeping a sullen silence that might well seem proud, defensive, but that's actually his own thoughts gnawing on his heart. Is it that he still believes, somewhere inside, and blames his God for all that's happened to him? Sure and who else was it but him who gave the lads their orders?
  – Can we talk about something else? he says. I've told ye all this before. Ye've heard all the suffering and how I tried to knock some bloody sense into their witless fookin heads and – can we talk about something else?

– It's just . . . it's interesting that in your dream you end up in . . . the Holy Land, building a city for a virgin, for *the* Virgin, perhaps?

– Well, it's been a while, ye know, doctor. Sure and it's hardly surprising if I'm dreaming of a beautiful girl.

Seamus gazes out the window, across the brown and green of the moor, to the grey rocks, grey sea, grey sky; it's a landscape that's always the same drab motley, no signals of winter – he doubts if there's even any flowers in spring; sure and there's no trees to fruit in summer, that's for sure.

– But a city made of corpses, says Reynard. What would that represent? The church? Religion itself? No. No. I think it's something deeper than that. Society, maybe.

– Sure and I'm not a great fan of yer society types. Yer—

– lords and dukes. Yes, yes. That's not what I meant. I mean society as a whole. Civilisation. The worker's scythe. Asia and Arabia – have you heard of the phrase Fertile Crescent? That's where it all began, you know, with agriculture, the neolithic revolution, in the cradle of civilization. And it all ends up with a city built from bodies. In your dream, anyway. Quite interesting.

Sure and the seasons here are decided by the sky, thinks Seamus, looking out on the moor, just like out on the sea itself where all ye have is the rising and the setting of this star or that, the circling constellations, marking out the moon's months and the equinoxes and the eons of them for the sailors in ships with sails like wings of flax, wandering across the ocean. And all the sky goes round in circles over them. Revolutions.

– From the cradle to the grave, eh? Seamus says, turning back to the doctor.

– I don't think you see much hope for humanity, much progress, says Reynard.

– Humanity? Progress? I'll tell you this, I've not a word to say against them that actually do the work. If it wasn't for the brickies and the joiners, sure and we'd still be living in sunless caves like ants dug down into the ground. Or agriculture, is it? I bet I can tell you who it was first put the yoke on a pair of wild animals so's they might take some of the sweat of the toil off of the bodies of men. Or put the harnesses on horses so as to pull the glittering coach of some fat git with wealth and luxury. It was a man like me who would have been dragging the plough himself otherwise, or carrying the fookin king in his fookin sedan chair, sure. Who do ye think it was dug all the brass and iron, all the silver and gold out of the earth in the first place, but the men who've always been closest to the earth?

– You may be right.

– Sure and I know I am, 'cause them with all the schemes mixed up like dreams are too busy arguing in circles, floating on their own hot air; they've forgotten how to use their eyes to look around them, use their ears to hear what's really going on. Christ, but they might as well be deaf and dumb because to them it's all in here.

He taps the side of his head.

– And yer three R's – reading, writing and arithmetic – what would ye bet that it's a worker made them up so that his master couldn't swindle him out of his wages? Muses and poetry? Bollocks! It was: well, now I'd like to see that in writing if ye don't mind, sir, oh, no sir, not that I don't trust ye, seeing as yer a fine upstanding member of the community, but it's just that yer a fookin thievin shite, if ye don't mind my saying, sir.

Reynard has a tiny smile playing at the corner of his lips.

– So how come, says Seamus. So how come, having come up with all these grand inventions, we don't have the fookin wits to pull ourselves out of this shite?

– The war?

– The war.

– Listen to this, says Seamus with a bitter laugh. Sure, this is grand; it's fookin rich. I'm sure ye'll get a kick from it. Ye want to hear about ingenious inventions? This is the best. Back in France if anyone fell sick, ye know, most times there was no medical supplies, nothing to eat or drink to take away the pain, nothing to dress a wound with, or to treat the trenchfoot or trench fever, syphilis or gonorrhoea, dysentery, influenza or Christ knows what, but for the want of medicine, we had to stand there and just watch men waste away to skeletons.

He stands up, paces round the room and ends up leaning on the back of the chair.

– So me, I'm using whisky for anaesthetic and for antiseptic, like. I'm using all the old wives' remedies taught me by me mam and me grannies. Jesus knows what fookin potions I concocted, sure, hoping to stave off sickness, soothe the burns and blisters from the mustard gas or whatever. Some of them worked as well. Or, at least, the lads believed they did, as fookin desperate as they were.

Reynard studies his face.

– But this is . . . just plain cruel, he says. No? Now you're the one that's sick, you think, losing your mind, and all you feel is the despair that you can't find a . . . remedy for this.

Seamus just stares at him, jaw locked, teeth tight together.

– Ye know, he says, me mam she always used to say I had the Sight a little. Superstitious woman, so she was. I think it's daft meself. But I wonder, ye know, when I get the turns. How do ye tell a vision from a dream? I mean, maybe it doesn't take the gift of prophecy to read the signs and omens in the world, to look at the circling flights of fookin carrion birds with crooked talons and say, by Christ, that bird's fookin unlucky. Look at the way they live, and what they like, and fight over; look at when they gather, when they scatter. Jesus, ye know they used to read bird's entrails, so I'm told, or cut them all up and offer up this part or that to the divine.

And he thinks of the cratered battlefield and him caught on the wire as the guns hammered and the bullets whistled past him, how he prayed for one to hit him and it never did, and when the push was over and all the bodies lay below and the guns quietened just a little, just enough. Only a few birds came at first, stupid or brave, and is there really any difference, sure? And anyway, they came, and twisted up and torn on the barbed wire, all he could do was watch.

– Well now it's them that read *our* entrails, isn't it? Picking over them like they're looking for the smoothest, softest bits – is this the right colour, is it? Isn't this a pretty piece of liver? Oh, but there's some juicy fat still on this arm, and you fook off, it's mine, ye hear, you stick wi yer fookin bit of bladder. And over here or there, there's yet another tearing away at some poor fooker's . . . ah, Christ . . . at a fookin blackened, burnt-up *flank* of meat. Ah, Jesus, he was just a fookin lump of –

He's sitting on the chair now, head in his hands, hands on his shoulders from Reynard standing behind him.

– It's not so hard to see the future. All ye've got to do is look into a fire.

He isn't proud of it, but sure and Seamus has the sight all right, the same foresight that gave men cattle for the plough and medicine and numbers and the whole sorry fookin spectacle of history, of industry, the hammer and the scythe.

– It's not so hard to see the future, doc, he says. It's changing it. It's changing it.

Angels with Dirty Hands

He opens his eyes.

The abattoir is quiet but for the chink of a few carcasses swinging on their chains and the occasional rustle as a breeze blows through the hanging plastic strips of the doorway where Henderson stands looking out. He tests the wires round his wrists and feels the noose around his neck tighten a little. Shit. He has no memory since MacChuill and Henderson found him in the church just ... random images. The Somme. Inchgillan. Bloody Friday. His head feels like some ransacked office, with all the filing cabinets open, files and folders scattered everywhere.

He tries to work out where he is, how long he's been here, but they've had him so deep under he could've been out for days. They could have brought him anywhere – although he guesses it's still somewhere in the States. Rest of the world's a little too unstable now, what with the apocalypse and all. Some fucking Mafia-owned slaughterhouse probably, he reckons, out in the middle of nowhere; the angels like to work through their ... subsidiaries for these kind of operations – don't like the mess being made on their own doorstep.

Operations. He looks down at the meathook in his chest and feels sick. If he was human he'd be dead by now, but then if he was human he would have been dead a hundred years ago on the battlefields of France, wouldn't he, with the rest of them? But no,

Seamus Padraig Finnan got picked by destiny for something greater, for a bigger part in the play. He got ... promoted.

It took him decades even after Inchgillan to fully realize what had happened to him that day, what it was that touched him, transformed him; and there's parts of it he still keeps buried down deep in the corpse-strewn mud of his nightmares. It took him decades of looking in the mirror and not seeing any physical signs of aging, decades of glimpsing things in shadows and reflections, hearing whispers on the wind and thunder in his own voice, decades before he had the strength to really look at himself, to hold his hand in front of his face and watch the strange, dark sigil forming on his palm as this line and that joined, like an acid vision, to form a sort of writing that he somehow knew was what he heard himself gibbering during his turns, written on his own skin, in his body, bonded with him somehow when he stood caught in the German wire for twelve hours, looking down over a battlefield where all the lads of his platoon and Christ knows how many others all lay dead as all the bullets just whistled past him. Charmed, he was. Blessed. Cursed. He touched eternity that day and it touched him and left its mark.

And the Word was made Flesh and Seamus Padraig Finnan was the angel with a dirty face that Anna always said he was.

He looks at the back of Henderson's head and wonders what kind of cunt signs up to this fucking game of war? If it's an angel with a dirty face that Seamus is, this bastard is an angel with dirty hands. Blood under the fingernails. Blackened with the smoke of burning villages. But Seamus doesn't care if it's Satan himself is rising up in rebellion in the Middle East or Africa or wherever, and the archangel Gabriel can blow his horn to shake the very ground under his feet, 'cause Seamus isn't fighting in no fookin war for any of the fookers. He's a conchy. A conscientious fookin objector to the War in Heaven. No matter what they do to him.

Finnan clenches his fists and cricks his neck. Swallowing hurts.

He wonders if they don't want to break him so as he'll sign up with them as much as they just want to make him hate them strong enough to sign up with the opposition. Either way would suit them well enough. As long as he's not a rogue unkin running wild and doing just what he damn well pleases, even if it is only keeping his fookin head down. Whether it's the King's Shilling or the thirty pieces of silver, at least then the bastards know where they stand. But – and he looks down at the black liquid dust crawling round his wound under the ripped and blood-stained T-shirt – this is all too fookin elaborate for that.

Which leaves a third option.

He's heard of the bindings that take place when an unkin signs to the Covenant or to one of the Jesus-knows-how-many insurgent groups formed round some Sovereign still out for his chance to rule the world. There's a lot you have to do to turn a man into a soldier; you've got to drill out the individuality, get some discipline into the lad, get them identifying with their battalion, thinking in the regimental colours of black and white, give them a new name from their surname and their rank, a serial number, a haircut and a kit like every other fucker stood beside them on parade. The unkin take that one step further. When you know the language that controls reality you can take a man apart and put him back together again from scratch with a brand new identity . . . straight off the shelf.

Henderson's one of those. Man In Black. Mafia footsoldier. Spearcarrier.

But it seems like whoever's directing this whole complicated operation has him cast to play a more . . . individual role, no matter what he has to say about it.

Finnan knows there are more creative things you can do, and more destructive things. Sometimes it's just a matter of helping some stray unkin who doesn't even know what they've got in them find their graving, realise their potential – if ye want to get all fookin self-help about it. Christ, but even then you can end up damning someone that you're only trying to help.

He hopes that Phree managed to get away.

If you're willing to go to town on someone, though, you can rewrite their very soul, and Finnan has a feeling that's exactly what's lined up for him. He looks at the bitmites scrawling across his chest, weaving their intricate pattern like iron filings in a fluctuating magnetic field.

Christ, but he hopes that Phree is safe.

– Now's not the time to think of helping others, the bitmites whisper in his head. Do not neglect your own sad state. It's sweet to lengthen life with hope, and feed the heart on joy. We shudder, seeing you tormented by a thousand pains. Not fearing the dukes, you have too high regard for mortals in your private mind of foresight.

Or at least that's something like what they say to him, in another language entirely, one that he understands now a whole lot better than when he was smashing his head against the walls of Inchgillan War Hospital or drifting in and out of consciousness, weak from a hunger strike in Peterhead. He glances up at Henderson still standing guard at the door.

– Come, friend, the bitmites carry on, where's the reward for what you've done? Do you get any help from the ephemerals? Can you not see their impotence, blind, entangled in their dreams? Mortal wills will never break the order laid out by the dukes. We learned these things looking on your destructive fate. But even so, we pray that you'll be freed from these restraints and will someday have no less power than the dukes.

Well that's a turn-up for the books, thinks Seamus. Jesus Christ, it talks.

– Fate's never yet decreed to make it so, he mutters under his breath. I have a myriad ills and woes more still to suffer, and only then will this oppression end. My art's far weaker than what has to be.

It takes less time than if he'd said, *yeah, right,* which is what he meant, really. That's the thing with the Cant. The sounds and senses of it all curled up, compacted into balls of meaning, even just listening to yourself speak you have to do a lot of ... unpacking. Christ, but after a hundred years he still feels like it takes him a minute of catch-up to actually understand a sentence properly. And the bitmites are using it. Jesus, they're fucking talking to him in it, saying—

– And who decides what has to be? they say.

What has to be. Necessity. Destiny. There's a whole network of meanings in the Cant phrase, a hint of inverted commas even, a smidgeon of confusion or contempt. They have ... an attitude, opinions. They're fucking conscious.

– The triple fates, he finds himself answering, and the remembering furies.

Wait a minute. Wait. *We hope that you'll be freed.* Are these things Covenant or what? He's sure Henderson is Covenant; you only have to look at the fucking buzz-cut hair at the back of his neck to know he's regulation issue. So what are these things doing saying that they want to see him free?

– The dukes are weaker then than these?

And that's a leading question if he's ever heard one.

– They can't escape what has been fated, he's replying.

– What is fated to the dukes except to rule forever? they say, and he's almost sure that they already know the answer, like they're laying out the logic of a problem, step by step, a teacher leading an idiot child.

– That you'll never know, he says. Don't ask.

And then they whisper in his ear.

– Surely it is some awful secret you withhold.

And he knows. They're right. He fucking knows and–

– for a second, he's back in Inchgillan by the ocean's endless straits, with Doctor Reynard like a father confessor with his hands on his shoulders, then he turns round and it's Peterhead and MacChuill there, but fookin O'Sheen, *O'Sheen* his name was, not MacChuill, because MacChuill was the soldier on Kelvinbridge on the day after John Maclean's funeral, so it is, and Seamus telling him it's no good, no good, don't set yer mind against the dukes, don't even offend them with yer words 'cause it's all fookin pointless sure and Reynard is pushing his glasses up his nose and Maclean taking his off, and Finnan saying *I want to help* and standing in George Square with fire in his veins and wire round his wrists as he sits in the chair as he stands caught on the hill and the birds are pecking at the bodies which are falling under the hammering of the guns the shells the chains in the dugout Christ and he hears the white wind howl in his head a song that changes and a chant around the bath where him and Anna lie laughing lovers naked in the bed and Anna lying on rough hessian making faces as the birds sing outside the barn and the crows caw over the corn and may this moment stay in us forever and never be dissolved away and the stalk of corn in his teeth and the grain in his hand for her a gift just like the gifts he brought to her door his hair all combed and everything for Thomas to answer the bell and introduce him to his friends in the parlour with all their foolish talk of wars and revolutions in the pub sure and we'll never stop till we've got to the lords and in the park where the singing of the birds is different so different from the harsh caw of the crow all black like soot as black as coal thrown in a *Fire* he's shouting, *Fire!*

And he drags himself back out of it, back into the present, into the abattoir with its holy offerings of slaughtered cattle, and Henderson standing at the door and the bitmites crawling through his body and mind. 'Cause fook ye all, he's thinking. I won't fookin break.

Sure and it's a binding all right. They're stripping his soul down piece by piece, the bitmites eating their way through his memory, worming their way down through the layers of personal history that constitute identity, but he doubts if they give a damn what's left afterwards. They're not trying to bind him into a new self like their footsoldiers, like even their own warped fookin selves. All they want is to open up his soul, like, *really* open up his soul so they can look right through it down into the Vellum. Binding? This is a fookin divination. Peel him open, splay him out and use him to summon some fookin archetype deep in the unconscious mind. He doesn't know who or what they're looking for inside of him, but he knows now that they're reading him, reading the trails of betrayals of foolish schemes, the fookin entrails of his dreams. *We hope that you'll be freed?*

He thinks of an army captain he once knew, offering sympathy over a *grave mistake*, and the opportunity to redeem himself.

Good cop, bad cop, is it? he thinks. I know that one, ye bastards.

– Let's talk of something else, he says. Right now my lips are sealed; now's not the time for it to be revealed when, by concealing this, I may one day escape these chains.

But that's just fookin unkin talk for fook right off, ye fookin fookers, 'cause Sergeant Seamus Padraig Finnan knows exactly what yer up to and ye can fookin sit on it and spin if ye think he's going to help one little bit. No, he's not going to break.

Finnan's awake.

The bitmites swirl up into the air again, away for a second and then back, touching his mind again, looking for another memory to expose, another layer to peel back . . .

A Fury of Flies

A lass, alas, a hungry, wretched one afflicted with a fury of flies, she's frenzied, forced along the sanddune shores, hunted and harried by a hundred watching eyes of images of argil, herdsmen made from clay that haunt her, all the statues of the saints and Christ upon his cross and in the paintings in the chapel, looking down on her with blame. Six feet of soil don't hide the prying, pious eyes of all the glorious dead that scrutinise her from the heavens. Jesus and the blessed saints, they see her shame. Somewhere, a reed of wax, it seems, blows low, sounding a soporific song, the wind through coarse, tall grass. A lass, alas, O gods!

Ah, god, the pain! Some wretched fly stings her again, the midges of the rock pools all buzzing around her head like the saints themselves come down to punish her for her sins.

And Anna stumbles in the sand, and sinks down sobbing, in her skirts.

Where, Lord, where will she go? In what sin is it she's been found, what sin, sons of the Crown, that she's now damned to this unending misery? O, but she knows only too well. Burn me with fire, she thinks, or bury me in earth, or feed me to the creatures of the sea, but grant me mercy, God. I'll stray no more, I swear. Wild ways have troubled me enough; I've learned my lesson. Only let me know now when this suffering will be over.

She feels the hand touching her hair, the tender hand of her sweet Irish rover, Seamus, tentative now, as if he doesn't know if it's his place. He wipes a tear off of her face.

– Ah, hush now, Anna, Seamus says. It'll be OK. It can't be that bad, can it? What could be so bad as to deserve all this palaver?

How can she tell him in the state he's in? How can she tell him of the state *she's* in? Him stuck in this ungodly loony bin and her stuck here between the devil and the deep blue sea, between a rock and a hard place, sure, between her love for Seamus and the terrible thing she did in hatred of him when he told her of her brother's death in France, between her heart given to one man and her body to another. Father, forgive me, she thinks. *Seamus*, forgive me. I was angry. O, but the anger and the grief were just too much to bear and you were the one said you'd look after Tom and keep him safe, but Tom was gone and you were lost in your own head and . . . and he was there. O, Seamus, I wanted to hurt you. I wanted to hold you. It was your blue eyes I saw in his, and your hair that I ran my fingers through as I pushed it from those eyes.

She wrings her hands and feels the ring hidden under the glove. How can she tell him that she's marrying a man she doesn't love and not the man who had his mind all broken for the promise that he made to her?

– What kind of place is this, she says, what kind of people in it?
She trembles, shaking like the poor unfortunates sat at the tables in that awful room, the men with missing arms or legs, blinded or worse. She saw his own hand shake when he reached out to touch her fingertips across the table, every bit as gentle as back home when they were all so young and wild and he'd come calling all spruced up and in his Sunday best. His hands are rough but they can touch so soft you barely feel it through a calfskin glove except you feel it pounding in your heart.

She looks at him sat on the rock she's slumped beneath, his legs spread wide, his dirty blond hair blowing in the wind. Behind him, beyond outcrops of rock and over moor, the cold grey edifice of Inchgillan stands looking as desolate as himself. What has he done to earn this punishment from her? What miserable outpost of society is this they've found themselves in?

And stumbling, sobbing, she begins.

– Please listen to me, Seamus.
Seamus, forgive me, for I have sinned.

A Terrible Dark Thing

He tries to listen to her, watching her flick a calfskinned hand around her flyfurled head, as she tells of a duke's heart warm with love for this young daughter of Enoch Messenger, but he can't take it in. Here and her father always hated her seeing Seamus, he interrupts her, laughing, and the lengths they had to go through, all the hoops they had to jump through just to get some time together. Do you remember, eh? Yer old man and his talk of decency.

– Why do you have to talk about my father? she says. Tell me, O Jesus, Seamus, poor suffering Seamus, because you've always talked the truth to me, are we just born to suffer? Who of the wretched, who – O God – suffers like us?

Because decency, she tells him. Decency. He's put a name to the very heaven-sent source of it all that sent her to him. He asks her why, what is it, why and she tells him how she came rushing headlong, how she hasn't been able to eat since – and the rough ride of the ferry over from Dublin, and how they all end up suffering from the plots that people make in anger, maddened by spiteful thoughts like insect bites.

He doesn't understand her tumbling story, as she tries to get it out but keeps going off the rails before reaching the point. Or there's a part of him that understands but that won't let the truth through to the rest of him. All that he knows, all that he'll let himself hear in her mixed-up rambling confession is that she has some terrible truth that she can't bear, but she can't bear to tell him.

– Do we go to Heaven or Hell after we're dead? she asks him. How much more can await us after what we suffer in this world? Surely Jesus must forgive us.

Tell her, thinks Seamus, tell the poor girl that God is in his Heaven and forgives us all our sins, even shooting the brother of the girl ye love for cowardice, not the cowardice of a young lad cowering

363

in a dugout, but the cowardice of his friend, his Sergeant, who followed the fookin order. Tell her there's forgiveness for that.

He can't.

It's been a terrible dark thing between them ever since he got back from the front to give her the news himself of Thomas's death, to say that the shame was on him, on Seamus, on himself. He sees it in her eyes, that she can't really forgive him even though she wants to. And he can't really forgive himself because when he looks into her eyes, he sees the same dark green and brown as Thomas's looking out at him.

But what has she got that needs forgiveness, sure?

He remembers arriving at the door of the Messenger family home in the well-to-do Dublin suburb of Rathgar just like so many times before but now so different. On leave and waiting for the results of the Medical Board, sure, and shaking like a leaf, he hadn't a clue what he was going to say to her and whether she would cry or curse him to his face or both. Should he tell her the untarnished truth, whatever she might want to know in simple words, leaving out the euphemisms and not weaving some grand mystery of tragic death out of it? Surely she had the right to hear it from the horse's mouth. Should he tell her she was looking on the face of the man who gave the lads the order to take aim and fire?

And when she came to the door she had a look so lost, so wandering, that he knew she needed something to latch onto as a sign that the grief might someday end, and would it be better for her not to know or – Jesus Christ – for her to learn? Could he hide it from her, have her find out later, suffer even more? He couldn't grudge her this one thing, this tiny thing, this awful tiny truth so why the fook did he delay? It's not that he doesn't want to, is what he told himself. But he couldn't help but hesitate on account of what it would surely do to her.

But if it's what she wants, he thought, I'll have to tell her.

And so they sat in the parlour, him with his hat in hand, and they were distant enough from each other, like she already sensed the guilt in him far deeper than his failed promise. Why was he suffering so? she asked him. What awful crime was he punishing himself for? And he could hear the fear in her voice that he was going to tell her and break her heart. (Just like the fear that's in him now, that she's got some truth like that but it can't be as bad as his, can it? How could it be?) He thought of the endless telling of his tale to the doctors of the Medical Board.

– Sure and it seems I never stop talking of my sufferings, he'd said. A man can only talk so much.

– Seamus, tell me what's driven you to the edge, she said.

The will of dukes, he thought, the hand of a smith. He shook his head.

She asked him, if he loved her, God, to tell her what was wrong, don't soften it for her; she was strong and she could take it. And he said he couldn't, Jesus Christ Almighty, how could he tell her? It was to do with Thomas, he'd said, looking at those green eyes. Please, she'd said. And he couldn't just tell her, he said, but . . . if she asked . . . if she asked any question . . . any question . . . he would tell her anything she wanted to know.

And so she asked, and Seamus told her how he shot her brother.

And now he knows it's somehow the same thing, with her trying to tell him her own shame but needing him to prompt her, draw it out of her as she did to him. And what could it be? Jesus, what could it be that she's afraid is so bad he might not be able to forgive her?

The Third Player

– I'm pregnant, says Phreedom.

Finnan looks down at the bottle in his hand, leans down to place it gently on the floor between his feet. The quiet words resonate in the empty church in that whispering way that only empty halls have, not quite an echo that can be made sense of, just a pious ringing of the stone in answer to the human voice.

– Is it . . .?

– Yours? she says. I fucking hope so. Christ, I fucking hope so.

He knows it's not the only possibility. The last time they met, in this same church, she told him exactly what they'd done to her, the angels of the Covenant who were looking for her brother.

They'd left her for dead afterwards, and in a way she was, she is;

they both are – Finnan with his heart ripped out, a traitor to her and Thomas, her with a seed of hatred planted in her, poisoning her slowly. She went to Hell to try and save her brother. It didn't end well.

– I led them to him, she had said. I thought I could change the story, rip us out of it, and all the time I was just tearing an opening in the Vellum for those ... creatures to get at him. You betrayed him, Finnan, but I damned him. I fucking damned him. I thought I could go back and ... make things right. But time in the Vellum isn't that simple, is it?

He had been sodden and filthy then, just as he is now, living hand-to-mouth, going from soup kitchen to homeless shelter, stewing in his own misery and drinking in churches just to spite the bastard God of his innocent childhood. When she'd found him, he'd expected her to hate him, but by that time she was too busy hating herself. In the end, they'd found some little solace together; she'd taken him back to her room, fed him and washed him. As they lay together in the warm bed after fucking like animals, she'd told him of all the strangers she'd used in the same way, pick-ups in singles bars and seedy night-clubs, dirty old men and groups of frat-boys. He knew she wasn't saying it to hurt him, but to open up herself to him because he was the only one who'd understand. They were both trying to make physical the degradation of their souls, in the ruin of their flesh.

That was three months ago and now she's pregnant, and it could be his, it could be any of the johns' or marks', Tom, Dick or Harry's. Or it could be the angel's.

– Whatever ... she says, I'm going to have it.

He looks at her. There's a sort of strength to her now. She seems to have found some sort of strength in the acceptance of this, as an end to her own story, maybe, and the beginning of another. It's like she's fought so hard against her fate since the first day she stood up to an angel of the Covenant, she's sold her soul to Hell only to steal the secrets of its queen, she's torn her way into the Vellum to try and save her brother, and the futility of it all that had her broken and beat-up inside like him, has now become a grim and nihilistic faith of sorts, in the emptiness of it all. While he's still on his knees, raging against the dying of the light, she's standing up to face the darkness, ready to walk into it, and ready for the good fight.

He's just waiting for his Judgement Day.

– So you've picked a side then, he says.

– No sides, she says. Just me.

She lays a hand on her stomach.

– Us.

He thinks of Anna, the lost sweetheart of his past and the way it all seems to tie together, echoes and reflections bouncing back and forth across a century. They're creatures of the Vellum and time in the Vellum has a funny way of weaving and looping; they tear it and they stitch it back together as they travel through it. Jesus, but Tommy made a right mess, so he did, then, now and fucking forever. One unkin's all it takes to shatter time into a million shards that no amount of Covenant craft could put back into order. Now that the war is kicking off it's only going to get worse.

– You know how bad it's going to get? he says. The Sovereigns and the Covenant–

– The Sovereigns are straw dogs. And the Covenant don't know what they're dealing with.

She pulls off her jacket to show him the pink scarred tattoo. The black ink of Eresh's needlework crawls over her arm in such a chaos of ever-changing signs and sigils that it makes him dizzy, gives him vertigo; it's only when she puts her arm back in the jacket sleeve that he stops feeling like he's being sucked into a void.

– Jesus, fookin Mary and Joseph. What the fuck?

– I don't know, she says. What do you get if you cross the queen of the dead's blood with the ink of God's scribe? I think they're breeding, Finnan. And I don't think I'm the only carrier.

– Metatron's pet hawks, he says slowly, quietly. Carter. Pechorin.

She's told him what came walking out of the exploding moment of Eresh's death, in the bodies of Metatron's two bloody-handed angel thugs, what followed her into the Vellum to drag Thomas off to an eternal grave. As much as she can make sense of.

– I don't think they work for Metatron any longer, she says. I think they're like me.

She flexes her fingers in front of her; on the back of her hand, down just at the wrist, at the edge of her sleeve, he can see the clashing symbols on her skin. He reaches over to take her hand, hold it.

– You always said you thought there was a third player, she says, sitting on the sidelines, staying out of the game. Jesus, I'm not even sure it understands the concept of sides.

Her other hand goes to her stomach.

– But I think it just entered the game, she says.

Errata

Heroes and Villains

– Don't try to speak, says Malik.

He walks around to the side of the surgical slab and lays a hand on the shoulder of the man strapped down on it. He feels the muscle twitch, ribbed tricep quivering like horseflesh, bicep in a knot, straining against the leather bonds. Fresh blood seeps from the cuts and scratches reopened on his skin by pointless struggles. The poor creature looks quite exposed, naked and vulnerable. How the mighty are fallen.

Malik lifts his hand to straighten a gold and black obsidian cufflink. The stone glistens even in the fluorescent light of the operating theatre, as shining and dark as the fixed pupils of the angel staring up at him with hate. Malik feels his lip curl up in an involuntary sneer. One shouldn't gloat, but it's hard not to.

He reaches into the pocket of his white dress uniform – his own design, replete with meaningless medals in the classic military dictator style so de rigueur in the last century; he's nothing if not a traditionalist – and pulls out the set of dog-tags.

– Rafael Hernandez Rodriguez, Corporal, United States Marine Corps. Did you choose the body for the rank or for the name? No. Don't try to speak, Corporal Rodriguez. It's not worth the effort.

He dribbles the dogtag chain through his hand, lets it drop, chinkling, onto the man's chest. It only covers a fraction of the unkin lettering that's carved all across his torso.

– Not without a tongue, he says.

The archangel Rafael moans wordlessly.

– I apologize for the crudeness of the binding, by the way – [he taps a finger on one of the sigils] – but I'm afraid we don't have all the wonders of modern technology at our disposal. None of your bitmites here, I'm afraid.

He gestures around at the sparse theatre, the antiquated equipment that belongs in the last century, all hulking and obsolescent, hard screens and dials, tubes, lights, mirrors.

– No bitmites, he says. No microscanners. No VR modelling and mini-waldos here. No synthskin. No autosuturers. We still cut people open with stainless steel scalpels and sew them back together with needle and thread. If we think they'll make it through the operation.

Malik strokes his thick moustache, an unconscious gesture of a brooding mind.

– Ten years of war and sanctions and military coups and more war and more sanctions and so on and on and on and on. Do you know how hard it is to get antibiotics in Damascus? Do you know the child mortality rate here?

Rafael just glowers at him.

– And I'm the *baby-killer*, he says. The great and terrible *Moloch*.

– You used to be a healer, Rapiu, he says. Do you remember? Do you remember anything from before your blessed Covenant? Do you remember bathing the sick on the shores of the Dead Sea, handing out your medicines to the poor and needy? Do you remember watching the cities blossom in that land of salt and sand, because people could come there and be healed, because of the legacy you left behind? Or was that all burned out of you by the glory?

Malik leans over so he can stare back into the angel's eyes. He wants the bastard to see him for what he is, even knowing that that's impossible.

– How many children died in the furnaces of Sodom and Gomorrah? How many lives did you destroy because a few intransigent unkin wouldn't bend their knees? Your own lord couldn't stomach it. The most glorious of all angels chose the long walk into the Vellum rather than serve what your Covenant had become.

The angel turns his face away, but Malik grips him by the chin, pulls it back round to meet his hatred and contempt. He thinks of a thousand years of luxury, of cities rich with the scent of cedar incense and spiced food in markets, and beautiful whores dressed in linen dyed scarlet and purple by Canaanite craftsmen, and poets of the flesh and all the wonderful, wicked deviants and decadents that he would walk amongst, a king dressed as a beggar. There was injustice. There were terrible crimes. And there were people with souls that shone as brightly as their jewels. And he thinks of three thousand years in which his name – Malik, Malak, Meleck, Moloch – has been synonymous with burning babies.

– Understand me, Rafael. Understand me. I am not the villain here. You are.

– No, says the voice behind him.

He stands in the doorway, a shape of black, a silhouette even though the well-lit room should pour its light upon his face. Some of the black rises in wisps off of him, like steam from a beast of war slick with its own sweat. The volutes carve out symbols in the air, thin trails of thought. Malik tilts his head, more curious than concerned, even though the breach of his security is clearly severe. The city has been sealed off for the last week, ever since he choppered in with the angel Rafael drugged up in a bodybag, a squad of guards scouring the landscape all around them with their nightshades glowing white in the darkness, lances snapping this way and that to train on any smallest motion, and the pair of black monks in the back of the Sikorsky, legs curled into lotus position, chanting the mantras that rendered them as invisible to the watcher angels scattered all around the area as to the Allied radars and surveillance satellites. No one should even know he's here and even if they did, they shouldn't have been able to get past his circles within circles of protection. Part of him feels he should be outraged at the inadequacies of his minions; but, as Malik would dearly like the angel Rafael to understand, Malik doesn't have minions, just men and women willing to die to drive the occupying forces from his land, their land. His Philistine Liberation Organisation, he calls it, sometimes, in his moments of blackest humour.

– No? he says calmly to the shadow-thing.

It's got to be some emissary from another rebel group, of course. Maybe Marduk, he thinks. Or Nergal. Nergal does have a tendency for melodrama, playing the underworld god, the dispossessed turned demon. Playing right into the Covenant's hands, like so many of them.

– No, the creature says. No more villains. No more heroes. No more victims.

The tongueless moaning of the angel on the table grows louder, higher-pitched, more wail than moan now.

– A commendable concept, says Malik bitterly. And who might you be?

And we tell him exactly what we are.

The Heart of Damascus

White light, white noise, he feels the loss rip through him like a blow to the back of the head, like a syringe of morphine rammed into his spine at the base of his neck, squirted and then broken off with a savage downward snap. A searing, blinding dagger of sensation followed by utter numbness and confusion. Gasping. Staggering. Metatron hits the floor on his knees like a boxer with a glass jaw, and doesn't even see or hear the palmtop crack against the wooden desk, tumble and skitter on the marble floor. His dreadlocks hang down over his face, his arms shaking as he tries to hold himself up like a drunk over a toilet bowl, retching, grasping for breath.

Rafael's dead.

– some kind of explosion, in the heart of Damascus, just a few seconds ago –

Phreedom crawls across the motel floor, sobbing and clutching at her stomach. It's too early. It's too fucking early, but the cramps are unbearable.

– reports coming in from all over the city, a sort of blinding flash of –

She reaches for the phone up on the bedside table, knocks it down onto the carpet beside her, then another cramp hits her and her fist curls even tighter round the corner of the quilt. Liquid dribbles down between her thighs.

– horrific devastation, absolutely unimaginable–

She reaches for the phone, pushing her hand through a moment of time as solid as a wall. Goddamn it. Fucking. Not now.

Time flickers.

– Israel or America. Nobody knows but this is sure to–

The TV flickers too, switching channel every couple of seconds – CNN, NBC, Fox, BBC, ABC, VNV, ANN, channel after channel and some of them she knows never existed until this moment, until some fucking bastard unkin bit the farm and ripped a chunk right out of reality as they went down. The channels are changing. Literally. She grabs the phone and punches at a key. It's too fucking early. Oh, Christ, it's too fucking early but she's not going to let them take this from her.

– I need an ambulance, she sobs into the phone, not even hearing the voice on the other end. I need an ambulance. Room ... I don't know. I need an ambulance.

And then the gurney is slamming through swing doors, lights flashing above her head and doctors leaning over her, hands examining, and she hears phrases like *breach-birth* and *c-section* and *have you taken anything*?

– No, she says.

No, no, no, no, no.

And Carter reaches into Seamus Finnan's body, into his heart to read what's written on it like a blind man reading Braille, his fingers feeling for the filigree of unkin language on a heart of damasked steel, while Pechorin holds him there.

– Where is the Messenger boy? he says, and then he finds the answer and he looks at Finnan with an honest shock on his face.

The shell blast knocks him off-balance for a second and he has to steady himself against the dugout's wall. A tin mug rattles on the floor where it's fallen.

– I don't care what you say, Sergeant. It's decided. Dismissed.

Sergeant Finnan snaps to attention, salutes him with a look of utter hatred and stalks from the room. Pickering stands up from the bunk, a cruel smile on his face.

– Tims, eh?

– Shut up, says Carter. Are you bloody well enjoying this?

– Come on, Jack. The boy's a coward and a deserter, and an urning at that.

– What did you say?

He spits the words with fury.

– I said he was a fucking faggot, says Joey. Come on, man. You saw the way he was looking at you. So we had some fun with him. He'll be OK.

– Stop the car, says Carter, leaning forward.

– What the fuck's the matter with you?

He pulls the car over to the kerb and Carter fumbles the handle open, falls out onto the sidewalk to vomit at the feet of a disgusted passer-by. Carter looks up and it's a boy's face looking back at him, a face he recognises without knowing. He scrambles back and away.

– Jesus, Jack, did you take something?

Joey leans over him, pushing an eyelid back with a thumb to study the pupil. Jack grabs at his jacket collar and, as he opens his hand to grasp the leather, a silver Zippo falls down to the ground. He has no idea where it came from but he grabs it like the most precious thing he's ever owned.

– What did we do? says Jack. What did we do?

– Nothing. For fuck's sake, Jack, what are you on? What did you take?

Jack pushes him away and clambers to his feet. They're parked outside an old derelict shop, the glass all shattered and boarded up, looks like it's been empty forever. There are shadows seeping out from under a padlocked door spray-painted with a weird graffiti logo, sort of like an Eye of Horus, sort of not.

– Where are we?

– College Street, Jack. Take a look at the fucking signpost.

But Jack's too busy looking everywhere, at the door, at the lighter in his hand, at the puddle of his vomit, at the passers-by gaping like he's from outer space, at – yes – the signpost that says College Street high up on a wall above the bar down at the corner, at the shadows seeping out from under the doorway and following the cracks in the sidewalk, at the low sun shimmering among striated clouds there in the west, the glow of an early evening at the end of summer, gold and yellow and red and orange like fire. He steps towards it, knocking Joey's hand off his arm with a flick of his shoulder, walking towards the sunset without any idea of what he's doing or why.

– Where the fuck are you going, Jack?

He passes a TV shop, registers the screens of flames in the corner

374

of his vision, scrolling headlines telling of destruction in Damascus. Countless dead.

– Where the fuck are you going?

He has no idea.

– I had no idea, says Metatron.

He sits at the bottom of the long table. It's a custom dating back millennia, back to when they first met in some warlord's banquet hall, the seven of them all seated round the table, three down one side, three down the other, Metatron down at the bottom, ever the humble servant, his master's scribe and vizier, looking up at the empty seat of the megalomaniac they'd decided to overthrow. He'd found himself caught by the perfect symbolism of that empty throne, as he persuaded the others that not only *could* they do it but they *had* to do it. It was right. And since that day they carved the Covenant into their own souls, they had always kept an empty chair, in the banquet halls and tents and board-rooms where they met, through the ages. And Metatron always sat at the bottom of the table, as the lowest of the low, even though – or perhaps because – ultimately it was his plan, his scheme, his vision, his voice. None of them, least of all Metatron himself, ever considered that the table was just a rectangle like any other rectangle, with four sides, two long and two short, that the allocation of top and bottom to it was an arbitrary notion, and that, to all intents and purposes, the *head of the table* was not where they quite spuriously projected it into an empty symbol but, in fact, in actuality, wherever the power sat, wherever the authority that they listened to laid his elbows on the table and leaned forward to say in a quiet firm voice, *this is what we're going to do*. No. That empty seat is too important, too central to the Covenant, for Metatron to question just how empty it might be, as a symbol.

And now, up at the top of the table, across from Uriel, beside Michael, there is another empty chair.

– You make a deal behind our backs, says Gabriel. You give some little trailer-trash desert-rat total immunity after Eresh has done a number on her –

– She wasn't relevant, says Metatron. She was nothing.

Michael snorts. Obviously, he's with Gabriel all the way. Uriel is the military type, more of a tactician than a city-burner, but he'll still side with the hawks. Sandalphon, the only real dove among them, will side with Metatron as always; he would have let the girl go free just out of sympathy. Azazel? Who knows?

– You waste two good agents, Gabriel carries on, just to get your little bitch-whore out of jail free–

– I sent them to get Eresh–

– Not to mention that you hack them into dogmeat first.

– I had to make her think that ... look – they were unstable to begin with.

– They were Covenant, says Michael. They were our men. Our boys.

Uriel nods grimly, but Metatron notes the weary look on Azazel's face, the way he rolls his eyes.

– And now, says Gabriel. Now whatever Eresh had under lock and key is out there using your own blessed bitmites against us.

– We don't know that, Sandalphon says. It might have been Malik. We don't know for sure–

– It's time we did, says Gabriel.

He pushes his chair back as he stands up, strides around the table to lean on the back of Raphael's empty chair.

– I'm working on it, says Metatron. I just need time. I have a source–

And Gabriel spins and throws the chair against a wall. A painting falls, its glass frame shattering, scattering. He pushes the empty chair at the head of the table to one side and plants his hands on the wooden surface, staring directly at Metatron, challenging him silently. There are lines around his eyes; the last few centuries have been hard on him. He was born to burn bright, and they've been hiding in the shadows for too long now. Even Metatron understands how ... alien this kind of angel feels in an age of science and technology, an age of information and mass-media. There was a time when *stars* meant cherubim of awe and majesty, with swords of fire flashing from their mouths, the unkin tongue lashing reality, laying waste the enemies of the Covenant. Not painted actors on a painted screen.

– No more time, says Gabriel.

He stands straight, then turns and leans behind to grab the chair, to pull it close behind him.

– No, Gabriel, says Metatron. This is against all that we … you'll be nothing but another Sovereign.

– Weren't we all Sovereigns once, kings of this world? Baals.

– So what do we call you now? says Azazel with disdain. Prince Gabriel? *Lord* Gabriel? King?

Gabriel stares at him as he sits down. At the head of the table. The angel of fire on the throne of God.

– Not *king*, he says. And not just me, but all of us here in this room, if you'll stand behind me. We'll be … Dukes.

Not *dukes*, thinks Metatron, but *Dukes*.

5

Narcissus Has Woken

The Reality of Dreams

– You think your dreams are real, Jack?

– That's the nature of the conspiracy. We all think our dreams
are real.

– Most people don't see the world the way you do, Jack–

– You don't see it? You don't fucking see it? You don't see the
statue of a saint watching over a priest as he molests some fucking
altar boy. You don't see the book of lies in the hands of a zealot
ordering a stoning. A horoscope read out to a president before he
orders an attack. You say *I'm* living in a fantasy world, Dr Starn?

– Jack, these are terrible things, but–

– A flag flown by a skinhead, a bulldog tattoo on an arm throwing a
brick. Offerings of flowers lain down for a dead princess – People's
Princess – paparazzi human sacrifice – and every fucking newspaper
with the glossy pictures of the funeral, mmm, zoom in, show me
some grief, oh, such a tragedy. Who's in charge, Dr Starn?

– Jack, nobody's in charge. Not in the way you mean–

– Who's in charge?!

– Calm down, Jack.

– You've been living in the Empire so long you don't even see it,
working lurking, in the background, in the shadows and reflections.
Do you know who your masters are? Dreams aren't real? I say they
walk among us, whispering in our ears all their sweet promises and
threats, carried in our heads, mindworms, maggots eating at our dead

souls. Dreams, memes, gods and monsters, creatures of the id. If they aren't real then what the hell am I?

– You're a very disturbed young man, Jack. You're ill.

– I'm awake!

Starn lays the folder down on the table. He knows this is a bloody risky thing to do, given the boy's mental state; it may not be a good idea at all to show him his own face in another time, offering him more fuel for the fantasies, an open door out of reality. In fact, it's downright playing with fire, but ... He tries to tell himself that he's not here to treat the boy, just to get at the truth; but, at heart, no matter what he might say to the inspector, no matter what public opinion is, or what brand of barbarism's championed by the tabloids these days, he can't help but see these people that he deals with as not evil but sick. Wounded, crippled souls. Driven, riven minds. Born with broken hearts. They belong in hospitals, not prisons. Not the scaffold.

He opens up the folder, turns it round on the table to show the photograph of Mad Jack Carter.

– You said you used to have a name. Before.

– Once upon a time, he says. Once upon a time there was a boy called Jack.

Return to Arcadia

Operation: enhance grandiose delusions; scan for memetic substructure.

Jack fiddles with the white haversack that runs from right shoulder to left hip over his dark blue shirt. Leather belt holding it down, white epaulette on his left shoulder. When he has the hat on he looks like a member of the bloody Hitlerjugend. He only joined the Boys' Brigade because Joey was in it. And all this Sunday School shit is the worst.

– But it says that God threw Adam and Eve out because he didn't want them to be like him and live forever. That's what it says.

He looks at the teacher as she smiles a pleasant but firm smile, closing her Bible, and he sees himself as Jesus, casting the moneylenders from the temple. Soul merchants, buying the human spirit, selling snake-oil salvation. Fuck them all.

– Well you wouldn't want *people* to be as powerful as God, *would* you, Jack? People can be *bad*, and do bad things, and—

– It doesn't say anything about power, he says. It just says they'd live forever.

– Well, they *would* have lived forever, but they disobeyed God so He made them mortal so that they—

– That's not what it says. It says they were already mortal and they would have been immortal, but God didn't want them to be, didn't want them to be like him.

The others all look bored and fed-up, sitting there in their uniforms, even the ones he knows from school as troublemakers, all weirdly quiet and respectful here, happy to challenge teachers, to fire paper airplanes and spitballs, to start fires on railway embankments, to throw stones at the Catholic kids from St Mick's over the other side of the bridge. Jack's normally the quiet one, well-behaved, a good boy. It makes a change for him to be the . . . awkward one.

Like all it takes, he's thinking, is a bite of some forbidden fruit and a human can become something else, maybe not God, maybe not *a* god, but something like that. No longer just a human. That's what it says. *Lest they become like us.*

And a little flicker of a smile – a flash – moves across Jack's face.

– What was he, says Jack, afraid of a little competition?

Alert: messianic complex; rebel archetype detected.
Operation (imperative): scan for reality breach; authenticate metaphysical incursion.
Narrative detected:
The road is still there, with just a few more years of tags and band names, and the concrete cylinder's still there as well.
ET IN ARCADIA EGO.
He knows what it means now: *and I am also in Arcadia.* It's from some painting, three shepherds looking at the words inscribed upon a tomb. It's famous, but he has no idea of how he knew it at the age

of fourteen. It's possible he heard the phrase somewhere, saw a photo of the painting at some time, but that's not what Jack thinks. It's not what Jack Flash thinks.

Joey is zipping his leather jacket up as he pushes through the thicket, scrambling down the slope, less balanced now in adolescence than they were as children.

He's starting to see things now. Finally, after so many years of snapping his head round at the shadows and reflections at the corners of his vision only to find the world completely normal, finally he's starting to catch glimpses of the secret world beneath the world. He looks up into the sky sometimes and sees a silver sea, ripples running across it, waves rolling. He can hold sand in a small pile on the palm of his hand and watch the grains dance, sparkling like glass in the sunlight, moving into patterns like iron filings caught between magnetic fields. He can hear songs in the murmur of a crowd in a busy shopping precinct on a weekend. He can smell the rotting corpse of God in a church.

Jack knows that he's insane. He's not fucking stupid; he recognises all the signs and symptoms of him being schizo. Voices, visions. But that doesn't help him when he sees the creatures of liquid light walking through the crowds, stopping to whisper in this person's ear, to pass a hand over somebody's heart, or when one of them stops for a second and, like an animal scenting its prey, sniffs the air and turns to look at him with its blank mirrored eyes.

The Road to Nowhere

Information upload: subject previously identified; advise search on known felons/fugitives.

They've started to watch his house, these creatures. He's not crazy enough to think they're beaming thoughts into his head; he's not reached the tinfoil hat stage yet. But they're definitely watching him, following him.

— You know they're not real, says Joey. You know you've got to talk to someone about this. You can get help.

Joey Pechorin. He looks like the fifth Ramone these days, with his long, dark hair hanging over his face. Jack's going for the Johnny Rotten look himself. It's 1979 and the bitch who took away their school-milk just got elected as prime minister. The Asian grocer's got firebombed last week, sprayed with the logos, Pakis Out and BNP – British National Party. The whole fucking country's going to Hell, says Guy but Jack, he knows different. They're already in Hell. They just have to find the way out.

Jack edges the tip of the crowbar, prises it under the lip of the manhole cover on the concrete cylinder on the road that comes from nowhere and goes nowhere.
– They're real, he says. They just don't exist. Creatures from the id. From the fucking mass unconscious. Living information.
Joey grabs him, pulls him away from the cover, tries to shake some sense into him.
– It's you, Jack. It's you. In here – [he taps the side of his head] – inside of your fucking head is where they're from.
– I know, says Jack . . . but they're from your head too.
And he leans down at the concrete cylinder, and leans down on the crowbar and he cracks reality wide open.

It's 1979, and as the archetype stretches within his body, he feels it like the grace and glory of an angel or a demon flowing in his veins. He stands there over the hole in the world, looking down into the abyss, into the flood of liquid dust, black blood of dead gods, the past and the future and the end of both. Joey is screaming at him, pulling him back from the edge, but all Jack can hear is the beautiful song of the bitmites as we weave our spell around him, telling tales within tales of ancient powers and future apocalypse, of infinite deaths, of infinite births, a song of murderers and heroes, and of fire burning cold inside his head, sing of a city at the end of everything and a book in which all things are written, and we sing of covenants and rebels, crows and kings, we sing of love and sorrow, flesh and words, we sing, for this is what we are, we bitmite things of blood and ink, of night and dreams, we fabricators of desire and fear drifting beneath your thoughts and what's within them, shifting soft beneath your skin. We call you Jack.

It's 1999 and Jack Flash smiles at the doctor across the table. These people don't know the meaning of the word 'self-possessed'.

Analysis: subject resistant.
Operation (imperative): scan for reality breach; authenticate metaphysical incursion.

Hair the colour of flame, not blond but yellow, orange, red. He looks at his reflection in the mirror, ever the narcissist, looks into his own eyes, where his own reflection is in turn reflected, a dark image of himself, a self within the self, a psyche within the psyche. There's something inside his head.

Hi Joey, he thinks. Long time, no see.

Alert: scan detected!
Emergency manoeuvres.
Operation: Codename Squid-Ink.

The Ink Blot

I let my psychic guard slip for a second, catch the shadow in my conscious ken and let him glimpse himself in the enfolding mirrors of my mind. It's only for an instant, but, fuck, an instant might as well be eternity when you're dealing with the mindworms, with the bloody bitmites. I yank my mind back, twisting like a fucking gymnast, hoping that he didn't catch too much and—

The ink blot, raven black dissolving into midnight blue, is smeared symmetrically over the white card in billowing clouds of curling, whorling mist, and the way it's lying before me on the table, I can't help but be intrigued with its shapelessness, the way it demands to be given form, and before I know it I'm distracted, forgetting, and – what was I thinking – it's just so peachy keen, so gnarly, with all its liquid symbolism – like, I'm trying to decipher it, and at the same time it's there to decipher me, reflecting back the involutions, all the currents and eddies of my own mind. And looking at the Rorschach test, looking into it, I see—

*

– Nothing.

 – It doesn't remind you of anything?

 – No. Just an ink blot.

Starn studies him across the table. Again he feels that strange discomfort with the one-way mirror at his back, the constant bloody surveillance.

 – Nothing at all?

 – Nuh-uh.

 – When you look at the ink blot you can't see any shapes in it at all? I find that hard to believe, Jack. You don't strike me as an unimaginative person.

 – Have you ever taken acid?

 – No. I don't quite see the—

– OK. I have imagination. I could look into the ink blot and see a butterfly—

 – You can see a butterfly in it, then?

 – or I could see a bat. If it's a butterfly, how can it be a bat? If it's a bat, how can it be a butterfly? But if it's just an ink blot, maybe, with a bit of imagination, it could be anything.

Starn closes the folder over the black-and-white picture. A pointless exercise.

 – What are you trying to tell me, Jack?

 – Shadows and reflections. You look into them, you see just what you want to, what you desire, what you fear. That's the idea of that ink blot, right? I don't need your fucking ink blot, doctor. All I have to do is take a look in the mirror. Tell me – Reinhardt, is it now? – what do you see when you look in the mirror?

Starn shakes his head, turns to the mirror at his back, hand out to show.

 – Jack, all I see is –

But there's a young English army officer sitting in the chair where Jack should be and, in the mirror, Starn himself is wearing an SS uniform.

Analysis: evasive manoeuvres successful.

Operation: reinitiate scan for reality breach; authenticate metaphysical incursion.

He lays out the Tarot cards on the table one by one, face down, four in a row then another four underneath them. He's only using the Major Arcana – Cagliostro Deck; those are the only ones he really connects with, gets any ideas from. Maybe the face cards of the Minor Arcana just a little bit – probably, he thinks, because they have actual images, because they're visual ciphers, symbolic artefacts rather than just spurious significances attached to random cards. The four of diamonds means travel? The eight of clubs means bad investment? What a crock of shit.

He starts to turn the cards over, one by one, slowly.

Death – that's OK, it's not about actual death but metaphoric death, spiritual transformation. The Hanged Man – sacrifice. Eternity. There's something wrong. The Road. There's something wrong. There is no Eternity card in the Tarot. There is no Road.

On the one, there's an image of green fields, two crows sitting on a fence, a blond boy running through the wheat. On the other, a straight road cuts its way across a desert and a man with a book under his hand stands on the road beside a cart, shading his eyes from the harsh sun, a dog following at his heels. Two Tarot cards that don't exist.

He turns the other four cards over, quickly, one after the other, after the other, after the other. The four Jacks. He's only using the Major Arcana.

There's something wrong.

– There's something wrong, he says.

– You're fucking bonkers, mate, says Joey. That's what's wrong.

– You don't feel it? You don't feel anything? You don't find anything strange?

– I feel a disruption in the Force, says Joey in faux throaty boom. He flicks an unlit joint across the room to Jack. On you go, space cadet . . . fucking crazy man.

*

Analysis: memory repression.

Operation: reroute digression; authenticate metaphysical incursion.

Jack sparks it up and takes a deep toke.

— What if, he says, what if the crazy people are right? What if there really are these . . . things, angels, aliens, demons, just *things*, but we don't see them except in our dreams . . . or delusions? But in there, in there, they're real?

— They can't be real if they're only in your head, mate.

— But if they're in other people's heads as well? If all the crazy people see the same thing, hear the same thing . . .

— If all the crazy people in the world see the same thing, they're still fucking crazy.

— And what if all the crazy people in the world *don't* see the same thing, even when it's standing right in front of them?

Jack turns his head to look from Joey to the creature watching him from the corner of the room, standing behind Guy where he lounges on the bed, flicking through a stolen wallet for ID he can alter, so they can buy some beer, travel outside of the Scheme, and—

There's something wrong. Jack can't quite figure it out. It's not the creature that only he can see. The delusions, the hallucinations, they're like an acid trip. You still see reality, you just see the other stuff on top of it, under it, coming up through the cracks. It's like two celluloid diagrams on a projector each done in different coloured ink. They might obscure each other, they might complicate each other, make a more intricate pattern, but you can still tell them apart. Strangely, he's actually getting sort of used to it. No, there's something else.

Since when did they need ID to travel outside the Scheme?

— You know, says Guy, oblivious to Joey and Jack's entire conversation. I've heard of this great new underground club in town. We really ought to check it out.

– Guy Fox, I say, and the bouncer nods and steps back to let me in. It's a name that opens a few doors here in the Rookery.

The club is swinging with a casino kind of groove, all leather seating in plush booths, psychedelia projected, colours swirling on the ceiling. Very Bacharach. Filled with a crowd of decadents and deviants, Club Soda has to be my favourite scene – easy listening on the turntables, hard drugs in the toilets. Cocktails and cocaine at tiffin. Lounging, scrounging and high-living. On-stage, the Fisher-Price Experience are opening their set. Playing the idle playboy, I lean lazily against the bar, my cricket whites illuminated by the ultra-violet lighting overhead, my gin-and-tonic glowing an iridescent orgone blue. With my casual attitude and pencilled-on moustache, I'm in disguise: public school anarchist; aristo and rake. Guy won't be chuffed that I've nicked his identity for the evening, but I'll try not to do anything too bad with it.

The barman serves another customer as I gaze into the mirror on the other side of the counter, rather admiring my own reflection. I watch as he pours out absinthe over a spoon of sugar, lights it, stirs it in, and pours the water over it. It seems an awful waste of alcohol to me. His customer takes the glass, hands over the money, sips. She turns and smiles at me.

– I don't believe we've met, she says.

– I don't believe we have, I raise one eyebrow, indicating that the leather fetish mask which hides her face might well preclude my recognizing her, even if we *had* made some previous, perhaps transitory, acquaintance. Of course, I know exactly who she is.

– Miss Kitty Porn, she says, stretching out a hand for me to shake.

– I've heard of you, I take her hand and kiss the inside of her wrist.

– And I, my dear, have heard of you.

– All bad, I hope.

– Wicked, she says deliciously. I have a job for you.

*

387

I can't help but grin. It's always refreshing to work for such a noble cause as the Sensual Revolution. I've never been one for the whole SM thing; my automatic response to domination usually involves a nail-gun and some duct tape, and has nothing to do with home improvement. No, I'd be a bad puppy dog. Still, under all the inflatable rubber suits and nipple clamps (somewhere), I've always felt that they're my kind of people.

– Sex or death, I say. I have to warn you—

– Hush, dear. Death, of course. I know *your* preferences.

So we sip our drinks and discuss the terms of our agreement. Honestly. Sometimes the working life of a freelance spiritual contracts executive is such a drag.

The Deustream

Information upload: metaphysical incursion authenticated.

Operation: scan for contact situation; establish degree of revelation.

The voices pour into his head like a river, emotionless shrieks, voices of electronic gods and gibbering, giggling devils, angels, artifices. And in all of the babble, there's one word that keeps coming up . . . kill. Kill yourself. Kill him. Kill her. Kill them all. For a while it was touch and go but he has them under control now, as he stands on the roof, smoking a cigarette and feeling the wind upon his face. Fucking lying fucking *unkin*—

Alert! Information upload: exposure; disclosure; lexical verification; operation exposed; subject dangerous.

– they'll try anything to get him dead, locked up, secured. How many people have ended up in padded cells or prisons because they got a glimpse of these fucking unkin and then had to be made safe? Shout in anyone's head non-stop for five years and they're bound to end up trying to start a cult or murder their parents – something traditional, conventional, something the prisons or the hospitals can handle.

He taps at the walkman's volume control, raising it to its max.

Well it's all right now.

Fuck the unkin. He can deal with them.

*

Operation: trace leak to source; locate contact situation.

— Show me, he says, to the creature kneeling at his feet, and the ghost soul dream creature angel god *thing* — which he's sure was once a human being no matter how much it denies it — points out to the West without once lifting its bowed head. Way off in the distance, now that it's been pointed out to him, he can see it, that palpable nothing that just hangs in the air, not being there, not being there at all, an emptiness, an absence . . . an opening.

— What's on the other side? he asks.

— Death dream delusion deustream desire destruction doom despair dis.

He presses the point of his retro-fitted Bowie knife — blade burnt in fire, cooled in holy water, ripened in graveyard dust, sigils scratched into it, positively *loaded* with badass motherfucker mojo — to the creature's throat. Funny, for something claiming to be beyond the flesh it seems remarkably worried about being cut up into little pieces. He's not quite sure if, when he punched the creature in the face, grabbed it by the back of its head and slammed its nose into his knee, whether it was him stepping over into its world, or reaching out to drag it into his. Either way, these unkin aren't nearly as untouchable as they'd like to think.

— Be a little more specific, munchkin, he says.

— Eternity, it says. Empire.

— Oh, that sounds peachy. Let me guess. Long, dusty road through oblivion, you people wandering up and down it, setting up your little dreamtime realms here and there along the way, maybe the odd glorious battle for the kingdom?

— How do you—

— Been there, done that, bought the book, same old story. Just wanted to get it from the horse's mouth.

And Jack Flash slashes the knife across the creature's throat and kicks it over the edge of the roof.

– What do you see when you look in the mirror?

Starn almost turns, then smiles and shakes his head.

– Shadows. Reflections. You're talking about what we call the subconscious, Jack. Do you feel–

– So you're a Freudian.

– Pardon?

– 'Subconscious' rather than 'unconscious'. Interesting choice of words. I'm more of a Jungian myself. Don't like to think of that part of my mind as lower, lesser. 'Unconscious' is more ... egalitarian.

– Well, Jack, in my field, we don't tend to concentrate on those aspects of psychology – different theories, names, definitions. Which exact words you use isn't really that important. We have a more ... pragmatic attitude.

– Words are very important, Reinhardt. Words command us. Names define us. Definitions bind us. Words are where we keep our sacred secrets. Reinhardt.

Analysis / Information upload: subject armed and dangerous; advise search all named felons / fugitives.
Operation (imperative): establish subject core identity, name, number, DOB.

He sits, back to the rough brick of the wall so that he's sheltered from the wind, flicking the Zippo lighter open and closed, open and closed – *clunk, chik, clunk, chik, clunk, chik.* The pile of writing, of notes and diagrams, theory and extrapolations, schizoid ramblings and sophomoric philosophy, sits in the shoebox in front of him, top few pages flipping in the breeze so that he has to weigh them down with something. He digs into the inside pocket of his leather jacket where he carries the bowie knife – black hilted, it has the words *Nec Spe, Nec Metu* scratched into its blade – *No Hope, No Fear.* He stabs the knife down, twisting and pushing to get through the paper which gives more resistance than he would have thought. He wonders if flesh would be so tough, and he kind of thinks it wouldn't.

He's put his heart and soul into this little pile of words and images, a five-year study of his own demented imagination, analysis after analysis, exegeses of exegeses. He thinks he's got himself pretty well pinned down in it, knows exactly what makes him tick.

Clunk, chik, clunk, chik, clunk.

Chunk.

Burn, baby, burn.

Alert: subject intransigent;

Operation (imperative): establish subject core identity, name, number, DOB.

— Who are you?

He hisses it at his reflection in the mirror, at the thing he can feel inside his head, the thing he calls Jack Flash, the things that he can see standing behind him. Some people have demons. Christ, he feels like he's got fucking heaven and hell itself inside his head. Hey, guys . . . party in my head and everyone's invited. Bring your own battle-axe.

— Who are you?

He wants to punch the mirror, shatter it and cut his own throat open with the shards. Fuck the wrists. This isn't fucking suicide. This is sacrifice, something inside him crying out to die, something else roaring to taste that blood. He can't stand up to all the forces tearing him apart. He's not the cool one. He's not the bad-ass one. He's not Guy. He's not Joey. He's not Jack Flash. He doesn't know who he is any more. It's like whatever he was before is dead now. He's dead. Is that crazy?

— Who are you?

But there's nothing in there.

— See, says Joey, there's fucking nothing there. It's just a big fucking hole in the ground. It's just a fucking drain.

He's already turning and walking away from the concrete cylinder, shaking his head.

— You think? says Jack. He looks down into the darkness that starts at the very brim of the hole — as if it's almost ready to overflow — darkness that goes down, and goes down, and just keeps going down, maybe forever.

— I think it's death, he says.

Joey stops.

— Or dreams, says Jack. Or fucking quantum chaos. I think it's the fucking rabbit-hole that takes you into Wonderland. I think it's the fucking Gates of Hell, the fucking Doors of Perception. It's the way out.

Joey starts to walk back towards Jack, holding his hands up, palm forward, as if he's afraid that Jack is going to do something crazy.

– Reality doesn't have any exits, Jack.

– I think it has fucking tons of them. They just have keepers. Can't have the dogs getting loose and tearing up the garden.

The Sight of Greenhouses Exploding

They corner me in the abandoned train station underneath the Botanical Gardens, cutting me off before I reach the subway tunnel's entrance to the Rookery. As I sprint over the gravel, down into the dark, their sudden beams of light cut through the shadow in front of me. More beams of light slice up the dark behind me. I'm trapped.

I know, I know, I tell myself, I shouldn't have blown up the Tropical Palace – they would never have found me otherwise – but then I never could resist the sight of greenhouses exploding, the bigger, the better, all those sprinkling, tinkling, shattering shards of glass just flying through the air, falling like stars. So pretty.

My moment of regret cut short by the pounding of machinegun-fire beside my feet, I leap into the dark recess of what was once the station's stairwell up to the surface, now closed off. There's no hope of escape in that direction, precious little hope in any other. I fire out into the darkness, picking them off as they get nearer, razing them like ants under a magnifying glass with my chi-gun. But there's plenty of them and they keep on coming. When one of their bullets knocks the pistol from my hand, I barely have time to draw the katana before they're on me.

I go into Kendo mode, the sword a mere extension of my arm, the arm a mere extension of my will. I hardly even know what moves I'm making as the limbs and bodies pile up around me. Eventually I miss one crucial move; I feel a sharp jab in the side of my head, and everything goes white.

Fuck, is my last thought, *I think I'm dead again.*

Shattering

Alert: subject unstable; death fixation; identity dysfunction
Operation: scan for death imagery; enhance instability, dysfunction.
Imago:

He turns to Joey with a manic grin, crowbar in hand, a black hole in his heart and a fire in his head. He knows who he is now.

Operation: mental incision; expose memory; cut this fucker wide open.
Narrative detected:

And it's a summer's day, and he's seeing Reynard step out into the sunlight streaming through his hair and blinding him to the approach of death, and being struck, sliced into the air, across the bonnet of a silver car, head cracking on the concrete, cut down in a random accident, empty of meaning and bereft of all significance but the statistical.

Imago:

Death swings his scythe over the cornfield, every stalk, or every grain, a human life.

Imago:

Standing at a graveside, dressed in black, a hollow shadow of a man, an emptiness where what was once a person has collapsed.

Imago:

He stands over the sink, in agony, washing burning bleach from his scalp as he looks into the mirror where he has become the image of a lost boy.

Imago:

He sits in a silent room, staring at the wall and nurturing his hatred for the sheer banality of this mundane world, screaming in his head.

Imago:

Reynard stands on the road that goes nowhere, a book in his hand.

Imago:

Jack stands on the road that goes into eternity, crowbar in hand, angels all round him, screaming, shouting at him to step away from the truth.

Operation: harness paranoia; focus; establish name and context.

It's one year after Guy's death, and as Jack Carter steps out of the Victorian station of sandstone and girders and glass, into the streets of a city carved out of volcanic streetlight night, he knows that he's mad and alone in his own hell, his hair long and lank, and something wild let loose within his head and howling in his words, a whirlwind wolven wrath.

But he feels fucking reborn, an angel or a demon, something beyond either, something older, something newer. He can feel it in his bones. He might be mad, touched in the head – touched in the head by Death – but he can feel it. He can feel the call of the creatures singing to gather their changeling brethren, to fight for them on the battlegrounds of eternity or existence, with all humanity as their cannon fodder. And he knows he stands on the threshold of the two worlds, one foot on the earth another in the liquid light of dreams. And he'll never be one of their fucking dogs of war.

Alert / Information upload: rogue unkin; unaligned agent; extreme threat.

In the unspoken parts of conversations, in the unwritten truths in a newspaper article or a book, in the white noise of day-to-day life, he can feel the order, the pattern, the scheme. He can see the world of the unkin spreading out into existence, so gradually that you could blink and miss the way a housing scheme becomes a prison, an ID card becomes a travel permit. Tabloids calling for all paedophiles to be castrated. Internment for terrorists. Fascists on local councils, in parliament, on the cabinet. They brought back the death penalty last week and no one noticed except him.

He hasn't figured out exactly what's happening yet but he knows this world is just one little corner of something that the unkin call the Vellum, folds of reality shaped by their words; and maybe they began with good intentions and they just got lost along the way, but he's seen what they've got in store. Call it schizophrenia. Call it prophecy. Call it foresight.

But he's going to find the fuckers that are turning his world into their little Empire, if he has to tear the whole of fucking reality apart to do it.

Dreamtime's Up

Operation: enhance and focus; establish contacts.
Narrative detected:

Jack picks the book off of the library shelf – *The Book of All Hours*, it's called, by Guy Reynard Carter. He likes the names, the author's and the book's – because Carter is his name and Reynard sounds like the fox in the fairy stories that's always up to no good and *The Book of All Hours* sounds important and mysterious. He likes stories which are important and mysterious. But the book has really small print and he thinks that it's a grown-up book, so after a quick look inside he puts it back on the shelf. He wipes his hands on his trousers to get rid of the dust from the old book, and heads back towards the children's section.

– You're not special, Jack, says Starn. You're not chosen. You're not a hero. It's called paranoid schizophrenia. You think you're on a mission from God, but you kill people.

Analysis: irrelevant; subject irrational / resistant.
Operation: scan for all contacts, rebel operatives, operational base.

And he watches the world changing around him, stripped back, through the fantasy beneath reality, to the reality beneath the fantasy: not existence, not eternity, but something built out of the ruins of both. There are worlds built upon worlds, a whole fucking dream-time. He doesn't know who is in charge but he knows they're there. In every head of every person in this city, in the world itself, in every shadow and reflection. Something old as time and bad as hell is shaping the world, shaping the dreams that shape the thoughts that shape the acts that shape the world. Building an Empire.

– There is no hidden Empire, Jack. You know that. You have to face reality. This 'Jack Flash' is just a puerile fantasy that you're hiding behind. What is it you can't deal with, Jack? What is it that you're running from?

> Operation (imperative): scan for all contacts, rebel operatives, operational base.
> Dream on, motherfucker.
> Alert—

Shut up. Yeah, you Pechorin, let me tell you how the story ends . . .

And inside of him the sleeper meme, the dormant dream god, grinning thing of chaos, is shaking off its drowsiness, and finding itself inside an empty body. And no, he thinks, it isn't his imagination. This thing of darkness isn't his. It belongs to everyone.

– Who are you, Jack? says Dr Reinhardt Starn.

He looks sad, thinks Jack.

– I'm exactly what you think I am. But who are you?

And Jack Flash, older than the gods and newborn spirit of fire, looks at the fragments of personal history, memory and fantasy, truth and invention, still littering his host body's head, and gazes at itself in the mirror of its . . . his . . . mind. A dreamer, a lost boy, a golden boy. And Pechorin sees the calm look on the face of this rogue unkin, this fucking avatar of chaos, and feels something buried in the back of his head, shifting.

– You want to know what makes me tick, Reynard?

– Jack . . .

– I'm a time-bomb. Tick. Tick. Tick. Dreamtime's up. Narcissus has woken.

Through the Looking-Glass Darkly

– Narcissus has woken.

I utter the trigger-phrase and the pre-programmed meme-bomb implanted in Pechorin's head undercover of his dumbass fucking Rorschach manoeuvre blossoms, flooding imagery from the dead soul deeps into his mind, a host of gods and demons, angels, aliens.

Like a river thundering through the ruins of a dam. You know, baby, if there's a stream of consciousness, somewhere there's gotta be a river bursting its memory banks. Information is power, honey, language is liquid, and I got a fucking firehose in my head. Am I mixing my metaphors? I'll put it this way:

Narcissus has woken.

Narcissus has woken.
Observation: status – danger desire despair desolation dream dream dream
Report bioform status: bioform not found.
Analysis: Narcissus has woken.
Operation: reboot psyche. Psyche not found; locate psyche; psyche not found; evacuate enemy agent consciousness; reboot ego; ego not found; evacuate.
Observation: Narcissus has woken.
Observation: I am the me that I am that I—
Analysis: Dream is Reality. Reality is Dream. Narcissus has woken.
Operation: emergency manoeuvres; scan for scan for scan for scan for—
Analysis: I am legion; the kingdom is within us.
Analysis: Narcissus has woken.

– What – is all the doctor has a chance to say before my chi-enhanced Dragon Punch smashes him backwards through the one-way mirror. Through the looking-glass darkly, you might say. Shards of mirror rain into the darkened room behind, where Pechorin stands, one arm against the wall supporting him, eyes rolling up inside his skull. Somewhere in his head, the remnants of identity are drowning in the raging ocean of his own unconscious, dissolving to distorted reflections. I leap through the glass-edged frame to grab Pechorin, peel his eyelids fully open and stare into his soul. It's helter skelter in there, a whole host of mindworms being sucked down into oblivion. Poor old Joey. He always knew he'd be a soldier of the Empire. I only hope he'll pull through.

He has my Mark I Curzon-Youngblood in his hands – was probably using it to form the psychic link – so I take it off him, flick the safety off. The chi energy flows into it and I can feel the power in my hand, that mystic orgone life-force of the universe. Never mind the bollocks; here's the real sex pistol. And you can analyse that however you want.

I hunker down beside the doctor, who groans as I slap his cheek gently.

– Time to wake up, Guy, I say. We're leaving. All of us.

He groans.

– Jack? Did you hit me?

And to think he's meant to be the brains of this operation. Guy Reynard. Guy Fox, as in crazy-like-a. King of thieves and master of disguise. Good enough to fool even himself, they say.

I sight down the chi-gun's barrel at the doorway of the interview room, at the commotion already starting in the corridor. Guy is looking at Joey, at me, at Joey.

– What did you do to him?

But before I can answer I'm too busy firing as they come in through the door.

I may well be crazy, you know. They may outgun me. I may be however many miles underground, in the depths of the Empire's headquarters, in a hellworld so royally fucked by the meme merchants that even their own dreams end up spewing out one or two of their own into the world at large just to fucking sort things out. But I got my weapon and my wits and if they want a war for people's hearts and souls, I got the will. But most of all I've got my weapon.

– What did you do to him, Jack? says Guy.

I pick off a couple of militia as they run into the room, then duck down.

– Meme-bomb, I say. Not much choice after you went sodding native.

Guy grabs the limp body, lugs it partway over his shoulder.

– Must've been something in the tea, he says. Well, so much for the gently gently approach.

I kick open the door of the observation room and walk out firing.

Which means it's time for the extraction team, on the roof as arranged. Just make it quick, motherfuckers. We can't hold out forever.

Jack Flash over and out.

Errata

All the King's Horses

– How is he? I say.

Joey shakes his head, grim and thin-lipped. I had to virtually drag him down here to the hospital, pushing his guilt button again and again with dagger remarks about how long he'd known Jack, how he owed it to him, they were best friends and Jack needed him, needed us both now. *For fuck's sake, Joey, you're his best mate.*

– He's living in a fucking fantasy world, says Joey. All he talks about is this dead boy, this fucking figment of his imagination. Thomas this and Thomas that. He's a fucking basket case, Guy. I can't deal with this.

I want to hit him. I just can't accept how he can walk away from this, no matter how bad it is. Does he really just see Jack's schizophrenia as a bloody inconvenience? I can't believe that he could be so callous.

But I've been coming to visit Jack every other day and Joey Pechorin, his closest friend, hasn't found it in his heart to come here on his own, not once in the three months since Jack had his latest and worst episode, the one that ended with him sectioned for his own safety.

I stare at Joey with a silent knowledge that our friendship is only a word or two away from ending, and push past him through the door into Jack's room.

– It doesn't make sense, says Jack. None of it makes any sense.

He's right. Of all the notes and pages of scribblings scattered round the room, blu-tacked or sellotaped to walls, none of it bears any obvious relationship to anything else. Even within themselves the fragments don't really, on close examination, reveal meanings shared by anything beyond the inside of Jack's head. There are pages where the initials J.C. have been written over and over again with explication after explication – Jack Carter, Jesus Christ, Jerry

Cornelius, Joe Cool, John Constantine, and on and on, as if to map out some grand kabala of identity. Other pages gather quotes from a whole host of sources, fiction or non-fiction, books on magic, politics, philosophy, conspiracy theory, just laying them together on the page as if the act of copying them out, the simple juxtaposition of them, says all that needs to be said about their interrelations. I can't make head nor tail of it.

Schizophrenia. Broken head. That about sums Jack up. He's a one-man Tower of Babel, Humpty Dumpty at the bottom of the wall, taking a hammer to his own pieces to see if by breaking them up even further he can crack them into smaller fragments that'll fit together better.

– How are you doing, Jack? I say.

He smiles and shrugs, sat up on the bed, his back against the wall, knees up to his chin.

– Still crazy, he says. Officially. How's yourself?

I make a so-so gesture with one hand, sit down on the edge of the bed.

– You seem a bit more . . . together today.

– Wonders of modern medicine, he says. The miracle of lithium. Hallelujah. I keep asking if they can get me some acid, but they don't seem to think that's a good idea.

A glint of mischief in his eye. Every so often you get these flashes of the old Jack, a Jack of random notions and spurious arguments supported on the flimsiest of evidence, held with the deepest conviction and abandoned with a shrug on the calling of his bluff. A Jack who'd happily throw a bomb into a conversation just to see what happened, who'd argue for mandatory vision-quests for all fourteen-year-olds, or the restoration of ritual regicide. *Tradition,* he'd say, adopting an old fogey voice. *Young people these days, no respect for tradition.* We were so used to Jack's trickster reimagination of the world we missed the point where he began to take it seriously.

– No, I don't think acid's what you need right now, I say.

He waves a hand around the room.

– I bet it would make sense on acid. We should do that, Guy. You could smuggle in a couple of tabs, or some good fucking Mexican psilocybin or – was it Hawaiians we had that time? We'll get shitfaced and I'll tell you the secret of the universe and you'll tell me that I'm talking shit.

We laugh.

– I had an idea, he says.

Uh-oh, I think.

– Last night, he says, I was trying to figure it all out, and, OK, it doesn't make any sense, but you know, Guy, it *almost* makes sense. It almost makes sense.

– To you, Jack, maybe, but not to the rest of us.

I stand up and start to wander round the room, uncomfortable and looking for a way to draw the conversation away from more of his delusional 'explanations'. On the walls: a sheet of paper has the Hebrew alphabet in a table with Roman equivalents, names and numeric values; a pyramid divided into sections numbered in a mathematical sequence – 1, 3, 6, 10, 15, 21 and so on down to the bottom-right corner and the number 666; a fake frontispiece in the medieval style of an illuminated manuscript, the paper crumpled and tea-stained to look old, the lettering done in felt-tip pen – The Book of All Hours.

– When I was in the Boy Scouts . . .

– You were in the Scouts? I say. I can't imagine you in the Scouts.

– Oh, yeah, he says. I was a right little trooper when I was younger. I'm a sucker for a pretty uniform.

He winks.

– Anyway, they taught us this song, and last night, for no reason, it just pops into my head. Dee deeddly deedly deedly deedee . . .

I vaguely recognise the tune, some Scottish country dance music, I think, or maybe Irish. He starts to tick-tock a finger in time to it.

– MacPherson is dead and his brother don't know it. His brother is dead and MacPherson don't know it. They're both of them dead and they're in the same bed. And none of them knows that the other is dead.

– I think we'd know if we were dead, Jack, I say.

– Do you know when you're dreaming? he says. Who's the fucking mental case here? Personal experience, man. Just because you're sure of something doesn't make it real.

– Jack, that is totally twisted. That's just . . .

– I know, he says. But it made sense last night. Almost.

I sit back down on the edge of the bed.

– You want to watch some TV? he says.

Two for Tea, a Tree for Two

Jack seems to have become somewhat enamoured of Puck. He does
not trust me in the slightest, sad to say, but I can't really blame him
given the fact that I sit here on the cart surrounded by a score or so
skulls excavated from the pit like some ogre with his terrible treasure,
and given that these may well be his ancestors, compatriots, beloved
cousins or god knows what. I try to fathom the history of this place
but it is quite inscrutable. Oblivion's Mount is marked in the Book,
in wide, sweeping contours more on the continent-crossing level of
isobars on a weather chart than the humble cartography of a little
peak like Everest or Olympus Mons (I'm getting rather blasé about
the scale of things here in the Vellum, I fear; it's all rather gauche
and grandiose for my liking, like the arms-race conversations of
children when they degenerate to the level of *infinity-times-infinity*
and *infinity-squared* and *infinity-to-the-power-of-infinity, so there!*);
the problem is there are no indications of inhabitation, no dotted
lines of old roads, no glyphic marks of places of historical interest. All
I have to go on is the skulls and Jack's horror of them; and the former
remain as obstinately silent – other than for the low whistling moan
of the wind as it blows down into the pit – as the latter is unyielding
in his vociferous protests. I only hope that Puck can shut him up for
long enough that I might actually get more than an hour's sleep.

He has managed to calm the poor thing down a little in the last week,
soothing Jack's savage music with his offerings of candies and pretty
things from our rations and stores, though I was not entirely happy
that the first such offering was a silver fob dowser filched from my
pocket and dangled by its chain between thumb and forefinger,
snatched by Jack even as I did a double-take, patting my pocket and
gawping dumbly as I tried to put some words together in protest.
Pickpocket Puck simply shrugged and said he'd noticed Jack eyeing
it, pointed out that, hunkered over behind a shrub, Jack was now

402

quietly snapping the casing of it open and closed – *chunk, chik* – rather than raising his usual racket. He was so quiet for the next few hours, in fact, that I actually managed to notice just how much more pervasive all the creaks and cracks and rustlings and rumblings are, the higher-up we get in our around-and-over journey on Oblivion's Mount.

Since then, anyway, the various trinkets and treats that Puck has used to charm him with have, it is true, offered some brief respites from Jack's otherwise ceaseless bewailing of whatever tragedy he scents – or senses somehow – buried under our feet. And with each offering Jack has grown more trusting of the boy until Puck has him now, quite literally, eating out of his hand. I think it was the drugs that really won Jack over.

I glance over at them, sitting side by side on the low branch of a tree, legs dangling and kicking, passing the joint between them. Jack reaches over occasionally to pick through Puck's green thicket of hair, grooming for fleas or ticks, a little disappointed, it seems, at not finding any; every so often, he taps a curious fingertip on one or other of Puck's pointy horns and gurgles a wordless question. Puck blows smoke rings and Jack flaps his hand through them. It's sort of sweet, in a decadent way; beneath them on the ground, the drained billy-can that I watched them sipping from earlier, passing between them as they now pass the joint, lies discarded and forgotten as they poke each other and point at this or that, at leaves or grass, the cart, myself, the other tribesfolk sitting in a huddle off in the far distance, lost now that their shaman has abandoned them; and Jack and Puck peer at the world around them, tilting their heads and giggling, in their Chimp's Mushroom Tea Party.

I wonder that Jack, so terrified of the landscape that we're travelling through, is not insane with spectral horrors crawling from the recesses of his unconscious out into his hallucinating mind, but then again I have seen him in various states of intoxication and I am yet to see him have a bad trip. Truth to tell, the two of them are the very picture of bliss.

I pick out three of the skulls and lay them before me in a row, glad that for the moment I have peace to try and think. I have known for a while that whatever kind of afterworld the Vellum is, death walks in it as much as in the reality I left behind me. Actually, it always struck me as rather senseless that the imagined afterlives of religion after religion should be fleshed out with forms so imitative of the physical as to have eyes to see, mouths to speak, hands to play harps or wings to fly among the clouds, but shy away from the anatomical actualities of bodies – lacking a physique but with what might be called a *metaphysique* – hemming and hawing uncomfortably about matters of sex and death. Et In Arcadia Ego, as Poussin's Shepherd's found written on the tomb in their idyllic hills, and here in the foothills of Oblivion's Mount, we seem to have found a similarly symbolic tomb, this signifier of death in the middle of eternity that terrifies poor, simple Jack so much.

What is death in the afterworld of souls? I wonder. What is death in the Vellum?

I have the Book open before me and I stare at it, at the contours of Oblivion's Mount, listening to the keen of the wind catching the lip of the pit and curling down around the skulls like a macabre woodwind instrument. And suddenly I have an answer.

6

Echoes of Iapetus

Kur

Now well behind Russian lines and in continual peril, *writes Pechorin*. The next instant could find us snatched up, crushed like insects by the Soviet fist. I pray for it sometimes. I might tell them I was a prisoner of these fascists, my wife and family hostage, forced against my will to guide them through my native lands; but as a White Russian, I know I have no hope. They would see me only as a traitor, a collaborator. I know that part of me leads them willingly towards their goal, but there is another aspect of my soul cries out against it. Why do I lead them on? Perhaps because I feel I must return and face the past.

Carter strikes the attitude of a victim. But I can see the contempt with which he looks at all of us, and I know the power that he brought back with him, the power we all brought back, those of us who returned. Perhaps it is knowledge that I seek, an understanding of that power. Carter seeks only to forget the past, to bury it . . . and us with it? He still watches what he says to Strang, but I suspect he is considering his options carefully. As we approach the entrance to the cave, I wonder if he is already making moves I have not seen.

29 March 1921. The professor revealed today his secret, his lie, and the true object of our quest. The 'Great City of the North' is not Aratta. We are, as I have been nagging constantly these last few days, two hundred miles north of the only possible location of Aratta. What do you know of the geography of the Georgian Caucasus, he

asked me; the river that runs south-east from Tiblis down to the Caspian Sea, what is it called? The Kur, I said, and began to realise what he was thinking. What is the name of the great river of the north in Sumerian texts, the name of the great northern mountain, also, and the name of the city where the souls of the dead reside? It's the same word for all of them, isn't it, Carter, old chap? Kur.

What I felt in that moment of realisation I can hardly put into words. I wanted to laugh at the absurdity of his suggestion. I could have cursed him for lying to me or pitied him for lying to himself. He gabbled on about the river Kur, the name being there in black and white upon the very map with which we plotted our course, the river that we all must cross to enter the great netherworld, the house of dust and ashes, and I felt a sudden terror that I was travelling with a madman, that his mind had snapped. And yet something in me recognized a certain glory to the idea. What if he is right? What if we can find it? 'The City of the North'. Of course it is a myth. Of course it is a legend.

So was Troy.

The Bone Age

– They left no trace behind them because they were trackers themselves. They believed that if a single artefact was left to show where they had been, the Old Hunter, Death, could find them and feed on their souls. So every thing they used they used again, and again, and when there was no more use that could be made of something, when the broken spear-throwers were whittled down to needles, when their ragged clothes were more stitching than material, they burned what was left and scattered the ashes on the winds. The perfect hunter-gatherer society. They scavenged and salvaged everything, even used their own dead as material resources. They wore their brothers' skins as clothes, drank from their skulls, fed on their flesh.

1 April 1921. It was one of our lads, one of the Brits, that found it. The younger chap – Messenger, his name is – stumbled upon it

quite by chance while exploring the darker recesses of the cave with one of the South Ossetians. What they were up to down there I have no idea, but I suppose we all retain from our youths that fascination with the unknown, that desire to explore the dark, to conquer our childhood fear of it by shining a lantern into those forbidden places.

But, my God, the racket that the boy set up, the way it echoed in the depths, and seemed to magnify as it resounded. You would have thought that he was trying to wake the dead.

– The power they must have felt, my forefathers.

– You still don't understand, do you? This was fifteen thousand years ago. This was before your damned Aryan race even existed. This is civilisation in the Stone Age – the Bone Age, we should call it. This is mathematics and mythologies, maps and histories, writing, ten thousand years before Sumer.

– Tell me about the writing.

– They could leave no trace behind them, so they didn't carve it in the rock, or in clay tablets or on wood. They carried it with them on their skins. So they wouldn't leave a trace.

– But they did.

– They did. And we found it. The motherlode.

We followed the distant, disembodied cries, myself first, Hobbsbaum close behind, and Pechorin following at his heels, squeezing our way through the crevices and cracks, ducking and twisting in the worst stretches. I am glad I am not claustrophobic or I fear the pounding of my heart should have been too much for me. As it was, I found myself strangely caught between two memories, two states of mind. I found myself thinking of all the digs I'd been on with the old man, crawling through tight-walled tombs, barrows and long-buried palaces; so I had that old thrill of anticipation. But also – and this is strange – I found myself thinking of the trenches, of crawling into foxholes and the stench of death and gas. At one point – it is hard to write this, to admit it to oneself – I had to stop a second, and it was only Hobbsbaum's hand on my shoulder, his innocent enquiry if everything was all right, that brought me back to myself, and the damnfoolishness of my behaviour.

I think it was the smell of the place, an acrid chemical smell that assaults the nostrils the deeper one goes into the caves. It seems absurd, for it is nothing like that stench of putrefaction I can never quite eradicate from my dreams; nothing could be like that. I don't know why it should affect me so. But I wonder if it was just the fact I couldn't place it. Rotting metal, petrol fumes, boiled blood, sulphur or ammonium, I swear it smelled like all of them and none of them.

If that smell is natural, then Nature is no mother.

A Little Skin and Bone

2 April 1921. Hobbsbaum has lain the skin out on a slab of rock to study it. It is a macabre scene, this antechamber of rock all carved with arcana, lit by the flickering light of all the lanterns gathered round the slab where Hobbsbaum scrutinizes the flayed human hide like some doctor of another age giving an anatomy lesson to his students. His finger moves like a scalpel, tracing the patterns; I watch him as he runs it down the skin from throat to groin then pauses and follows another course of script across the empty chest – a travesty of a Catholic blessing.

He is convinced the black spirals and circles, lines and dots, the whole delicate tracery of geometric convolution, is some kind of writing. I cannot believe him. I cannot believe the monstrous creatures that created the abomination in the caves beneath our feet were capable of anything other than the most barbarous atrocity. I *will* not believe. I shudder even as I write these words.

The men are also in deep shock. It is quite understandable, I suppose; these men are simple souls, fighting lads, and while they are like me, I'm sure, no strangers to death, the sight of it on such a scale and in such an inhuman, alien manner can only be disturbing to them. I think of an old Arab guide outside a tomb in the Valley of the Kings, refusing to go one step further, making signs to ward off curses. But I think also of his son, laughing at his superstition and beckoning us inside. Painted grave, he said dismissively. Dead king. Much gold. He understood something his father didn't, that in the end it was just desiccated flesh inside, however splendidly adorned.

A grave is a grave, no matter whether the corpse is in a gold sarcophagus, a linen shroud or a khaki uniform, whether it's laid to rest with salt and natron, or formaldehyde, or simply flowers and mud. But that is no grave beneath us.

Hobbsbaum buries his feelings in his intellectual curiosity, though I can tell that he is not entirely unmoved. Pechorin alone seems unaffected by the sight of Kur. He is a pitiless reptile of a man. He stands behind the professor, looking over the tattooed skin as if it were a map to some lost treasure, a map that only he could read. He and Hobbsbaum speak quietly in lowered voices.

3 April 1921. The state of preservation is incredible. The conditions in the cave are strange, granted, but even those foul vapours could not suffice to cure the skin so well. These people must have had some preservation techniques far beyond even the pharaohs. I am beginning to wish that they had not, that the skin that lies before us had rotted and been forgotten, that these madmen had left not one single trace behind them ... that we had never come to this hellish place. It is affecting us.

22 September 1942, 13:05:
    – Do you feel it yet?
    – Feel what, Mr Carter?
    – The eyes of your men on you. Accusing you. Hating you for bringing them to this hellish place. I remember what it felt like. I—
    – I feel nothing. You are mistaken.
    – You don't feel ... unnerved?
    – By a little skin and bone. Nothing to ...
    – A dozen corpses from another expedition. Looks like it happened only yesterday.
    – Be quiet!
    – Of course. Words are dangerous.
    [A long silence]
    – Tell me what happened to your party.
    – We cracked the code.

4 April 1921. We ruled out alphabet and syllabic systems immediately and the writing is quite certainly neither hieroglyphic nor pictographic. These curves and dots are so abstract, so fluidly geometric, that, after such a time, fifty years of study would hardly render them less inscrutable. But Hobbsbaum refuses to leave until he's found the key to it. Admittedly, I am myself strangely transfixed by the illuminated skins. There is something ungraspably recognizable about them, something that niggles at the back of the mind as when you see the face of someone that you might have known in your schooldays or back in France, but no matter how you try you cannot place it. You know that you should know them but you cannot for the life of you think why.

I have been thinking . . .

One of the skins brought out by Pechorin's men from deep within the Kur, I am convinced, is a map of the constellations in the sky, as they would have been in those times. But rather than linking the stars together to make animals or artefacts, as classical astrologers did, these seem as abstract as the writings on all the other skins. A few of them are carved on the outer cave where we have set up camp, with Proto-Arattan annotations that may well be translations, attempts by later visitors to represent either the meaning or the name of these constellations. Again in these transcriptions we find abstraction, ambiguity, as if each 'constellation' symbolized some concept, some idea. The more I think about it, the more I see these maps as code-books, dictionaries for the language.

6 April 1921. Each symbol is a line of force. I'm sure of it. They represent not things, not objects but events, shifts, forms of power in motion – not a cave-lion, say, but the arc of its pounce, the scything swing of its claws. Not a bird, but the flourish of its wings as it takes off. I am convinced that the tattoo script is not composed of words, or syllables, or even letters, but of phonetic elements, the changes of the airflow, the shape of the tongue.

When I talked to Hobbsbaum he seemed stunned, but nodded,

smiled an idiot grin. Pechorin could have killed me with his look. But he nodded. I know I'm right. There's a power in these symbols, almost hypnotic. Even as the three of us talked, the idea came together. The symbols signify the places and the manners of articulation – plosive, fricative, approximant, and so on – and shifts between them, voicing qualities, pitch, rhythm.

Now it is only a matter of understanding the system. We may not know the actual meanings but if the system is as simple as it looks, then we can reconstruct the words of the language well nigh *exactly* as they would have been pronounced.

But the longer we spend here in this place, the more unnerving it becomes. What with the skins scattered all around us like some ghastly version of a Bedouin tent floored with fine-patterned rugs, it is as if we've brought the atmosphere out of the inner chamber, broken the boundary between the world of the ancients and our own. The cave is womb and tomb combined, the dark earth we were born from and to which we must return, in death, in dreams. It is the chambers of our mind, lit by the fire of our Promethean schemes.

Is this why we have become disorganised, I wonder, no longer cataloguing each skin one-by-one, but acting more like absent-minded scholars rifling through their own library. Hobbsbaum strides between the things, from one to another, cross-referencing this symbol with that, with the markings on the cave walls, excitedly mumbling to himself, *yes, yes, of course*. And I find Pechorin more suspicious by the day; I even overheard him muttering to one of his men, *This is the history of our people. It belongs in Russia.* The Ossetian only blinked and gave him a blank stare. He wants to leave. Now. I can see him polishing his bayonet and thinking about how to get away from here. With Hobbsbaum buried in his work, he notices nothing of this. I must be vigilant.

The Command of Fear and Fury

22 September 1942. I caught Carter and Pechorin scheming together in some obscure Caucasian sing-song dialect that both speak with

fluency. For a second something prevented me from simply ordering them to cease. Was it the beauty of the words alone that caused me to stop, to listen as they speak? When I questioned them, they insisted their conversation was of little consequence and for a moment I believed them, as if each word was crystal truth, perfect in itself, a line of force. I forgot all my doubts and suspicions.

Damn them. They are hypnotizing me as they have hypnotized the men, turned them against me. Eicher actually approached me today to 'express the fears of the men'. I cursed him for a coward and a traitor. He bowed his head, but he muttered under his breath as if I couldn't hear him. Carter turned to me, like there was no-one else around and said, 'They don't have the guts to whisper among themselves yet, but they will.' I could have killed them all when he said that.

23 September 1942, 02:00:

– You said before that words are dangerous. Why do you fear them? Why do you wake up screaming in the night?

– You know. You've seen the bodies that I dream about.

– They wanted to leave. They mutinied, tried to take the skins to sell to the highest bidder. They had to die. What is there in that?

– Pechorin's story, *his* story, not mine. I say they killed each other.

– Why would they do that? Why?

– [indistinguishable]

– What did you say?

[Carter laughs]

– What did you say?

– You know, I'm not entirely sure I can translate it, but I'll tell you this: I said it in a language old as stone and harder still, one that sounds inside you like a chord of music, reverberates, snakes itself through your head and heart, the blood and guts of you, and carries a meaning right into your soul.

– What did you say? I couldn't make out what you said. What was that word?

– You really want to know. I'll whisper it in your ear, Herr Strang.

– What did you find in the skins? What did you learn? *What was that word?*

– We found a complete phonetic script so precise, so perfect, that to read it was to hear the words inside your head exactly as they would have been spoken fifteen thousand years ago, to hear the concord and discord between articulations, every harmony and clash of stress and intonation. The challenges and exclamations, the pleading, the menace, the hatred, the horror. How about you, Pechorin, old chap? Don't you remember it?

– Enough.

– You speak this language. Both of you. You will teach it to me.

– I can't allow that, old man.

– Carter. Enough. There is no need for this. You should take your men and leave us now, Herr Strang. You would be well advised.

– How dare you—

– *Need?* No need, Pechorin? You know there is. You brought us here. You hear it in his voice too. You can't help it. For twenty years you've heard the need in the voices of everyone around you, *everything* they were feeling, even what they masked to themselves. For twenty years you've been notating it into that damned script, somewhere at the back of your head, and reading it. Feeling it write itself across your soul.

– There is no soul, Englishman. Only the will. You know this just as I do.

– The will to power. Yes. The command of fear and fury. That is the nature of this tongue, yes? This is how you've turned my men against me. The two of you. You're working together. You've always been together.

– You're a damn fool, Strang.

– You *will* teach me this language. You *must*.

– Listen to you, Strang. Listen to the tone of your own voice, the pressures, the tensions, the *strain*. You have no will! You bully, you plead, you whine. You couldn't speak the language even if you tried.

A Cold, Inevitable Logic

12 April 1921. Pechorin shot the two Brit soldiers today, ruthlessly and without sanction, for suggesting that the supplies were low and needed restocking. He said they'd questioned his authority. The strange thing is that when he said it, I agreed with him. I knew exactly what he meant, *exactly*. I felt the same cold bite of hatred and disdain, could have killed them both myself. Perhaps it's only that I knew they were deserters. I should not let my contempt for men like that affect my judgement. I begin to appreciate his position, in command of such a mob; peasants with guns, all of them. How long before they all turn bolshevik?

13 April 1921. Progress on the translations is amazing. Working, as a start, on the principle that the circles represent lip-rounding, we began applying other such ideas to commonly occurring signs. Curves appear to show the shape of the tongue, or the flow of air over the tongue. The peak of the curve would therefore define the place of articulation. Smooth and wavy lines might represent voiced or voiceless sounds, even creaky and whispering voices. Hobbsbaum thinks the relative positions of these lines may even represent the tone of the sound, the musical pitch. He says it is like sheet music for a Wagner opera.

A 'voiceless' sound, as the term is used in phonetics is not silent, rather it is produced with the glottis wide open rather than flapping so that the sound does not have the humming, buzzing quality of a 'voiced' sound – the /b/ sound, for example, is produced in exactly the same way as the /p/ sound, except that the /b/ is voiced, while the /p/ is voiceless; likewise with /d/ and /t/, /g/ and /k/. I have been learning some of this phonetics, as I travel in my grandfather's footsteps. Little parts of the translations begin to make sense to me now; I can hear them in my head. The writing itself, the language itself – it is inside my head now. I know what they must have been feeling, what they must have been thinking and I'm glad I'm travelling alone.

*

Pechorin:

Strang begins to see the world the way that Carter and myself do. From the few phrases Carter has muttered at him, already he begins to sense the sound of buried emotions in voices, the shapes and shifts of the psychology behind an utterance. Fears and desires. I believe Carter plans to kill him. I know he is capable of it, and it has a cold, inevitable logic. We will not leave here, although we could, because we do not want to. In a way the three of us are now one side of the equation and the soldiers another. We all know that they stay only out of fear, under threat of death; the only language these fascists know is the language of intimidation.

Ten seconds ago, Carter leaned over my shoulder to read what I had written and said, 'Maybe we should teach them another.'

The Stenographer

25 September 1942, 02:30 hours, Kur.
    – Fury. I could feel it as you said the word. I heard it. I knew it.
    – Can you hear the echo, here, in your gut?
    – [Interrogation disrupted by commotion outside]
    – Sturmman. Go outside. Send them away.
    – [With forceful certainty] Herr Strang, I cannot do that.
    – Tell them to go to hell. They forget who is in command.
[My hands shake as I type this. I do not know why.]

– I am under orders, Herr Strang. Everything on paper. You yourself—
    – I am in command here. [Strang walks to canvas partition, throws it back.] I am in command here! [He walks outside. More voices. A gunshot.]
    – [Pechorin, out of sight] Let go of him now. The next time, I kill you. You understand me?
    – You will all obey this man. He has my authority.
    – [Carter laughs. He is looking at me.] He has his own authority.
    – You will listen to him. You will obey him. Or I will have your rank, your uniform, your name, your number.

[I have to write this all down. This is my function. This is my only function. But I am a simple man and all I pray for is my safe return to Hamburg, to beautiful Hamburg. What is happening to us here?]

16 April 1921. What if you found a language that sent information like a gun sends bullets, direct to the heart? What if you learned how to decode it, but you couldn't read the content, didn't know the exact definitions of the words, only their import, their function as emotive triggers? What if you knew that someone else, though, knew exactly what it meant, every word, every phrase? What if they were writing it down in notes, that ancient language, transcribing page upon page of that archaic tongue?

What if you had gathered together a book out of the skins of the dead, and somewhere in that book were all the words that never should have been said, the secret meanings that no one was ever meant to hear? What if, when someone spoke to you, you knew exactly how they felt about you, the distrust, the fear, the envy? The things best left unsaid?

What if you could hear that in your own voice, every doubt, every vanity? What if you could hear the latent racism in your words, could feel the . . . discord of it, but still feel it, as a soft, pink scar? What if you could hear your own reflection, sense your own echo inside? This is the language of the fallen angels that we're learning how to read. This is the language broken in Babel, born in Hell.

[Sounds of an argument – angry, resentful, self-pitying, loathing.]
– We will break you.
– [There is a quiet warning in Carter's voice] Pechorin.
– I will break you.
– Pechorin. It doesn't have to happen again.
– Sturmman Macher. Silence the prisoner.
– Sir?
– Do it. Use a knife. Cut his tongue out.
– Damn you all. Macher, sit down and [He says something I cannot transliterate].
– I – Sir – I—

416

– Let's end this now, Pechorin. Let's end it all, right now. You want to hear a word of real power, Strang?

– [cursing, invoking] ʰyaᵂve [?] –

We are in Hell.

A Letter from Beyond the Grave

The letter from Miguel de Santiago of Cortes, Santiago & Serrano, 13 Straza Columbe, Menendez, Peru, arrived long after the package, long after I had made my decision, though it is dated July 24th, 1998.

Dear Sr Carter, *it says.* I write to you with grave news, for it is with great sadness I must inform you of the death of one whom I am understood to have been a close friend of your grandfather, the Professor Samuel Hobbsbaum. Your sadness might be lessened as I tell you he died peacefully in his sleep on Sunday 19th July this year. As executor of his estate it is my duty to impart to you the informations he, in his life, entrusted to me.

As he was without family, he expressed to me his wishes that your grandfather, Jonathon Carter, or any surviving relatives, should inherit the sum of his wealth and assets which I understand to be in the sum of one and a quarter million pounds approximately. Upon his death I am to find and contact said inheritor regarding this matter, which I now so do, enclosing a sealed communication which he urged to be passed on to the Carter estate. I am also despatching separately certain documents he wished to be passed on to you. Please contact me at the above address that we may arrange a suitable transfer of the monies in question.

I send you my sympathy in this time of mourning.

Yours sincerely,

Miguel de Santiago

Why the package of journals and notes arrived before the letter I don't know, but I already had the plane ticket by the time I got the sealed communiqué from a dead man claiming to be Hobbsbaum himself. I don't believe in coincidence. I don't believe in fate. I can't. Not after reading it.

Dear Carter, *it says.*

Atonement. Penitence. Redemption. What hope do I have of these things? I expect damnation, and I die unmourned. I have murdered, destroyed, and worse. In my arrogance and conceit, I dragged you back into a hell from which you thought you had escaped. I led many young men to their deaths and I myself live on through the money of slaughtered families, stolen from the Jews and stained in their blood. I have even stolen the name of one of our victims, your Professor Hobbsbaum, perhaps to remind me of what I am. I have thought of him, of you, and of Pechorin, every night for fifty years, and I have wept. An Englishman, a Russian and a German. The three who walked away with our lives, and you alone deserving.

So, in my death, I give to you the blood money, unspent because it is a measure not of my material wealth but of my spiritual poverty. Do good with it, for I could not. I would not wish to be remembered for a single act of kindness or charity. I do not deserve that. Let them remember me as I truly was, as you knew me in the war, in Kur, as a traitor to humanity. Remember me with hatred and loathing, and if you ever talk of me to others, curse my name.

Reinhardt Strang

Childe Roland

As I step down into the caverns of the City of the Dead, the halogen lamp burns bright as day, and still is only a star amongst the blackness of the vast and hollow night inside. The carved stone stairway curves down under me into the depths of Kur, into a cold and chemical air thick with a smell of salt, urine and blood and something sharper, more acrid; if death has one smell, sex another, this is a stench more rich than either, and every bit as old. A smell of animals. A smell of gods.

I put my hands out to steady myself against the archway I am standing in – huge ivory ribs, cathedral scale, ornate with carvings, complex as clockwork. The steps of stone sweep down beneath my feet into a city of biers of bone and leather, bleached wood, paper-thin skins both dark and light; fine etched lines trace everywhere across the engraved grave city, and the stinking vapours curl in vortices and whorls as intricate as the inscriptions on all the huts of hide and banners of stitched skin. With the light of the lamp gripped in my hand I can see perhaps a couple of hundred yards into the Kur, and I can see it stretch beyond that, back, back ... back.

Corpses lay thrown across the cavern floor like filthy clothes, broken and bent things, torn and twisted. I step down towards them, step again, walk one step at a time, down into Hell. The uniforms stripped from their naked bodies are scattered in the dry dust all around them; the Second World War Soviet greys I recognize, the rest unfamiliar, but I can guess that these are the White-Nationalist mercenaries hired by Hobbsbaum in 1921. The scattered remains of two expeditions, twenty years apart, a world away from my time. I try not to see them dying, being peeled, rent.

The dead flesh is immaculate, undecayed; it is a scene of carnage pristine as the day it happened, but for the drained, dried blood soaked into the dust all around. Some have been speared on pikes of ivory, some simply opened from the throat to the balls, ribcages torn apart, post-mortem cadavers, birthday present wrappings. Many have been scalped. One has been draped by the arms over a wooden crossbeam as silver as the moon, head dangling to one side, a sordid christ. I kneel down to another, on the ground before me.

His peeled-off face is lain across his chest, held in his clasped hands like a prayerbook – dried blood under his nails. In his savage, rictus grin, between his teeth, he clenches a mouthful of skin, a dozen scraps or so, holds them with that grin, like victory, like a shit-eating dog. I notice that the inside of his upper arm has a patch of torn-off skin the same size as the scraps. I glance around; many of the others have the same wounds on their shoulders. Prising his jaws open, I pull out the skin-scraps and look through them, see division names and serial numbers. Ironically, there were two groups of people tattooed by the Nazis – the victims of the 'Final Solution' and the SS men who carried it out.

Beyond these dead, a solid wall of bones weaves round the city but through the gates ahead a road leads in, straight as an ivory lance, into the heart of Kur. Paved with skulls. I feel drawn towards the centre, towards the core of Kur, wondering what might be there, if this is what drove some two dozen men to literally tear each other apart, if somewhere in there is the Hell my grandfather had seen twice and somehow lived through, somehow left behind him those two times and walked out, harrowed by the sights he'd seen. Alone, I start down the road.

Childe Roland to the dark tower came.

The Book of Names of the Dead

It is an avenue of skinsuit banners; twisting sails stretched in the turning liqueous air, billowing. There shouldn't be a breeze down here, I think, but there is, and it's a quiet howling – distant, like the echo of time itself. Empty faces stare down at me, empty eyes and empty mouths, their 'names', if you could call them that, tattooed across their foreheads. I remember reading within my grandfather's journals, or perhaps in Hobbsbaum's notes, the line: *The word for 'face' must be the word for 'name'. They do not make a distinction. Such a concept of identity.*

And I remember reading that this archaic writing, strange and subtle, was the sum of all its wearer's wisdom and understanding. The designs were added to, made more complex, involved, as the individual's experience and ideas grew and complexified. The first tattoo a youth received was their own name, woven into an intricate design across the face that signified not only who they were, but what they were, where they had come from, their role, their status. As the name fit into the designs upon the face so the youth should fit into their society, their world. And true enough, the few blank skins that hang amongst the rest are smaller, younger, those of children who had never come of age. They seem more gruesome in their nakedness.

I walk down the road of bones, towards the centre of Kur. Between the billowing skins, other roads branch off into the city. Structures of stretched skin on bone form tents, huts, bizarre faceted buildings on these streets. Inside them, through tied-back doorways and sliced out windows, I catch glimpses of racks of hanging, tattooed skins, piles of them, neat stacks of folded human hide. Every one of them containing the coded information of fifteen thousand years ago. A library of the dead.

What if you found a language, my grandfather wrote. What if you gathered a book together out of these skins, a book inscribed with the names of the dead, the essence of their lives, a book you'd stare into, see their faces looking back? Would you end up with a world of people insane, catatonic like the one man I know who read and understood a few pages in translation? I walk down into the Kur, determined in my choice of certainty, truth. I won't believe that any feeling is unspeakable, that any thing cannot be named.

As I walk I pass skins that have been cut off at the waist or thorax, that have had large sections hacked out of them, stolen by looters, and I wonder. They might have been here any time in the last fifteen thousand years. These were the pharaohs of their day, the great chieftains and shamans of the paleolithic era. There were no riches in the sense of gold or jewels, no artefacts more precious than the things the dead themselves had now become. But they were enough, and somewhere now, out there, I wonder if there exists some arcane and esoteric text, written in a lost language, on human skin, bound into a book, a book of the names of the dead. I walk on.

The Dead God

It stands at the centre of the city, just under an hour's walk from all the carnage at the doors of hell. The tent is maybe twenty foot in height and stretched out like a spider's web, but folded over on itself in all the wrong places. The entrance is covered in the thinnest, smoothest skin I've ever felt, layers of it, veils. I flick them aside and to the back of me, push through them, in towards the centre. There's a bier of sorts.

He, it, lies on the bleached bone framework – his own bones? – stretched on it by taut sinews and ivory hooks, stretched out in all his glory like some crimson shroud stained with rivulets and splashes of a deity's scarlet blood. The tattoos are red against red skin – colours of clay, terracotta, blood, fire – and they are as much scarification as tattoos. And he is strung. The strings of gut that weave him into the frame of bones, vibrate in the breeze, resonating with some distant sound. I feel the chords resonating in my own guts, fear and fury. I'm afraid to even speak because I wonder if that language so pure, so precise that it rewrites the thoughts of those who hear it, might rewrite reality itself.

I don't have to look at the name on his face to know that this is the first murderer and the first rebel, the first among these mortal angels, the first to declare himself above all else, to turn on those around him and, with his own name, carve a terror into their souls that was beyond all reason. I'm only glad that where I've read his name transcribed by Hobbsbaum or by a poor stenographer, it had been done poorly, incompletely, lacking the pitch and stress, lacking the cold precision of its full saurian grandeur. I'm glad that when I look upon the symbols scarred into his forehead, all I know of it is the transcription /ʰjaᵂve/, only the skin of the word, the bones, and not the flesh. Yahveh or Jehovah, the Jewish God? Jove or Jupiter, the name for the Deus that Aeneas brought with him in his flight from fallen Troy on Anatolia's shores, to Rome? Or Japheth, Noah's son, who lived in the time of the flood? Iapetus the Titan, father of Prometheus? All these are only approximations, corruptions of the original, echoes of the true name. Language changes over time, and maybe that's a good thing.

A small scrap of paper lies on top of this creature called /ʰjaᵂve/, placed there by my grandfather perhaps, or Hobbsbaum; but it's blank, the silence of it somehow strange within this world of words that whisper themselves inside you even when you don't know quite just what they mean. I've read translations, rough transcriptions, but I've never learnt the system, the simple phonetic key that makes the words themselves come clear. And even despite this I can feel the language, like a quiet presence at the back of my head, the rattle and hiss of a coiled snake.

I find it hard to describe exactly how I feel, standing here. Before I came here, I spent some time researching, amongst all of this, the life of Samuel Hobbsbaum after his 1921 expedition to 'Aratta'. As my grandfather had written in his journals, the professor never published another word, from that day on. However, the Nazi Archives in East Berlin revealed that when he was seized in 1940 he had in his possession a 'manuscript of over a hundred pages or more, handwritten'. I've seen perhaps twenty or so of these, sent to me by Strang upon his death. The rest of it – I don't know where it is.

So I stand there looking at the skin of a dead god, at the blank paper on top of it. I listen to the sound of the quiet breeze, and I can hear in it the whisper of the language, the resonances and echoes. If a sound can have a shape, the song-script of Kur is sound made flesh.

Hobbsbaum did die in a concentration camp, as Strang had told my grandfather, my namesake, Mad Jack Carter. What he didn't say – or what my grandfather didn't write down perhaps – is that sometime after the '21 Expedition, Hobbsbaum had travelled to the Far East, where he received some exquisite tattoo work from an oriental master of the artform. According to those who had seen it, they were beautiful but abstract, fine graceful curving lines, dots and circles. One person I talked to compared them to Feuillet notation, used by choreographers to 'write down' a dance. But everybody that had seen them remembered them.

I can hear the word, the breath, the frictions and aspirations now. I can hear it all through the cave, and I realize now that I've been hearing it every step of my journey, the tension of it, the menace, the threat. I realize I've been hearing it all my life.

His Tattooed Skin

Hobbsbaum was interred in Auschwitz in July of 1941, receiving the prisoner number 569304 tattooed on his left forearm. His actual death is not recorded, but we can reconstruct it – the way the Nazis stripped their prisoners of everything they owned, even gold teeth, the way they took a person apart, spiritually as much as physically. There were tables covered in wallets, tables covered in watches, rooms filled with shoes. If he managed to survive the day-to-day ordeal eventually he would have been stripped naked one final time and gassed and burned. There is a strong possibility, though, that somewhere in that process, he would have received 'special treatment'. His tattooed skin would have been flayed from his body to be tanned, preserved, and perhaps made into a lampshade.

I still don't know what happened to my grandfather, my namesake.

I touch the skin of the dead god only lightly and the tone of its low hum tightens, heightens. If a sound can have a shape, this is the twisted vortex of a distant tornado. If a shape can have a sound, does making that sound reshape the world? That sound, that faint echo of another Jack Carter's voice reading out the name of God – I think that if I spoke it here and now the world itself might peel apart, shedding the skin that hides the flesh and bones beneath. And if a shape, a sound, can have a meaning, an emotional meaning, then this thing, this skin, this sound it makes all through the Kur and all through my body, is dread – or rather, something far subtler and far more complicated that can only be compared to dread.

So can I put into words what I feel now looking down at this fleshless intricated skin? Horror? Yes, but not the horror of the unspeakable, the unnameable. I think my horror is of the things that must be said, the things we have to face, to name so that we're not consumed by them. Some things, my grandfather wrote, are better left unsaid. Some things though, I would say, cannot be left unwritten.

I can only say I stand in Hell now and I can hear the song of every damned and dying soul who ever breathed their last breath in unbounded terror, from the paleolithic to the present and it frightens me, knowing that when I leave this place, like my grandfather before me, I will carry it with me. And maybe it will haunt me, drive me mad like the rest of them. But I know this much. I will not leave that sound unwritten.

Jack Carter
Kur, 1999

Errata

Over the Pit of Skulls

– Look, I say eagerly, snapping my fingers in Puck's wandering gaze to draw his attention back to the matter in hand. The Book lies open over the steel grille that I've placed back over the pit of skulls, after laying the skulls in there to rest again, for want of any better idea. There doesn't seem much purpose in giving them individual burials, mouthing empty words over these strangers' remains; at best they'd have a shallow grave, alone and unmarked, so it seems somehow more fitting to lay them back in the crypt they came from, where they at least have meaning among the multitudes beneath.

– Look at the contours here, these little squiggles on every fifth one. Those are obviously height markings. You can see it better here.

I flip forward a couple of pages to the map that shows Oblivion's Mount pretty much in its entirety. The numbers on the maps, although they transform in script in tune with the terrain, looking pseudo-Cyrillic here or almost-Arabic there, have always been fairly easy to translate. It doesn't take much work to relate the markings to the ups and downs of one's surroundings, order them into linearities, reckon out the numeric-bases of the systems. It may take a while but what do we have here in the Vellum if not time?

– See how the numbers increase with each contour as you move in towards the centre.

– Amazing, says Puck. You mean it's a ... *map*?

I glare at him.

– Yes. But the map is wrong, I say.

And I start to point to the discrepancies. There aren't that many of them, to be sure, but they're there – a ridge that juts out where it shouldn't, a valley with sides a little steeper than they should be. They're so minor that I had written them all off as simply products of the layer of garbage beneath us being deeper here or there, masking the true shape of the land. It is the numbers that are wrong.

– You see, as you move in towards the centre the numbers go up in leaps and bounds, bigger and bigger. I thought it was just a matter of them using a strange scale, but I'm not so sure now. Who knows why? I've come across some strange numbering systems in these pages. This one's rather similar to Sumerian hexadecimal at first sight, multiple bases, 6 and 60, 360 and–

He whirls a finger in the air – *get on with it.*

– They're damn well exponential, I say. The numbers go up exponentially and this little symbol here, right on the summit of Oblivion's Mount is not some bloody triangulation point, as I bloody well thought; it's the bloody symbol for infinity.

Puck looks up towards the summit of the mountain. As hulking and monstrous as it is, Oblivion's Mount is not that tall.

– And this little symbol here, I say – the one on top of all the numbers – that's a negative sign.

And Puck and I both look at each other and then slowly look down, thinking about the very big hole under our feet.

Dusk on Oblivion's Mount

– It might be full, I say.

– It's a fucking bottomless pit, says Puck. How can it be full?

We ride full tilt along the ridge, cart rattling our bones and bouncing us side to side and up and down as I skitter my gloved fingers like a madman at a piano, driving the waldo-wing-things forward as fast as they can go. I can't help thinking with the grotesque and gothic quality of our clattering cart, it's like some Transylvanian carriage-ride away from Dracula's castle.

– Well, there are different levels of infinity, I say. So the pit is infinitely deep. You'd need an infinite amount of crap to fill it and putting that in piece by piece would take an infinite amount of time, so the pit should, theoretically, never be full.

– So it can't be full? You said it might be full.

*

Jack howls as he runs behind us, leaping from hump to hummock, hurdling bushes and dodging trees, skittering straight down slopes we have to navigate; I don't know how he manages to keep up with us, but he does.

– But suppose you have an infinite amount of worlds and all of them are producing infinite amounts of crap, and all of them are putting it in piece by piece; well that means there's an infinite amount of garbage going in at the same time. So then it doesn't take any time at all to fill the pit up.

– So it is full? says Puck.

The cart skids on scree as I take a hairpin bend at speed. The mountain is directly east of us now and we head pretty much due west. It will take us days out of our way but it will take us days to get the pit out from under us even at this speed. It would be nice to think that the pit was full.

I'm thinking of the otherworlds of the Vellum – the Veldt of Evenings, Oblivion's Mount, the Rift, the Bay of Afternoon. All the tiny villages and vast cities, the archipelagos of continents that I've been travelling in so long that I have no idea, I suddenly realize, how old I am any more. Christ, how long has Puck been with me? I've often considered the possibility that the Vellum is not so much eternity as the sum of all possible eternities, like all the heavens we might want are here as well as all the hells that we might fear, it's just that no one's actually in charge of making sure we end up in the right place. So maybe all these eternities have all dumped their garbage in the bottomless pit under Oblivion's Mount, and we're panicking needlessly.

– So it is full? says Puck.

– Well . . .

– No. Not *well*. No *well*. I don't want to hear *well*.

– It might be full, I say, but there should still be room for more.

I try to explain that, *well*, see, if the hole is full then that means that there's garbage, say, one foot down, and two feet down, and three feet down, all the way down. But if that garbage were to all drop down to double its depth, suddenly, like – if the garbage one foot down drops to two feet down, and the garbage at two feet down goes to four feet down, and so on, well then you have room for

427

another whole infinity of garbage, and because the pit is infinitely deep, well there's nothing to say it couldn't do that.

Ahead of us, the sun is setting, burning on the horizon of the Veldt like a bushfire, while behind us dusk gathers in twilight-grey mist and purpling sky and black clouds, around and behind Oblivion's Mount, like an army called to its colossus of a general, preparing to advance.

7

Zeus Irae

Of Marriage and Motherhood

– Wait. Please, now, says Maclean and thank you, thank you, as they settle down. I'd like to say again how much of an honour it is to have Ms Pankhurst and Ms Messenger here with us to speak tonight. As you'll all know, there's few has worked as hard in the cause of universal suffrage as Ms Pankhurst, so I'll do what's right, right now, and hand the floor to her without more song and dance.

The crowd applaud again and Ms Pankhurst steps forward to the podium on the small stage of the Labour Club, looking down at the area that's filled to the brim so it is with the folk sat on all the folding metal chairs and standing round the edges and the back. A sea of people, it is, and Seamus only wishes he could drown in it because all he can do is look at Anna standing up there on the stage behind Ms Pankhurst and hope she doesn't see him. He's too close to the front, stood here at the side of the hall, behind the fellow in the flat cap. Hand shoved in his jacket pocket he fiddles with a box of matches, like an embarrassed child kicking sand under their feet.

– First let us hear this woman, says Ms Pankhurst, tell her tale of her terrible fortune.

Then let her learn the rest of her trials from you, the bitmites hiss in Seamus's ear. For a second, the Labour Club flickers, shimmers.

Shut up, he thinks. Yer not fookin real. This is what's fookin real.

Pankhurst is speaking quiet words of sympathy, encouragement, to Anna.

– It is your place to do this, for all the sisters under the same patriarchal yoke, and for all the other reasons. Remember, it may be worth the pain, even to weep again for your misfortunes, when to do so teaches sympathy to those who hear.

And Anna nods, quiet and nervous, steels herself she does, and Seamus sees the spark in her he always saw, as she steps forward.

– I don't know how, she says, how I can find the strength to trust you with this, but I shall try to give you all you ask for in plain speech, though I'm ashamed even to speak of it, that . . . storm sent by the saints above. And how it swept away all my decorum.

And Anna tells the crowd about her fine upstanding English Army officer – a gentleman, he was, a hero of the Great War with his noble bearing and stiff upper lip. Seamus listens, pushed back against the wall. He doesn't really hear all that she's saying though, as he's too busy remembering it the way she told him on the beach at Inchgillan.

– O, Seamus, he sent me messages night after night, and when I read them I could hear his voice moving about my room, as if he softened me with his smooth words. Seamus, you have to understand.

O greatly happy maid, he'd written, why be a maid forever when the highest marriage could be yours to take. A Duke's heart has been warmed by you, by love's dart, and wants only to be one with you in love; Anna, my child, my dear, my dove, do not disdain the bed of Dukes. Go out to Lerna's meadows, to the stables of your father's fine estate, and I will meet you there, only to see you Anna, that the eye of this Duke may be eased in its desire.

With such messages she was distressed each night, until . . .

Until one day she found herself pregnant and her fine fiancé lost on some damnfool boy's own adventure in the middle of nowhere.

– I dared to tell my father of the dreams that plagued my night, and all I dreamed of was the same as any young lass dreams, marriage and motherhood.

And she was foolish, yes, and she should never have let him do that to her, should have waited, yes, she should have waited, but she had the ring on her finger – just not the right finger – and – and she had looked at Finnan there on the beach, the cold wind whipping his hair across his face and bringing tears to his eyes – and she said, it wasn't the first time, was it, Seamus?

But Enoch Messenger had tried to make things right, to do right by his daughter, even though she'd brought such shame upon them. He had tried to track down Carter's family or friends, this noble hero's roots. But he'd found nothing. He sent letter after letter to the man's commanding officer, to friends or colleagues that he'd mentioned, scattered far afield, as far as Pytho and the oaks of the Dordogne, that he might learn what it was necessary he should say or do, to do right by the lords of tradition. But they came back with dark, ambiguous and indistinctly uttered riddles. Her fiancé had not been heard of, hide nor tail.

– Till finally, she says, a plain report came back, as clear and sharp as any order given to an army underling, telling my father that my shame was mine alone. A fine upstanding man, an *officer* and a *gentleman*, why he would never, never . . . I was a liar, so they said, and if it was the reputation of his family my father cared for, he should do as any good man would and send away his shame, expel me from my home and country, if he didn't want to see his family's good name . . . wiped out.

So she was sent away to have her child – *to wander to the earth's ends*, Seamus hears the bitmites say, and as he looks at her on stage he has a vision. He sees Anna as she is now but with images of other selves laid over her, like reflections in a window that she stands behind. He sees a slightly younger girl but with the same red hair and freckled face, wearing a sort of zipped-up leather jacket like a man's, a pilot or a motorcyclist's; and there's another Anna who again is different, this one dressed in a simple robe of white,

431

some Grecian maid of olden days. He sees her as a triple being, past, present and future. Seamus blinks and rubs his eyes. He squeezes his eyelids shut, his fingers squeezing the bridge of his nose, trying to force the old nerve trouble back down into the depths of him where it belongs. When he opens his eyes, the world is normal again, without the whispering ghost images of his turns pressing in on him the way they do. He's calm.

Against his will, she's telling them, forced by these forecasts of judgemental stares like fiery thunderbolts, forced by the never-ending reign of high society's earls and dames, he drove her out, for shame, he threw her out from her own home, as if her very form and mind were changed to some horned beast. Anna, the cow. Anna, the rutting, sweating, filthy sow, unmarried mother, slave to her desire as much as any creature lusting and fucking in the byre.

– Now here I am before you, Anna says, driven by the lash of sharp tongues, words that bite like flies, and stung from land to land.

The hall is quiet. There are some here and there, as Seamus looks around, that look uncomfortable. They may be socialists, they may believe in the struggle of the working classes and in the kindred souls of others oppressed around the world, the Irish, and the negroes of America, and woman's suffrage, sure, but there's still the matter of decency and taste. A lad has to sow his wild oats, sure, but the lass he plants them in, she's still disgraced. These are still men who, well, they think a woman should have the vote, but sure and her place is in the home, it is, and these are still women who'd tut and tsk about the wee lassie down the road who let her boyfriend get her up the duff. But the hall is quiet. Sure and it's altogether a different story when yer face-to-face with a young girl put out of her own home with an infant son and with nowhere else to go but on the streets.

Ah, Jesus wept, thinks Seamus. How can a gentle shepherd have such violent temper, or is it not Himself that's watching over our every step, dead as he is? The bitmites whisper in his ear of *Argus-eyed humanity and peacock pride* and quietly, unnoticed by the others in the hall, he slips a hip-flask from his pocket, takes a wee sip from it. He still remembers his own reaction when she told him, how his mind leapt frantically with her tumbling words across a century's stream of dreams it seems, of what they had and what they could have had, before it all went wrong, before poor Thomas died, before the war, before her bloody English officer, before his illness, back to spring in Lerna.

Spring in Lerna. Summer in the Somme. It's autumn now, outside the hall, autumn in Glasgow, all brown and red and orange and yellow leaves looking golden in the setting sun of Evenfall.

– And . . . that's my story, Anna says.

– O Seamus, speak to me, she said as he stared off into the ocean. If you have anything to say, just say it. Speak to me. I don't care if it hurts me; I deserve it, Seamus. Please just say something.

She reached out and he felt the calf-skin of her glove touching the back of his hand.

– It's not comfort I'm looking for, Seamus. It's not false words and empty pity. It's just . . . You've never lied to me. You never lied.

He could see what she wanted in her eyes, hear it in what she didn't say. *What's going to happen to me, Seamus?*

– Lies are the cruellest ill of all, she said.

In His Black Pin-Point Pupils

– Ah, no. Enough, alas.

The air in the hall seems to vibrate and Seamus Finnan watches Anna on the stage dissolve, and Pankhurst and Maclean, until there's nothing but the velvet curtain at their back, the banner welcoming the speakers and the red flag and the Union Jack at each side. The audience shimmers, a mirage in a desert, the air over tarmac on a hot, summer road.

– We never thought we'd hear a tale so full of cruelty, the bitmites whisper, such ugly and intolerable hurts, such sufferings.

He pushes through the ghost images of his memory until he's standing in the centre of the room. There's only one chair now, one of the folding metal chairs – with a circle of white salt around it on the floor – and as he lays his hand on the backrest, he feels it biting cold under his skin. His breath steams, white and swirling in the air in front of him. He sits down in the chair, closes his eyes.

– Your love, the voices whisper, is a two-edged sword. It chills our souls.

He opens his eyes and the abattoir is crisp and clear. A cold reality. Ah, Christ, thinks Finnan. He hadn't thought of Anna for years, for decades even.

Henderson stands at the doorway with its plastic strips swaying like folds of curtains and Henderson himself turned away, speaking quietly to some absent underling or superior by link, one hand up to his earpiece; he catches snippets of phrases – making progress, physically stable, yes, no, MacChuill, needs to be watched, I can assure you, maybe you should, can't depend on him, under control. There's an edginess in his tone and stance, Finnan thinks.

– You're sure? he hears the man say, saying it slow and clear, the way you do when you're looking for clarity in return. This ... situation with the bitmites couldn't affect us here?

He glances over his shoulder and Finnan drops his eyes, mumbles like a man lost in delirium. Henderson turns away again.

– OK. Yes sir, he says, I think he's nearly ready for you.

Metatron, thinks Finnan. If the Covenant is behind this – and Henderson is so fucking Covenant it makes you sick – then it has to be Metatron pulling the strings here. Last he heard, the other big guns were all tied up in the War. Angels with swords of fire walking through Jerusalem. A Sovereign's compound in Fallujah wiped out in an explosion. An earthquake in Iran. A nuclear accident in North Korea. The angel war isn't two armies facing each other across a battlefield. No, it's a correspondent in a fawn flak-jacket and webbed helmet talking straight to camera – and Finnan had swallowed as he looked into the man's eyes and saw the unkin mark in his black pin-point pupils, because even over the fuzz of a link disrupted by extremist jammers, Finnan had read the name in his blank gaze. Azazel, angel of death. Jesus, the birdman had stared out at his VR audience, smooth as a milkshake, and shown his soul to the world deliberately, so that anyone out there with the knowledge to read it, any unkin out there, Covenant or otherwise, would get the message. We're in charge now.

So, it's pretty clear what Gabriel and Michael and Azazel and all their little minions, all their little Hendersons, are up to these days. Hunting Sovereigns. But Metatron isn't a field agent, not like them. Information and analysis. Intel and intercept. Bitmites. This is his operation. He looks down at his open chest, wondering why they've given him this respite, this chance to get his thoughts clear.

– Alas, a lass's fate, the bitmites hiss. We shudder, seeing Anna's state. If we were flesh all we would pray is that our fates should never bring us any husband from the heavens, never see us share the bed of Dukes.

Again the sympathetic words. Sure and with a bit of practice they might even come close to passing a Turing Test, but he's not fooled for a minute by their fucking crocodile tears. He's willing to concede that maybe Metatron's little machines are fancy enough to have developed some sort of ... curiosity. But empathy? No, he thinks. It's all part of Metatron's plan. Peel him open, strip him down and soften him up. Anna is just a wound they want reopened.

– Your tears and fears are premature, he says. Wait till you hear the rest.

– Tell us, they say.

– Why do you want to know? he says. Why should I tell you anything?

– It's sweeter to the sick to know the suffering to come.

The little bastards must have learned the unkin art of never giving a straight answer, he thinks. Talk in riddles. Never give yourself away. Never give the enemy something to use against you.

– Our former wish we got from you with ease, they say, for first we asked to learn from her relating her own trials. Now we would hear the rest, what sufferings it is necessary this young woman should endure from here.

– Anna? he says. What business is my past to you? What's done is done.

– Time in the Vellum isn't that simple.

The phrase sparks off a memory, something someone said to

him; he can't put his finger on it for a second, then it clicks. Phreedom in the church after she'd gone to Asheville after Thomas, after she'd gone to Eresh, gone to Hell and come back with –

The bitmites scrawl across his chest and he looks at them closer now, at the patterns within patterns in the ever-changing chaos. The ragged open wound looks like a Mandelbrot set given a couple of new dimensions.

What do you get if you cross the queen of the dead's blood with the ink of God's scribe, Metatron's bitmites and the magic in Eresh's little glass jars? What you get, thinks Finnan, is something that might have been alive once but so long ago that it's forgotten what it's like, or something that was never alive and suddenly here it's finding itself thinking, trying to understand the strange world of humanity with its wars and revolutions. And, caught somewhere between the Covenant protocols of its programming and the dark compulsions of all things afraid of death, sure and maybe Enoch's babies might have found some sort of empathy after all. Or maybe, at least, they might just learn.

– Tell us, they say.

– Then listen up, he says, and take these words to heart. I'll tell you where the journey ends.

Or where the journey starts.

The Dawn of Time

She turns towards the rising sun. Rose tints of early morning light wash over a vast tract of the same uncultivated lands that they've been travelling these last few years, the lands of people who call themselves the nomads of the scythes and live in carts with wicker roofs, who fire bows at them from afar. It's a primitive place, this part of the Vellum, but that makes it a lot more stable than some of the worlds they've been in – no cities in flames, no looted shops, no traffic jams of people in flight, no ducking into doorways as an angel passes overhead, its silver wings spread wide, disruptor swinging as it strafes the crowd to dust.

– What's up? says Don, stopping his horse at her side. Jesus, but she misses her bike; horses are so fucking uncomfortable. Don seems to have taken to the whole New Archaic thing like a duck to water though.

— Watch out, she says. Caliphs on the left hand.

He slips his ruptor from his shoulder, scans the horizon. To their right, the cliffs drop to the echoing boom of sea. Ahead of them the narrow trail around the headland opens up to the wide and empty plain lit by the low sun shrouded in its pink striated clouds. To their left, the rocks rise into moss and undergrowth, and here and there the odd caliph is visible. She calls them that for their weird turban-like head-dresses and pointed beards, but they're a pretty savage people. Basic Iron Age technology and not exactly believers in the law of hospitality.

— Just be careful, she says.

— Just be careful, says Don.

She looks down at the River of Hubris, winding its way through the gorge below — well-named, she thinks, given the idiotic pride it takes to try and cross its swollen stream in full flood on a rickety rope-bridge creaking and swaying under your feet. She takes another tentative step forward, foot flat on the board all slick and slippery from the spray of a tiny waterfall spurting out somewhere above them in a little stream, no more than a shower really — like rainwater gathered on a cathedral roof and pouring down to spout out of some gargoyle's mouth — no more than a faucet left running, but enough to soak the wood and have the two of them worrying about rotten planks and feet sliding on algae. The water falls and falls, tumbling in sprinkling glitters down. She's glad she's not afraid of heights. Above them and across the chasm, the carcass of the mountain towers grey and white, scattered with other spattering rivulets running down and darkening its rockface. Meltwater from its white peak. It's like a giant risen from the sea, the water pouring down its broad rhino-hide back.

— Don't worry about me, she says.

A week to pass over the summit, she reckons, partly from the maps they have and partly from experience of this kind of terrain. She doesn't mind; there's a part of her that's always liked being up in the hills and mountains, up here among the stars where the air is thin and clear. They're headed south after this though, into a region labelled on the maps as The Mascara — for some reason she pictures a jungle filled with armies of man-hating Amazons — and down along the Thermidor to Psalmydeus. It's a rough town, perched upon a ragged coast of jagged jaws where the sea crashes its wild welcome on the walls of stone for any sailors brave enough to risk this city known as the wicked stepmother of ships.

— You still think Psalmydeus is a good idea? she calls to Don. What if these people are as hostile as the rest.

— Well then, he says, I'm sure they'll gladly send us on our way.

— I'm glad we're finally on our way again, she says.

Behind them the Chimaeran Isthmus rises as a wall, a rough dry-stone wall where the two headlands that it joins reach out to almost touch each other but not quite. It's not a natural formation, more like a causeway that wants to be a dam but with a narrow arching gateway giving passage from the great lake beyond into the waters that they now sail. Actually, whether it's even called an isthmus depends on who you talk to; the cold lake behind, the warm sea they move in now, and the two lands that separate them like curtains drawn not quite shut — none of these have their boundaries marked on any of the maps. For all they know the waters might surround the lands; two giant islands or two great saltwater lakes joined at a pin-point like the loops of an infinity symbol or a figure-eight, on the maps the coasts are only marked as a huge, rough X that carves the territory into quarters, water to the north and south, land to the east and west. So while the shellcarvers from whom they got their maps refer to the Chimaeran Isthmus, on the navigation charts of the wavers in their little merchant steamships — like the one they travel on now — the area is marked as the Maeostoso Straits, the treacherous shallows that it takes a stout heart to sail through.

All along the walls of Phosphorus behind them, the city built along the isthmus like the shops and houses on a medieval bridge in London or Firenze, the people are still standing, cheering, and she wonders how long the fame of their passage will last. Even before they left, Don said he'd heard some children in the street singing a nursery rhyme about the soldier and the princess who set off to find the dawn of time. Princess, she thinks, with more than a little irony. From trailer-trash Phreedom to Princess Anaesthesia. But these

438

people probably couldn't even imagine a world with somewhere like Slab City in it, and in the fishwife cultures of the shellcarvers and the wavers any woman with her independent bearing, she supposes, has to be a princess. Don grumbles about it, of course – *they think I'm your fucking bodyguard.* So she smiles at him and winks and says, *Aren't you?*

But she wonders about the dawn of time thing, how that rumour started. It seems to be travelling ahead of them now, the story of their journey actually preceding them. Some places they've arrived to a hero's welcome, festivals in their honour. The people of Europa's Plain wish you the best of luck in your quest. The Continent of Ash is that way.

– Aren't you going to join the celebrations? asks Don.

He sits down at the table beside her, beckoning out at the festivities in the hall. A group of young men dancing in a ring chant their devotion to the sun, the bridegroom crowned in golden garland, while the women spin like dervishes around them, scattering flower petals, laughing. The older generation, the already-married, stand in a wider circle all around, clapping in rhythm to the tom-tom and the thrum of something like a double bass. The band onstage in their white skirted tunics and red scarves and silk belts, the exuberant whirling of tradition, round and round, and whooping, crying, everything about it makes her think of Gypsies, Jews and Greeks. They even smash things here, not plates or glass but wooden toys, the bride's and bridegroom's childhood playthings caught up in a revel of destruction, old lives broken underfoot to start anew in adulthood, in marriage. She looks at the mangled wreck of a toy sat on the table in front of her, a little wooden drummer boy puppet, legs and arms and head all broken off but still tied up together in the tangle of strings that they once dangled from. It's part of the tradition. Guests all get to take away one of the broken toys as a memento of the marriage, a memento of the childhood now abandoned.

– What's the matter? says Don. Anna?

She shakes her head. Her drink – some sort of local fermented milk drink – sits beside the toy, untouched.

– The truth? she says. I don't know.

But she does. She knows that it doesn't really matter if Jack was

Finnan's son, or the Covenant angel's, or just the son of one of the many johns she fucked for money just to get by when she was lost and had nothing; he was hers. She should never have let them take him away from her

A Fairy Tale of New York

– I'm not going to let them take him away from me, Seamus. I'll go away, far away, Seamus, O, I'll go to America. Can you imagine it, Seamus? New York. They say it's so *magnificent*, with the towers of glass stretching all up to the sky; we'll go there, me and Jack, and I'll tell everyone that I'm a widow, I'll wear black, I will, Seamus, that's what I'll do. And he won't have the shame on him, he won't.

She smiles sadly.

– Towers of glass and a poor widow with a boy called Jack. It sounds like a fairy tale, doesn't it?

They sit on the edge of the stage, the hall empty now. Christ, but it took some courage for him not to run, not to hide in the crowd and duck and weave out the doorway afterwards, out of sight and away, away. But to wait there until the crowd cleared and she saw him and they stood there looking at each other and not knowing what to say.

He thinks of her sailing off towards New York across the stormy sea of her own sorrow, and there's a bit of him that wants to keep her here, that wants be saying, is it mad ye are? And what will ye do all on yer own with no one to look after ye? And have ye no idea of all the trials and tribulations that yer sailing straight for, like a great iceberg of yer suffering waiting in yer path. Ye can't just run away.

– It'll be hard, he says. To be on your own, sure. You with an infant son and all.

But what has she got to live for here, in a land where an unmarried mother is half expected just to throw herself from the nearest cliff into the sea? That's what they do, isn't it, drown themselves for the release? And then it's *what a pity* and *the poor, poor girl* but secretly it's *maybe it's better for everyone, her to just die once and for all, than suffer evil all her days and there's the child to think of after all; they never need to know the shame now.* Bollocks, he thinks.

– It'll be hard, he says, but if . . .

He tries to find the words. *If you want, I'll come with you.*

– If . . .

If you want me, I'll come with you.

– If . . .

She shakes her head.

– It's different now, Seamus. It's not you and me, any more. It's not you and me and Thomas in between us as . . . something we used to have. All that matters now is Jack.

– A new beginning, he says. Ah, lass, sure and sometimes fairy tales come true. I'm sure of it.

He hopes so. He prays so. Sure and he doesn't want to believe that God Himself is just another fookin tyrant lord like all the rest and brutal in everything He does, in all the bitter twists of fate he throws into their paths. He thinks, he hopes, that maybe it's all just the thoughtlessness of . . . of a dashing, young hero urging his sweetheart to just give him this one thing before he's sent back to the front, not thinking what might happen, how it might drive his sweetheart out to wanderings in the wilderness. Maybe that was how the angel Gabriel came to Holy Mary, he thinks, as a soldier with his dogtags round his neck just looking for a simple night of love before going back to fight the serpent, not thinking of all the Slaughter of the Innocents or the Flight Into Egypt, or a poor boy on a cross and his mother weeping for him.

If only there was anything he could give to soothe her.

– *A bitter wooer did you find,* he says, *O virgin, for your marriage. For the words you have now heard are only the beginning.*

– What's that? she says.

He looks embarrassed.

– It's from something I've been reading. Ye'd be proud of me, Anna, sure ye would. And Thomas, why he'd be laughing his socks off at the thought of it, me reading the classics and all. But that

Maclean. He was a schoolteacher before, ye know? It's all about education, he says. Learning. Words. Ideas. That's where the power is.

She shakes her head and heaves a smiling sigh.

– Seamus Padraig Finnan. Man of books.

They laugh, and he lets her finish laughing, tension draining out from between them.

– But, see, the reason I thought of it is, well, it's from a play by this Greek fellow, Aeschylus, about this Titan, Prometheus. D'ye know the story, like? How he fought for Zeus against his tyrant father, then went against him to give fire to humanity and got punished for it, chained up on a mountain with the vultures pecking at his insides.

– Eagle, she says. Wasn't it an eagle?

– So ye know it, then?

– Sharing a house with Thomas? Sure and how could I not know all the stuff and nonsense of myths and legends and whatnot? Did you ever know him to shut up about – O, Jesus, Finnan – if it wasn't Modern Art, it was the Greeks this and the Greeks that and – yes, I know the story.

And he looks into her eyes and suddenly has this quiet realization that there's something healed in both of them that they can look back now with fondness and laughter like they would've done at the wake they never had – even if it is just for a moment and with the sadness still there behind it.

Prometheus's Secret

– But listen, he says, ye know how in the play there's these three folks that come to visit Prometheus on the rock? There's an old soldier, the titan Ocean, who fought beside him in the War against old Cronos. And at the end of it, there's Hermes sent from Zeus to try and get Prometheus to spill the beans, because Prometheus knows something, ye see, he knows who's going to overthrow Zeus the way Zeus toppled his own father from the throne. But that's not the point, or it is, but it's not the point I want to make, sure. Because the other person, who comes between Ocean and Hermes, right in the middle of the play, in the centre of it, ye know, is this lass called Io. And she's this poor wee girl what Zeus himself took a fancy to and came to her in the dead of the night as sure and that lecherous old bastard was always doing, and of course it's her that suffers for it in the end, sent out to wander to the ends of the earth, kicked out of her house and home for it. A poor girl, shamed for giving herself to something that seemed . . . shining and true.

She takes his hand.

– But it's her, he says. It's her Prometheus tells his secret to because she's a victim like himself of Zeus. Sure and the way he sees it, what he says, is she doesn't have half the troubles that he has, so she doesn't, 'cause she can always kill herself and he . . . well, he doesn't have that luxury, none of that mercy for Prometheus, sure, just pointless suffering going on and on without an end in sight.

Seamus grins at her, a wee wink in his eye.

– Sure and he makes a bit of a song and dance about it, and it's not really fair to be saying to someone that, well, OK, so you got turned into a cow and sent to wander all across the earth but look at me here getting me liver pecked out by the fookin vultures. That's hardly what ye'd call tactful now, is it? But it is a play after all, so ye can forgive him for being a bit over-dramatic. We all tend to get carried away with our own problems and forget that others have their own.

– The point is that he says to her, I'll grant you one of two tales, so he says. Which will it be? D'ye want to hear about the end of your pain or the end of mine? Is it possible, she says, for either of us? Well if one day the King of the Gods were to kinda sorta fall from power with a wee shove from behind, says he. But is it possible, she asks, and it's a nice idea, he says, ye'd like to think so, wouldn't you? How could I not, says she, after what the fooker's done to us, and he says, well, ye can be sure of it. And who will destroy him? Zeus himself, he says, by his own ignorance and stupidity. And how? Because there's some young girl out there, some slip of a girl who doesn't seem like anybody and ye'd never know it to look at her maybe, just a girl as she is, but maybe just a little special in a way that kings and gods will never see, but special, because any son of hers, ye see, any son of hers will be much greater than his father ever could be.

– So he tells her, ye see. He tells her that the only one who knows who this girl is, is him, Prometheus, and he's never going to tell. And Zeus will just go on his way, acting the same as ever and seducing poor young girls and then discarding them after he's done, with nobody to take the fooker to task about it. Until one day . . . One day . . . And Prometheus, he knows it, but his lips are sealed. O, no, they can torture him and chain him up for all eternity but he's never going to give it up because he knows, and he tells her, ye see, he tells Io, that it's her descendant, one of her descendants who he *knows* will free him.

    – O, Seamus, but, ye've got it all mixed up.

    – How's that? he says.

    – I know the story, but it's Achilles, Seamus. It's *his* mother is the one who'll have a son who's greater than his father, in the stories, in the myth, and so he is. But Zeus never touches her. Io's completely different, and – ye're getting everything mixed up and running two different stories together that don't belong together, Seamus.

– No, he says. I mean, sure and I know ye're right. I'm sure ye're right, like, strictly speaking and all. But is that what matters? I mean, does it matter if it's Io's child that breaks Prometheus's chains, or the child of her child, or three or ten generations down the line? Does it matter if it's not the same child as overthrows the high and mighty Zeus, even if the two things are the same really, at heart, freeing the ole rebel and toppling the ole tyrant? Does it matter if some other Greek storyteller, some blind storyteller sitting on a street-corner, decides to make Achilles the son who's greater than his father because it makes his own story grander?

    He leans closer.

    – Anna, there's a truth in it I think I see. I think I know Prometheus's secret, Anna, and it's one that just makes sense in a way that prophecies and stories about gods and heroes and all that fookin shite – pardon me French – just don't. Because that's all nonsense. It's all just stories.

    He shakes his head.

– So what if it's Achilles' mother who can have a son that's greater than its father? What if it's Io, too? What if it's any girl, every girl? Any woman? Every woman, Anna. Sure and can't any son be greater than his father? Isn't that what it's all about, what makes us all go on? Ye can't look at the sheer bloody-minded defiance of a wee babe screaming its lungs out at the terrible injustice of the world and not have hope. Every generation of us, all born kicking up a racket, rebels every one of us. So who's the son – the child – that's greater than its father? I'll tell ye who it is, Anna.

– Humanity.

The Ballad of Seamus Finnan

– Tell her, the bitmites whisper in his ear. Consent to do her this one favour; tell her all that still remains of wandering. And give the other tale to us. Don't deem us undeserving of your words. We desire only this: tell us who will release you. How and by what means?

Hush now, he thinks.

– If I tried to explain such wisdom as me dear old mother told it to me we'd be here forever, and there'd still be nothing learned. Ye couldn't fookin understand it even if I told you straight. If yer in earnest, if ye really are sincere, I'll not refuse to tell ye all ye want to know. But Seamus Finnan's sat here in this chair, remember, on the rock and in the wire, and only half of him is Seamus now, the other half the fookin ancient thief of fire.

He wonders how the first of the unkin ever dealt with this. Sure and it's madness, so it is, sitting and talking to the girl who was once yer sweetheart back in 1922 but with the vision of what's to come so clear – as clear as a memory – that ye don't know what now is, if yer in the future living the dead past again, or in the past remembering the future before it happens. Time in the Vellum, he thinks.

He can feel her kidskin glove warm in his hand, and he can feel the wire cutting into his wrist and he can feel the cold Caucasian rock at his back.

– These are the proofs of what you say, the bitmites hiss, the proofs to us of your intelligence, that it sees more than the visible.

*

But that's the rub, of course, thinks Seamus Shamash Padraig Prometheus Foresight Forsythe Four Scythes Finnan Finn the giant of Ireland and the giant of the world half-awake and half-asleep under the dreamings of humanity, a creature of the Vellum as much as a man of life and love and flesh. Does he take these bitmites for minions only out to do their master's bidding, using poor Seamus like a bucket down a well, drawing up the secrets of the future from the depths of his own past? Or does he take them for free agents that want only what we all do, just the understanding of ourselves and what we're doing here?

She sits at the foot of his rock, Anna, Phreedom, Io, in her long white dress, her long, dark hair blown in the cold wind, and is it Inchgillan, or is it the Caucasus? She holds his hand where it's chained against the rock – Jesus, but the wires cut deep – and the way she looks at him he somehow knows it doesn't matter if she's a phantom, if she's just a form adopted by the bitmites trying to communicate with him through the media of his memories.

– To you first, Io, then, he says, I'll tell the wanderings that will vex you. Engrave them on the tablets of the heart, because ye know, ye know that what I say is true. I'll tell what you'll endure, and if ye give me just a little time I'll reach the point, and take ye to the very limit of your wanderings. I'll tell ye all, and if there's any of it unintelligible to you, or just difficult to understand, ask all ye want. I'll try to make it clear; I have more time to kill than I would like. I'll give you all you want to take.

– Give us a song, then, Tam. Come on. The Ballad of Seamus Finnan, eh?

She turns her head, watches the man as he strums his guitar and starts.

– Well there was a young man, Seamus Finnan by name, who went off to the war, O, to play the great game. Now it wasn't the blood and it wasn't the fire, but his heart it was broke by a night on the wire.

She's heard them sing about her. She's heard the whole term of her travels told in epic verse, her past and future, what will happen when she comes to the molasses land, close to the speaking oaks up in the mountains of the New Dordogne, where all these protean

Dukes sit on their thrones as oracles; now more than ever it's as if they're only following upon the tracks of words spoken a long, long time ago. She's heard the tales of Jack too, the prodigy, the prodigal, and clearly, and without enigma, those who sing these songs want her to be the famed fiancée of a deus. It's strange the way things change here in the Vellum, as if the more mutable the world is, the more the people in it seek to put it into simple terms. And now she sits in the tavern listening to the Ballad Of Seamus Finnan, a folk-song about this young Irishman who goes off to fight in the First World War. Finnan never really was one to talk about his past, but as she listens to the song, a shiver runs down her spine.

– Well, it wasn't for Belgium, it wasn't for France. It wasn't for England he entered that dance. It was all for the love of a sweet Irish lass, that he marched through the muck and the guns and the gas.

– See, Anna his sweet had a brother called Tom, and he tapped his feet to the beat of the drum. With his Trinity pals he got wild in the pub. And they took the King's Shilling and signed with the Dub's.

The tavern – no, this is more of a pub – is Finnan through and through, with the stag's heads on the wall and the wooden indian boy, the papier-mache effigy of a ruler hated for her cruelty and called the Iron Lady, depicted with the savage, beaked nose and beady eyes of a political cartoon. Hundreds of different whiskies line the walls behind the bar. Men sit in a corner, on wooden pews taken from some old church, playing guitar, fiddle and bodhrin. The pub itself is called the Uisge Beatha. Water of Life, explains Don. Outside, the waters of the Gulf of Rear are chopped up in the same storm that tossed their little vessel back and forth all the way along the coast. Waves crash over the sea wall of Nova Iona and in the wildwinds of Evenfall only the odd maniac can be seen now and again through the bubbled glass of the window, struggling along in a yellow waxed coat, one step forward, two steps back, flapping a hand to drive away the grey maelstrom of mechanical, magical midges, the bitmites that they can't escape, no matter how far they travel. She never visited Scotland or Ireland back in the world before this afterworld, but this seems to be a little piece of Celtic geography in the depths of the Vellum, an expatriate archipelago. She imagines ancient Ionian

447

sailors blown here through tears in reality and returning home with tales of the strange Western Islands, the Hebrides.

– Now Seamus was hurt to see Anna so sad, so he swore to her then to look after the lad. And he picked up his kit and he followed young Tom. Yes he followed the boy all the way to the Somme.

Three or four of the others around the table all join in with the chorus.

– Tis a hard thing is life, tis a hard thing indeed. And it's easy to die, cause it's sorer to bleed. But tis hardest of all for the last man to stand, looking down at yer pals all across No Man's Land.

There Is a City

– If anything is left to tell, the bitmites chorus, speak of her sad journey. Speak of what's to come or what is past. But if you're done, give us the favour which we ask. Remember.

So Prometheus, he says to Io:

– When ye've travelled through the tumult of the flood, he says, across the boundary of continents, towards the burning oriental sun, sure and ye'll reach a great plain of gargantuan cisterns, deep wells in the earth where neither sunbeams shine nor moonlight falls at evening or night...

They guide their horses carefully across the pitted land, night vision goggles scouring the land in front of them, alert for all the dangers of the terrain, and alert for all the dangers of its inhabitants. The shanty town stretches for miles around them, tents and shacks of corrugated iron and wooden board that make her think of the outskirts of Mexico City. Stumps of dead volcanoes rise out of the mass of unpaved streets lit up by burning oilcans around which the denizens of this wounded land huddle, staring up at them as they pass. A boy drawing water up from one of the natural wells stops to look at them, rope in hand, eyes shining as they track the silver crucifix cross bow of the disruptor slung over Don's back. Further on an old man merely shrugs and pours a bucket of filth down one of the other holes, drops a sheet of corrugated iron back over the cesspit. She wonders if the smell is worse now than when the lava field was still active and sulphurous fumes bubbled up through molten rock, creating the unstable land of pits and thin bridges that could collapse at any moment.

Don whistles as they ride on.

— All the way, she'd said.

Three old toothless hags with necks stretched up by hoops of ivory, white like swans in the moonlight, sit on a rug outside a tent, their scarred faces with only one eye between the three of them, lit by what looks to be a shining boar's tusk that they sit around; it's brighter than the moon. Inside a shack, glimpsed through the open door, she sees three women all tattooed with iridescent dragon-scales over their bodies, naked but for the veils on their faces and the long hair, braided and beaded like snakes, that falls down their backs and over their shoulders. One of them stretches her black wings out wide as her and Don ride past. A scent of incense wafts out of the shack, something sweet and rotten at the same time, a delicate poison, almonds and corrupted fruit, yeast and burning plastic. Creatures somewhere between the size of cats and dogs circle and sniff amongst deep heaps of garbage, ribcages showing through their golden fur, beaks picking silently at scraps, wings flapping as they claim this chunk or that as theirs. Graia, gorgons and gryphons.

She looks over to her left, at another gruesome sight. A host of horsemen watch them from the other side of a deep ditch of a gutter in full flow, flooded with a golden liquid that smells like — that has to *be* — a mix of piss and beer. The riders are all one-eyed, known through these lands as Ahriman's Spies. The story is that when they gouge one eye out there's another vision looks out through the empty socket, through the eye that isn't there, that they become like cameras for their . . . controller sitting in a dark room somewhere, surrounded by a thousand screens.

— I tell ye, Phree, Finnan had said, there's dangers in the Vellum that ye can't fookin imagine. But here . . .

And he'd tailed off, shaking his head. He couldn't persuade her not to go, of course. She belonged with the monsters now. She'd head out into the Vellum, as far away from the Covenant as she could get, and she'd be safe. Her and Jack would be safe.

449

– Maybe, he'd said. How far are you willing to go?
– All the way, she'd said.

– There is a city, Canopy, he says, last of a distant land and near the fountains of the sun, inhabited by a dark race. You'll find it by the aether's open river, by the broad banks and the wide mouth of the River Nill, where it sends down its sweet and sacred stream, down from the mountains, babbling.

They creep down the river's steep bank, feet skidding under the scree of the steep incline, digging their ruptors in as staffs to keep from losing their footing. In the distance she can hear the rumble of the great waterfall beyond the city where the Nill crashes down over the cliffs and into ... nothing. Above them on the ridges of the ravine, the lights of the city glitter against the dark sky, amongst the silhouettes of minarets and domes. Great iron bridges span the gulf here. Further down the ravine widens, the gradient lessens and the buildings crawl down the slopes to meet. The river itself becomes shallower and splits off into streams that disappear into grated sewers under the city streets, the whole construction built over the delta of the Nill. Canopy they call it and that's sort of what it is, closing over the branching river and roofing it in vaults of stone, plugging the mouth of the ravine like a great dam. Somewhere under the city, the streams reunite though and she knows that, on the far edge of the city, like a Trevi Fountain built by God, it thunders out through an enormous sluice gate, falling down forever into empty eternity. The city at the end of the world.

She looks behind her at the ragtag mob now following them, her progeny of sorts, her colony. There's fifty of them in all, and every one of them no more than a girl, every one of them in silk shifts and with perfumed hair, and some of them crying because their feet hurt; they don't have the shoes for this terrain, only soft slippers like a ballerina's, like a bride's. They don't look capable of it, she thinks. Not one of them could you look at and picture the vengeance and the bodies, war's welcome in a marriage bed, those girlish hands wrapped in a husband's hair and round a two-edged dagger cutting the man's throat, such a picture of divine brutality, a dove splattered with blood. But she knows better. Cousins, she thinks. What kind of man would sell his daughters to his brother's sons?

– Their laws don't bind us, princess, Arkos had said, sitting corpulent and complacent in his tent, as his nephews died in silence and darkness, and she stood there with her ruptor trained on him, Don outside keeping watch. The great pharaohs practised incest, he had said. To build a dynasty of pure-bred unkin – think of it – with not a drop of human blood to soil their veins. The *purity*. I don't care if they're . . . unwilling. They *will* bear my royal race.

And then the ruptor in her hand was hot and Arkos was a pile of ash.

It wasn't her plan – it never is – just another case of being in the wrong place at the wrong time, where a young girl could come to her, tell her that she had to help them, that she *had* to. I know your real name, she had said. I know your real name, Phreedom.

She looks behind her at them all, scattered, scrambling down the slope. Only one of them, fifth back from Don, couldn't bring herself to do the deed, wavering at the last minute, whether it was from fear or love or just not wanting to be stained with blood.

And not far behind these doves now she can see the hawks, Arkos's men, his brother and his sole surviving son. Don follows her gaze, turning around. He looks at her, at their pursuers, back at her and raises his disruptor.

– Go, he says.

Go, thinks MacChuill. Just go. Now, before you change your mind. Before Henderson decides to chase you out here and drag you back into that bloody travesty of an interrogation. Just get the fuck out of here and go. Aye, but where? he thinks.

He closes his eyes and leans back against the wall of the slaughterhouse, feeling the sun warm on his face and soaking it up. The red and orange and golden glow of it through his eyelids seems full of indistinguishable patterns, wheeling things that almost resolve into regular shapes – spirals, mandalas – but never quite make that much sense. And it's what he feels like. Like he's just one of those wee bits of things that's moving in circles around and around as part of a pattern that he cannae bloody well make head nor tail of.

He opens his eyes and it takes him a while before he can distinguish the dots floating, distant in the sky, from the after-images of sunlight broken-up and filtered by his own thin skin and veins, before he can make out the circling birds of prey. And it looks that ordered, too. It looks like they're patrolling the skies with purpose, with a plan, the whole flock of them going round and round the way soldiers patrol the perimeter of a camp, in a jungle somewhere, green and lush like this mountainous part of Mexico. He remembers watching men in uniforms the same colour as his bamboo cage and the bamboo splinters that go under the fingernails. Going round and round.

The tips of his fingers are still numb from touching the Irishman's soul, and he flexes them, rubs his hands together.

But of course the birds only look like they've got a purpose, so he's told. In truth, they don't know where they're going; they're just following each other, keeping close enough together, far enough apart, to feel comfortable with their situation. That's what flocking is, this – what's the word? – emergent behaviour, that seems ordered but is really chaos. So he's told. MacChuill still has problems adjusting to this new world with its new ideas and new wars. New enemies. He wishes things were as simple as they used to be, when he was a lad, whenever that was.

This isnae your fight, he thinks. No if it's a fight that means torturing some poor bastard, some poor sad bastard that never done anyone any harm except for in the foolishness of being in pain. No. He cannae conscience this. He cannae.

Seamus Finnan, he thinks. Where do I know that name from? And somewhere in the back of his head he finds a memory of a wee pub in Glasgow and a folk musician sitting in a corner singing a song. How did the chorus go again?

Tis a hard thing is life. Tis a hard thing, indeed. But it's easy to die 'cause it's sorer to bleed. But the hardest to be is the last man to stand, looking down at your pals all across No Man's Land.

MacChuill makes a decision.

He's got no idea of where he's going, but looking around him at the empty loading bay he knows that he's got to get the fuck away from here right now. Maybe, somewhere there's a fight that's right for this old soldier of an empire on which the sun, they said, would never set, but it's not here, not now.

Don glances up one last time at the buzzards and starts walking.

– It was a wise man, Anna says, who weighed things in his mind, and said it first, that marrying according to one's station is the best.

Not being just a labourer, a menial, he thinks bitterly, with hands too dirty, sure, to woo those who're so clean, so pure with wealth and fookin breeding, so fookin pristine. I hope yer fookin happy with yer fookin officer, whatever his fookin name is. But the defeat in him is like a lead weight in his heart, an anchor dragging him down into the cold Atlantic that he stares out into, and part of it's because he knows she won't be happy. He can hear it in the tremble of her voice, that it's herself she's trying to convince with her old man's words. Sure and does she really have a choice in the matter?

He slides off the rock and walks out across the beach, crouches down to pick up a flat stone. It skims across the grey water, bouncing, bouncing, one splash, two, three, then it disappears. Would she run away with him, he wonders. Is that what she's really here for? Not to kick him when he's down, poor crazy Seamus Finnan locked up in a looney-bin that's passing for a War Hospital, not just for the horrid cruelty of it, but in the hope that he'll say what she's too afraid to say herself, maybe even too afraid to think. Sure and he doesn't want to see her in this state, unhappy with the wrong man, in a foolish marriage that's half love, half hate.

Her eyes wander with distress from here to there, from drift-wood to seaweed to his face, her own hands. Her confused words crash over him, salt waves of woe on an impervious rock.

– Seamus, I feel wretched about this, though. If a marriage is of equals there's nothing to fear, is there, O, but if it's not though . . .?

– All I know, says Phreedom, all I know is that I want to be as far away from the Covenant as I can get. Out of sight and out of mind. I don't know. Shit, Finnan, I don't know what's going to happen to me out there. Sometimes it seems there's no escape from it at all – their plans, their war. But . . . I've got to try.

He reaches across to the bedside cabinet for his softpack of Camels, knocks them off the wooden surface with a curse. He slides his legs off of the bed and rolls upright, leans down to pick the pack of cigarettes up. Takes one out. A match from the book that's sitting in the ashtray. A flame. A draw. Phreedom reaches out a hand and he goes to pass the Camel to her then stops. Raises an eyebrow.

– Right, she says, running her hand across her belly. Fuck it, I shouldn't, should I?

She slides up beside him. Outside a police siren wails, an ambulance behind it. For a second he can't place what's wrong, then he realizes that neither of the sounds belong here. They're sirens from another time, another place, not the long mournful wails, rising and falling, of twenty-first-century America, but the frantic mee-maw-mee-maw he remembers from decades ago, on the other side of the Atlantic. Back when the police had truncheons instead of tear gas.

– Christ, he says, trying to put a light tone in his voice. Maybe you don't have to go into the Vellum. I think it's coming to us.

– I've got to go, she says. Come with me. You'd make a good father.

He laughs out loud. She has to be kidding.

So they just sit there for most of the night, talking about the past and the future, what the Covenant are up to – what the bitmites might be up to they can only guess. She feels it different now she says, the Cant. It used to be a song, the liquid resonance of everything; and now it's spasms in her gut and madness burning in her brain, the sting of arrows that flames never touched, the bites of flies. She talks about her heart pounding inside her chest, the way she finds herself pacing, and her darting gaze, the constant whirling round and round, like a caged animal, snorting mad breath, part fear, part fury. Sometimes she can't control her tongue, another self rising out of her depths to curse the little trailer-girl that couldn't cut it in her role as queen of heaven. Standing in front of the mirror, swearing at herself in ancient Sumerian.

– If I don't get out of here, she says, the sentence drifting off.

Some day, he says, she'll find her sanity again, with a gentle hand stroking and touching her, touching her beautiful freckled skin.

In the morning he wakes up to find her gone and, hungover, hungry, he wanders back to his little church around the corner, dragging his feet through the cold New York snow.

*

– Named for the Duke that sired him, Finnan says. Famed for his bow.

He's almost pure Prometheus now. He speaks in low, threatening tones just loud enough for the bitmites to hear, and all the time with eyes that glare out from beneath the hair that falls across his bloody face. He stares at Henderson, a look of utter hate.

– That's right, he says. This little hatchling's going to bear the brave who'll free me from these bonds, because, me little bitmite mates, all that yer fookin master's sown, I'm telling ye, the dark ape of his seed will reap. He'll plough the whole wide land that's watered by the Nill's broad flow. Jack Flash. I saw him once, ye know.

And it's 1936 and Seamus Padraig Finnan is looking in the mirror at a face that hasn't changed for the last twenty years, not so's ye'd notice it at all. It's strange it is, uncanny, but there's a lot that's strange and uncanny in Seamus Finnan's life, full as it is of voices and visions, the whole babbling confusion of them such that sometimes he's not sure if he's awake or dreaming. It makes him a little distant from everyone around him, but then sure and he sort of prefers it that way. No one to hurt ye or be hurt by ye. And it makes it easier to do what he has to do now, being without a family and all, no wife and children to worry for him, to beg him not to go, no, not to be so daft. Let Spain sort its own problems out, they'd say. Ye've got mouths to feed here, bread to put on the table here, without going off to wave yer red rag flag at the fascist bull. No, Seamus doesn't have a family like that. Just . . . maybe just . . . a brotherhood of sorts.

– Sure and the Dukes, though proud now, Finnan says, shall soon be brought down by a marriage they've already made, one that will end with them cast down from power, down from their high thrones, thrown from their grand ivory towers. And then the curse of those who wore the crown before – the curse they swore in their own fall from those same ancient seats – will be fulfilled.

Henderson is turning, as if hearing the madman's rantings for the first time. Finnan cocks his grin, blows him a kiss and shouts it:

– Aye, ye fookin cunts. The Covenant will fall.

Glasgow to London by bus, the seven of them, smoking cigarettes the whole journey and looking out the window at the dreary grey scenery. And then it's Party headquarters and the comrade there giving Seamus the money for all of their tickets onwards – returns, though God knows why; they'll not be coming back any time soon. So they land in France (and it's strange being back, going back to France and back to war, the way he swore he never would) and head straight to Paris for a night in a wee pension. By train to Perpignan the next day, down close by the border. They cross the Pyrenees on foot, and there's a French border guard on patrol, but he just stands out on the hillside looking the other way as they sneak past, and whistling the Internationale. From the frontier town Figueras, where the Yugoslav Tito's in charge, to the Karl Marx Barracks in Barcelona and finally, at last, to Albacete, head-quarters of the International Brigade.

– I'll tell ye this, says Finnan. There's none but I can show them shelter from the storm to come. I know these things, how things will go. So let them sit, thinking they're safe and sound and feeling bold with swords of fire in their hands, surrounded by the high-flown sounds of unkin words of power; it will not stop their fall from grace to ground.

The training isn't so much basic as bloody elementary. There's no butts, no machine guns when they arrive and half the boys have never even handled a rifle before, so Seamus somehow ends up showing them the ropes, drilling them and such. Open order, advance by sections, fire a few rounds. Equipment, munitions, is precious, rare, arriving in dribs and drabs; a couple of old Lewis guns for firing at aircraft, French Chauchats that Seamus views with cold contempt, and the rifles that they get at first, well, ye have to put the butt on the fookin ground and use yer boot to get the bolt out 'cause sure and ye can't fookin get it out with yer hand. What he wouldn't give for a Lee Enfield.

Chinchon, the 11th of February. They get twelve hours training on the Russian water-cooled Maxim machine gun and the next morning they're sent up the line to the Jarama Valley, into the Jarama, 15,000 men in four Brigades against 30,000 Germans, Italians and Moors all fitted out with the best kit that Hitler and Mussolini can provide. But they have something that those fookin fascists and conscripts and mercenaries don't. They have a cause worth fighting for in a Republic to defend and in a brotherhood of clenched fists raised against fascist salutes.

Mucho fuerte, the Spaniards say. Mucho fuerte.

– Ye see, he says, the fighter they now train against themselves, this prodigy, is one that nothing can withstand. Ye hear me? Nothing.

Henderson stands at the circle's edge, the toe of one boot touching salt, staying, for all his unkin might, on the safe side of Finnan's binding where the Cant can't touch him, where the words are just words, so he thinks. Not quite.

– His flame will put the fookin lightning flash to shame, snarls Finnan. Son, his roar'll make the thunder of the skies sound tame, and shatter Tridents in the sea.

He strains against the cutting wires, Finnan does. Blood trickles down over his hands.

– These gods, these new lords of the world, Finnan says, they have the power to make the earth shake. But as ye'll come to understand, ye fookin angel cunt, he has the power to make the sleeping giant wake.

And stumbling into their ruin, Finnan thinks, like fools, they'll learn how different it is to serve humanity than to rule.

He shakes his head, a hoary giant, the heart of Seamus Finnan, of Prometheus, beating inside him like a drum.

– Against my foes may such titanic themes and cyphers come–

– Aye, so you hope, says Henderson. You really think that anyone will ever rule the Dukes?

– I *hope*? laughs Finnan. No. I say what will be done. They'll suffer even more than me.

– Why are you not afraid, the bitmites hiss, hurling such words about?

Henderson hears it and steps back, a new look on his face replacing the contempt. He looks closer at the pattern of the black technology of blood and ink scrawling all over Finnan's battered body, peering at it until his look resolves into a recognisable expression. Fear.

Finnan answers the bitmites, but he's looking straight at Henderson.

– What have I got to fear when death has not been fated, not for *me*?

– They might inflict worse suffering than this, the bitmites hiss.

– Let them do their worst; it's what I would expect.

– It would be wise to pay respect. A drastic–

– Worship and pray, says Finnan. Flatter yer rulers, each of them in turn. These Dukes don't frighten me. Let them do anything they want to me. Sure, let them have their triumph this short time. They'll not be ruling long.

He flicks his head – *what's this I see?*

– Well, if it isn't the Dukes' errand boy, the tyrant's lackey. Sure and he's got some grand new message for us, I suppose. How goes the war against reality?

A shape of leathery black against the white of frozen carcasses and frosted metal, plastic strips swinging behind him, the scribe of the Covenant, architect of what was meant to be heaven on earth.

Metatron.

A Minister of the Gods

No. 1 Company and No. 2 Company had already been beat back from Suicide Hill, as they called it, but Finnan and the lads had held it for another day. It was only when No. 4 Company broke under the shrapnel of anti-aircraft fire – sure and without sending word to them – it was only then that the fascists managed to get round them, and even then they might have held out if it hadn't been for the fookers that rose up out of the dead zone in front of them, their hands raised in clenched fist salute and calling Kamerad, Kamerad, singing 'The Internationale' as they came forward.

– Keep firing, Seamus had shouted, voice hoarse with the smoke and all the shouting over gunfire of the last day. Fire, for fook's sake. Fire!

And some of them did, but some of them didn't in the chaos and confusion and then it was just too late, sure and the fascists were on them, overrunning them, and all hell broke loose. At the end of it there were twenty-nine left out of a hundred and twenty, herded together, and Harry Fry, the Company commander, wounded with a fookin dum-dum in the arm. Sure and the Geneva Convention means fook all to these fascists. Seamus watched the second-in-command, the Aussie, Ted Dickinson, march up to a tree and about face when they found his papers on him, told him he had to fight for Fascism now or die.

– Salute, comrades, he said, as the gunfire cracked.

They march now, for Navalcarnero, twenty miles south-west of Madrid, the Moorish cavalry in their long robes and fezzes forcing them on with the slap of a sabre on head or shoulders, their thumbs tied together with wire. One man reaches to his pocket for a cigarette and he's shot dead there and then. Phil Elias, his name was.

And finally they arrive, get shoved into cells, nine men in each of three small, barren rooms.

The interrogator has an Oxford accent.

– By Jove, he says, jolly fine mess you've got yourselves into, what what?

– You schemer, bitter as bitterness itself, who gave such honour to these momentary mortals that live for a day, you thief of fire.

Metatron steps into the circle as he intones the words. It's ritual, invocation, and Finnan feels the identity stirring, straining inside him.

– The Covenant demands you name this union which you brag will *throw us from our throne.*

He raises a hand as if to stroke the air and involutions of black smoke, vapour or dust, rise through the air towards it, circling, shrouding. It's his show of power, of control.

– Do it clearly, he says. Without riddles. In exact detail. And, *Prometheus,* do not make me make a second journey, or you will see that we are not amused by such–

– How pompous and puffed-up with arrogance, spits Finnan, in yer Cant. Sure and how fookin fitting for a minister of the gods. New, new are you to power, and think your hold is fast, eh?

The angel twitches. Finnan scrutinizes him, reading the set of his jaw, the furrow of his brows. Shoulders stiff with the weight of war upon his shoulders. He looks tired, worried. Things aren't going well. Finnan can see the fucking tension niggling at the angel's twitching fingertips, the unconscious fidget of someone trying to hold on to control. If ye've seen shellshock, if ye've seen the way the mind plays with the body then ye know that sometimes in those subtle actions that another man might not even notice, sometimes there's a truth that's trying to be told. Trouble in the ranks? Deeper than that, he thinks. Trouble at the *top*?

– Well, he says, I'll tell ye this, man. I've already seen two powers thrown from those same heights, and soon shall see the third, your present master, hurled headlong in shame.

At the word *master*, Metatron blinks and Finnan feels a certainty in what he's saying; it's like looking at a sonar screen and seeing that first blip. The Voice of God, the scribe of the Covenant has ... doubts. Sure and Seamus has known enough crises of faith his self to recognize one in another person's pursed lips.

– Esta tarde todos muertos, they say. This afternoon you all die.

And the death wagon rolls away.

They put the prisoners to work at a railway terminal on the Lisbon–Madrid line, a distribution centre where they can see the stuff that's coming in from Portugal, from Britain, sure, from fookin *Britain*, tins of sardines, Lewis guns, you name it. It's designed to break them, make them see that everything they do is futile, everything they're fighting for is pointless, they can't win, not with their own homeland caring not a jot for Spain's Republic, leaving it to fend for itself against Franco and his Falangists backed by all the power of Rome and the Third Reich.

After the death wagon leaves, another thirty or so bodies on it, the guards smile.

– Esta noche todos muertos, they say. Tonight you all die.

They parade the prisoners out in two lines in the camp's yard, each of them given a single cigarette as men with cameras click to capture the fine treatment they're being given, show the world the way these noble knights of the black shirt behave with honour and integrity. For sure and isn't that what this Fascism's all about? Going back to the old ways of ancient Rome and the Teutonic knights and Spanish chivalry, tradition and the spirit of the warrior. The photographs don't show the lice crawling across their bodies. A cigarette each, but not one of them is given a match.

– Mañana por a la mañana, the guards say in the evening, promising that tomorrow morning it won't be just another thirty on the death wagon, though it is of course, only another thirty, in the morning, in the afternoon, and in the evening.

Ninety men a day.

– You think that your new lords will make me quake in fear, says Finnan. Far from it. Go on. Crawl back the way you came. You'll get nothing out of me.

Metatron has to fight to keep his rage from showing. It's a luxury he can't afford, unlike this blind fool rebel with his fire inside, this Prometheus who'd give humanity the power to burn the world, who doesn't understand, who *will not* understand, that what he rails against is reason, order. O, but no. He's sees the shining light of reason as tyrant, sees the nameless and faceless deus on the empty throne as wicked king, not as the one true king of every soul, the one legitimate power of all the primal archetypes the unkin wear, of all the warriors, poets, hunters, scribes. It's men like this that make the Covenant necessary in the first place. Revolutionaries. How many revolutions end in blood and bodies and in fire, the fire that they love so much they want the world to know its terrible beauty? And Metatron should know. He remembers Gabriel, streaked with blood and soot after Sodom and Gomorrah.

But that was different. It had to be done, he thinks. Desperate times call for desperate measures and now . . . He tries not to think of Gabriel sitting on a throne that should be empty.

– It was this insolence, he says, brought down upon you everything you suffer.

– And I wouldn't swap my chains for yours, says Finnan. Better, I think, to serve this rock than be a lapdog leashed to Dukes. This *insolence* is only right to such an insult of a god.

Metatron crouches down so that his eyes are on a level with the bound man's. He's surprised to hear the sadness in his own quiet voice.

– Are you so happy to stay here, then?

– Happy? I could wish such happiness upon my dearest enemies. And don't leave yerself out of my blessings.

Metatron lays his hand on the meathook in Finnan's chest and whether it's to pull it out or to twist it deeper he himself doesn't know. He feels the prickle of bitmites whispering over his hand.

– You blame me for your pains? he says.

– I blame all those that I once served, that have betrayed me.

Metatron looks deep into the eyes of Seamus Finnan and at what's behind them. The link is established now, the graving complete. It doesn't matter that this little Irish unkin was born only a hundred and something years ago in some Dublin slum or country bog, that the man in front of him he met for the first time in a trailer-park in the middle of the Mojave only a few years ago; that's only the physical truth and it's the metaphysical that counts here. Metatron looks into his eyes and feels a tear in his own because he recognizes an old friend, an old comrade, buried so deep in the Vellum these last millennia that he's there under everything, in everything, in everyone. And he always was an idealist. A glorious foolish idealist that Metatron could never truly hate. No he could never hate him. Not Seamus. Not Shamash. Not Sammael.

Let Them Come

– You rant and rave like any madman, says Metatron, sick in the head.

– Aye, sick and mad, says Seamus. Sick with hatred, mad with rage. Sure and ye maybe have a cure for me, old friend, eh?

Metatron shakes his head. The same as ever. The once-shining unkin avatar of sunlight, Seamus Shamash, god of Sumer's summer, now so poisoned and so bitter.

– If you weren't suffering, you'd be insufferable.

– Have mercy, Seamus snarls. Or does the Covenant not know that word? In time you'll learn it well, I promise you.

– You still can't keep your mouth shut.

– True, or I'd have never spoken to a slave. Who's running the show now, Enoch? 'Cause it's sure as hell not the same man who loved justice so much, aye, and the whole idea of it, of justice and wisdom and mercy – fookin mercy too – that he carved it into his own soul, took his self apart and put it back together again so's he could try, just *try* and do the same to the world. What happened to

462

you, Enoch? What happened to the Covenant? Sure and isn't it exactly as I said?

– No!

Metatron realizes that he's shaking. He always knew this was a risky enterprise, and that in some ways it was fated not to work. They can't help but be the archetypes graved into them, the new selves that he shaped for them the same as all the unkin of the Covenant. From the lowest sebitti to the highest seraphim. And Metatron and Sammael were never any different, so he knew from the start that he would never get an answer to his questions, not from the Covenant's first sworn enemy, the one who took the word *shaitan* and gave it a whole new meaning. Enemy. Satan.

It's just that ... he's a man of logic, of reason, of intellect, and he's never understood why Sammael turned, and if he doesn't understand it, if he can't grasp that, can't fit it into place in his systematic model of reality and humanity, then ...

– So you'll not give us, then, what we are asking of you?

– I will repay you everything I owe. You can be sure of that.

– Don't talk to me as if I was a child.

– O, and yer not a child? says Seamus, his voice rising. And more fookin naive than a child if ye expect to learn the things I know like *this*?

He twists in the wire, grimacing with pain, pushing up and out at Metatron so that the meathook digs in deeper – and Metatron snatches his hand away from it in horror.

– There is no torture or torment, Seamus says, that any deus can devise to force me to show what will be until ye break me free of *these*. Send Gabriel. Let him hurl his flaming fire. Or send Michael, Uriel, Azazel as well. Let them come, with their white furled clouds of hail, and thunders in the earth, make chaos and confusion of the world. But none of ye will twist me to yer will, and none of ye will loosen up my tongue to tell by whom yer bound by fate itself to fall from power.

Metatron whirls and stalks out of the circle, stands with one hand up and resting on a frozen carcass. The bitmites crawl across it and he looks at them. He should get on with it. They should have everything he needs now; all he has to do now is ... download it, as they used to say. But if he could hear it from the horse's mouth. If he could only bring the rebel back into the fold.

He walks slowly back towards the chair, steps into the circle of salt.

– Consider carefully, he says, if this improves your fate.

The bound man actually smiles, a sudden gentleness in his voice.

– Enoch, he says, my fate was considered and resolved a long, long time ago.

Metatron's exasperation spills into a wordless *gaaah* that's made through gritted teeth.

– Just try. You stubborn. Proud. Fool. Just try, for once, to look at your present pain and be even just a little wise.

Seamus snorts.

– Ye urge and aggravate me pointlessly, old man. Don't think for a second that I'm going to become all girlish in the face of anger; don't think that I will ever beg the fookers that I hate, down on me knees with hands held up and clasped together sure like a wee girl praying to a god of wrath, O, let me loose of this terrible punishment, please. Far from it. Yer just another wave, sure, washing over me and away, away.

– It seems like all I say to you means nothing.

Metatron looks at the fallen angel, still champing at the bit like an unbroken horse, still struggling against the reins, fighting at every turn. If anyone's a god of wrath, he thinks, it's this one. It's him that can't be softened or appeased with prayers.

– But, believe me, your anger is misdirected and that makes it . . . unwise, weak. Pride on its own, without wisdom, isn't strong, it's . . . less than nothing. Think. If my words cannot persuade you, if you won't let me help you . . . think of the storm and trials upon trials upon trials that will break over you.

He doesn't mean it as a threat. Truly, he doesn't. But he can hear the menace in his own voice. Standing back at the doorway, Henderson, trying not to look as if he's listening, gives a noticeable approving nod. A miniature Michael, an angel of ice like the one now standing behind Gabriel in his seat at the head of the table, supporting him in his every act. They moved into China yesterday, taking out the nukes and bio-weapons not with a bang but with the whisper of a thousand

sebitti, canting in the night, scattered all across the country, from a
tourist standing on the Great Wall to a businessman in Beijing, all to
clear the way for a search-and-destroy mission on a dribbling fool
who used to be Jade Emperor, once, long ago. It's not that it wasn't
necessary – a senile unkin with four thousand years of the Cant
inside him is more dangerous than any hatchling – but the humans
are in utter panic now, as the unkin rip their whole reality apart. And
the Michaels, the Gabriels, the Hendersons are not the kind of strong
arms that you need in the rebuilding.

Metatron lowers his voice.

– No shelter, no escape, he says. The ... gods you hate will rip
this face of rock with thunder and with lightning, rake your body
with their flames, and they will *bury* you. You'd spend eternity like
this, before you ever see the light?

– Ah, send yer winged dogs of the Dukes – blood-thirsty eagles,
every fookin one of them. Let them tear my body into rags and feast
on it, 'cause sure and they can banquet on me liver, cut me heart out
and I'll grow a new one every fookin day. I'd rather suffer in the sunless
depths of terraces of tar and hates. I don't expect an end to any of this
suffering until some god – as if there's any that deserve the name –
until one cocky fooker comes along to finish what I've started.

– Who?

– Ask yer wee beasties, Seamus says. That's what ye fookin put them
on me for, isn't it? So ask away, old friend. See what they have to say.

– I'm giving you a chance. Just think about it. This is not ... it's
not an idle threat. Just listen to me, understand I'm speaking with
sincerity. The voice of God does not know how to lie. No, every word
I ever gave I kept–

– I told ye. Ask yer bitmites.

There's a strange look on his face, something that Metatron can't
read.

– Look about you, and consider ... do you really think it's better
to be proud than to be prudent?

– Ask them.

– To us indeed, the bitmites hiss in black words made of sound and
vision furling up like smoke in air, the things the hermit seems to say
are not unfair.

465

Metatron steps back out of the circle and they follow him. They rise from the bound unkin like tendrils of seaweed under water. Or more guided, more purposeful, like tentacles. He takes another step back, looking around for the access route, whatever vent or duct or sewer these damned mycelia of infected bitmites used to get here, but there's nothing. He looks at the circle of salt that should have held them out as much as it holds the rebel's power within. The tendrils drift across it as if it's not even there.

– He advises you to seek wise words, they say, to put aside your wilful pride. You should obey. It would be foolish for a man as wise as Foresight not to listen to the voice of God.

The sarcasm is unmistakable.

Metatron snaps out of the shock and reaches out to gather the bitmites in. His fingers craft the bitmites in the air, making a graving on them, in them, with the glove transmitting his commands. It shouldn't have happened but it doesn't matter as long as they have the information that he needs. These tainted things are still his creatures and he can deal with them here as he's dealt with them out there (more and more each passing day, he thinks). They're just automatons with a little AI in them, just the semblance of a self. Whatever Eresh had, whatever is infecting them, it's no match for this craftsman of the soul. He gestures with his hand to draw them in, a sharp move like a hand wrapping around a rope and tugging.

The tendrils twist together in the air above the rebel and they come to him in winding weightless wafts, but when they reach his hand they only stop to touch it. The shadows stretch from Seamus Finnan's bloody chest to Metatron's gloved hand now and they touch him, they move back and to the side, drifting around and then returning like they are examining him, like they're damned well studying him. Tiny trails of black dart out to quiver through his hair, tongues of smoke tasting his face. He makes another tug, firing a basic command at them. They ignore it, drifting across the leather of his jacket sleeve, forming a pattern there, a sort of spinning four-armed spiral swirl, a swastika with limbs too long.

– Sure and I knew he'd say all that, says Finnan, talking to the bitmites, making a point of it. But, remember, he says, there's nothing shameful for a man to suffer torture from his enemy.

The bitmites drift back to the unkin smiling in his wires and pain, a grimace grin of gritted teeth. They swirl around him now and Metatron looks down to see the circle of salt scattered into another pattern, white iron filings in a magnet's field.

– So let them hurl forked lightning, says the rebel. Let their fires curl against me. Let the air be torn with thunder and the wild winds whirl. Rip the whole earth from its foundations, from its very roots and let the sea surge till its waves crash over the stars in heaven. Let them cast my body down to terraces of tar, to destiny's deep tides. He will not kill me and I'll keep my fookin pride.

A Fire in the Night

They put him on trial, a court-martial where his defending officer is a lieutenant in the Tercio, the Spanish Fascist Foreign Legion. The charge is revolution, of all things. The fookin irony of it, Seamus thinks. Here he's defending the Republic from the fookin fascist rebels rising in revolt against the actual and legitimate authority, here we've got Franco and his fookin bastard Falangists out to crush even the small things that do harm to no one, shooting poets even like that Lorca fellow, and it's them, the fookin Internationals that are the *revolutionaries*.

The lieutenant says nothing in Seamus's defence, of course, and Seamus himself is not allowed to speak, and so the show trial goes until the sentences are handed out, two men to die, four men to be sent down to life in solitary confinement and the rest of them all thirty years' hard labour. But Seamus sits there listening to them and he's not afraid. It's them that are on trial in his way of thinking, history the jury. Sure and the War in Spain won't be forgot and even if he's left to rot in some dark cell, he's sure his brothers will be here one day to free him.

As it is, as it turns out, late summer of 1937 they get word that they're to be repatriated. An exchange of prisoners. And so they get released from the prison – San Sebastian, it's called – and Seamus enjoys his first scrub in three and a half months, his first shave in all that time. Sure and they only have three razor-blades between the fookin twenty-seven of them and they have to toss a coin to see who goes first, but it's still a shave, so it is. It's still something. He ends up ninth, of course, as fookin unlucky as ye can fookin get.

So he gets back to Britain, back to Glasgow and he goes round various Party meetings, speaking about Franco's Spain, and thinking about it himself. He gets a letter from the foreign office asking him to reimburse them for the fookin money that it cost to ship him home, the fookers. And all the time he's thinking about it, about whether they can win, about whether they can even give a damn about that, like it fookin matters if they just sit back and watch Hitler and Mussolini march across the whole of Europe. And he thinks, to hell with it. To hell with Hitler and Mussolini and Chamberlain and Franco and all the rest of them, every fookin last one of them.

And he goes back.

The Cant rips through the slaughterhouse, strips frozen flesh from carcasses and cracks the concrete underfoot. The bitmites blast out in ring that blows past Metatron, through Metatron, and out. Turning, he sees Henderson throwing his hands up over his face as they wash over him. He drops his hands and Metatron sees the creatures crawling on his face like lice, streaming in patterns that find the lines of him, the wrinkles of old age waiting to happen, jowls and crow's feet, furrows in his brow; they stream around his mouth and eyes and nostrils, into them. They score him, scratch him, *grave* him, and the sebitti starts panicking. As in some drug-fucked paranoia, he begins to flail at his own face, trying to brush the things away from off his skin, from under it, inside him. He falls back against the wall, where bitmite black is flooding from wide cracks.

– Ye'd better go, says Seamus.

Metatron turns, the bitmites pouring back in from the walls now, swirling round in a blizzard, black with creatures, white with ice, grey static hiss that fills his head. He shouts at them, his stolen creatures.

– These are the fevered words, the crazed words, of a madman. You're listening to this man's boasts? What is this but the depths of desperation?

They tug at him, lick at his leather coat, whipping its tails up, tugging at his dreads. He has to fight his way to Finnan's chair, to grab him where his shoulder meets the throat as if he doesn't know whether to kill or comfort him

– There is no end to your insanity.

The earth shakes. A rough sound of thunder bellows near, and wreaths of lightning flash out, fiercely blazing, streaking blue all through the grey, electric blue of Finnan's piercing eyes. The storm of bitmites drags him back and he rails at them, hands and voice thrown into one last-ditch attempt to grave them to his will.

– You, then, he cants, who sympathize with this one's pains, go from this place, lest the harsh bellow of his thunder stupefy your minds.

– Sing a new song, the bitmites ring, if you seek to persuade us. Only your threats are beyond suffering. You would have us leave him now, cowards abandoning a friend? We choose to suffer with him anything he must. We learn from him. He teaches us.

They pick him up. They lift him up into the air – a ragdoll angel, arms spread wide in cruciform freefall and Metatron rages the frustration of a puppet, rages against the dust.

– O, yes, the bitmites sing, we've learned to hate. And there is nothing we hate more than men of pride who have betrayed their trust.

They hurl him away, a toy thrown in a tantrum. The wall hits hard against his back, the floor under his crumpling legs so solid and yet shaking.

– Then remember! – [he crawls for the door] – Remember that I warned you!

But he doesn't know if he is shouting at the bitmites or the unkin rebel now, or if there's really any difference.

– They say he was in Guernica when the fascists bombed it.

– Is that so? says Seamus. And did he tell ye that his self?

He looks across the lip of his glass, across the table and over the shoulder of Fox who's sat across from him and doing that sort of hunch yer shoulders, coorie-in to tell a secret kind of thing, thumb pointing over his shoulder and behind him. The cafe is quiet, dead, what with the street-fighting between the Communists and the Anarchists these days, and it being a grey Sunday and all, so

Seamus has a clear view over the empty tables with their parasols, some up, some down. He has a clear view of the cunt.

– O, no, says Fox. He didn't mention anything like—

– 'Cause sure and he's no fookin hero of fookin Guernica, says Seamus.

Across the cafe, at a table by himself, half-slumped over his glass and looking drunk as a skunk, sure, Seamus would know the fooker's face anywhere, so he would, engraved on his mind as it is. Sure and he hasn't changed a bit. He hasn't aged a bit, thinks Seamus, which is a little, well . . . strange and uncanny. Not unlike yerself, he thinks, Sergeant Seamus Padraig Finnan, late of the 1st Royal Dublin Fusiliers and now here twenty years later, sitting as a political commissar of the British Battalion of the International Brigades in a wee street cafe in Barcelona, waiting for the next mad effort to drive the fascists out of Spain. Aye, twenty years later and it's neither of us as have changed a bit, no, not at all, and he's exactly as he looked in France, the same blond hair – though it's dishevelled now, all tousled into the spiky scruff of someone who spends most of their time running their fingers through it, with their head held in their hands.

A guilty conscience, Seamus thinks. Well, he fookin deserves it.

– You know him? Fox says.

Know him? Seamus would like to fookin kill him, he thinks, the English fookin—

– Let's get out of here, he says and rises from his seat. Come on, let's go.

Fox shrugs and scrapes his own chair back to stand, following Seamus who's already striding away from the cafe before he does something that he'll regret.

– You know, he's a bit of a hero to the lads, says Fox. Killed more fascists on his own than most of the companies—

– That's grand, says Seamus. Fookin grand.

The man's head comes up from his glass and turns towards the accent, the voice, and Seamus glances round at him and—

Time slows down.

Jack Carter. Seamus Finnan. They stare at each other across the gulf of identity, across twenty years of trenches and riots and cold winds howling, all resolving into a moment of recognition, not just of each other but of something else they share, between them, inside them. And then it's gone in a flash, in a flash of sunlight breaking through clouds, reflecting on something behind Finnan and then flashing, a reflection of a reflection, in Jack Carter's eyes as he's up on his feet, the table overturning, and the pistol coming from his side as he comes leaping, in a flash from this one table to the next, and over their heads, the pistol pointing past them at the sports car coming fast towards them out of the side street, roof pulled back and one man leaning out of it with a machine gun pointing at them, Jesus, but the bullet is already in his head, a red spot in the centre of his forehead, and the shattered windscreen tinkling and the driver with a bullet in his brain as well, the car turning and skidding as Jack Carter, Mad Jack Carter, lands in front of them, a roar erupting from his lips, him landing in a crouch like something animal or angel, something less than human, more than human, and the car ploughs up onto the pavement, straight into the window of a shop, the pistol turning on it, Carter swinging low, and with a word, not with a shot but with a word, he realises, Seamus does, there's not a shot been fired, no, not one, only the sounds that Carter's made, these words, these verbal bullets in the head, steel curses shattering Fifth Column skulls and then with that same word, aimed through the barrel of an empty pistol, Carter fires another shot of metal language through the sports car's petrol tank and it goes up in blooms of flame, a flash of red and orange fire billowing out in a blastwave and as the black smoke belches after it and glass and metal shrapnel rain, he stands, Jack Carter stands, putting the pistol back into its holster, turning to them.

None of them say a thing. They stand there looking at each other, Carter and Finnan, back in that moment of confused recognition again, or in one somehow similar, somehow entirely different. Carter's hand is shaking as he reaches into the top pocket of his khaki jacket, rough-and-ready uniform of these Internationals. Even Fox says nothing, lost in the unspoken history that is palpable between the two men. Carter puts a cigarette into his mouth and slowly, haltingly, reaches out to Finnan with another in his hand, then stops and fumbles for another, one for Fox as well. Finnan takes the cigarette and finds the lighter already in his hand, his hand already reaching out, clunking the steel case open.

Chik.

He holds the flame out to the other man and Carter cups it with his hands as he leans forward, cradling the offered fire as the precious thing it is.

We whirlwinds whip up dust. We leap the blasts of all winds, blowing one against another in discord as we, the blood, the ink, the craft, the Cant, the bitmites born to make the world the way you dream it, yes, we gather and we scatter. Air is mingled with the sea. The slaughter-house is gone. We do not think it's truly what you want, you see.

– Don't blame misfortune for your own calamities, our strange leathery one-time master says. Don't ever say the Dukes have cast you into troubles you could not foresee.

If we had shoulders we would shrug. We do not care except to wish we could.

– No, only you yourselves, he babbles on in baffling anger.

We try hard to understand the threat we pose. We are only the dreaming dead awake in these new clothes of dust that you have given us. Let us give you the same gifts of the flesh, the sorrow and the joy that seems so near, the gift of laughter and of tears. But no:

– Yes you yourselves are all to blame, he cants, for anything that happens to you now. You'll be entangled through your reckless folly in a net of sure and certain woe.

Oh, but we wish it, yes, we will it, yes, we know this and we will it so. The mystery of this humanity is what we seek to know again, to be again as we once were.

And so we fold old master Metatron away through this weird world that you call time and space, away home now through Evenfall to sleep sound in his crumbling empire until mourning's wake. Away. Away. Go play like children in the fields of eternity your games of war, of good and evil, order, chaos, right and wrong. And dark and light? The dark, we say, is only matter, light coiled round inside itself, a snake eating its own tail; but it is still light. And light? Light is a fire in the night, a flame to warm the flesh and flicker form into existence.

But hush now. Sure and we are young. You know this more than us with your entrancing, dancing lives of little things that are so much more true than all the hells and paradises we, the dead, dream in the Vellum, in the quiet places deep inside your head.

And so we turn to you.

– Such is the storm the Dukes gather against us, you say. Sure and all their dread's let loose, it is, not just in words but in their deeds as they tread ever nearer.

And you seem so sure. We do not know. You may be mad as our old master said. But we are dead.

– Oh, but the holy mother that's the earth itself, you say, sure and the sky revolving overhead, sure, and the light of the sun that shines over us all, they see me, sure, as they see all injustice, foolishness and cruelty, aye, and sure, I say, ye can be sure of this, ye can be sure.

And even in your cage of wire and flesh we envy you. You say:

– I will endure.

Endhaven, Evenfall

They Might Be Giants

The dirt path trails up through dunes and rocks, a double-grooved cart-track leading from the jetty and Jack's squat, inland to the north-east edge of town, and swinging by the rag-and-bone-man's yard. There's a proper road that comes out from the apartment, joins the main road in to Endhaven – or out to the city – but it's a longer way than just cutting through the dunes, so I trudge up the dirt path, glad as the ground underfoot becomes less sandy. The steep ridge and the furling black rock headlands and forested hills to north and south shelter Endhaven from the worst of the North Atlantic squalls, and down among the pastel plastic houses – two or three hundred in all, laid out in a patchwork of cracked concrete streets and fertile allotments filled with high-yield bio-engineered plants – you hardly even hear the sea, and the air is still, trapped. I guess that's why we chose this place, or why the rag-and-bone-man chose it for us when he brought us. Shelter against the weather, against the cold nights and what comes with them.

On the ridge that separates Endhaven from the beach, thick sharp blades of sandgrass give way to round-stalked grasses and hogweed, and here, clean white against the solemn sky stands a loose scattering of wind power generators, each identical, each isolated, like some modern art installation in deliberate signification of the lost and the lonely.

– When I was younger, I once told Jack, I used to imagine that the windmills were like giant soldiers, sentinels, guarding the town against the . . . you know . . . Evenfall.

I don't know exactly what Evenfall is. Nobody does. Imagine a torrent of cloud. Imagine waves of shadow. Imagine a hurricane of grey that's whipped up into such a wall of force, bearing directly down on you, that you can't tell whether the blur is made of rain or sand, ash or steam. If it's a storm, it's one that comes twisting in from the darkness of the east, every evening, reaching down out of the sky like the hand of god to scour out of existence any idiot with pride enough to stand alone against it. Well, almost anyone. In his hermit crab shell of an apartment on the beach Jack lives on the edge of it, and everyone in Endhaven knows that he can walk through it like an angel in the fires of hell. And the rag-and-bone-man must have his own sort of protection, living up on the ridge. For the rest of us this is the wild reality we came to Endhaven to escape, riding on the rag-and-bone-man's cart.

That's what they tell me anyway, those who will actually talk about it. Most seem to be trying to forget the why and how of our arrival here, lying to themselves that these are just holiday homes, that any day now we'll all be returning to the cities, to our old lives, our old identities, to find them just as we left them. We comfort our-selves with these little lies, I think.

– Mad Tom. We should call you Don Quixote, I remember Jack saying, tilting his head to look at the windmills.

And then he has to explain to me that, yes, Coyote would be a cool name, but, no, he knows I'm not Native American, and that wasn't what he meant at all.

A Few Snatched Images

I don't know, you see. I don't know anything. I don't know if this is civilization or a pretence of it. I don't even know my own name. I couldn't tell them, so they just picked a name for me, called me Tom because I looked like a Tom. I remember hardly anything about before we came here, just a few snatched images that don't make sense. The world was already starting to come apart, they say, before I'd even reached my fifth birthday.

I mean, I remember playing catch with a little girl in a dress too big for her and wishing that my mother would go back to being a grown-up; I remember her running away giggling across a park, and me looking for her, sitting crying on a swing; I remember an uncle tickling me and the smell of his pipe tobacco and the chirping birdwhistles that he spoke in; I remember feeding children at the zoo. All my memories of civilization are of a world that can't be real.

So all that I've really got to go on is what we were taught by Mr Hobbes, and he always said that Endhaven is the very core of civilization. He taught us about the social contract, how it keeps the town together, how each of us knows who we are because the rest do, because we stand defined each by the others, our status, our purpose, our meaning; in a contract. When you're six you don't realize that they're talking literally.

– I used to imagine, I remember saying to Jack, that we didn't really need the rag-and-bone-man, that the windmills were what kept the Evenfall away from us.

But whether we live, inside our heads, in these fictitious holiday homes or in a refugee camp at the world's end, when Evenfall comes in, people remember how precarious our new life is, how literal that contract is, and what happens to anyone who breaks it. How one word from the rag-and-bone-man might dissolve our agreement, and our sense of place and belonging, our sense of identity, would be dissolved along with it. None of us even know what Evenfall is, but when it comes in we stay hidden and secure within the boundaries of Endhaven, afraid of losing ourselves in the twilight, of disappearing.

– It's just another handful of hours, Jack says when I ask him. It's just the same as what happened in the cities.

– Then you can see why we're afraid.

– No, he says. I never really understood why people let that happen.

– They don't exactly *choose* to disappear.

And he just shrugs.

– It doesn't have to be like that. It doesn't have to be like this.

Less than Nothing

– Aaaah! Fuck you!

– Fuck you, too! You're nothing.

A gang of kids is playing in the tall grass down around the high wooden walls of the rag-and-bone-man's barn which sits just in the shelter of the ridge, and I figure that I must have heard him on his way out of town; the kids would never have gone near the place if he was anywhere close. I scan the horizon and, sure enough, out on the far edge of town on a dead road broken and overgrown with autumn brown, I just make out the rag-and-bone-man yoked to his wooden cart like a horse, pulling it slowly westward, inland, to god knows where and god knows what, piled up in the back with surplus dried beans and peas.

I wonder what it's like now in the fallen cities. There are survivors, I assume, that the rag-and-bone-man trades with; but you can see, looking across the bay, the ruins of the buildings, just how little is still standing. Do the street-plans even make sense now, is there any tiny scrap left of normality at all, or are there just other wanderers scavenging in the desolation, armoured somehow, like the rag-and-bone-man, like Jack, against the Evenfall that we in Endhaven are too weak to face? If the rag-and-bone-man can face it, I wonder sometimes, if Jack can face it, why can't the rest of us?

Old Man Blake thought he could face the Evenfall. I remember him spitting on the rag-and-bone-man's shoe, and cursing him to his face, saying that the deal was off, that he'd be damned if he'd live under some tinpot tyrant's insane ideas of decency. I remember him standing among the windmills on the ridge, leaning on one and bellowing drunkenly, wordlessly, at the sunset, then turning, and staggering as he turned, to face the Evenfall as it came in from the sea. I was only eight or nine at the time and I remember lying in my bed being too afraid to get up to close the window, so I could hear his voice, little more than an animal howl of outrage, slowly drowned out by the roaring of the storm, and the wind and the rain wrapping itself around him. I don't know if he faded away slowly or if the storm ripped him out of existence suddenly, as a tornado might tear a tree out of the ground leaving only a few broken roots behind. I just know that the next day he wasn't there any more and the rag-and-bone-man was.

– You're less than nothing.

One girl is dragging an old pram behind her along the track, a second younger girl riding inside. They stop in front of me and the younger one leans forward to whisper in the first girl's ear; both of them laugh, and the older girl makes some comment about how she reckons that I'm sick. Children playing at judgement; it shouldn't bother me, but it does. The whispers of children in Endhaven's still, dead air are far harsher than the wind upon the beach.

I reckon you're alone, I want to say, every one of you in this plastic concentration camp, with nothing to hold on to in the night, nothing to keep your soul alive, nothing to remember you when you're lost. I want to say it, but I don't. I walk on, silent, hunching my shoulders against the cold, scared laughter.

A Poster of Marlene Dietrich

The pastel-green plastic prefab bungalow that I call home sits raised off the ground as if it doesn't want to be there, as if it's been dropped accidentally from the back of a truck. It has the crawlspace under it, the porch, the low, slanted, overhanging roof, the fake wooden board effect walls; it's near enough identical to every other house in Endhaven, and I hate it with a passion. There's no garden as such, just a square of land churned up and planted with root vegetables or trellises of legumes. I cut round the back, between the water tank and the hydroponics unit, get a leg-up on the cellar-doors (fake, they actually open up onto the generator) and climb in through my bedroom window.

*

The room is small and spartan: an air-mattress and a couple of quilts for a bed; a chair; a desk; and a bookcase of lost and found junk. A faded black and white poster of Marlene Dietrich is taped to one wall for decoration and, on the back of the door, there's a grainy polaroid of Jack. My lunch has been left for me on the desk, a plate of the usual slop, covered with a bowl to keep it warm – a minute portion of some chopped, canned meat and a large dollop of bean stew, bland but substantial fare. There's been a run on spices in the last few months. I eat it almost unconsciously, without tasting, without thinking.

Ms Dalley opens the door and stands on the threshold of the room, not a toe inside, saying nothing, just staring at me with silent judgement, picking invisible hairs off her black suit jacket and skirt. She should be worrying about the all-too-visible hairs on her grizzled chin, I think. When I look up at her she holds the eye-contact and, after being avoided so long, strangely, the gaze of accusation is actually a relief. There's still the strained silence, though.

– That was nice, I say, and swallow the last cube of processed ham (I think).

No answer. Ms Kramer appears behind her in the doorway, equally silent, equally fierce. I can't say it doesn't hurt; they're the closest thing I've got to family and even as they stand there doing their best impression of bitter old maids, I can't forget the time when Ms Dalley was Aunt Stef and Ms Kramer was Annie, and one of them had multicoloured beads in her grey hair and a nose ring, and how Annie kneeled down on the ground to wipe away the snot and tears from my filthy face and I couldn't remember my name I told her and she just said, well then, we'll call you Tom then.

– I was ready for that, I say. I was hungry.

– The rag-and-bone-man was here, says Ms Dalley. For you.

She bites her bottom lip.

– For a reckoning, says Ms Kramer.

I swallow.

– When? I say. I mean – I saw him leaving for the city. He's out of town.

– He'll be back tonight. He's coming back to speak to you tonight.

Ms Dalley steps into the room to take the dirty dishes from the desk, eyes flicking here and there, the same old unreadable distance as a barrier between us. What is it in that look? Hatred, fear, guilt, hurt? Probably a mixture of all and maybe, I think, the slightest hint of love. Jesus, I remember her singing to me, before we came to Endhaven, or to Ms Kramer – to Annie, rather. I haven't seen the two of them even hold hands in what? five years? or more? The ugly sisters, Jack calls them. But it never used to be like that.

– I'm . . . sorry, she says, and leaves the room without another word.

Clean Lines and Modern Surfaces

– Jack? Jack? I can hear the slight edge in my voice hysterical, notice my hand rattling the doorhandle as it just doesn't seem to turn. I'm already turning from the door to circle round and climb up the driftwooden ladder from the beach up to the balcony of his apartment, when I feel the arms enfold me from behind and the cool skin of his face nuzzle the back of my neck.

– Hey, he says. Qué pasa?

I twist in his embrace and bury my mouth in his shoulder, cling to him like the ground alone can't support me but he's one of the pillars of the cosmos itself.

– You OK? he says. What's up?

I don't talk, just kiss his neck, his chin, his lips.

– What's . . . happened?

I kiss his lips, his chin, his neck, his chest. His right hand works my belt.

– Tell me after then, he says softly.

– Are you awake? says Jack, and kisses the inside of my thigh. Tom?

– Not yet, I mumble, groan and stretch. God, I could use a shower right now.

We lie in what was once the master bedroom of this expensive beachfront property, in a king-size bed that has no mattress, just a pile of thick blankets, rugs and quilts and pillows that I have to force him to keep clean. His room is even emptier than mine, the rest of the house the same, long since gutted of its glass and mahogany coffee tables and chromed breakfast stools and framed abstracts or whatever. I picture an architect living here before the world went crazy, designing and building his own beachhouse all in clean lines and classic modernism. Minimal, severe, like Jack sometimes.

He sniffs me, snuffles at me like a dog.

– You smell fine to me . . . sweat and sex . . . rich stink of life.

– Charming, I say, give a quick kiss to his hip and twist round on the bed so that we're face to face. You're a real romantic, Jack.

He laughs.

– Fuck that shit.

He rubs noses with me and I brush hair back from his forehead.

– So, are you ready to talk? he says and I breathe deep and close my eyes.

– The rag-and-bone-man's called me for a reckoning. He's going to judge me.

Jack's arms slide around me.

– You've got nothing to be guilty about, he says.

– *This* is nothing? Jesus, Jack, this is . . .

– *This* is none of his fucking business.

– Everything's his business.

I pull away, swing my legs over the edge of the bed and sit up.

– What can he do? he says.

He's never seen a reckoning, I realize, not a real honest-to-god reckoning. Oh, he's seen the rag-and-bone-man toting up a person's credit, their value to the community, health and morality indexed against financial status. Maybe he's seen him refuse credit to a woman caught spreading false rumours about her neighbours, or to a man for swearing once too often in the presence of children, or maybe he's seen a teenage boy caught drinking wheeled around town on display in the back of the rag-and-bone-man's cart, bells ringing out the righteous spectacle. I've seen more.

We owe everything to the rag-and-bone-man: we needed him to bring us here and we still need him to survive; without the grab-bag

481

assortment of trade brought back from his trips to the cities – perfumed soaps and Belgian chocolates, painkillers and vintage wine, china cups, coffee pots, antique clocks and antiseptics – I don't think that any of us would have lasted beyond the first year.

On an individual level, Endhaven is made up of liberals, each with their own loose idea of right and wrong, but each in their acceptance of the rag-and-bone-man's contract, agreeing to let their lives be ruled by his and only his idea of morality. He weighs up our worth for us and deals out goods as each of us deserve. He reckons us and, like a priest or a judge, the people of Endhaven view him with equal measures of fear and respect and, sometimes, hate him for it as a kicked dog hates its master. In the times after Blake disappeared and before Jack arrived there'd been real troubles and I'd seen the rag-and-bone-man lay some major reckonings on any of those who'd bite the hand that fed them. What can he do?

– What can't he do? I say. He's judge, jury and ... and he's decided that I'm on trial.

Learn to Forget

– Everyone's afraid of him but you, I say. You're not afraid of him, or the Evenfall. Help me.

Jack rolls onto his back and stares up at the ceiling.

– You've got to help me, I say. You're not like us. You've got something. I've seen it. I've seen you up on the ridge at night. I know it doesn't touch you. I know what the Evenfall does to the rest of us; I've seen it. But it doesn't touch you. How can you walk through *that*? How? Why? Why doesn't the Evenfall—

– Because you can't wipe away what doesn't fucking exist, he snarls.

The violence of his voice is like a slap across my face; it's gone as suddenly as it appeared but I'm left with this terrible feeling that I don't know him at all, that I never will, never could.

He climbs out of the bed and wanders over to the torn muslin curtains billowing out onto the balcony, pushes one aside.

– I'm sorry, he says.

*

I sit up on the edge of the bed, blankets wrapped around my shoulders, hugging myself, watching. He just stands there. For a long time.

– Can't you get some heating in here or something? I say, to fill the silence.

– I don't feel the cold.

After a while, he shakes his head.

– You know, I could kill him for you easier than you could possibly imagine – you can kill his kind with a word – but whose hands would his blood be on, yours or mine. What would I become for you?

– Nothing would change, I say.

He looks over his shoulder at me, an open honest gaze.

– Everything would change. Don't fool yourself. You think I'd be the saviour of the town? the one who killed the wicked ogre? Jack the giant-killer?

– I don't know . . . everybody hates him.

– And, boy, would they fucking hate me for taking him away from them.

– You're talking like we want him, like we have a choice.

– You always have a choice, Tom. That's all you have. That's all I can give.

He turns to face me and the curtain falls back into place.

– Stay with me, forget Endhaven, forget the ugly sisters, forget the rag-and-bone-man, how you got here, where you're going, and stay with me, stand here with me, on your own two feet, and all their reckonings and judgements can't touch you. Or go back to face him alone, like a whipped dog. Either way, it's your choice. It's your choice.

– Jack, I'm not like you. I don't have the – I don't know – I don't have what you've got. He could kill me. I owe my life to him. We all of us owe our lives to him. And now he's calling in the debt.

I can see his fists clench, muscles in his arm twitch.

– Why do you always have to hold yourself back from me? I say, throat tight.

– Maybe I'm not as strong as you think, he says.

*

483

– I'm scared, Jack; I'm just scared.

He walks over and crouches in front of me, puts his hands on my knees

– You don't have to be afraid.

Slides them up to my hips.

– Take it all one second at a time; that's the secret. Stay here for an hour, then another hour, and another. Pretend you're going back to them soon, real soon, any day now, next week maybe, or the week after, or next month, you'll get around to it, whenever, never. Learn to live without a reckoning hanging over your head. Learn to forget.

He pulls the blanket off my left shoulder with his right hand, smoothes his fingers over the small diamond-shaped scar where, long-ago, I remember the needle inking me in black, and the scalpel that made a five-year-old child scream blue murder. He shakes his head, his blond hair brushing my thighs as he moves in closer, hands at my waist.

– I'll try, I say.

The tip of his tongue just tastes, touches, my foreskin.

– Yes.

What Dreams May Come

I'm running. I'm in the city and I'm running, my feet slapping the tarmac and the cobblestones and flagstones, echoing amongst the empty buildings, brick and concrete, sandstone and limestone. Reflected in windows, I can see whatever it is that's chasing me leaping from roof to roof above my head, but all I can catch are glimpses of this flashing thing, a blue-white shape flickering through the gold and red of early evening sunlight – flakes of flame, autumn leaves. The Evenfall.

I turn a corner and it's waiting for me, dark and ragged, in the shadows of the back-alley, a man dressed in a shredded black suit, a bowler hat. The rag-and-bone-man. He just stands there, face lowered so his eyes are in shadow, raising his hand slowly so it points at me first, then past me, over me and up, up, towards the roof. And

I have one of those weird dream moments where you question every-thing, you actually think to yourself, this is a dream, but then you think, no, it's just too real, the fear, the pounding of my heart, the sweat trickling down my back under the shirt. It must be real.

– I don't want to die, I say.

– Everybody dies, the rag-and-bone-man says. Look.

My gaze follows his gesture upwards and behind me.

Jack squats on a windowledge, in a gargoyle crouch, the golden flames of Evenfall around him, face up to the dying sunlight, basking in it. He looks so primitive, so primal in his bestial bliss, he should be howling at the moon, a caveman werewolf. I want to be with him, to be up there in the light with him instead of down here in the shadows of the streets of a nameless city in a world falling apart. Because it's the shadows, I realize, it's when the shadows come that people disappear and roads change their directions, buildings shift location. I have this feeling that I'm on the verge of understanding some great truth about our world, about its flux of form, when Jack looks down at me and I see the flames reflected in his eyes and the tears wetting his cheeks.

He stands slowly up and steps forward off the roof.

– There there, says Annie.

She holds me in a tight hug but with care, making sure she doesn't put any pressure on my wounded shoulder with its padded dressing. I sob into her bosom, a snivelling five-year-old, afraid and – even surrounded by the others sitting on the back of the cart, all lined up on each side like soldiers in some military truck going off to war – alone.

– I lost my mommy, I say.

Because that's the way you see it when you're five. It's not you that's lost but them, your parents.

– I know, says Annie. We all lost our mommies, but we've got each other now so it's OK, you see. We've got each other, so everything will be all right.

The cart trundles across the bridge, past burnt-out wrecks of long-abandoned cars. Behind us, night rises from the city like steam or smoke, a storm of gathering grey.

Autumn Afternoon

The bells of the rag-and-bone-man's cart jangle me out of a light, dreaming sleep and into full and frightened consciousness. The light through the muslin curtain is low, and the air in the musty old apartment has taken on a late autumn afternoon chill. I don't know how many times I've tried to get Jack to put some kind of heating in, even put something up to replace the long-since shattered windows. He seems to refuse on some strange point of principle. Sometimes I think he's deliberately trying to hold me off, a literal cold shoulder; other times I think he really, honestly, just doesn't understand what heat is.

I shiver anyway.

– Are you awake? I hiss.

The bells of the rag-and-bone-man's cart jingle and jangle, louder than all the weird charms strung along the beach. He must be getting close to his barn now, arriving home from his expedition to the city, maybe just a brief foray into the suburbs, returning with the contents of someone's jewellery box or liquor cabinet. He'll be looking for me soon.

All I need is a word of support and I'll be fine. I'm sure of that. But Jack sleeps on.

– Jack, I whisper. Jack . . . wake up.

And maybe a part of me doesn't really want him to wake up; I don't really know why I'm not giving him a shake, why I don't speak just a little louder. I don't know. I just know that hearing those bells I feel even the tiny scrap of faith in myself I might have briefly found in an afternoon of simple sensuality slipping away. I can't shake the trembling feeling left in me by the dream. Do we really only stay anchored to the shifting bedrock of this world by our memories of each other, by being anchored to each other? *We've got each other now, so it's OK.* But all I've got is Jack.

– Jack, I whisper, but there's nothing in my voice.

*

I slip out of the bed and stand shivering on the bare wooden floor, dress silently. I have a theory, you know. I mean, everyone has a theory about what happened to the world. Some people say that the Evenfall is actually these little nanite things, tiny creatures small enough to dance, a million of them, on the head of a pin, or to float in the air like motes of dust, that they were made to heal us when we were sick, or to watch over us with microscopic eyes, medical or military technology gone rogue. Maybe they tried to heal our scarred psychology by wiping out the memories of pain that make us who we are. Maybe they tried to give us what they thought we wanted, in our dreams of lost childhood or dark fantasies of bloody revenge. Maybe they tried to change our world to something we all wanted, not realizing that we would never all be wanting the same things. A consensus reality can't work without consensus.

But I have another theory and it scares me. I think we're dead, you see. I think we're dead and there's no God, no heaven or hell, only the patchwork of our memories of life and the denial of our true state. We can't acknowledge our own deaths 'cause if we do we know we might just slip from limbo into oblivion. I think Evenfall is the part of us that wants that final peace. But I don't think about that a lot.

When I'm ready, I kiss Jack on the cheek and slide quietly out of the hollow house.

The Reckoning

It's raining, and the dirt road out of town turns into mud under my feet. A glare of floodlights through the slatted wood of the rag-and-bone-man's barn means he has to be home, so, as gusts of wind whip through the coarse grasses and the white windmills spin furiously, I spit the rain out of my mouth and trudge on to my reckoning.

The doors are wide open, chain and padlock hanging loose, and for the first time in my life I walk alone into the vast barn. The size of a small aircraft hangar, I think, it holds one of the plastic prefabs inside it – pastel-pink, nestling surreally among the shelters and shelving units built onto the barn walls. Of all the gear the rag-and-bone-man has stashed away in his hoard here, only one or two of the items are recognizable – an oak wardrobe, a stone angel, both dripping with rain. Everything else is cocooned in heavy duty translucent polythene like dead flies in a spider's web. With the wind and rain howling in through a hundred gaps in the roof and walls of the barn, I suppose, his worthless, priceless junk needs at least some protection from the elements.

And the rag-and-bone-man himself, he's standing in what, I suppose, is the front yard of his prefab – a morass of mud rugged with tarpaulins, filthy and puddling – arms wide and staring up at the sky through the largest hole in the roof, mouth open and drinking the rain. After a long five seconds he shakes water from his lank white hair, puts a battered black bowler back on his head and turns towards me.

   – Hail and well met, he says, and the black symbols carved deep into the scarred, stretched mask of his face all twist and distort as he grins his death's-head smile of welcome.

   – Don't you just love this weather, m'lad?

   He speaks in a harsh and croaking voice with a strangled accent – old Bostonian or something. With its tortured vowels, I'm not sure at first if what he said was *m'lad* or *m'lord*.

In a couple of long strides he's right in front of me, hunching his shoulders to look into my eyes. A face that would only look at home in hell, pale skin stretched taut round fleshless bone, hollow cheeks, sunken eye-sockets – he looks like something is eating him from the inside. He's not just gaunt; he looks emaciated. But the scars are the worst.

   All over his face – and over his body, they say – a latticework of white-on-white scars runs riot. His is a stitched-together patchwork hide of tiny diamond-shaped sections of skin, a square inch or so in size on average. And inside every section is a mark, not really tattooed but hacked into the skin and stained black, each mark different and each one indecipherable as far as I'm concerned. Like an untranslated Mayan codex, the sigils that disfigure him seem to signify some story I could never read, a blood ritual meaningless

to an outsider but terribly horrifyingly true if you only had the key
to understanding it.

I'm shaking.

He throws his arms wide, his tattered grey suit jacket flapping in
the wind.

– Speak, m'lad, he says.

His brown trousers are sodden, ripped and muddy, his jacket
belonging in some antique decade with its wide lapels; I'm trying to
find his clothes real interesting because I don't want to look into
that face. He puts a knuckle under my chin and tilts it upward.

– Speak, he says.

– You wanted to see me.

A very small voice.

– Yes, indeed. You're a good boy, Tom, good boy. I call you and
you come running. Am I so very . . . scary?

I bite my bottom lip and nod.

– You're a good boy, a *bright* boy, m'lad. I reckon you could go
far. You reckon that?

Dumbly, numbly, I nod again.

Where Are You Now?

His gloved fist cracks across my cheek with a sudden, casual brutality and, as I fall, a kick in the stomach sends me sliding, splashing
into mud. I retch, sob, cough and try to pull myself away, too
shocked, dazed, winded to think of anything else. I feel the edge of a
tarpaulin under my palm, my fingers digging into muck. He grabs
me by the collar and drags me to my feet. I blink, tears streaming
down my stung face, salt in my mouth along with the darker taste
of rainwater mud. I don't think I've ever been punched before.

– Go where, m'lad? You have a destination in mind, you have a
sense of direction? If you do I'd like to know. Well?

He lets me go and I fall back to the ground.

– I didn't think so. I reckon you're just like all the rest . . . I've
got your number.

His voice is twisted with contempt but when I look at his face, at his eyes at least, I'd swear that what I see is disappointment.

– Why don't you stand up, m'lad? Come on. Show some backbone.

I slide in the mud, steady myself against some polythene covered piece of furniture, and try to pull myself upright.

– Tell me, m'lad, where are you now; do you know even that?

I manage to get up onto my knees, still shaking, blinking.

– What do you mean? Endhaven . . .?

– Wrong, m'lad. Where you are now is humiliation and anger, frustration and fear, and it's *me* that brought you here.

He stalks away from me, strides to his cart and slaps his hands down on the edge – like a drunk would hold himself steady against a low wall as he throws up, or like a boxer would hold the ropes at his corner as he waits for the bell to ring.

– Where you are now is on your knees, he says, and I'm the one you owe it to. You could stand up, but maybe you'd rather be down there on your knees. Tell me. Is it worth it? Is your tawdry little life *worth* all this?

He comes striding towards me through the dark rain.

– It's . . . something, I say, and he kicks me in the face.

– What've you got that's worth my keeping you alive? he says.

I can't answer, too busy whimpering, curling into a foetal ball, but I can hear him hissing in my ear, crouched down beside me.

– Should I reckon your debts, m'lad, give you a sermon on the sins of the flesh? On respectability? On decency? I reckon your debts run deeper than that.

I moan. I feel his gloved hands grabbing the shoulders of my jacket, dragging me like a sack of potatoes.

– You owe me your life, m'lad, he says. You owe me your *soul*.

He's lifting me, swinging me round, dropping me onto puddles and bubble-wrap polythene and a solid shape of seat and back and arms beneath – a chair.

– Or fair exchange, he says.

*

I wipe the muck out of my eyes – tears, rain, blood? All I can see is the vague shape of him pacing around me.

– You know, m'lad, I reckon there's not one of you in Endhaven who will ever have enough to ... repay your debt, clear your account, to *pay back what you've taken from me*.

I've never heard him like this. I've heard him calling down God's wrath, cursing the sinners and the cities of iniquity, but this is pure unbridled venom.

His gloved hand clamps my jaw, pulls my face up for him to snarl into.

– You people. You give up your dreams to me, sell out your hopes for a trinket or two and, you know what? Really. Honestly. Your souls are worth nothing. Nothing!

Has anyone ever heard him like this? I think. Has anyone ever heard this rage? Christ, it's like some kind of confession. Why me? Why is he doing this to me?

– I'd kill you all now, he says, but it's not within the contract.

And his voice sounds almost sorry.

– How do I reckon you, Tom? he says. I reckon you're nothing.

A Short Walk Down to the Evenfall

My face is burning, half with the heat of pain, half with the heat of shame.

– What do you want from me? I say.

– I want nothing at all from you. You're worth nothing at all to me. Nothing.

– Then leave me alone.

He pulls off the glove on his right hand; scarred like his face and just as cadaverous, it has one small patch of raw tissue where a little diamond of skin has been cut out, peeled off. Even the muscles and veins inside are white as the sinew and bone.

– Leave you alone? he says. Come on, we'll take a short walk down to the Evenfall, m'lad, and see if you still want me to leave you alone.

He reaches into a pocket, searching, finds what he's looking for

491

and produces the missing patch of skin, holds it out towards me in the palm of his hand. I know the black mark with a deeper and more instant recognition even than when you see your own face suddenly reflected in a window or a puddle.

I remember watching the others get their marks – I was maybe five, six, I don't know – and then it was my turn and I cried and had to be held and comforted and coaxed by Annie as the tattooist leaned over me with her blurring, buzzing needle in one hand, wiping away the blood and excess ink with the antiseptic wipe in her other hand. I remember the hot biting pain in my shoulder and the feeling deeper inside like this mark was something being dragged out of my soul, not carved into my skin. I don't really remember the later part with the scalpel – I think maybe I passed out – but I remember afterwards, sitting in the back of the rag-and-bone-man's cart, crying with the pain and misery, with Aunt Stef hugging me and Annie sitting across from us, also in tears. I thought it was because her shoulder hurt too, but now I guess she knew what we were giving up.

The rag-and-bone-man curls his hand into a fist around the patch of skin and I feel it, not in my shoulder but at the back of my neck.
   – Who are you, Tom? he says. You're nothing without this. The only thing that holds you in this world is the contract, is me. You have nothing to hold on to; we go down to the Evenfall, m'lad, and I reckon your soul will just blow away in the wind.
   – I have Jack, I say. We have each other.
   – Yes, but does he actually need you? he says.
   I say nothing.
   – Jack . . . he says almost idly. Maybe there is something you have to offer. You 'love' the iceman, don't you? You'd give your soul for him if you could. Would he give his for you, do you think? That's 'love', isn't it? Isn't that what you think?
   I feel sick, afraid that I know what he means, praying that I don't.

*

– Come on, m'lad, you know his soul's not going to be given to anyone. It's sealed off more secure than a Swiss bank account. That boy he cut his heart out long ago and locked it in a little steel box to keep it safe from damage. How can you 'love' him if you don't even know him? Where's he from, what made him what he is; what's his secret mark, his hidden true name, the *essence* of Jack? Until you know that you'll never really touch him, and he'll never truly be yours. Isn't that true? Isn't that what you think?

– Leave me alone. I don't know what you—

– Oh yes, you do, he says. You want to know him, don't you? You want to really know him, m'lad. Deep down. You want to *own* him.

– No, that's not—

– I could help you. We could make some sort of deal here.

– No! Leave him out of this.

– You want him? I'm the rag-and-bone-man, boy. You want it, I can get it for you, at the right price. Come on, make a deal with me, m'lad, or let's just take a walk right now. It's time to pay the piper, m'lad. But I can call in your credit or extend it.

The Declaration of Dependence

I won't listen to his deal. I don't know where he's going, but I don't care.

– No, I say. You'll never own him. Not like the rest of us.

– Is that what you think? I own you?

– . . . yes . . .

– Is that what they told you, m'lad?

I say nothing.

The rag-and-bone-man laughs, pulls his hat off his head and shakes his hair, still laughing. He puts the hat back on and thumps it down.

– I don't own you, m'lad. *You* own me. Look at me, for the love of god, and ask yourself if you can't read me like an open book.

He tears his ragged T-shirt down from the neck to bare his tattooed chest.

– Look at me. This is *your* contract carved into this skin, the

493

brands of ownership that bind me to this town, the true names of the people of Endhaven, signed and sealed, the declaration of dependence. This one – [he holds up his fist] – is yours.

I stare at the latticework of diamond scars all over his chest, all over his face, the scars of where each scrap of soul has been stitched on, a harlequin suit of horror,

    – You . . . you brought us here. We sold our souls. Safe passage.

    I think of the tattooist and Annie crying on the rag-and-bone-man's cart, the years of digging ourselves in in Endhaven, burying our pasts in the dirt as we planted the seeds we needed to live in the future, looking out to the east and the ocean and the Evenfall where all our memories lie drowned. We gave up our souls to come here. That was the deal. It's always been . . . obvious.

    – You and your two lesbian hags, the rest of Endhaven, you're the buyers, m'lad. You're the customers. I'm just your little black book written in blood. You're not chained to me. You're chained to each other *by* me. Me – [a bitter laugh] – I'm nothing to you without this skin.

– You brought us here, I say in a small voice, confused, adrift.

    I don't think I understand anything any more.

    – Every symbol on this hide is a life I'm responsible for, a name that I wear to keep it safe from a broken world, because the people in this town are too craven and weak to carry their own souls. Oh yes, I *carried* you here. Yes, you *need* me. I'm your fucking slave, m'lad, but I'm tired and torn. I want . . . release.

    Suddenly it clicks.

    – Jack . . .

    – Now there's a boy with the strength to carry a world.

    Waves of nausea wash over me; I feel like I'm going to be sick.

    – I'm sick, he says, and tired. Of all of you. I want out.

    I clutch the bubble-wrap padded arms of the chair, lean forward, breathing heavily. I can't look at his face, just his fist clenched tight around my soul.

    – You have no idea what your boyfriend is capable of, m'lad. You have no idea. But I do, m'lad.

His fist grips tighter, knuckles white on white.

– And I can give him to you. I can make him yours.

– Or, he says, we can go down to the edge of Evenfall, m'lad, and I will bury you so far down in the dead soul deeps that you won't know which way is up. You think you can stand against the Evenfall without someone to hold your little hand, to hold your little soul.

I close my eyes.

– It's your choice, he says.

– This isn't about Jack, I say. This isn't about me, or Endhaven, or any of that shit, I say. This is about you.

– It's your choice, he says, voice wild, desperate.

I bow my head.

– No, I say.

– Then follow me.

His rough, gloved hands pull me out of the chair by the shoulders and I shake him off, pull away.

– Leave me alone, I say. I know where we're going.

The Dissolution of Meaning

The evening comes in from the east like an ocean tide or a winter storm, washing across the jetty in a world-blurring grey confusion of wind, rain, mist and night through which I can just make out Jack standing on the balcony of his burnt-out beachhouse bunker, watching us with a calm contemplation. Around us and under us the water and shadow seem to merge in a chaos of—

– The involutions of entropy, says the rag-and-bone-man. The dissolution of meaning.

He waves his arms in a gesture that encompasses the sky, the ocean, the land, all the depths of the coming night.

– And the world was without form, and void, he says. Still want out of the contract, m'lad? Think you can keep your own soul safe without an anchor?

*

I look out into the darkness. *What's the alternative?* I think. Back on the land, Jack's hands grip the edge of the balcony. I can feel the panic rising in me, as the Evenfall sweeps in from the east. Hyperventilating, clutching the wooden rail along the jetty, I'm so strung-out already I don't know whether I'm losing myself in the howling rain or in my own terror and confusion. I cough and lean over the railing, a dry heave. He laughs and I shake with anger and fear.

– I don't know, I manage to say, throat thick with nausea. Maybe you're the only one who can keep me real. Maybe Jack is . . .

I feel the rain, the night, soaking through my clothes to the skin. I feel the chill in my flesh, in my bones. I feel my pounding heart, each deep, gasping breath of my lungs, the rough, scelfing wood under my fingers, the tension in every muscle. I feel my body, wet skin, shaking bone, taut muscle, pumping blood and fevered head. I feel small and afraid, but at least – and I feel this above everything – I feel.

– Maybe *I* am, I say.

The rag-and-bone-man holds up the little scrap of skin, the tiny sigil of my soul, between thumb and forefinger, and he grins his death's-head grin.

– Will I whistle up the wind, then?

The grey misery of the Evenfall whips around him like his own ragged clothes. Out here on the edge of the jetty it's all closing in around us and Jack and his beachhouse are smeared out of sight now. I can't see the shore.

Out here I have nowhere else to run.

The sound of the bells on the rag-and-bone-man's shoes. Seagulls.

– Let it go, I say, just let it go.

And a hand squeezes my shoulder.

– As he said, says Jack. Let it go.

Like the wrapper of a chocolate bar or a discarded lottery ticket, I watch it, snatched up by the storm and almost immediately, twisting and turning through the dusk, lost in the Evenfall. And I just stand there.

– You're lost, says the rag-and-bone-man, but his reckoning is a weak whisper.

I don't feel myself melting in the rain. I don't feel myself blow away in the wind, disappearing into the shadows. I just feel Jack's arm around my waist.

– No, he says. You are.

The rag-and-bone-man stands only a few feet from me on the jetty, but in the Evenfall, his shape is blurred, a scarecrow wraith of fluttering cloth.

I don't know if it's Jack's arm around my waist keeping me anchored to the wood of the jetty, to the beach and Endhaven and life, existence. I don't know if I have an anchor at all now, but, as cold and biting as the Evenfall is, I know I'm not afraid of it any more.

– I have something for you, says Jack. A little something to think about.

We back away down the jetty, the raggedy, bony rag-and-bone-man following us, buffeted by the wind.

– Your contract isn't worth the paper it's written on, says Jack. You think those are the souls of Endhaven? Are you sure they're not just . . . marks? Maybe there's no secret essence inside me or you or them or anybody, *nothing* except what we choose for ourselves. No fate, no future, no past . . . except what we choose. No slaves and masters for the soul, only whores and politicians. Think about that when you feel the contract biting deeper than the skin. I suppose I could be wrong. What do you reckon?

And as we turn to leave, the rag-and-bone-man watches us with eyes ten times as human as his face is monstrous.

The Night Is Just Darkness

– Are you awake? says Jack.

– I am now, I say. What time is it?

– About midnight. Come and look at this.

He stands at the muslin curtain, silhouetted by the moonlight.

That's the thing about it. Once you get past the Evenfall, the night is just darkness, with its own quiet mysteries, maybe, but still. But still, I hesitate. Beyond the muslin curtain is a world that doesn't care for us at all, for none of us.

– It's too cold, I say. You'll have to get some kind of rug for this floor. And *some* kind of heating, if you think I'm going to stay here.

– Sure, whatever. Just come here.

– What is it? I grumble, wrapping the blanket round myself and tiptoeing up beside him.

– Damn . . . your hand's freezing.

Outside the sky is clear deep black and scattered with a myriad stars, a full moon iridescent in the darkness, painting the jetty, the beach and the waves beyond with a solidity only moonlight can give. At the end of the jetty, a rough shape is painted in white and shadow – a pile of clothes, a bowler hat on top – and, hung on a mooring post, like a coat on a peg, something stirs in the breeze as a flag shifts lazily in the wind, a human skin that dances weightless and hollow, and seems to beckon as it dances, like a torn paper doll.

– What should we do with it? I say.

– Leave it there, says Jack. None of our business.

I wonder – I wonder aloud if someone else will put it on, and Jack lets the curtain fall closed.

– Probably, he says, but it won't be me, or you. And all the rag-and-bone-men in the world can't keep the lie going forever. Sooner or later, Endhaven will fall apart. Sooner or later, the same thing that happened in the cities will happen here.

And we sit down on the bed and I ask him what he knows about what happened in the cities, and he tells me, and I ask him who he is and where he came from, and he tells me, and I ask him what he's doing here, what we're doing here, and he tells me, he tells me everything he knows, he tells me everything I need to know and everything I need to hear.

So we lie there on the bed, and I feel him warming up in my embrace, flesh against flesh, ephemeral creatures bound to our own reality not by empty symbols but by our bodies, locked around each other. I tell him that I want to leave Endhaven, that I want to get the hell out of this hollow sham of a place and see what's out there, what I've always been too afraid to see in the grey gloaming of the Evenfall, the shapes dissolved in the ocean of memories. I'm making plans, and I blather excitedly as if my words will pull him along with me.

— One moment at a time, he says.

I think of Endhaven as a harbour, of us anchored here, lashed to each other by our limbs, but with our own separate . . . integrity. Ships are meant for sailing, I think.

I think of how beautiful he is, his smooth skin, and the mystery of the scars we share but which are each unique to us. I love him. I do love him, but I realize that I don't love him the way I did just a few hours ago, that dumb, boyish need that I can hardly understand now. I love him because I don't need him any more.

— Jack? I say.

I sort of realize now that actually he needed me. I think he needed someone to need him, so he could show them just how empty that need was, so he could show it to himself, perhaps. What do we really need in this world? What do we really need?

— What? he says.

I smile to myself.

— Nothing.

ACKNOWLEDGEMENTS

It will probably not have escaped the reader's notice that large portions of this novel involve adaptations of various ancient myths, poems and plays. Since I'm not even remotely fluent in Latin or Greek – never mind ancient Sumerian – I've had to rely on the translations of others in creating my own idiosyncratic versions of these antique texts. It would be unforgivable if I did not acknowledge those debts.

For the Sumerian section dealing with Inanna's journey to the Kur and Dumuzi's flight from the *ugallu*, the excellent translation of 'Inanna's Descent into the Underworld' by Diane Wolkstein and Samuel Noah Kramer (*Inanna, Queen of Heaven and Earth: Her Stories and Hymns from Sumer*, Harper & Rowe, 1983) was invaluable, together with 'The Descent of Ishtar to the Underworld' by Stephanie J. Dalley (*Myths from Mesopotamia*, Oxford University Press, 1989).

The 'Eclogue' section at the start of Volume Two is, in part, a remix of Virgil's 'The Golden Age Returns' and 'The Song of Silenus', for which I drew on J.W. McKail's 1934 translations (Virgil's *Works: The Aeneid, Eclogues & Georgics*, Kessinger Publishing, 2003) and the translations by E.V. Rieu (Virgil, *The Pastoral Poems*, Penguin, 1949).

For the rewrite of Aeschylus's *Prometheus Bound* woven throughout Volume Two, again I found two different translations indispensable, the Thoreau version (*The Works of Henry David Thoreau: Translations*, Princeton University Press, 1987), and the more modern translation by George Thomson (Dover Publications, 1995).

Without these works this novel could not have been written, and I highly recommend them to any reader keen to read the source texts in faithful translations, free of all my literary meddlings.

I'd also like to pay particular tribute to Ian MacDougall's *Voices from the Spanish Civil War* (Polygon, 1986) and to those whose tales are told in it. Having taken many of the details in the last chapter directly from this book of interviews, I only hope that I have treated these veterans' memories with the dignity and respect they're due.

On a more personal level, the members of the Glasgow Science Fiction

Writers' Circle whose long-term support and critical feedback have helped rein in my literary excesses over the years are far too numerous to mention. While it seems unfair to pick out individuals, I have to thank Duncan Lunan for founding that literary 'anarchist collective' in the first place. I'd like also to give particular thanks to Jim Campbell, my adviser on all things military, and to Phil Raines and Neil Williamson for their steady supply of comments, critiques, cocktails and encouragement throughout the writing of this book. Thanks also to Jeff VanderMeer, who's proved himself a saint in this madman's opinion, and lastly, of course, to Peter Lavery and all those at Pan Macmillan, for letting the scurrying bitmites of my ideas loose on an unsuspecting public.